GemQuest
The Twins
Book One

Gary Alan Wassner

Windstorm Creative
Port Orchard § Washington

GemQuest The Twins: Book One
copyright 2001; 2007 by Gary Wassner
published by Windstorm Creative

ISBN 978-1-59092-078-7
9 8 7 6 5 4 3 2
First Edition February 2005
Second Edition September 2007

Design by Buster Blue of Blue Artisans Design.
Cover artwork by Robert Sammelin.

All rights reserved, including the right to reproduce this book or portions thereof in any form whatsoever, except in the case of short excerpts for use in reviews of the book.

Printed in the United States of America.

For information about film, hardback, reprint or other subsidiary rights, please contact legal@windstormcreative.com

Windstorm Creative is a multiple division, international organization involved in publishing books in all genres, including electronic publications; producing games, videos and audio cassettes as well as producing theatre, film and visual arts events. The wind with the flame center was designed by Buster Blue of Blue Artisans Design and is a trademark of Windstorm Creative.

Windstorm Creative
7419 Ebbert Dr SE
Port Orchard, WA 98367
www.windstormcreative.com
360-769-7174 ph

Windstorm Creative is a member of the Orchard Creative Group Ltd.

Library of Congress Cataloging-in-Publication data available.

Acknowledgments

Eternal thanks goes to my family; my wife, Cathy, whose endless love and companionship for the many years we have been together has always been an inspiration; my son, Brien, who was the first person to read this manuscript, and whose thought-provoking suggestions have made it a better book; my son, Cristopher, whose kind soul and casual innocence always stoke the fires of my heart and imagination; my son, Cole, whose incredible mental imagery and poetic creativity provide me with an endless supply of ideas.

Thanks must also go to Judy Kronish, my friend and associate, for her noteworthy suggestions and comments, her invaluable editorial assistance, and her continued and unselfish support of my work.

Thanks to Jeff Grippe for helping me to properly phrase the series title, a task that had been eluding me for so long.

Finally, thanks must go to Windstorm Creative for believing in my work and for giving me the opportunity to present my story so cohesively by releasing the first three books in the series simultaneously.

Dedication

For Wendy.
She would have been so proud.

GemQuest
The Twins
Book One

Gary Alan Wassner

Chapter One

The rock surface still seemed real. To any observer from the outside, a casual glance would reveal only a large, gray boulder. Unfortunately, though, Mira's ability to maintain this illusion was growing weaker by the hour. The young man in her arms was sound asleep, and she had made sure that he would sleep for quite some time. He had no idea just how much effort was being expended on his behalf. But, surely he was worth it; if anything or anyone was, he was! Just how much longer she could continue to support the environment she had created to keep them alive, she did not know.

The space inside their shelter was cramped and dark. She knew that the small light she suspended in the corner was a waste of her waning power. But, it eased the boy during his waking hours and was therefore infinitely worthwhile. Mira allowed it to remain even now, to lend to the sad atmosphere a bit of warmth. Fatigued as she was, she meticulously brushed a strand of her long, brown hair from her face and tucked it into the loosening braid that hung down the middle of her back. Her almond shaped, green eyes sparkled with love as she gazed upon the inert youth, and the contemplation of his calm face soothed her momentarily.

Nevertheless, she knew that her strength was ebbing and mental fatigue was setting in. The two of them had gone so many days without sleep, surviving on two Lalas leaves every twenty four hours, with no easing of the tension or of the exertion. And now, the leaves were almost gone. Mira had at best two days supply left, and only if she barely used any for her own sustenance and devoted the majority to the boy. Even then, it would be just enough to keep him alive.

The boy would last a few days after Mira's passing and then he too would fade, too young to defend himself against an enemy of this magnitude, and tragically, still unschooled. The rock shelter would dissolve, and the enemy outside would find him and rejoice in its final victory. Mira knew that whatever it cost her, she could not let this happen.

With the passing of this young man went the only heir to the throne of Gwendolen. The great and noble line would forever disappear from the planet, its foretold destiny unrealized. He was the last. Mira shuddered as she recalled the horrid demise of his parents and sister Lara. Her weakened state allowed the tears to well up in her tired eyes unbidden. It was tragic enough when the boy's twin died as his life was just beginning, two tiels and two years ago.

Queen Lewellyn so wanted the two boys. It broke her heart that at his birth he had to be removed from the grounds to die alone and bereft of a nurturing hand and companionship, but the illness he was born with was incurable and it could have infected his brother if he were not removed from the palace immediately. The risk was too great, so he was left to die in the Spiritwood, near the Lalas, hopefully to be reclaimed by the trees when his own life force passed from his body. Sometimes, the fabric of life weaves of its own will, and there is nothing anyone can do to alter the design or prevent it. Yet, each new thread subtly affects all the succeeding ones and incontrovertibly changes the patterns.

No one but those few attending the birth itself, Mira, Fiona, the midwife who died herself shortly thereafter and the King and Queen, ever knew that he even existed. They did not want their surviving son to bear this sad knowledge throughout his lifetime. Superstitious as the common folk were, the family was concerned that the people may have blamed the fit child for the ill one's demise, for he, not the healthy sibling, was the elder one if only by mere minutes, and would have been the true heir as the law decreed.

Tragedy seemed always to mark this beautiful and good family's life. It was only due to Mira's sharp wits and her forethought that she was able to spirit the remaining heir himself out of the castle these many years later, as the shields came down and the black hordes of the enemy swarmed inside the fortress.

In her lifetime she thought it would never happen. Their lives should have been so perfect. Never had they all experienced such joy as at the birth of the beautiful child, his sister Lara. And the marriage between Queen Llewellyn and King Garold was so inspiring. But, there were signs that they should have recognized. Surely the warnings were there, but the advisors to the King kept him veiled and apart from the truth.

Were they part of the conspiracy? Did they really think the enemy would protect them afterward? Those fools! Such treachery, and such a beautiful family, she recalled.

Mira wiped a salty tear from her cheek, as she thought of all that was lost. *Stop!* she chided herself. *Do not squander what energy remains on regret. The shields must be maintained. If I weaken even for a moment, they may be able to sense our presence.*

Mira cast her mind vision outside the shelter and carefully searched the surrounding hill top. Nothing! Not even a bird was flying. Surely they were coming. What else could frighten away every sign of life from the area? She would preserve the boy as long as she could, and in the final moments she still had one option; If she had the strength, and she must if the time came, she could cast him. With the limited energy she had left, Mira knew not where the casting would leave him. More than likely he would die of exposure to the elements while still unconscious, or worse yet, he would fall into the hands of the enemy. Fortunately for him, her spells were woven well, and he would not awaken in either event. Courageous as she was, she consoled herself with that thought, at least, since all of the other possibilities were so much more grim and painful to contemplate.

Mira removed her loden cloak, embroidered with the crest of Gwendolen, and lovingly wrapped the boy in it. She knew that she would have no further use for it, and perhaps it would keep him warm just a bit longer and ease his discomfort somewhat.

Fate often has a cruel heart, she thought sadly as she folded the ends of the fabric securely around him.

Mira had reconciled herself to the fact that when the time came she would use the last moments of her life to attempt to save him. At least there would be a chance someone would find him and help him if she was incapable of casting him where she hoped she could, or perhaps someone or something would be there when the moment arose to guide him on his journey if she failed. She would not despair and give up hope. Not now! Not after she had come this far.

There were still some enclaves of safety at the far reaches of the countryside. If her memory served her well, far to the north, over the Thorndar mountains was a protected area still watched over by the Lalas. It was always said that the northern reaches would forever be safe from the gathering clouds. The air was too thin to support the minions of the Black Lord. It was too cool for their furless hides. All of the tales told to the children of the kingdom since the beginning of time, referred to the safety in the north. In the back of everyone's mind all believed that they could flee to the north if the enemy swarmed the borders. But, when things appeared to be going so well, they all forgot about the danger. They grew complacent and thereby sealed their own fate.

The King's sorceress was able to keep the skies blue despite the growing darkness that was encroaching upon the countryside. So much time and energy were spent on maintaining the image of safety that the people started to believe that they were truly safe. Even the King, wise as he was, was persuaded to let his guard down. No one except Mira expected the deceit and treachery that befell the kingdom. Mira knew. She knew!!! She pleaded with Queen Lewellyn to be careful—to retreat to the safe rooms of the castle, and clear her mind of the fog that the sorceress was spreading over everyone. There were still some areas that were not infiltrated and reduced by the sorceress.

Trialla was her name. "Trialla the Ugly" the children used to call her. She was ancient and unbearably ugly, but her magic soon made her appear learned and sweet natured, and even the children forgot what she was really like. Mira ranted and raved, but all of her warnings fell upon deaf ears. Everyone seemed to see beauty in Trialla where Mira saw ugliness. The children who at one time feared and taunted her, overlooked their concerns and flocked to her side. Soon enough, Trialla appeared as the savior and Mira the outcast. She despaired but she knew the truth, and the truth kept her alive. The truth would protect and inspire her. She would never give in to the powers that engulfed her beloved homeland.

The seduction of the city was so obvious to her, yet to no one else, and the frustration therefrom was unbearable. Eventually, she forewent trying to warn the people and she began to set down her plans for her escape when the proper time came. She did whatever she could for the young boy. From the time of his birth until now, she had been his protectress and teacher. She imparted whatever knowledge to him that she could, and she hoped against hope that some of what she taught him would be absorbed. She never really knew how much time she had left.

Mira grieved for the others knowing it was too late for them. It hurt her so to face that fact, to be so helpless. Yet, they had practically driven her out of the inner circle. Fortunately, Mira always maintained access to the royal child, and she guarded and guided him as best as she could. She had hoped that she would be able to maintain her closeness with him and continue to oversee his growth until his formal training could begin. She made herself as inconspicuous as possible; humble and silent. Mira moved about the palace like a shadow, caped and hooded, ducking into corners whenever the enemy was present. By the age of thirteen the boy was certainly ready, but her time with him was becoming restricted despite her efforts, and Mira feared that she would shortly be forbidden to see him at all.

As time passed, her premonitions grew stronger. She poignantly felt the end drawing near. The dreams and visions plagued her at night, and she awoke often, choking on her sorrow and regret. Trialla had successfully isolated her and kept her separate from all of the court decisions. She was too strong to combat by herself and all of the others were already under her spell. The sources from which she drew her powers were seemingly endless. Whatever Mira did was virtually fruitless, and she feared that her continued efforts to warn the royal family would jeopardize what little time she still had with the boy. The spells cast upon the city were so well spun that the people of Cinmarra barely heard Mira's admonitions, as they fell upon deaf ears time and time again. Trialla wove her evil plans so well that the fabric of illusion that she created mesmerized even the smartest of the Kingdom's citizens. Fortunately, she did not feel the threat of time passing.

Trialla was comfortable with her successes, and she basked fawningly in the glory of her works. Her hubris, Mira hoped, would serve to be the weak spot in the old witch's plan. It gave Mira time to prepare. The people of the kingdom who had at one time revered and loved Mira, did not resent her now; they showed no anger whatsoever. They simply ignored everything she said, and like puppets, they smiled and said, "Hush. Hush. You worry too much." Trialla believed that Mira would seethe from such behavior, but in fact, eventually she reconciled herself to it and learned to use it to her and the boy's advantage. She was left alone to do what she felt she had to do; plan for her and the heir's escape.

By the age of nine the boy manifested a clear and distinct awareness of his power, extraordinary at so young an age, but his ability to use it consciously was severely limited. He was still young and far too innocent. Time marches on nonetheless, regardless of whether or not one is prepared for what is to come. And, how could an innocent child ever be prepared for what Mira feared might be in store for this boy? She wept openly now, and frequently, but not in the child's presence. No, never in front of him. Mira would spare him from her misery at least. She still had time to plan.

As the years passed, Mira did what she could, a valiant effort nonetheless, but not nearly enough, as she dreaded. At fourteen, the young man was strong, surely, and heading in the right direction, certainly, but he was still no closer to understanding and controlling his powers than an untrained animal, no matter its brute, physical strength or instinct.

The time was growing near now. Mira would try her best to save the heir. She hoped that she could cast him as far north as she needed to.

Preserve your strength! she mentally rebuked herself. *Concentrate. The moment is almost upon us.*

The boy slept peacefully. He knew nothing. Mira watched his chest rise and fall with his breath, totally unaware of the grave danger surrounding him. She wove a powerful spell over him, hastily yet perfectly. It would insure that he slept. Even if the worst were to happen, Mira would be able to spare him the pain of knowledge, of awareness. He would sleep forever, if need be, until the precise words of power were spoken. The First willing, whoever found him if her casting went astray would not recognize him, and he would pass from this world innocent and unaware, never to awaken again. Come what may, he would be spared the agony of being at the mercy of the enemy, even if that meant that he may never be brought back to consciousness, that his destiny would remain eternally unfulfilled. That was the best she could do for him now, and the prospect of this deed sat comfortably, if sadly, upon her soul.

Knowing that the end was near, she removed a thin, woven chain from her wrist and secured it around the boy's limp arm. It was made of a substance that carried no lasting scent, and it could not be used to help an enemy identify wherefrom he came should he fall into the wrong hands, but he would recognize it if and when he awoke. It would comfort him to have it, she believed, and she had no further need for ornaments.

Despite her vigilance, without a warning, her senses reeled. It seemed as if she had been slapped in the face, and she recoiled violently from the evil touch. They were approaching, and the horrifying power she felt was practically overwhelming. Mira knew it was inevitable, and yet she had hoped for a little more time; just a tiny bit more. All she wanted was to rock the boy in her arms and say goodbye in the proper fashion. There was no time now for that. If she had any expectations of casting the boy to safety, the process would have to begin immediately. Her mind sight told her that she had only moments left, that she must act quickly before her emotions distorted her actions. Mira lifted the inert young man in her arms, and she struggled under the dead weight of a physically mature adolescent. Maintaining the rock illusion for a little longer was essential.

She began to hum. With one part of her mind focused on the facade surrounding them, she began to relax her body. The casting spell had to be done properly or who knows where the boy would end up. Her teachers told her countless years ago that all you needed to do was form a picture, however obscure, of the destination in your mind, concentrate your energy upon the image of the person at the other end, and force the power from within to blend with the image. As the power flowed into the image, a feeling of warmth arose in her abdomen. Mira knew that it was beginning to work. The moment in which the power and image became one together would just about be her last. Of that she was sure. She would have no strength left afterwards to protect herself further. But, if she could only reach that moment her life would have been worthwhile.

The image of the northern reaches grew brighter in her mind's eye until she felt as if she had to squint in order not to go blind, even as the dead weight of the boy made her legs crumble beneath her. The strong features of the face of the noble man she sought to cast the heir to began to sharpen before her, surrounded by an ephemeral image of a mighty castle. Suddenly she felt a tugging at her arms. The boy was fading slowly. He was being drawn into the light that was now filling the entire rock shelter that served as their home for these past weeks. Strangely enough, Mira was reluctant to release him, and yet she knew she must. She was tempted to hold on more tightly, to keep him with her.

With a silent prayer for his safety and a last moment's hesitation, she let go, and she felt the weight lift from her weakened arms. The boy vanished into the shimmering vortex of light with a swooshing sound. Allowing herself one last instant of sadness, Mira watched as the rock illusion dissolved around her. With barely any strength left in her, she stared out into the daylight, thick with smoke and emanating evil, and she shielded her squinting eyes. No sooner did she regain her balance and force herself to her feet, when out of the woods to the east came a shrill cry and a bloodcurdling pounding on the ground. They were here.

Mira looked at the approaching enemy and knew exactly what she had to do. Her thoughts were strangely clear and sharp. She felt no fear, only sorrow. Focusing her energy once again inwardly, with the remaining power she had gathered inside her, she said the words she had hoped she'd never have to say. The blood that suffused her skin and kept it porcelain-like and normally rose-colored withdrew from her extremities. She appeared now as white as a blanket of newly fallen snow, staid and calm. Abruptly, the leader of the rancorous enemy halted. As he reached out to clasp the arm of his prey, it shimmered and appeared to burn. A thin, slippery, green-skinned arm reached toward a benumbed and helpless old woman, and recoiled with a virulent yelp as it came into contact with a white hot, glowing statue.

For Mira, it was over. She had transformed into a substance that would never again feel pain or experience remorse. Perhaps she had won after all in a strange way. But, what of the boy; what of the beautiful boy? Just as Mira's mind slipped away forever, she sent one last streak of power outward in search of the heir. Hopefully, it would find him safe and envelop him in its warmth. If so, Mira would live forever within him and always be a source of hope and guidance for him. She smiled to herself, a smile that remained frozen upon her face for eternity; an enduring affront to the enemy before her. With that final thought, her cognitive entity was gone along with its physical identity.

Chapter Two

"The boy has arrived, my Lord," was all that the messenger said in such a matter of fact way that one would think that this sort of thing happened every day.

So, Baladar mused. *It has finally begun!*

Walking slowly to his burnished stone table, he felt an immense wave of satisfaction envelop him and soothe what he had come to believe was to be an ever anxious mind. Four such simple words as "the boy has arrived" held so much meaning for him. A lifetime of anticipation, a generation of hoping and a century of planning were coming to fruition. Finally! The boy had arrived!

Baladar sat in the high backed, rune-carved chair, and truly relaxed for the first time in years; perhaps for the first time in his lifetime. He laid his head back upon the hard, elfin wood, and breathed a deep breath of relief. Knowing fully that the work was just beginning for him and the boy, he felt so wholesome and buoyant, so filled with pride and dreams for the future that he could barely contain himself. If he was not careful, he knew that he would drift off in this reverie, and perhaps not return for days. He had not allowed his mind to travel outside of his body for years. It would be wonderful, once again, but now he had too much to do. He did not have the time for such luxuries.

Ah, if only Briland could be here to see this, to experience the elation of having the boy among the protectors after all these years of preparation and prayer, Baladar mused. *She would have brimmed with joy. It would have made her so, so happy. Yes...but, such are the ways of this world,* he thought sadly.

Briland, Baladar's stunningly beautiful wife, passed into the after world at least two tiels prior. She was so full of life, and so kind and loving that she was sorely missed by the entire kingdom of Pardatha. Her death marked a low point in Baladar's life. Never before had he felt so unsure of himself and so alone and abandoned as just after Briland passed on. There was nothing he could have done to prevent it. She was a child of the trees, and without the ability to live in the proximity of her Lalas tree, she was doomed. He knew this, and as a Chosen one, so did she.

Presently, only a small number of the grand and wonderful trees remained alive on the planet. Their roots tunneled into the earth, and searched one another out. From distances of thousands of miles, they had always been able to find their same, and wherever they met, a new tree sprouted to the surface. Yet, today no new trees grew. Perhaps the distances had become too far between the remaining trees for them to make contact and regenerate, or as Baladar truly suspected was the case, the trees lost the will to search and rejuvenate *themselves* for some reason not known to man. Nevertheless, the Lalas had stopped perpetuating themselves, and the entire planet mourned their continuously dwindling numbers.

During the peak of their growth and development, all of the trees were intertwined with one another, and they were able to pass on information instantaneously. Centuries ago, there were many, many of these trees reported to have been seen all over the populated areas of the world, and most certainly in unpopulated areas as well, all rumored to have sprung from the one history referred to as simply "the First", whose whereabouts was reputed to be shielded from detection, and protected from all harm.

Years and years of questing for the First became the grist for the mills of legend. Yet, no concrete report of its discovery ever reached the ears of civilized man. The First was said to harbor the Gem of Eternity, the most powerful and sacred of the tools of the gods brought to the planet aeons ago with the golden seeds of the First. It was said that the Gem was placed in the soil by the gods when the golden seeds were planted. Thus, legend has it, as the tree grew, the Gem remained nestled within its heart, sheltered from all evil, and radiating its power from this position of comfort and security.

The First was so enormous, and endowed with such unimaginable power that no living thing could ever conceivably reach its heart as long as the First lived. The Gem was the most holy and revered relic on earth, and was thus given sanctuary in the safest place possible. Had anyone been able to procure it, they too would have been blessed with eternal life and unlimited power. The First was the guardian of the Gem. Legend decried that the First would relinquish its guardianship of the Gem to only one charge, the one chosen by the First as its bond mate. This would only occur at the most crucial time in history, one of great threat or great triumph, before the end of the current cycle. No one had yet attained that title, "the Chosen of the First."

All of the leaves of the Lalas trees possessed the gift of nourishment, and had superlative healing powers when properly prepared and administered correctly. The trunks were at times so enormous that entire villages could thrive within the hollows and branches of the oldest of the Lalas, but only the leaves were ever utilized by living things. The branches were never cut, and the trunks were never chopped down. Such was impossible, and any attempt at what was considered to be a defilement of the tree was strictly forbidden.

Everyone believed that the trees would live forever. One day, though, during the third year of the ninth tiel of the sixteenth century, only four tiels ago, with no warning whatsoever, slowly and painfully, the leaves began to wilt, and one by one, a small number of the trees proceeded to shrivel and die. There was no visible sign of decay or disease anywhere on any of the trees, yet there was a clear and audible sound that echoed throughout the land whenever a tree was dying. It sounded as if the tree was screaming in a high-pitched voice. The sound terrified the children, the animals ran around scared as when a storm is rising in the west, and all grown men and women stopped whatever they were doing and remained still as statues until the sound ceased. It just seemed as if the Lalas has made a conscious decision to die and leave the earth.

Briland's tree, Snihso, was one of the first to quit the world it had been born to, and thus, quit its bond mate as well. As each tree died, and shortly thereafter its Chosen, it was deeply mourned as was its human partner. A great sadness engulfed the towns and cities in the vicinity of the dying tree. The population surrounding the doomed tree was awash with feelings of abandonment and doom. When the trees first started to die, the skies darkened and rain fell unceasingly for weeks. Floods resulted, and many deaths ensued. The circle of life was being threatened with each death, and everything imbued with the light of life, revolted from and reacted to the loss.

A precarious balance was soon restored, but during these first tiels, each time a Lalas tree fell, the crash and the subsequent echo were said to be so incredibly loud that the mountains and lakes surrounding it suffered severe damage. Avalanches, tidal waves and untold horrors were unleashed on the land upon the death of a great Lalas. The vibrations when the tree finally fell were so severe that great rifts in the earth resulted.

The hollows left after the root structure rotted away had become a forbidden maze into which no one would dare venture. Legend said if one followed the tunnels one would either end up at another tree whose roots were intermingled with the dead giant, at which point the clash of opposite forces was understandably stupendous and deadly, or more likely, you would die in the process.

The Tomes of Caradon, the mysterious and often unfathomable recorded history of the land, bear no clear records of anyone entering the caverns of a dead Lalas and returning safely anywhere on earth. The juncture of the living and the dead was a maelstrom of power, an enduring battlefield, barring all manner of life.

The Lalas were considered to be gentle giants, affording comfort and security for the peoples of the planet who served the light whilst they lived. They were formidable enemies of anyone or thing who was driven by evil motives.

Although they were sentient beings, they communicated in a language known only to a few whom they selected by methods unknown to man. Once selected by a Lalas as its bond mate, that person was forever tied spiritually and emotionally to the tree. Those few lived incredibly long and fruitful lives, although often apart from the rest of mankind in spirit. They rarely married and raised families, but when they did, they bore exceptionally gifted children who quite frequently became Chosen themselves.

The Chosen came and went mysteriously, and rumors about their longevity and magical abilities spread rampantly throughout the villages and towns and cities of the nations. They attained the status of demigods in the eyes of the common man. They were almost always benevolent, and endowed with leadership qualities that mesmerized the populace.

In all of recorded history, there was only one known aberration to this pattern, in the form of a renegade Chosen named Aracon who in the sixth tiel of the Seventh century, subverted the will of his tree in an abortive effort to promote his own authority. He failed miserably, and was literally sucked into the earth by the joint and concerted effort of the Lalas while he was proclaiming his superiority before a gathering of the peoples of his city, Nescon, on the southernmost coast of the continent. The timing of his demise was absolute perfection, and no other incident of such subversion has ever again been mentioned in the Tomes. This incident is celebrated every spring during the holiday of Mantal, named after Aracon's tree, and is a source of great entertainment for the children of the nations, as they act out the final moments of Aracon's life dramatically and in forever new and unique ways. The child picked to be Aracon is always one of great potential, and this choice is meant to teach him or her humility, and to be a reminder of the futility and great sin of any effort to not serve the tree truthfully.

Each Lalas was said to be able to engulf an enemy if it entered its territory with bad intent. Once taken by the Lalas, death was imminent and said to be terribly painful. There are accounts in the Tomes of entire armies being absorbed by the trees. Their vengeance was legendary, and their power seemingly limitless. It was thought that the Lalas held the earth together and that when the last of the great trees finally died and the light from the Gem of Eternity was extinguished forever, the earth would disintegrate and its fragments would be spread all over the universe. That day, named the Great Dissolution in all of the legends, was feared by all who served the light. Only if and when evil prevails could such an event be possible.

The ancient diaries of the gods of Caradon devote chapters to the great dissolution. The powers of darkness looked forward to it as their means of salvation. The fragmentation was viewed as a renewal and rejuvenation though completely antithetical to life itself. The dissolution was the means by which their ideas and seeds would be spread all over the universe, and by which they would find eternal peace and freedom from the cycle of human suffering. They had no feeling for the lives that would be lost or the pain and hardship that would inevitably precede the final days.

Baladar shivered at the thought of how few Lalas remained. Of course, he was not certain of the count, but his powers allowed him a good sense of the weakening of the chain of communication which could only be the result of a lessening in the number of the trees. The sadness which engulfed him and his people so infrequently years ago was more and more common nowadays. He knew what it meant each time. With his wife gone, he had to strain his abilities to the limit in order to fight the sadness and depression. Reports of citizens jumping from cliffs and into rivers for no recognizable reason were much more prevalent recently. Nature sadly but necessarily began to strike a balance of sorts with the continuing loss of the trees, and although the power that renewed and sustained the Lalas was ebbing, the earth had girded itself against the terrible consequences of their deaths.

Baladar's own sense of desperation at times seemed overwhelming and unbearable. Yet, he had the strength to fight on, particularly as his hopes were being rekindled by the arrival of the boy, the Child-King; the only remaining link to the ancient Gwendolen family. This noble family was probably the oldest of all of the blood lines in recorded history, and oh, what a history of achievement and accomplishment! The myths are rife with stories of triumph and goodness, so frequently traceable back to a Gwendolen family member.

Baladar knew that somehow he had the noble blood streaming through his veins. He, like many others with the gift, instinctively knew that he was tied to the family, yet his mother had been a regal though simple woman, a healer who labored day and night if circumstances required, and his rise to power was seemingly achieved by hard work, and intentions that were honorable, true and just. His father had died when he was quite young and little was known about him. He was not a local man, and whenever he attempted to discuss his father with his mother, she avoided the subject, and she made it clear to Baladar that it was not something she wished to talk about. She indicated to him that there would be a time and place for that conversation, and that he would have to remain patient, but alas, she died of the fever that swept the city when he was only two tiels and three without ever having had the opportunity to impart that information to her son.

Orphaned at a young age, he was taken under the wing of the city's Lord, Breamar of Ashton, and raised as if he was his own kin. His talents as a statesman were always evident, even as a child, and he readily assumed duties that heretofore were reserved for older, more experienced individuals. When Breamar died without an heir to succeed him, Baladar was chosen to assume the exalted role, and he was installed in the office of Lord of the city as if he was of the blood. The people of Pardatha gratefully accepted his leadership, as he had performed in a civic capacity almost his entire adult life to date and he was well respected, and more important, thoroughly trusted.

Ever since he assumed the role of leader and protector, he had managed to maintain a civil society that prospered and remained fair and generous to all of its citizens. That was no mean feat in a world that was constantly degenerating, with reports coming in to him and his advisors from every corner of the world of ensuing darkness, depression and disintegration. Yet, his kingdom of Pardatha was a shining jewel in a sea of dull and lifeless objects. In fact, he feared that his domain was becoming too obvious in its success, and that the wrong eyes would stumble upon this aberrant example amidst the mundane landscape of accelerating decay.

His efforts to conceal from the rest of the world his land's prosperity and relative contentment were painstaking and a constant strain upon his powers. But he remained ever vigilant, never letting his guard down. He fortified the city over the years by painstakingly constructing an exterior wall of the strongest stone, quarried nearby, and an inner wall surrounding the castle that was twenty feet thick, and able to withstand even the fiercest of assaults.

Unlike most cities, the gates of Pardatha were hewn from the Elfin tree, the Noban, the wood of which was given to the city as a gift from Lormarion, the kingdom of the Southern Elves, some fifty tiels ago. The timber of this tree was harder than stone and had to be carved with special tools by skilled craftsmen. The great planks were preserved by Baladar's predecessors and only utilized when the outer walls to the city were completed, sealing it with a magnificent gateway that when closed, was virtually impenetrable. The inner wall, too, was secured by the sculpted Noban, carved with Elfin runes and characters from Lormarion's glorious past, its awesome strength disguised by its sheer beauty and delicate gracefulness.

Even in these times of relative peace and prosperity, the battlements were manned and kept in the best of repair. Baladar's armies were well trained and equipped, regardless of the apparent safety that prevailed throughout his land, for every time a Lalas died, the people of Pardatha were sorrowfully and painfully reminded of the creeping danger. And, Baladar would never forget the ultimate price that his wife paid for being intimately connected to the changes occurring all around them.

He made certain that there was room inside the outer wall for most of the city folk to gather in times of trouble. The storerooms and cellars were always prepared and well stocked, for Baladar would not leave a single person or even a helpless animal outside of his circle of protection if circumstances required it. The city could endure a siege of many months, and its battlements could withstand the onslaught of a formidable army.

The Thorndars protected Pardatha against a direct attack from the south, and the city abutted the very base of one of the tallest peaks in the massive range. The outermost wall itself was built right into the mountain, and thereby provided Pardatha with one perfectly secure boundary. Baladar had the lands surrounding the northern and northwestern most approaches to the city cleared and leveled, allowing his scouts to see the approach of any force well in advance of its arrival at Pardatha's gates from their vantage points atop the high towers built for just this purpose.

Baladar, being the practical man that he was, made sure that the fertile ground was utilized for grazing and planting. He also made certain that the fields that were cultivated thereon would pose a substantial obstacle to any advancing army. Cloudberry bushes flourished there; incredibly thick and dense and covered with sharp thorns. Bergenbane vines, the fruit of which was used for medicinal purposes, grew in compact, winding clumps tangling around the feet and hooves of anything that tried to walk over them, and low growing Rasteria bloomed in abundance, whose sweet-smelling flowers attracted the dangerous Tsenso bee, which, when disturbed, stung in fierce and furious waves, but whose honey was sweeter than that of any other drawn from flowers in the land.

The eastern front was shielded by the forbidding Spiritwood which grew high on the crest overlooking the dry river bed below. The dense foliage made it difficult for a force of any strength, transporting wagons and the machinery of battle, to easily navigate through to the city. Baladar fortified outposts at the eastern most edge of the forest, and he created a network wherein messages and information could securely be passed back and forth between the city and the front. It would be difficult for any sizable army to advance unseen against Pardatha from that position.

The only remaining direct approach to the city was through the gorge, and unfortunately, there was little he could do to prevent an attack from thence. A former river bed, the valley to the southwest was wide and barren. It ran almost to the gates of Pardatha themselves, the city being perched on a bluff above it. He could only hope that due to the fact that it was so exposed, nothing other than a massive force would dare advance through it, knowing they would be seen long before they reached the city gates.

Prior to the demise of his beloved, the work of protecting Pardatha from the envious eyes of its would be enemies was effortlessly carried out by Briland. She was a true beauty, in body, mind and spirit. Her blood could be traced directly back to the High King Breardan, and his beautiful and mysterious Queen Lanatrae. The Tomes devote chapters to the glories of the reign of the High King. During his time, the Lalas trees were everywhere, and accounts of his Queen's close relations to the one who chose her, provided numerous and uplifting stories that are told to children today at bedtime, and during times of crisis. They still comforted the people of the kingdom, probably more so than ever these days, with their accounts of the beauty of the High Queen, and her soft touch and healing nature.

The Tomes recount her miraculous ability to transport herself instantly to the bedside of the seriously ill and dying. Lanatrae was said to be able to heal with her touch. More than one story recounted the words of the healed on the brink of death as remembering a vague image of Lana's body taking on the sinuous simulacrum of her tree, her arms like soft, leaf laden branches as they enveloped them and brought them back from the very edge of eternity to the healthy impermanence of life.

The domain of the High King Breardan was seemingly limitless. He ruled over most of the known world, with harmony and gentleness. Yet no one ever doubted his strength, as was most needfully demonstrated during the bitter battles precipitated by the marauding Trolls toward the end of his fifth tiel. Rarely though did anyone or anything threaten the peace of Gwendolen in those days.

The network of communication created by the trees and the Chosen was sturdy and comprehensive. It was even rumored that somewhere, known only by the great council and the Lalas, the high ones, including Lanatrae and Breardan, met and planned the course of events to come. The contemplation of these council meetings invoked images of mystery, beauty and power in the mind of each person and being devoted to the light, while it precipitated immeasurable fear in the hearts of the disruptive and the evil.

Alas, though, those times are long past, he thought sadly.

Baladar shrugged and literally brushed his hand over his brow to settle his thoughts on the hopes of today, rather than upon the glories of the past. The boy needed to be trained, educated, loved and nurtured. He needed to be prepared. And, he would be, he averred. Baladar knew that the time was ripe and the boy would be everything and more than he and the world had hoped for. If he should fail in his teachings, or if the boy should fail in his future quests, the world was doomed and dissolution was inevitable. The boy was given unto Baladar to train and to protect. This vast responsibility weighed heavily upon his shoulders, but he accepted this charge with pride and gratitude. He would see it through to the end, at the expense of his own life if need be.

Baladar walked across the softly lit room to the darkness of the sheltered alcove at the far side of his work table. The chamber in which he worked was at the very top of the castle. It was octagonal in shape and the windows, edged in stone and clear as could be, surrounded him. The sun shone through them from many angles, glittering and sparkling upon the furniture and implements that filled it. From here he could see as far as anyone on earth without the aid of either any instrument or of magic. The majestic Thorndar mountains to the south glimmered in the distance. The snow capping their summits looked like icing upon an enormous cake.

Baladar removed from the ornate wooden cabinet in the alcove a round piece of what looked like burnished stone. He moved across the chamber, back to his large desk that occupied a prominent place in the center of the room, and cleared off a space upon its smooth surface. He placed this object in the middle of the work space and walked around and took his seat. The stone was highly polished and it shimmered as if made of liquid within its sharply defined borders. Baladar placed his palms upon the center of the stone and closed his eyes. The designs in the stone seemed to swirl and spin as Baladar hummed quietly.

In fact, this object was not a stone at all. What Baladar was working with was a disk-shaped piece of Briland's deceased tree. Briland had left this to Baladar after her death. With it, Baladar was able to gaze almost anywhere on earth. All he needed to do was concentrate and mentally request a location. He neither had to have been to the place previously, nor did the disk require an image in his mind in order to locate the spot. All that was necessary was that at one time a Lalas had been in the vicinity of the desired location and that Baladar knew approximately where he wished the disk to search. If he could provide the disk with rough coordinates, an idea of the location he sought, it utilized his thoughts and intuitions, as well as its own special "instincts," and provided him with images almost instantaneously.

At this time, Baladar was seeking out the origin of the boy's casting. If he could find the place from whence he came, he might be able to determine if his casting was observed by the enemy. The dilemma was how to instruct the disk and how to accurately guide it to a location that Baladar did not yet know even remotely. He concentrated on a point south of the mountains, for he knew that the boy had come from somewhere in the immense southern regions of Gwendolen. He had to be more precise than that though if he wished to find anything of use to him, the area he was searching was so vast.

Suddenly and abruptly he stopped and placed the disk hastily into his inside pocket. He strode across the floor quickly and threw the door to the chamber open.

"Dalek! Come here quickly. And bring the boy!" he shouted to his aide on guard outside the room.

"Yes, my Lord," Dalek responded, a bit startled by his liege Lord's animated behavior. "At once, my Lord!" he answered as he leaped down the winding staircase to the room below where the boy was sleeping.

Baladar hastened back to the table with the disk and smiled to himself.

If the traces are still fresh on the boy I may yet be able to locate the casting ground. Oh, I hope that they have not yet bathed him. These doting nursemaids of mine, they probably couldn't resist immersing him in water as soon as they got their motherly hands upon him.

Baladar paced the room impatiently while he awaited his aide's return.

Dalek entered the room where the boy lay sleeping, and told the attending women of his Lord's orders. They reluctantly handed the prostrate youth over to the soldier, whose large and awkward hands received their portentous bundle with some discomfort. Hastily retreating from the room, Dalek began the ascent to Baladar's study once again. He clumsily tripped over the corner of a soiled, green cloak the meddling women had apparently wrapped the boy in to keep him warm in the chilly castle. Dalek grabbed at his feet, not wishing to disturb the youth, but also unwilling to delay in fulfilling his lordship's orders, and pulled the cape from under his boots. Hurriedly balling it up without taking even a moment to glance upon it, he tossed it into a corner, out of sight behind a large piece of oaken furniture.

As rapidly as he could, Dalek bounded up the stairs and into the room, carrying the boy as awkwardly as anyone could imagine, his arms outstretched in front of him as if he were holding a snake at bay and out of striking distance, straining under the weight.

"I have done as you asked, Sir, as fast as I could. Is there anything else you require?" he appealed, breathing heavily as he thrust the child into Baladar's waiting arms.

"No, not now. I appreciate your haste, though, Dalek. Wait outside. I may need you later."

"Yes, my Lord." He bowed as he returned to his post outside the door, relieved that he no longer had the burden of the child in his arms, and anxious to take up his post once again *outside* of the room.

Dalek was a country boy at heart and though he was as loyal to Baladar as any man could be, he was still unaccustomed to the use of magic. As uncomfortable as it made him, he nevertheless trusted his Lord implicitly. But, he still preferred not to be in his company when he wielded his power.

Baladar received the boy lovingly. It was with much sentiment that he carried the unnamed and helpless youth across the room. The boy's head rested peacefully on Baladar's shoulder, and he misted over with emotion. His almost navy blue eyes were clear as crystal and wide open, though empty of any awareness. The thick, long, blonde hair was matted against his skull. Baladar wiped a single tear from his cheek as his thoughts skidded between the sorrow at the absence of his wife and his joy at having the young man in his presence. He felt the true weight of the boy for the first time, in all senses, and he was precipitously aware of it.

Lord Baladar set the boy down softly upon the grand work table in the center of the room, and then he gazed upon him attentively. He was quite tall for his age, though thin and pale from his past ordeal, and his skin was almost translucent looking. He carefully placed two large, sausage shaped satin pillows on either side of the boy so that he would not fall. As he pushed the support carefully and snugly into his body, he noticed a crude bracelet around his wrist and pondered briefly on its origin and meaning. It was clearly not of appreciable value, at least in a monetary sense, so he was certain that it bore some other significance. Before Baladar had an opportunity to closely examine the trinket, he was suddenly distracted by the feeling of the disk emanating power from the confines of his cloak.

He reached inside another pocket and removed a modest suede pouch. Loosening the drawstring, he took from it four small stones, one ruby red, one sapphire blue, the third a deep, deep green and the fourth as black as night. From his right hand, he removed the large gold signet ring he always wore on his index finger. It bore the seal of state, and had been passed from generation to generation, from leader to leader, during the ceremony of succession. Although the ceremony was public, the secret of the ring was conveyed in a very private ceremony, or rather, ritual at which only the privileged few were welcome. Pushing up his tunic, he carefully placed the ring on the tender belly of the boy.

Reciting the words of power taught him that fateful night, Baladar concentrated on the rune carved into the ring. The carving abruptly came to life, and hovered over the adolescent child. Baladar took each of the four stones and placed them singly in a corner of the table. The rune image appeared to solidify about two feet above the boy, and as if tiny spiders had escaped from each corner of it to spin a web to the stones, lines formed of an apparently solid nature that reached out to each of the four corner gems. Upon touching the stone, the web like strings blazed with the full color of the gem to which it had attached itself.

The wide eyed yet unconscious boy was totally oblivious to the vivid colors swirling and sparking all around him. Baladar removed the concealed, warm disk from his cloak and placed it on the table just outside the sphere of power encircling him. As if the Lalas disk inhaled a full and deep breath, the colors began to twirl together and merge into one as they headed for the polished instrument. Baladar, beginning to feel the affects of these exertions on his person, sat himself down at the foot of the table. He gazed as intensely as he could at the disk.

An image began to form immediately above it as if a miniature play was being enacted before his eyes. In a trance-like state, Baladar witnessed the last moments of Mira's efforts. He felt the intense rush of sentiment and his body stiffened in response. He instinctively recognized the enormous sacrifice she had made and he perceived, as if he had been present in real time at the scene of this heroic deed, her great sorrow in the leave-taking, as well as the tremendous joy she experienced at the seeming success of her casting. He was awash with the warm feelings of elation and relief as he experienced her final emotions.

Without warning, Baladar recoiled from the sickening touch of evil. He felt the hot breath of the vicious beast upon his face as he leapt out of the nearby trees. The pallid skin and slimy appearance he'd chosen that day only enhanced his unholy aura. His long, pointed fingers grasped with a lustful and desperate urgency toward the boy. Baladar witnessed the boy's disappearance and he saw the agony on the distorted face of the Evil One as he recognized that the boy was gone from his reach. He momentarily swayed in his seat as the flood of anger permeated his soul and the sickening sensations infiltrated his consciousness. With an enormous effort, he shielded himself from the emotional onslaught and continued to observe the final moments of the casting.

The hordes of animal-like beings swarmed out from the nearby trees and surrounded the Evil One, but clearly, not too closely and in considerable fear of his wrath. They were accustomed to his arbitrary lashing out, and none wished to be too near if he was not successful. As Colton dar Agonthea, one of the most reluctantly uttered names of legend, realized that he had lost the boy, his mouth, dripping with venomous saliva, opened in a constricted circle and he let out a wail of agony that hurt Baladar's ears.

Baladar realized that Mira was more successful than she had ever dreamed she could have been at her life work. There was no sense of a trail and no trace of a direction. The boy was so safely and solidly cast by Mira that no other man or god could have done better. Colton struck repeatedly at the stone statue that was once Mira, and disregarding the gashes that the stone left in his arms and fingers, he continued until a greenish blood began to flow from his body in a steady stream that soon covered the statue with its putrid essence.

Baladar watched with much satisfaction as the statue reddened with heat and burned the gore off of itself in a sizzle of vapor; a fitting final slap in Colton's face. The plaint that emanated from Colton's mouth continued for quite some time. The gathering armies of his subjugated mutants fell to the ground and covered their heads with their arms. Eventually the Evil One became silent, turned abruptly from the stone statue, closed his blood red eyes and rose two feet off of the earth, suspended momentarily in the air. As if in a trance, he glided over his prone minions and retreated into the darkness of the forest.

Baladar slumped over the table in a state of exhilarated exhaustion. The boy was safe for the moment. Colton could not pursue him now for Mira had done her job well. She had granted him the time he needed to begin the education and training of the still unnamed boy. This "seeing" had accomplished much, and in addition to the knowledge he had been granted by virtue of it, he had also been granted the means with which to name the boy; Davmiran Dar Gwendolen it would be, thus granting rest and eternity to the great woman that was Mira.

The boy would not remember who he was or where he came from when he finally awoke. The process that Mira used to shelter him and protect him if the worst happened required that she erase the past from his young mind. She deeply regretted the fact that his parents would disappear from his memory, along with all of the other good and kind people from his other life. However, she had no choice, and Baladar recognized that she had done the only thing that she could have done under the circumstances. He would also thus be spared the pain of the memories and of the tragic fate which befell his family.

Now that he had arrived safely, he could be told gradually and gently who he really was and where he came from. The great legacy would not be lost to him forever, while Mira's heroic efforts would be everlastingly memorialized in song and poetry, her namesake would honor her with his deeds and his memory of her would never totally abandon him. Yet as Baladar well knew, his trials were just beginning and the days to come would require hard work, love balanced with sternness, rigorous training and constant sacrifice.

The boy would be prepared by the best in the land. Baladar would send the guarded word out to all whom he required to impart the knowledge and understanding in all of the mundane as well as arcane arts to the boy, Davmiran. He would be ready when the inevitable time of confrontation arrived.

He will succeed! He struck the table with his fist.

Baladar would help him and guide him and provide him with everything that he could, including his own life force, if the need for that should arise. He would sacrifice all and everything for the boy, for without his success the world was doomed.

There were still a few more acts to commit before rest would be possible for Baladar and the boy. He gathered up the four colored stones from the table and dropped them into the pouch from whence they came, and reached down in order to grasp the still warm ring and slip it back upon his hand. As he bent to retrieve it and slide the tunic back into place over the exposed skin of the sleeping youth, he noticed with astonishment that the tiny letters of his new name were scored into his skin above his navel: *Davmiran dar Gwendolen* in ancient script glowed reddish and bright. This did not appear to have harmed the boy at all, but rather the words radiated their glow throughout his body, and bestowed upon his inert form a shimmer heretofore absent that turned his skin from a pallid color to a healthy hue. He smiled, pleased with the ring's acknowledgment of his choice.

After finally maneuvering the great ring back onto his finger, he moved the disk slightly to the side so that it could witness, in its own way, what was about to take place, even though it would not be partaking in the following exercise. He then reached into the selfsame pouch and removed a small, pure white diamond. Barely was it out from its suede comfort when the room seemingly lit with energy. This tiny stone was a powerful relic, purportedly hewn from the same block as the Gem of Eternity, and truly it acted with a will of its own at times, frightening even Baladar with its compelling but silent instructions. It had been his mother's, and he had found it amongst her possessions only after she died. She had shown it to him once and explained its history to him, emphasizing its healing powers to which use she had relegated it. She also warned him of its enticing potency. It seemed as if the gem actually directed Baladar, even though there was no verbal or audible communication between them.

Baladar had an instinctual feeling that the small and beautiful stone was responsible for many of his ideas. Oft times he would be inspired to do or say something that he was not consciously aware he had any prior knowledge of. It was easy to attribute these moments to forgotten lessons of childhood, or to some other coincidence of a similar sort. Nevertheless, whenever Baladar held the stone he was certain that it communicated with him and inspired him in many unaccountable and often surprising ways.

He placed the white stone at the head of the sleeping boy. No sooner was it set down upon the table than it began to emanate a visible, clear light. Immediately, Baladar felt a sense of pleasure and peace envelop him. He relaxed for a brief moment in the satisfaction of the feeling, and he actually felt renewed and rejuvenated as if he had just awoken from a long and restful sleep. The light engulfed the silent boy and wove a cocoon of tendrils around him.

The gem had such power that Baladar momentarily gave in to its dominance and refrained from directing it. This could be incredibly dangerous, as the power was often raw and unpredictable, and it required a concentrated direction on his part. His fear from the day the stone was received unto his protection was that he would give in to its dominance and lose himself in the wondrous feelings that it generated in him whenever he unleashed it. It required such strength and control to focus his energy upon the task at hand. It was so easy to relax and let the heavenly sensations carry him away. Yet, Baladar was well trained, and if he had not given in to it yet, after these many years of possession, he would not give in to it now when the limits of his strength were being tested and the need was dire.

He sent a mental direction to the stone. *Cal mara timathor. Cortan deuxte indiran druidenter.*

The gem sparkled with energy and the forces encircling the boy were spinning rapidly. As suddenly as it began, it ceased. The diamond returned to its dormant state but Baladar knew that the spell had been properly cast. He reluctantly placed the gem back in the pouch with its brethren. From this day forward, or at least until Davmiran's powers manifested themselves and he was strong enough to protect himself, he would be invisible to all human eyes upon leaving the confines of the city gates. Neither would he be heard nor would his presence be detectable in any manner by any human being outside the walls of Pardatha. The spell would cease by itself as soon as the boy was ready. This would hopefully give them more time to train him and prepare him for what was to come. Word of his existence would not spread so rapidly, and therefor the period of learning would be able to run its own course. Those in the palace who knew of his existence would forget entirely about him upon stepping outside the city, as if they had never seen him, and only Baladar and the few whom he would choose, would be his guardians at all times and would not for a moment forget about him or his primary importance.

Finally, Baladar needed to send out the message of bidding. He needed to inform those whom he had long ago chosen to be the boy's teachers should the time arise, that their presence was now sorely needed; that the moment had finally come. For this, he would require the disk once more. Its powers of communication were once limitless, as it was a piece of a Lalas. Now however, although still strong beyond measure, the demise of so many of its brethren had weakened the network of communication somewhat. Baladar had no fear, though, that they would not receive his message. He also knew that it would not be received by anyone other than the ones for which it was meant. The Lalas never made those mistakes. Their messages were never intercepted inadvertently. Baladar bade the disk to send out the call. It promptly and eagerly responded, and as he heard the high-pitched hum, he simultaneously witnessed the slight vibration of the disk. Cairn of Thermaye, Robyn dar Tamarand, and Filaree Par D'Avalain were summoned and were sure to respond as soon as they possibly could.

Baladar need only wait now. The fabric would weave of its own will and nothing could stop it short of dissolution, and for that to occur many events of an obvious nature would need to precede it. They still had time. The trees were yet alive and the First might even be found by the likes of Davmiran. His hopes were rekindled with the presence of the boy, and the future once again took on the many faces of possibility, not all of which were bleak. In fact, the arrival of the boy at long last had perhaps recast the future entirely. Now he could only await, anxiously, the arrival of his cohorts, and hope that nothing serious would impede their progress.

    The spell was complete and Baladar felt the satisfaction that he had done as much as he could have in this small amount of time. He was exhausted and although the presence of the white stone had at first made him feel ripe with energy and youth, as soon as it was out of his sight, the true weight of his years began to wear upon him. With barely any energy left, he returned the disk to the cabinet in the alcove and then he proceeded to collapse on his resting divan in the corner, and to sleep and sleep with heretofore unanticipated abandon.

Chapter Three

Cairn of Thermaye, shaven-headed, grey robed, humble and reserved could do nothing to hide his strange yellow eyes that sparkled in contrast to his attempts at being inconspicuous. For him, the contradiction was not obvious, but it was curious that his personality embodied similar differences in its nature. It was indicative of his attitude toward good and evil; the world is full of dichotomies, and all standards for measuring such inexact ideas are arbitrary, he would say. Yet, Cairn had an innate sense of right and wrong that surpassed any impulse to reason his way clear to anarchic thoughts.

When the call came, he was ready, as if he had been expecting it his entire life. He rose immediately, wrapped his cloak around his legs and went to gather his belongings. Although he never really knew when his thread would enter the weave, this moment felt proper to him; it felt right. He glanced circumspectly at the sky as he jogged to his cottage, expecting it too also appear different, as he knew that from that moment forth nothing else in his life would ever truly be the same again.

Cairn was a brilliant man, schooled by the masters of the Carnesian order, the son of a Duke who at the age of one tiel and one recognized his calling and renounced his birthright in order to enter the league. He had studied ever since, and he had visited all of the seats of learning, renowned throughout the world. At Thermascon, he studied metaphysics with the master, Cosacteris. There he learned to think in broad strokes, and to see the beauty in the patterns that governed the once-removed aspects of everyday life. In the wastes of Pertas, he studied ethics with Durmas de Borea. This was his most cherished subject, even though he found it to be the most taxing one mentally. It oft times confused him and forced him to question so much of what he had been taught as a child. But, he learned to use his broadened concepts of right and wrong, and good and evil constructively, as it seemed so easy to misconstrue the lessons of objectivity.

He learned ethics from the viewpoint of the "question mark." His teacher's primary conceptual starting point was that good and evil were simply definitions of ideas that changed from society to society, and age to age. Though he honored his mentor, this concept of ethical relativity appealed to his intellectual senses, but it was unacceptable to his instincts. He recognized how dangerous an idea this was, and he was aware of how often it led to blatant abuses of power. If good and evil could be redefined within specific contexts, then base and depraved actions could be justified semantically. Cairn *felt* the difference between good and evil! To him, it was imbedded in nature itself, neither the product of reason, nor subject to the whims of society.

Cairn learned to think of consequences and to begin to define good and evil based upon consequences and possibilities. His primary objective was to educate so as to enhance the quality of life on the planet. In a world where magic overtly manifested itself, and historically the gods made themselves evident, both in positive and negative ways, one would think that the true path would be obvious. Yet, the gods acted in ways beyond the comprehension of even the most brilliant of men, and their actions could only guide the learned. Cairn was attuned to the pulse of nature and he sensed when its fabric was flawed, when its weave was unstable or a stitch had been inadvertently dropped. He allowed reason to help him choose but never to determine the choice entirely.

Cairn wholeheartedly believed that the standards for behavior should be based upon what would promote the welfare of living beings. To him, even though he had an eclectic mind and could convincingly argue many and diverse ethical points, his heart was convinced of the one path, and his style of teaching allowed his students to think and reason, but inevitably led them to the conclusions that he hoped for. His success as an instructor in ethics was measured not by virtue of creating disciples who mimicked his style or his thoughts, but by virtue of generating thoroughly rounded thinkers who intuited their way to the conclusions that they supported, but could support them logically nonetheless.

Cairn's primary teacher, Durmas de Borea, was a skeptic, the fact of which influenced all aspects of his concepts of right and wrong. Durmas cultivated the minds of his students, and he forced them to develop their own codes and to theoretically carry them out to their logical conclusions in reference to a society governed by them. He then had his students evaluate the success of this society and analyze what consequences these rules of ethical conduct and standards of good and evil would have upon the rest of society. Of course, this was only done on paper and in the minds of the students. The method did force Cairn to think, and he was particularly good at this type of thinking. Durmas loved him as a son and he had hoped that he would carry on for him after his death. Yet, Cairn had a different calling, and his talents and years of study would now be utilized by others to a far more serious end than the mere pleasure of learning.

Logic, the subject he liked the least even though he acknowledged the inherent beauty in the correctness of its methods and the clear definitions of truth that it embodied, Cairn excelled at. It bothered him that he had such natural proclivities toward a subject that was so limited in scope for him. Yet, his teacher, Bora C'al Thomasan, taught him to expand upon the simple tautologies and proofs, and apply the concepts to life itself. Although Cairn did not see the logical patterns that he learned in these books repeat themselves in everyday life, he gladly accepted the teaching and hungrily absorbed them into his psyche.

Cairn was the best student that the masters ever had. He was humble and studious, yet he was full of life, and he demonstrated a healthy arrogance that comes with such talent and confidence. He was unequivocally the most fitting teacher for the boy. Cairn would school him in philosophy and help the boy to learn to think. Although perhaps one such as Davmiran would oft be tested in ways that would not allow for the luxury of deep thought and time, Cairn hoped to instill in him an attitude, and a spontaneous understanding of what needed to be done and to what purpose. He hoped to teach in a way that the proclivity for good became instinctual in the boy. And to do so, he needed to teach all of the consequences of evil, as defined in the context of the current world. The boy must *feel* and *taste* the differences between right and wrong. He must be able to act without hesitation, and with the confidence of a moral leader. He could not make a priest of the young man. There were many occasions wherein the inherent act that needed to be committed would not and should not be done gleefully. The lines drawn between these deeds of good and deeds of evil were so thin. Murder or self-defense? Execution or righteous removal of a criminal? War or surrender? Domination or victory? These were some of the issues that the boy would have to face in time, and Cairn was determined to provide him with the intellectual means that he would require in order to deal with the decisions.

He needed to gather only a few things before his journey could begin. First and foremost was the object which had served him so well during his own search for answers to the ethical questions which had tormented him so often as a youth. Although an object possessed of great magical power in its own right, it required only strength of mind to activate it, not the powers of a mage. In fact, it only responded to thought, pure and simple. No magic could animate it. Thus, Cairn was fully capable of utilizing it, perhaps more so than anyone else. And utilize it he did, to the point where he thought of it as his friend and confidant, rather than the inanimate object that it appeared to be.

This ancient wooden box filled with beautifully carved pieces that resembled many of the beings alive on the planet, was similar to a chess board in design. Yet, these pieces had lives of their own when properly directed. They served to instruct the user on the many and varied outcomes of his speculations, and had been of immeasurable assistance to Cairn during his philosophical endeavors. The figures were so lifelike that they served to mitigate the cold and detached perspective that a thinker oft times assumes, and they reminded one of mortality and the reality of flesh and blood consequences. They aged and died and were reborn, and they constantly transformed themselves. This box was a tool Cairn would, under no circumstances, be without during the schooling of the boy.

When the call came, Cairn of Thermaye was sitting cross-legged on the edge of the stream that curved around his small house, deep in the woods. He was not surprised by the summons and he was thoroughly prepared to respond. He had not had contact with any humans for half a tiel now, yet there was no reluctance on his part to resume his worldly life.

"Baladar of Pardatha," he repeated to himself. "I should have known it would be he!" The scholar smiled a portentous smile.

Cairn was content with what he had been doing, and he knew that such feelings of contentment lead only to a lessening of the mind's activity and to mediocrity. He needed to be challenged and he was thus stimulated by the call. His entire body was immediately rejuvenated and he required only a small amount of time to prepare himself for the trip at hand. As he neared his house, he brushed the grass and twigs from his tunic and went inside to gather the box and the few other things he would need to take with him on his upcoming journey.

He had been preparing his entire life for this call, even though unbeknownst to him, the threads had only now been woven together in the pattern that allowed for his assistance. It all seemed so natural and correct that Cairn barely broke the stride of his thought as he prepared for his sojourn. Having no magical abilities of his own, the journey would not be a short one, but he looked forward with enthusiasm to the time he would have while traveling to think and plan.

Of course, he would need to call upon his dearest friend and soul-mate, Calyx, whose strength he always relied upon when need reared its possessive head. He was a Moulant, the mysterious benefactors of the tree's love and affection for time untold. The Moulant were so few on this planet that each and every one was revered and held in the highest esteem by all who knew of them. For Cairn to have been befriended by even a young offspring of one, spoke volumes about his integrity. He was honored to have Calyx as his soul-mate and he celebrated their relationship every moment of his life.

The Moulant heretofore remained the friends of the trees and their Chosen only, and breeding outside their own race was a thing practically unheard of. Yet, Calyx befriended Cairn, and no one ever thought to question the mysterious beast's choice. Though anomalies both, it was accepted that their union was rooted in purpose. Calyx was a giant, catlike animal, red-eyed and almost iridescent, and his fur shimmered in colors of silver, blue and copper. He stood on his hind legs perhaps ten feet tall. His jaw was hinged like that of a snake, and it gave him the ability to open it wider than seemed possible, thus exposing his enormous white teeth to his enemies sight. When in battle, his roar was so loud and resonant that it sent shivers through the bones of anyone within hearing distance.

When Calyx was born, he went immediately to live with Cairn. He arrived unbidden upon his doorstep one day, and both Cairn and Calyx knew instantly that he was there until one or the other passed on, though neither perceived at the time just why they were meant to be together. They lived their lives hand in hand and waited for their calling, not knowing what form it would take.

The Moulant were known to protect their own and their companions with a ferocious possessiveness, as they were so few in number to begin with. They developed a common call, the "plea of aid," utilized only under circumstances of the greatest mortal peril. When sounded, aid of one form or another would surely arrive in a timely fashion. Their lives were very long ones, and although they usually remained separate and apart from the world of humans and human events, Calyx entered the world of man with design and little trepidation.

Calyx and Cairn shared a bond of love and protection as intense as any parent and child could hope to have. They communicated in their own unique manner, and although Calyx could not speak, he made his feelings known. Cairn had little difficulty understanding his friend, and it often surprised Cairn just how attuned to his thoughts Calyx had grown.

Cairn needed only to sit and think of his need and Calyx would appear, prepared and fully aware of the intention for which he was summoned. Cairn could hear the water splashing a bit upstream as Calyx crossed the current behind the cottage. Within an instant he was at his side, waiting for instructions. The enormous, red-eyed cat with a subtle resemblance to a wolf, a slightly elongated snout, long shimmering fur and a catlike tail that moved slowly and gracefully back and forth, gazed knowingly at his friend for life.

Calyx and Cairn were both ready for the journey ahead. No words of explanation needed to be spoken in order to remind either one of the significance of the occasion. Strangely, Cairn, with Calyx standing majestically next to him, felt as if his life was only now verily beginning, as they gazed apprehensively yet longingly, northward toward Baladar and the boy.

Chapter Four

Robyn dar Tamarand, the profligate and prodigal son of the Baron Calipee dar Tamarand, was an adept at the arcane arts, though not always so. It seemed at one time that Robyn had come very close to getting lost in his power, and only when his father, the Baron, ostensibly forced him to choose between his life and his proclivity toward mischievous exhibitionism, did Robyn apparently recognize how far astray he had wandered. Nevertheless, he maintained the cover he had inadvertently created during this dark period in his life, and he hoped to utilize even this to his benefit.

He and his father allowed everyone to believe what they would about Robyn, as they always had. They did not attempt to alter anyone's perceptions. In fact, they subtly encouraged the negative reputation he had gained in order to provide him with an excuse to remain aloof from the prying eyes and minds of those who could ultimately endanger him. Only his father and a few chosen others knew the truth about this ruse. At a very early age, Robyn's ample powers were acknowledged, and to protect himself, he continued to manifest a frivolous and carefree attitude so as not to be taken too seriously by anyone whose intentions toward him may not have been healthy.

He was a beautiful boy and an even more handsome adult. He needed no magic to enhance his appearance. Jet black hair hung in thick waves upon his broad shoulders. His dark brown eyes glinted with excitement at whatever task he took on. His skin was of a rich golden-tanned color that highlighted his piercing eyes. Perhaps six feet tall, he was average in height for his part of the world, yet his bearing made him appear to be much taller and broader than he actually was. He carried himself with majesty, as his father proudly recognized.

Robyn was the dream of every young girl in the province, and his aloofness and private ways only enhanced his desirability. His flippant personality masked a somber and serious side that few people witnessed. Even his father portrayed him as a carefree bon vivant, which was partially true. Yet Robyn was far deeper than he appeared to the outside world to be. No living being who had such a mastery of the arcane could be superficial without being extremely dangerous, and although Robyn was quite dangerous himself, he was by no means superficial.

Robyn's instinctual understanding of magic and the ways of the supernatural far exceeded anyone's expectations or surmising. He had a natural comprehension of the art, and there was little that he attempted that he could not accomplish. An avid reader, he made considerable use of the vast library at Triesma, the university city south of the capital of Concordia, where his father presided. He was constantly starved for knowledge, and the need to learn was so great in him that it kept him restless and striving. His instincts coupled with his intelligence and commitment to learning created a formidable character. Fortunately, he also sensed the alignment of sides and he incontrovertibly chose the side of the light.

His rapport with the tree who had chosen him was intimate and productive. He never had a doubt in his own mind that he would be chosen by Promanthea, the name he appended to his bond-mate, though the circumstances surrounding the process in his case were unusual and unprecedented. As a young child, he communicated with it and felt closer to the tree than anything or anyone else. His tree was a central and essential part of his life for as long as he could remember. Even his father was excluded from the circle of intimacy that he closed with his tree. Such was the way with the Chosen, and families were often left out of what would be the most important relationship in their child's life. Promanthea allowed him his diversions when he was young, and Robyn came to believe them as intentional. Had he not neared the precipice early in his impetuous life, he may neither have understood its compelling danger nor recognized its shameless threat.

Robyn received the summons with glee, as if he had been waiting all the while for just such a call. He was well prepared and more than ready to attend to the task at hand. Sitting in the soft and aromatic cleft of a large branch of Promanthea, Robyn lifted his head and gazed at the ceiling of leaves above him. As he did so, the softness of the cushion supporting his head solidified immediately into a rough branch, reacting to the absence of his body warmth. The canopy of branches and the foliage above him shivered in anxious anticipation of the travels in store for him.

He immediately closed his eyes and began the trance inducing humming that brought him into synchronization with his tree. Shortly, he was carried, like a leaf caught in the rapidly moving water of a rushing river, into the surging energy of Promanthea. Together they traveled for some time, as Robyn liked to describe his communication with his tree. Although he remained in a state of stasis during the process, it felt as if he was traveling, and traveling at mind-boggling speeds. When he finally came to rest, although no words were spoken, he was full of the knowledge that he needed and he had the answers to the questions that he never even consciously asked.

Such was his relationship with his bond-mate. But, this time there was a subtle difference. Robyn was not sure exactly what that difference was, but he was certain that he sensed that something was being kept from him. Never before in all of his communications with Promanthea did he ever walk away with such a feeling. It was neither fearful nor joyful, but his bond-mate was keeping things from him, the awareness of which even Promanthea could not fully suppress.

Normally, Robyn returned to the physical world after merging in thought with his tree, relaxed, infinitely calmer than before the experience and prepared for whatever lay ahead. In this case, he was rather anxious even though there was no sense of foreboding or danger, simply one of mystery. Try as he might, Robyn could not merge with the flow of thoughts that generated this feeling. He was purposefully being excluded for the first time ever!

He sent to Promanthea barbs of protest, only to have them gently rebuffed without any sense of explanation, as his frustration mounted unbearably.

"Have I committed some grave misdeed that you should treat me so?" he finally and piteously said aloud, knowing full well that verbal communication would gain him nothing.

Robyn was immediately overwhelmed with the calm and comforting caress of Promanthea's mind-touch, and he understood without further regret that yes, there was something un-communicated, something so monumental and far beyond his understanding at this point that knowledge of it would only serve to prejudice the future. His tree felt similar remorse at the need to conceal anything from Robyn, yet he remained steadfast and determined, and Robyn resigned himself to that fact, relinquishing his feelings of hurt and abandonment in favor of his greater trust and respect for Promanthea. Yet, the nagging presentiment would not wholly disappear, and Robyn was certain that it had something to do with the calling.

"Aha! The boy!" he gasped. "You know more than you are telling me!" he said, but just as quickly as he formed the words around this thought, Promanthea retreated to an incommunicable state. The conversation was over.

Robyn knew that the task to which he was just recently called upon to lend his aid and knowledge was one of primary importance, and his role was a crucial one. With his strength and Promanthea's, he began the preparations for his journey eastward to join Baladar and the others at the side of the boy.

Chapter Five

She turned abruptly and parried his thrust. With the flat side of her broadsword, using all of her body weight, she slammed into the exposed portion of his arm above his gauntlet and knocked him off balance. Before he could recover, she grabbed the staff lying on the ground nearby and swept him off his feet with one circular motion. As he fell heavily to the hard, dry earth within the circle of combat, Filaree Par D'Avalain stood over him triumphantly with the staff across his throat.

"You fool!" she exclaimed gleefully. "You should never have come at me so quickly when you thought my back was turned. It was just what I expected and hoped for. Next time, do not be so predictable."

Cameron pushed her to one side, then stood and brushed the dirt off of his clothing, concealing his reddened face from view.

"Everything is predictable to you, my Lady. I don't think that I could ever surprise you with my attack," he responded rather sheepishly, glancing at her out of the corner of his eye.

"Well, nevertheless Cameron, try and be more creative, and never expose your sword arm to the enemy. It will eventually spell your downfall no matter how inept the opponent might be," she replied in a motherly tone. "If you always come upon your enemy square, you present to him your broadest surface. It is not unmanly to be discreet."

She hoped that she had not admonished Cameron too sternly with her harsh response. He was, after all, the best swordsman in the kingdom, next to herself of course. Her fondness for him was immeasurable, and if she could embarrass him into being just a tiny bit more careful or more aware of the subtleties of battle, it might just save his life one day. He was too good a man to die unnecessarily because she failed to properly reproach him in fear of insulting his masculinity.

Filaree smoothed out her green, suede tunic, straightened the silk belt which held it in place, and began walking back to the horses lolling nearby. As she approached her silver grey mare Nico, she nickered affectionately and knelt on her front two legs to allow her to climb on easily. She required no saddle or bridle when she rode upon her back. She gladly carried her wherever she wished to go and responded to her needs as if she could read her thoughts.

"Come, Cameron. Ride with me back to the castle. The sun will soon set and I am ravished with hunger. Tonight the moon will be full and the lake sprites may be out and about. You know how they love to find a handsome, young man alone after dark," she teased. "Or perhaps you would like to be seduced by the ladies of the lake, for all I know," she said, smiling into her sleeve.

Cameron frowned and hastily called to his mount so that he could accompany his Lady back and not be left here alone. There was little he feared in life, but the lake sprites made his blood run cold. He knew that Filaree did not share his concern, but, then again, what did really frighten her? He had yet to see her waver in the face of any obstacle. Neither did she ever express anything but sheer confidence whenever she was presented with what would have been insurmountable to most other warriors. Cameron shook his head back and forth. This Lady never ceased to amaze him.

Filaree Par D'Avalain was surely a warrior, in every sense of the word. Perhaps the finest at single combat in the kingdom, Filaree was never beaten. Her prowess with the broadsword and the staff was well renowned. Few had been privileged to witness her ability on horseback with a lance or crossbow. Nevertheless, it was extraordinary. Her opponents never walked away unscathed unless she chose to let them. If the enemy were real, they rarely walked away at all.

Cameron served his Lady for the past two tiels by now, and his respect for her as a leader and teacher, as well as his awe with regard to her continually astounding success against great odds, increased and compounded itself. He knew that he would do anything for her, including laying down his own life if need be. Such was his feeling for the Lady Filaree, and such feeling was mirrored a thousand times over by the men and women who served her.

As soon as he was mounted, Filaree clicked Nico onward and the two leapt forth at lightening speed in the direction of the castle. Cameron did all that he could to keep up with her and not be left in her dust once again. The sun would soon be setting, and it got rather cold and windy in the kingdom of Altair this time of year due to its proximity to the ice lakes. They were directly in the path of the breezes blowing southward across the vast expanses of ice, carrying with them a damp, cold air that settled on the city in the evening hours. Filaree, like usual, was too quick and was shortly out of his sight and into the forest ahead, and he spurred his mount on to regain her side.

As Cameron burst forth from the dense, pine, stockade-like forest surrounding the castle walls, prepared to gallop the fifty or so yard open expanse to the gates of the fortress, his mount suddenly reared up as he almost came crashing into Filaree and Nico. At first, his senses reeled with what he interpreted to be danger signals. With his broadsword already in his hand, he stared intently at Filaree, wanting desperately to know why she was seemingly frozen in stride directly in front of him. She neither moved nor reacted to his abrupt approach in any way. Nico pranced in place, her handsome head bobbing up and down.

He turned his horse so as to face the forest and give himself the ability to back toward Filaree. After scanning the space between her and the castle gate and seeing no sign of trouble, he focused his eyes on the sharp edge of pine trees, fully expecting that whatever had stopped his mistress in place to shortly pounce upon them as well. He slowly retreated to her side, glancing left and right.

"My Lady, can you hear me?" he asked while never taking his eyes off of the perimeter of trees in front of him. "Mistress? Try to break away from whatever is holding you while I guard your back."

Cameron was slowly backing up next to her so that he could just about grab Filaree from her saddle and flee to the gates, when she turned her face to him and simply said, "We must go quickly, Cameron. Please assist me to the castle. We have work to do before we leave here."

Cameron was so shocked he could barely respond. "Yes, my Lady, at once," was all he could manage, as he turned and grabbed Nico's mane and led them to the entrance.

"Do not fear, dear Cameron," Filaree said rather sweetly, sensing his concern. "I am quite well. I have only just received a long awaited message. The means of its conveyance was rather unorthodox, and I was momentarily unable to move. It has merely caused a bit of fatigue, that is all. I am fine now, truly I am," she continued convincingly. "We must prepare though and with as much speed as we can muster. We have been 'called'," she exclaimed with finality.

By the way she said "called" at the beginning and the end, Cameron recognized the auspiciousness of the event, although he had no inkling as to the why or the wherefore of the call. His first concern was to get his mistress safely behind the castle walls. There would be time for explanations later.

Chapter Six

Cairn, with Calyx by his side, departed from the southern woods on the very first day of the new year. He suspected that it would take them approximately eight or nine days to arrive at the border of the kingdom of Pardatha, just north of the Thorndar mountain range. The pass through the mountains would be difficult to traverse at this time of year, but with Calyx's aid, he knew it would be possible. Baladar's message was clear; "The boy is in need of training. Make haste. Waste no time during your journey."

He carried only a small satchel containing necessities, and of course the box. Cairn of Thermaye was accustomed to eating sparsely and traveling light. His needs were not great. He knew that as long as Calyx was with him, he would never lack for something to eat in the event that the nuts and berries were not prevalent enough along the route to the boy's side. He wrapped his robes around his long legs to facilitate his ability to jog at a decent pace, and without a glance backwards, he was off.

The days were short during the winter months, and although the air was only cool not cold this far southwest of the mountains, there was a considerable nip to it. Cairn wished to travel quickly, but he had no desire to take unnecessary risks and attempt to penetrate the forest during the evening hours. His plan was to proceed eastward until he reached the border town of Pardeau, about four days jog, and then to go northward through the Forest of the Winds, and then on to the feet of the Thorndars. He would have to cross lake Tamaran first, though, as soon as he emerged from the woods, and the thought of that did not amuse him.

The lake was a treacherous body of water, perhaps the deepest in the known world, and it could only be crossed during the evening hours when the Selgays were asleep. Sometimes referred to as the guardians of the lake, the Selgays were the giant bird-like beasts who made their homes in the large crevices of the sheer walls of the Thorndars surrounding the lake to the north. They attacked mercilessly, and they craved flesh. Their beaks were sharp as razors, and their claws were long, hard and honed on the rocks to lance-like tips. The talons were barbed, and when a Selgay grabbed its prey, like a fish on a hook, the more it struggled, the deeper the wound became and the more damage it did.

No one ever escaped a Selgay attack. They seldom traveled with companions, though, so that if you ever encountered one, you could be almost certain that there were no others anywhere near. The Selgays fought bitterly and savagely amongst themselves over territory and they preferred to hunt alone. That was of little comfort to Cairn as he anticipated the long and arduous trip across the length of the lake during the pitch of night. He had four days to march in peace before he would need to really begin to worry.

After perhaps four relatively eventless days of keeping up a rather steady jogging pace, sleeping on his mat amidst the fragrant meadow grasses at night and thinking about the days to come, Cairn broke his stride and began to walk along what appeared to be a well-worn path that started about one hundred yards before the tall grasses of the fields of county Pardeau began.

There was very little evidence that anyone was living anywhere near here. The grasses were uncut, the fields unplowed, and as far as the eye could see, there were no buildings of any kind. Cairn hummed a comforting tune to himself as he now ambled down the path, thinking intently about the opportunity he would soon have to impart whatever knowledge he could to the boy. He was gratified that he could be involved in this prodigious undertaking. To be able to be of assistance, of whatever kind, was an honor.

As he continued to walk, the path narrowed and the grasses increased in height. He was now totally unable to see above them and he had to follow the trail, however indirectly it abruptly seemed to proceed. Calyx had been absent from his side for some time presently, as was quite normal, and he paid it little mind. Cairn never questioned how his friend arrived at the same destination as he did without taking the apparent route. Yet, arrive he always did, and Cairn took it for granted that he did so with more knowledge of the terrain than Cairn himself obtained by traveling the direct route.

The grasses, perhaps seven feet in height at this point, were dense and emerald green, shimmering and clicking in the wind as they bumped into one another. Cairn noticed the path widening and straightening out as he came around a sharp bend, playing tricks with his sense of direction. His sense of hearing was sharp from years of living apart from the harsh sounds of the cities, and he was sure he could distinguish human voices in the distance.

With caution Cairn continued down the path, not wanting to stumble into a group unannounced, looking as foreign as he must with his tied up robes and shaven head. Aware of his appearance and how it could be disconcerting to the country folk in this area, he silently approached the sounds in the distance. As he came close enough to the group, and a group it certainly was for he could clearly hear at least six or seven different voices seemingly arguing with one another, he kept close to the grasses bordering the sides of the path.

"I do not know why we were given these instructions, but follow them we must if we are to keep our jobs!" Cairn heard one of the men say in a heavy Pardeauan accent.

As he inched his way around the final bend, Cairn stepped into the grass just a bit in order to keep himself concealed while catching a glimpse of the crowd ahead.

"It goes against me to do so, Petro. I cannot detain a man just because he is a stranger. Our town has always welcomed travelers," a barrel-chested, tall man with a red beard responded.

"I do nay want strangers coming to my town no more!" said another short man with long tangled hair and high, muddy boots. "I need to protect me own. Me wife and child is scared 'nuf these days."

"Travelers are still welcome and always will be!" the man called Petro responded. "But, we have to be careful now. Mayor Steed has been *told* by the councilor to keep vigilant. I do nay know what they expect to come here, but they are mighty worried."

A fourth man, burly and silent up until now, spoke up with determination. "I trust not this councilor. He has our timid little mayor running around scared like a mother cackle bird who lost its babes. Why should we listen to this foreigner? Where did he come from anyway?"

"Trevor speaks the truth!" another man chimed in. "Where *did* he come from? We here never needed outlanders to help us run our business. He just appears one day and then is gone and we now have a new boss? Strange times are surely upon us, and I do nay like the feel of them."

"Borland is right. Ever since this outlander showed up in our town things is turned topsy-turvy. 'Strangers' as he calls 'em, have kept us alive for many a year with their trade and travel needs," said Constant the farmer. "If I am to feed me kiddies and pay me taxes, I needs to sell me grain elsewheres. Are you going to buy it all from me, Petro?"

"Nay, I cannot, Constant," he replied, shaking his head and toeing the ground petulantly. "But there is truth to the warnings.

Worse things may come of this than too few business partners, I fear."

"I do nay want trouble. We were told just to hold them up for a bit, not to harm anyone. I say we do as we been told," a dark eyed and sinister looking man named Marto retorted.

"I do nay like to be *told* by anyone how to do things, let alone some green skinned, slimy messenger boy from the south!" Borland exclaimed with finality.

"You defy him and you will bring evil things down upon us all. I swear to you Borland, I will nay allow it. Trouble is as trouble does, and trouble is coming. I do nay want to be in its way when it reaches here," the short, bearded man retorted.

"You will nay allow it? And how do you propose to stop me from aiding whomsoever I choose? You have always been a coward, Gumley, and I would nay have expected more from ye."

Marto raised his staff in front of Borland in a menacing way, and as the lines were being drawn amongst the parties present with a nasty fight seemingly inevitable, Petro smacked the hilt of his broadsword against the lone tree trunk in the clearing. "Enough now!" he said with authority. "There's no sense in fighting amongst ourselves. We can nay decide the matter here with our tempers red hot. Borland! You take Trevor and farmer Constant back to the town center and wait for us there. The rest of us will finish our scouting watch and meet you there an hour after the sun is down. We can sit at Parla's and talk this over later. Some good ale and one of her peppered hens will ease these tensions, I suspect."

"OK Petro, if *you* say so I will. But you can nay get me to go against my better judgement here and change me ways," Borland said, glaring at Marto.

As Borland left with the others, it was easy for Cairn to determine that however good the intentions of some of the men might be, if he entered the town now, then his journey would surely be delayed. Something was going on here, that was certain. The town of Pardeau was heretofore known as a haven for travelers, but not now!

Some green-skinned messenger boy from the south? Cairn repeated to himself. *The southerners so rarely travel this far north.* Cairn sensed trouble here, far more serious than the orders to merely detain all travelers indicated. *And could it be that Calyx and I are the two they were referring to?*

Cairn decided that the most prudent course of action under the circumstances would be to sit tight exactly where he was for long enough until the men left the clearing, camp for the night in the area that they had already searched and vacated, and proceed just before dawn, bypassing the town, and head for the shelter of the forest north of Pardeau. He was inured to sleeping out doors, and it was really of no consequence to him. Cairn's only regret was that he would be unable to gather any more information from the townspeople on any of the most recent, disturbing events. But, his curiosity was not worth the risks he now perceived.

When the remaining men had completed their cursory scouting and departed for the town, Cairn emerged from his hiding place among the tall grasses. He laid out his bedroll and sat cross-legged upon it. The sun was hanging low over the horizon, and there was perhaps twenty to thirty minutes of light left before it set completely and left him in total darkness.

The stars will be bright tonight, he mused, as the sky was as clear as a bell.

He would need no fire to give him comfort and his robes would keep him warm. He ate a few dried fruits from his satchel, relishing the intensity of their flavor, and he immediately enjoyed the feeling of rejuvenation that they offered him.

Cairn's thoughts kept drifting to the image of the "councilor" who was surely up to no good.

*Where could he have come from, and who would have sent him? What purpose would he serve stirring up doubt and trouble so far north? Who could he be looking for in this part of the countryside? Surely no one could have known of **my** journey already,* he thought with consternation.

Cairn lay down on the pallet and drifted off into a fitful sleep, disturbed by the unexpected turn of events he had just witnessed, and anxious for the sun to rise so he could be on his way north and away from here.

Cairn was woken abruptly when a bony hand, smelling strongly of ale was clasped over his mouth. A second hand had grabbed both of his arms and twisted them behind his back in such a manner that if he struggled he might just break them himself. He was lying upon his stomach, trussed like a spring chicken.

"Look at what I've found here!" he heard his attacker say. "A funny lookin' 'un. May hap our green friend will want to see this'n," the hoarse voice said.

Cairn turned his eyes sideways enough to recognize the face of the man who held him. Marto, the burly one arguing earlier with the others, spun him back and snapped his face forwards.

"No you don't. I do nay want those devil eyes lookin' on me. Come, Gumley help me out here. Do nay hide yourself in the woods."

"I am nay hiding. I'll do me job like the rest of ye. Here, let me bind him with this," he said as he unwrapped a bundle of stout cord.

"First cover the eyes of this stranger. I do nay like the looks of 'im," Marto instructed.

As Gumley was tying a dirty rag around the head of his prisoner, Cairn heard a loud thud followed by the sounds of a scuffle and a sharp crack. There was much grunting and scraping, when at last he heard a voice say, "Yes, run you old bat. Show me the tail of the coward that you are, Gumley. And do nay try to come back again tonight and cause more trouble."

The voice belonged to the man called Trevor, one of the dissenters from earlier. Cairn was certain of that. As he was helped to his feet and his blindfold was removed he saw the other man, Marto, sprawled out on the ground with a nasty wound on the side of his forehead. A small amount of blood was oozing from the cut, and he was clearly not conscious. He lay in a heap with what was certain to be a broken leg by the sight of it.

"I make my apologies for my countrymen. They are scared these days and they forget themselves. My name is Trevor Cortland. I am the blacksmith in the town, as was my father before me and his father before him," and he extended his broad, calloused hand forthrightly to Cairn.

The scholar reached out his own arm in response, as the big man was attempting to brush off the soil from Cairn's robes. Before they made contact, a tremendous gust of wind came out of nowhere and sent leaves and dirt flying in all directions. Trevor's eyes opened wide in fear as he reached for his staff with a look of sheer panic on his face. Into the clearing, from what direction he could not tell, a giant, catlike creature appeared with his jaw opened further than seemed possible, bearing rows of sharp, white teeth.

"I'm fine, Calyx. Have no fear. The man here has come to my aid. He is not here to harm me," Cairn said, and stepped quickly between the Moulant and the blacksmith.

Trevor, astonished, gaped childlike, at Calyx.

"I was stupid, my friend. I went to sleep too soon and I did not think I really needed to be so careful. I was wrong. But, Trevor Cortland here has saved me from a surely unpleasant fate at the hands of some roughnecks. I thank you from the depths of my heart, Master Cortland. My name is Cairn, Cairn of Thermaye," he said as he clasped Trevor's trembling hand, completing the greeting.

He bowed gracefully to the shaken and still frightened smith who obviously was afraid to move even an inch.

"You are perfectly safe, my friend. Calyx will not harm you now."

Calyx moved gracefully over to the side of his companion and placed one giant paw on top of the fallen attacker. He rolled him onto his back and put his face close up to Martos as the wounded man regained consciousness. Upon opening his eyes and seeing only the huge face of Calyx, Marto shrieked and tried to push himself backwards despite the broken leg, passing out once again.

Trevor had regained his composure by this time, and he waited as Marto opened his eyes once more and frantically looked around him. He caught the eye of Cairn who was smiling subtly with his arms folded across his chest.

"I do not think you should try to get up, even if you could. My friend here is not often generous toward those who wish me harm," Cairn spoke softly. "Perhaps you should help this fellow back to town, Trevor. Or, maybe not. Why don't we leave him here with Calyx while you and I go to town and fetch some help?"

Marto shook his head so quickly and violently, indicating that he did not think that would be such a good idea, that Cairn and Trevor laughed.

"I do nay think he will be so likely to bother you again, sir Cairn. If'n his leg did nay stop him, by the look on his mug, he be certain that your friend there would."

"I tend to agree with you, Goodman Trevor," Cairn replied with a grin.

"My cottage is nay far from here. Would you care to come back and have a warm cup of cider and get some good rest?" he asked.

"It would be my pleasure, Trevor. But what of this one over here?" he asked, pointing to Marto.

"Let 'im sit tight for a bit. His 'friend' will come back sooner or later, as least to see if'n he is alive or nay," Trevor replied, winking at Cairn. "Come, you must be weary from the greeting our townspeople have given you."

Trevor led the way through the brambles to a narrow path beyond, and Cairn and Calyx gratefully followed him, confident that this man's intentions were noble.

Chapter Seven

Baladar gazed out of the tower windows, scanning the horizon with both his eyes and his mind. His body sizzled with a quiet anticipation, and yet he could not calm the ever-present anxiety that wrestled with his soul. The pieces were falling into place, or so it seemed. The boy, Davmiran, was under his protection at last. Although still a child, he bore within him the seed of the future. He was the last great hope that the world had left, and Baladar would give his very life to nurture, support and enhance this hope.

Baladar could sense the coming of his friends. He could also sense the evil lurking in the background, just beyond his comprehension and ability to pinpoint it. It was surely there, nevertheless, and it was not going to go away by itself. He had seen its face and the memory thereof was permanently inscribed upon his consciousness.

His friends were quite competent and they were more than able to deal with whatever might come between them and their mission, but Baladar harbored misgivings nonetheless, for only a fool would not recognize the threat of a formidable foe just because its presence was not physically manifesting itself at the time. He knew that his vigilance was probably more important now that the boy was with him than it was before he even had him under his protective wing. Word would spread of his existence and his location. The spells that he cast upon Dav were strong ones and they would serve to shelter his essence from detection to a certain extent. Common people, people without magic, would continue to be innocent of the fact of his existence.

Baladar was no fool though, and he was well aware that the forces opposed to him and the boy were crafty, strong beyond measure and devious. The Evil One would eventually discover who was protecting him and where he was being kept. It would take considerable effort and a long, long time, but so would the preparation. The battle lines were drawn ages ago, and it was only a matter of time before both sides would have to meet and confront the dichotomy. Only one force could and would emerge victorious, and Baladar was going to give every advantage to the side of life and goodness that he had fought for so long, with all of the energy that he had and with the will of the righteous urging him forward.

As the sun set over the turrets of the castle, swathing the entire room in a crimson shower of broken light, Baladar hastily wrapped himself in his cloak and prepared to leave. He wanted to arrive at his destination before the moon rose over the mountains, and he needed to return before sunrise the next. While strapping his sword to his belt, he hurried over to the chest in the far corner and spoke the words of power that would activate the mechanism allowing him to open the ancient wooden box.

The latch sprung with a whooshing sound, like a balloon being quickly deflated by a pin prick, and the rim where the cover meets the bottom portion began to glow and sparkle ever so slightly. Baladar was accustomed to the reaction and paid it no mind. He pressed the two concealed buttons under the handles mounted on either side of the chest and then he waited the full ten seconds required before lifting the top. With little effort, he raised the lid of oak, burnished and shining as brightly now as polished steel.

Kneeling down in front of the box, he retrieved the small dagger from the tray suspended across the back of the box, the hilt of which harbored a ruby the size of a robin's egg and secured to the handle by a web of woven platinum and gold. He cradled the weapon in his palm, and he felt the warmth of the stone and the power it generated immediately upon its contact with his skin. Baladar placed it carefully within the folds of his cloak and let the nourishing heat penetrate his body.

As if in a trance, without needing to look, the Lord of Pardatha reached into the far left-hand corner and picked up a small, square black velvet box. It had no marks of closure and no apparent cover, yet Baladar knew very well how to open it. He had been waiting untold years in order to do so and only now was he able to. From his pouch of gems in his pocket, he loosened the drawstring and took out the white diamond. It sparkled with an awesome beauty, as if alive with hope and joy, and if he could ascribe human emotion to such an inanimate object, he would have believed it to be as expectant and excited as was he.

Placing the stone atop the velvet box and humming a deep and resonant note in just the right key, he sat down in awe and witnessed what he had never even anticipated. The white stone glowed with power. As if melting, yet clearly maintaining its shape, it enveloped the box in tendrils of white light, so very beautiful to behold. The black velvet shimmered under the diamond web and then vanished as if it had never been there to begin with.

Baladar focused his vision upon the stone as best he could, considering the brightness of the light, and he began to discern the clear shape of a ring suspended within it. It twirled and spun like a coin flipped by a child upon a table. Spinning faster and faster, the light from the ring filled the entire room with a dizzying, almost nauseating whiteness. As quickly as it reached its peak, the light abruptly vanished as the diamond and the ring fell to the stone floor with a clatter and jingle. The velvet box was gone without a trace. Baladar retrieved the stone and returned it to the pouch.

With a tremendous amount of trepidation, he deferentially picked up the glowing band of gold between his thumb and forefinger and held it aloft before his eyes. Ancient runes covered the ring, inside and out, most of which were not quite discernible to the naked eye. Nevertheless, he recognized a symbol here and there, as he examined it with care. It was warm to the touch and remarkably beautiful! He removed a thin, gold chain from around his own neck, slipped the ring over it and secured it once again, and although seemingly weightless, Baladar felt and sensed its presence against the skin of his chest. He hurriedly returned the implements of his work to whence they had come and left the chamber. With obvious purpose, Baladar rushed down the winding stairway from his tower room, barely taking the time to navigate the narrow steps with care.

Upon emerging from the stairwell into the great hall, he was immediately confronted by members of the court who had no idea of what was imminently unfolding right within their midst. The mundane tasks of running a rather large city seemed so far away and unimportant at the moment, yet no one else here was cognizant of that fact.

"My Lord, would you be so good as to sign this document? It has been sitting upon my desk for three days now and the families involved need to partition the land before the winter rains wash the markers we set away," the clerk of the 1st court said, thrusting a quill pen and a paper in front of him.

"I am sorry, my friend, but I have no time now. Perhaps later this evening. Or even better, bright and early tomorrow morning. I have some business to attend to now."

Baladar dismissed him politely although abruptly, and rushed through the crowd gathered in the great hall, perfunctorily responding to those who would take no less than some kind of acknowledgment.

I should have found a better way out of here, he thought, not realizing the time of day and just how crowded the grounds of the castle would be now.

Immediately in front of him, the door to the courtyard loomed, and in only a short time now he would be on his way.

Pushing the great oaken slab unassisted was a real test of strength, but not wanting to draw any more attention to himself, he did not call for aid. As it opened and he was about to take his first step into the passage just ahead, he felt a strong hand upon his shoulder.

"Forgive me, my Lord Baladar," the deep and resonant voice he recognized immediately said. "I must detain you from your obviously pressing calling for just a moment. A matter of importance, if you please."

"Yes, Darrel, what is it? I am late for an appointment with the new gelding in the outer stable. Before the sun sets, I promised the trainer that I would attempt a riding."

"Oh, I see. I will not keep you for too long then. But, I understand that we have a guest in the castle!"

Baladar's heart leapt at the last remark. *How could Darrel possibly have found out? This will change my plans drastically. It is just too soon.*

"Who is that you speak of, my friend? I know of no such person. Was I not informed?"

"Ah, and could it be that you have not heard yet? I thought for sure he was here at your invitation?"

"Who?" Baladar's suspicion rose.

Darrel smiled, looking like the cat who got the mouse, so proud for knowing something before his Lord did. Perhaps he did not in fact know of the boy, and some other person of significance had coincidentally arrived concurrently.

"See for yourself. You need only to turn around," he replied rather smugly under his breath.

Baladar turned and took in the sight of someone he never dreamed would have had the courage to enter his city.

"Baladar, my Lord and liege," the man said bowing low before him. "It is so good to see you once again. After such a long absence, I would have thought for sure that you would have prepared a welcoming for me." The dark haired nobleman made a disapproving sound, "Such a disappointment. But, I do forgive you, with the mundane affairs of state keeping you so busy all the time, I am sure you simply forgot that I was coming."

Baladar was so taken aback, his feelings awash with conflicting emotions; relief that his secret was not exposed, trepidation at the arrival of his rival, the Duke of Talamar's heir, at such an inopportune moment, and extreme wariness at the concurrence of the two matters.

Kettin Dumas, son of the proprietor of the southern reaches, sly and not to be trusted, flashed an insincere and toothy smile at Baladar.

"My father sends his fondest wishes and hopes that you are in good health, both body and mind. His only regret is that he himself could not be here at this time. Pressing matters keep him occupied at home, as I am sure you can well understand," he said, as if he shared a monumental secret with his father that he was unwilling to fully reveal.

Kettin never seemed to say what he meant. His inflections of speech could not help but lead one to believe that his seemingly simple words had far deeper meanings than they originally indicated. Whether warranted or not, he aroused suspicion and doubts even as he spoke.

"I welcome your presence at any time, Kettin Dumas, although I have to admit that my aides have been remiss in not informing me of your intended visit. How could they have been so irresponsible? Surely you will forgive me and kindly not humiliate me by conveying to your father my embarrassing yet truly innocent and regretful lack of preparation for your coming. I would be mortified if the Duke should learn of my faux pas."

Baladar almost choked on his words, as he fervently hoped the insincerity was not too obvious to those present. He was not afraid that the Duke's son would recognize his affectation. Kettin was not astute enough to sense anything subtle. But he certainly did not need to enter into a lengthy and wasteful argument with his southern "ally" over etiquette at this moment.

"Come, Kettin, embrace me and enter my court as a welcome guest."

With that, Kettin moved the few paces required to reach Baladar's side, and with as little physical contact as possible, hugged him as if he were infected with the trecco virus itself. Upon contact with Baladar, Kettin noticeably jumped back a pace. His expression changed from one of casual discomfort to one of startled fear. He looked at Baladar askew and then abruptly attempted to regain his composure.

"I could have sworn that something just shocked me, yet I know that I am not that unwelcome here Baladar. You are surely charged with energy this evening. It is in the air. I can feel it. I hope my arrival is not untimely?" he responded, looking around the court.

Kettin immediately regretted having uttered such a suspicion, but Baladar could not help but notice a flash of fear in the young man's eyes, coupled with his usual mistrust.

"I must have been imagining it." He quickly shrugged as if it was nothing, yet his cautious look betrayed to Baladar more than he wished at the moment.

"I have no idea what it could have been. A storm may be forming upon the horizon," he said, glancing at the darkening western sky, "or perhaps you are just tired from your journey and a relaxing bath and good dinner will calm your nerves. Please, aides! Come and relieve this young and tired Lord of his cloak. Sit, Kettin, sit and have some warm cider mulled from our own trees by the maidens of Balbor. That should certainly settle your nerves and put you at ease. The hour is growing late and you are clearly weary from your journey."

He momentarily contemplated slipping a sleep draught of nightspark into the drink so as to relieve himself of this troublesome development at such an odious moment. Of course, he knew such an action was impossible, as the young Lord would surely know in the morning that he had been the victim of foul play, but the thought lingered longer than it probably should have.

Kettin sensed the ring and that was dangerous beyond belief. He could not have known what it was he sensed, yet the fact that the token of power was emanating so clearly caused great concern. Moreover, the power rejected his touch and reacted in a negative way to his proximity. That bespoke more against Kettin than any feeling Baladar could have had about his neighbor's ungentle son.

The timing of the Duke's son's arrival could not be mere coincidence. *Beware!* it spoke to Baladar in its own subtle fashion. *Beware of the darkness approaching.*

A chill ran down his spine, as he attempted to calm himself amidst his growing consternation.

"Kettin, please relax. I must arrange for your comfort while you are with us. And by the way, how long do you plan on gracing my home with your noble presence?"

"Ah, my Lord Baladar," he replied as he drew him aside and

away from the ears of others. "Your warm welcome is so gratifying after my long traipse through the barrens that perhaps I will remain for a while. You and I have much to discuss. My father, the Duke, has sent me as an envoy in his stead as his health is recently questionable, something I dared not repeat earlier in common company. Who knows what advantage someone might take with that knowledge under his hat, and with his only heir away from his side and relatively unprotected. Well, you can definitely understand my concerns. Nevertheless, there are developments in the east that need our attention, and whom could he trust other than me to be his proponent in such delicate matters?"

"Ah, of course," Baladar nodded. "He has chosen well, Kettin, that is for sure! I know of no other who would serve in your lord's stead better than you. Let us plan a moment to sit and discuss these untoward 'developments', Kettin. Perhaps I can be of some assistance."

"Yes, we must. We need also speak of trade once more. It seems our merchants are rather disgruntled by the prices they are recently receiving for their polong oil. You know that it is the finest in all the lands."

"It is the only polong oil in all the lands, my dear sir."

Baladar tried very hard to conceal the sarcasm in his voice, although he did not really believe that Kettin was astute enough to sense his distaste anyway. He saw his opportunity to sneak away and he jumped upon it.

"As you surely need time to settle in, and as we can expect an extended stay, let us both retire until the new sun. You can bathe and freshen up, while I attend to some matters of state that seem always to press upon us. We will have ample time tomorrow to discuss these issues and do some much needed catching up on old times. By the way, how is your charming mother, the Duchess? I so enjoy her robust sense of humor."

He turned to his aide without giving Kettin any further opportunity to speak.

"Cristian, show Lord Kettin to the north suites and see that everything necessary is done to guarantee his comfort while he is with us. Also, arrange for his cortege as well. The barracks are more than comfortable in our domains and they are far enough away from the din of the city to allow the guards their well deserved rest. Stable the horses and see that both humans and animals are well fed. Make haste. My noble friend has ridden long and hard, and we have been remiss in our hospitality by obliging him to stand here for so long."

"Yes my Lord, at once," Cristian responded and leapt to the task.

A good man, that Cristian is. He will understand my meaning, Baladar thought. *The farther away from the castle that he leads these armed guards, the better.*

Kettin bowed to Baladar then turned and followed the aide, as Baladar seized upon the moment and headed out the archway toward the stables.

Baladar drew his cloak closely around his shoulders, concealing his attire as much as possible. The last thing that he wanted now was someone to notice his brocade glinting in the moonlight. He needed to travel undetected and unimpeded, and he wished nothing more than to slip quietly into the darkness and be off. Baladar entered the stables through one of the stableboy's back doors, slipping by the reposing guards at the front entrance. He made a mental note to chastise the guards for being so lax, though he was thankful for it now. Greater vigilance would have to be the rule in the days ahead.

He quietly saddled his stallion Porta, and without bit and bridle, coaxed him out the side doors. Upon clearing the corrals, he headed toward the castle gates. Once outside the castle grounds, he leapt upon Porta's back, headed for the Noban gate, and then north in the direction of lake Everclear. The night air was crisp and fragrant and the wind blew steadily but calmly across his brow. Porta was excited at having been aroused at this uncommonly late hour, and without the benefit of reins, Baladar exerted quite some strength in directing him properly. He was a good and noble horse, and although instinct led him to press onward unguided, loyalty and training kept him on the path that was expected of him.

Through the woods surrounding the city they cantered, weaving in and out amongst the low slung branches, the good Lord avoiding being unseated by a hair's breadth many times. As they neared the lake, the trees grew denser and the underbrush thickened, slowing their pace considerably. The moon shone through the canopy of brush brightly enough to illuminate their destination. It reflected off of the waters of the lake as if the liquid was a mirror in the sunlight. Yet, the path to it was not clear, and the closer Baladar seemed to get to his goal, the farther he realized he was. This was not unexpected and he ignored the appearance of distance, knowing that the illusion would pass. The lake was protecting itself from intruders, and although he was considered to be a friend, he was not of the same making and he would have to struggle with this confusion if he was to arrive at all.

After coaxing Porta through a particularly odious tangle of brambles, a clear pathway opened up before him, beckoning with the scent and appearance of comfort and warmth. He knew at that point that he had been admitted and that the test would only now be beginning. Baladar summoned what strength he could from deep within himself, preparing his mind for the onslaught that he knew would soon overwhelm it.

As the path narrowed, a portal appeared glimmering in the near distance. He headed straight for it, slipping slowly off of the saddle. Porta shied away from the light only slightly, and proceeded to drop his head and search calmly for some moist grass to chew. Baladar knew that he would remain there until his return. He walked up to the shimmering area of ambient emptiness, drew a deep breath, and proceeded to step inside.

Chapter Eight

Cairn and Trevor walked side by side, with Calyx trailing cautiously a few feet behind. The walk to his humble home was short and refreshing. Trevor was certainly a good man, Cairn could tell, and there was no question he could trust this woodsman. As they approached the thatched roofed cabin, an aura of warmth and safety enveloped him. A startlingly attractive, middle-aged woman, dressed in deerskin and linen, eyes as bright as the midday sun, bolted out of the doorway and to the side of Cairn's new found companion. The sight of Calyx lurking in the distance did not seem to disturb her.

She eyed Cairn with friendliness and openness, uncommon among strangers these days, and pushed her jet black hair behind her ears. He spotted a bright yellow stone glimmering from each lobe of her delicately carved ears, as if they were speaking to him, welcoming him. Cairn immediately liked this woman. In fact he felt strangely comfortable in the company of them both, even having been unaccustomed to communing with humans as he had become. Her smile was warm and welcoming and there was not a hint of hesitation in it.

The house was modest but homey, the walls hung with tapestries, undoubtedly home made and the floor was covered with a woven rug of dyed reeds. The furniture was heavy and well made, clearly carved by an artisan of no little talent, probably Trevor himself, if Cairn suspected correctly.

"I bring to thee a guest to share our food and grog, my dearest," Trevor exclaimed proudly, as he introduced Cairn to his wife Safira.

"Come in, stranger, and make yourself at home. Trevor, fetch a chair for the gentleman," she replied so casually and honestly that Cairn relaxed immediately.

The smell of something delicious cooking was most evident, and Cairn quickly forgot all that had been burdening his mind in the face of the prospect of such a good meal and the prodigious company.

"Should I prepare something for your friend outside?" she asked so naturally one would think the big cat was a friendly pet dog.

"No, thank you," he replied. "Calyx prefers to provide for

himself. He's quite capable, you know," Cairn replied grinning.

Safira smiled again, with an expression of understanding as if they were sharing a private joke. Cairn felt the goodness in her. It radiated from her eyes. In fact, he liked the two of them! He wondered if this meeting was mere chance, or if something greater was at work here, bringing this group together at this particular time. Lately, he had been questioning much of what he believed prior to the onset of this journey.

"Come, sit down. Be comfortable. You look weary, and I am sure a full belly will change that expression of yours considerably," Safira remarked as she pulled the high-backed chair away from the table.

Cairn joined the two of them for a tantalizing meal of stewed fowl and greens mixed with steamed flower blossoms, mulled cider and berries, and the hours passed comfortably and quickly amidst small talk and warm company. Refills of cider were plentiful, and after considerable conversation, soon enough it was time for bed. Trevor and Safira would hear of nothing other than Cairn sleeping in the only bed in the cottage, while they camped out on down quilts and woven rugs on the floor in front of the hearth. They seemed to enjoy the prospect so, that he could hardly refuse.

They said their goodnights and Trevor showed Cairn to the small room, filled almost entirely by a huge feather mattress and mile high pillows, where he was to sleep. And sleep he did, as if someone had slipped a considerable dose of nightshade into his cider.

Cairn slept soundly and thoroughly, waking with the dawn, only to find a warm breakfast steaming on the dining table as he emerged from the bedroom and Safira brewing a remarkable smelling tea over the fire. He felt refreshed and wonderful. After having slept upon a mat for so many years, the luxury of the bed was something he would not forget quickly.

"Ah, Cairn. You have slept well?" she asked, knowing the answer already.

"Yes, very well, good mistress. Remarkably well! In fact, I cannot remember a time when I have slept better. It must have been the excellent repast and the even better company, not to mention the softest bed I have ever seen. Only in a house where I felt totally secure could I have had such a good night's sleep. I thank you, from the bottom of my heart," he replied, and he bowed slightly to the woman.

Cairn needed to check on Calyx and he felt remiss in not having done so once more before he retired the previous evening, but he was confident that the big animal was as safe and as secure as he himself had been.

"I would like to step outside for just a minute before I am totally seduced by your cooking once again, mistress Safira. I need to find my furry friend and make sure that he is not concerned about my welfare."

"As I expected that you would, and the food will certainly wait for your return." Cairn stepped outside the humble house and was immediately taken in by the smell of the air. The trees were fragrant, and the unmistakable odor of Lalas was heavy on the wind, something totally unexpected in this part of the countryside. He felt as if he was in a paradise of sorts, for everything was alive and in abundant bloom. He wandered into the fringe of brush in front of the cottage and then followed a narrow, winding path further into the depths of the woods in search of Calyx, only to be totally shocked by the scene that soon overtook him.

Calyx was standing over a young boy, no more than fourteen years old at most, tugging upon a knotted piece of cloth that the boy held tightly between his two hands. At first, he was engulfed by a wave of concern for the child, but he did not sense any danger, and Calyx was astonishingly careful. He quickly realized that they were playing with each other, and the boy apparently had no fear of the animal whatsoever. This was truly a sight he had not seen before. Most people ran in terror from the big Moulant, fearing for their lives. This boy was playing with him as if he was a house pet!

Upon spotting Cairn, Calyx dropped his toy and leapt to his side. The boy stood up, clearly disappointed by having lost his playmate.

"Young man, I am Cairn. Who may you be?" he asked in an unthreatening manner.

"Is the cat your friend?" the boy asked first and forthright. "Because if he is, then I do not have to fear you as I would fear any other stranger in these woods."

This youth stood before him, eyes wide, and Cairn could not help but smile at his boldness and honesty.

"Yes, I can assure you. He is my good friend. My best friend in this world. And you have nothing to fear from me. Nor from Calyx, as I can definitely see. Since I have given you my name, now whom might you be?"

"I am Tomas, and you spent the night in the house of my uncle Trevor and aunt Safira. I know more about you than you do about me I wager," he replied with a voice so sonorous that it blended well with the smell of Lalas and the warm breeze wafting through the trees. A fearless, innocent boy indeed.

"And where did you spend the night? We did not share your company throughout the entire evening?"

"I slept in a tree, behind the cottage. I stay there whenever I can, when the weather is nice. Would you like to see it?" he asked with genuine interest.

"I certainly would! Lead the way."

Everything about this place was intriguing to Cairn. *I wish I had more time to linger here*, he thought as he leapt to go after the boy. Tomas briskly skipped his way through the underbrush with both Cairn and Calyx following closely behind. The bushes became quite dense, the smell grew more fragrant and the sun, although seemingly blocked by the thick vegetation, shone brightly, illuminating the twisted path and making it appear as if the sun itself was directing the lad to his destination. Cairn felt, or rather, sensed a change in the atmosphere. The fragrance in the air was heavier, more aromatic than before, and the air itself was thicker or denser it seemed.

As the bushes gave way to tall grass, a tingling sensation overtook him, strange but not at all unpleasant. He passed carefully out into the more open area, on guard against the prospect of anything unforseen occurring, and continued to follow the boy. Calyx bounded ahead, unconcerned; a good sign.

Soon enough, Tomas stopped, faced Cairn, with an expression of extreme pride spread across his young face. Behind him stood the most beautiful tree Cairn had seen in ages.

It must be a Lalas, he thought. *And this boy must be its Chosen, otherwise he could never be sleeping near it, let alone inside the shelter of its branches.*

Yet, Cairn was unaware that any of the great trees lived in this area, certainly not one as massive as this one. He knew that he had recognized its presence earlier, yet he was baffled as to how one could be here, now, without having been recorded by the elders.

"Tomas?" he queried, "Is this *your* tree?"

Tomas looked slightly perplexed by the question, bowed his head, chin to chest, and thought for an instant.

"How could a tree be mine?" he replied confused. "The tree is my friend, as Calyx is yours, if that is what you mean."

"Surely, I do, my son. It was only a matter of speech," Cairn responded, not wishing to confuse the child with terms he was clearly unfamiliar with. He thought to himself that this must be a very unique boy and an even more unique Lalas, certainly untraditional to say the least. The fragrance of the tree was obvious and as he thought this, some leaves wafted to the ground in front of him, an invitation not to be taken lightly. Cairn bent over and retrieved the leaves, bowed deeply to the tree, and placed them carefully in his belt pouch.

"Ormachon likes you," the boy said gleefully.

He twirled and danced in a small circle, singing in his melodious voice.

"Ormachon has a new friend, just like me. Before it was just us, now we are three."

He giggled and pranced around the trunk of the Lalas, until he was sufficiently tired and dizzy, then he fell to the ground and laughed some more. He behaved as a child, but his knowing eyes betrayed a wiser more mature young man hidden behind them. Nonetheless, the boy warmed Cairn's heart like no child had ever done before. He felt bound to him somehow, and through the boy, he felt a kinship to the tree. He was not a Chosen one, he had no magic and he never envied those who had. Yet, the feelings now taking over his very being were like none he had ever experienced and he was thoroughly enjoying them. Both he and Tomas reveled under Ormachon's protective branches for a short while, each in his own manner, enjoying the peace and comfort the Lalas afforded them.

There was no mistaking the sound that shattered the calm surrounding Cairn and Tomas. Calyx's growl was not one of friendship, as he bounded down the path toward the cottage. Tomas lifted his head and gazed in the direction Calyx had just run. His face lost its youthful color for just a moment, Cairn thought, and he felt rather than saw a sadness overtake the boy. Cairn also sensed that Tomas reluctantly remained where he stood, sheltered by a sweeping branch of the great Lalas behind him.

"Stay here, Tomas, something is dreadfully wrong and I must follow Calyx," he said worriedly.

Cairn peered once more at Tomas before he too dashed down the trail, and it appeared to him as if the soft branches were caressing him and holding him back.

Calyx was far ahead of him by the time he reached the brush and he could hear sounds of violence in the distance. Everything was happening so quickly, he barely had time to think about what he would do if he came unawares upon another group of belligerent townsfolk. Taking care not to burst into the open undefended, Cairn approached the house of Trevor and Safira stealthily. He felt the tremor of apprehension overtake his body, as his senses were assaulted by the scene that opened up before him. Calyx had already begun his pursuit of the aggressors by the time that Cairn was in view of the cottage itself.

He was unprepared for what he saw in front of him. Trevor lay on the ground, his staff clenched in his hands, partially concealing the body of his wife, Safira, in a protective manner. Both were dead. Trevor's eyes were burned out of his sockets and his hair and beard were singed from what could only have been balefire. His face was distorted and ruined. Safira lay under him, her eyes too were totally annihilated by the magic and her hands clutched a small piece of a branch, broken and charred.

Cairn rushed to their sides, knowing only too well that there was nothing he could now do. The house was in ruins, uninhabitable, stinking of burnt flesh and evil. Pieces of the door lay shattered, splintered and ragged, all the windows were blown out, while glass and debris littered the ground everywhere. As he peered inside, he noticed that every drawer and cabinet had been riffled through and that everything in the house was torn apart as if the culprit or culprits was looking for something.

"Whatever it was, I hope to the First that they did not find it!" he exclaimed consumed by anger and sadness.

If only I had been here before, when they so desperately needed me, instead of playing games in the woods. I could have come to their aid. Perhaps I could have prevented this, Cairn thought.

His regrets were too late now, and his concerns immediately turned to the boy and to Calyx. Tomas was clearly in more danger if he wandered outside of the protection of his tree, as Calyx was not afraid of magic and knew quite well how to defend himself against it. He could not leave his newly found friends in such a state, their memories desecrated by this depraved performance, chancing that Tomas would soon return to see what was going on and stumble upon this gruesome scene. He was safe with his tree for now, and Ormachon was surely wise to have kept him back and would continue to do so, Cairn assured himself as he proceeded to carefully lift and move Trevor off of Safira. The stench was awful, but Cairn was determined to provide these good people with a proper grave, if nothing else.

Who could have done this? And why? He located a spade and began to dig a trench in front of the garden by the edge of the woods. He wondered if Calyx had caught up with the murderous lot, and he grieved deeply for the two friends he had only just met. He would bury them together, hand in hand, as he expected they would have preferred. Cairn had known them for such a short time, but he was now bound to them forever.

The thought of the boy returned to his mind as he immediately recognized that Tomas was now in his charge. He could not help but feel that although everything had taken such a tragic and sad turn, some good would come out of it. Cairn was uncomfortable with that feeling, nonetheless, considering the circumstances, but it was only his conscience that was experiencing this discomfort, not his instincts. No matter how awful things were, it felt right somehow; not the deaths, not the loss, but the responsibility that he now assumed for Tomas. As he thought, he completed his grim task, laid the bodies side by side in the ground and began to cover them with the moist earth.

He finished his job as quickly as possible, anxious to attend to the child, and a bit uneasy, standing here exposed as he was. When the job was done, he said a brief prayer over the grave and then he turned to go. Calyx would see to it that the magic users would not return and catch him unsuspecting. He would have time to defend himself, unlike Trevor and Safira. They obviously had no warning. Trevor had not even had time to remove his ax from the wood in which it lay embedded next to where the front door had been.

Who would wish harm upon these good people? What secrets did they harbor, for surely they had done no evil in their lifetimes? What manner of being would want them dead?

So many questions swarmed around Cairn's brow, like bees around a waiting Queen, only to be frustrated by a lack of answers altogether. He knew so little of these people to whom he had become so intimately attached so quickly and so briefly. He would find out! In time he would determine who did this and why. But, no matter how pressing it seemed to him at the moment, he could never forget what brought him this way in the first place. He had been called, and he could not stray from his path now. Cairn of Thermaye would have to gather the boy, Tomas, find Calyx and resume his mission. He had to reach Baladar as soon as he could and he still had a long and dangerous trail to follow. Now he would also have the welfare of a small boy to protect, an innocent lad, whose life had just been turned inside out, a life that he had just entered and one that he was now bound to forever, albeit, through a tragedy greater than any other he had probably yet experienced in his short lifetime.

After hastily gathering his things from the cottage, he found his way through the bushes, back to the boy. He concentrated his thoughts upon Calyx, summoning him so that they could quickly inform Tomas of the new and harrowing circumstances and be on their way. As Cairn emerged from the trees and passed through the tall, green meadow grass, the beautiful Lalas once again in vivid sight before him, he observed the unmistakable motion of his companion bolting through the herbage to attend him. Almost simultaneously, he heard the distinct sound of a child humming, and only seconds later he felt the air crackle in response.

Chapter Nine

Robyn dar Tamarand knew how to travel and how to do it quickly. He was by far one of the best horsemen in the city, and his horse Kraft, was among the finest in the land. Together, they would make the long journey from Concordia in the north west, southward to Baladar's kingdom. Robyn always traveled without any other companions, entirely his own choice, so as not to frighten or confuse other humans who did not share his extraordinary abilities. He had few friends after all, and he had yet to meet anyone who measured up to his talents. He was anything but a fool, though, to assume that such a person did not exist. He had just not yet encountered him or her. That time would come, he knew, and he hoped that it would be under friendly circumstances.

As he slid down from the tree branch and bid a short and meaningful goodbye to Promanthea, certain that his soul-mate knew much more about where he was going and why than he had communicated to Robyn. But, he was also convinced that no amount of time or effort would serve to open the tree's thoughts to his mind when it came to this matter. Robyn dar Tamarand realized when to expend his energy and when to conserve it. He was no common dolt. He would make his farewells, suffer the pangs of separation with grace and dignity as always, and move on. He knew that Promanthea would commune with him as soon as need required. In the meantime, he would get no more advice or help from him, of that he was certain.

Robyn signaled for Kraft and the big horse attended him immediately. Together, they returned to the castle so that Robyn could make the preparations necessary for the journey. He wished to bid farewell to his father, too, before setting off for the southern reaches, even though the Baron was well accustomed to his unannounced comings and goings. He felt compelled to say goodbye this time, as he truly knew not how long he would be gone, nor what was in store for him whence he arrived at his destination. He desired to see his father, to be in his presence once again, and to leave with the memory of his spirit and soul upon him. Robyn was a good son, not the careless narcissist that many people were led to believe he was.

"Your Lordship, your son returns," Baron Calipee's aide remarked, having spotted Robyn trotting lazily through the gates outside of the windows of the conference hall. "No doubt, he had a pleasant evening," he commented with a knowing smirk on his face.

Ah, the indignities we have to endure to maintain this ruse, the Baron thought regretfully to himself as he attempted to hide his eagerness to be with Robyn once again.

"No doubt, Dustin. No doubt. I only wish he would put as much energy into matters of state as he does into women and wine."

"Do not blame yourself, your Lordship," Dustin replied. "Most men would trade places with him if they could."

"Yes, but Robyn is not 'most men'! He is of royal blood, and he has responsibilities. I have no other heir but he, and I fear for the kingdom should I grow ill or become incapacitated."

"We all pray for you, my Lord. I am sure many share your concerns," Dustin stated and quickly realized his words were not comforting, but rather brought to the fore the problem everyone dreaded.

"He is a good boy, you know? He loves too deeply and lusts too deeply, but that is only a sign of his passion. He will mature. He has no choice."

The Baron ambled over to the large, leaded windows, hoping to catch a glimpse of Robyn as he entered the outer courtyard.

He has such a way about him; such striking beauty and such seeming arrogance. His enemies will do well not to underestimate him, Baron Calipee thought with a great degree of comfort.

Robyn swaggered into the hall with such insouciance and indifference that only his striking looks would have caught the attention of an observer. He appeared to have not a care in the world; to be idly passing the time. He plucked a bunch of grapes from a laden table in the entryway, beckoned a servant to fetch a pitcher of wine and a pair of goblets and plumped himself down in a high-backed chair at the very end of the table of state.

"Father, I am exhausted!" he exclaimed. "I was up all of the night just thinking about it, or should I say her. The most extraordinary thing has happened."

"Pray tell," the Baron responded . "You met a woman?" he mocked.

"Not just 'any' woman, father. An incredible woman. A lady!" Robyn retorted. "How did you know anyway, father?" Robyn asked rather mystified.

"How could I not? I know you too well, my son. I wish only that your passion for the opposite sex was matched by your interest in your position and responsibilities," he said somberly.

"But is that not what you do, father? You are forever interested in nothing but your position and responsibilities. Is that not why I have no mother to comfort me?" he asked sarcastically, clearly meaning to hurt his father.

The Baron turned sharply toward his son, raised his head to speak, and then hesitated. The anger appeared to be rising within him, as he seemingly calmed himself and turned to Dustin.

"Please leave us. I wish to speak privately with my son. Have them bring the wine now, and be gone."

Dustin recognized the tone coming from his Lordship and he hastened to obey.

"As you wish, sir," was all he said as he went to the doorway, signaled for the servant with the refreshments, saw to their proper placement and turned to retreat to other quarters.

"I will be waiting for your pleasure, my Lord," Dustin remarked with an air of reluctance at having to depart and leave the Baron in such an agitated state, fully expecting it only to be exacerbated by a private conference with Robyn. Baron Calipee would be in a dreadful mood upon his return, of that he was sure.

As soon as Dustin closed the door securely, Robyn and his father stood and walked toward one another. Rather than fight, they embraced with such deep feeling it brought tears to the older man's eyes.

"Ah, my son, the price we pay for your safety. I pray for the day when we can be openly father and son, the way I would like everyone to view us, the true way."

"It concerns me not, father. I have learned to ignore the sneers and snickers. The ones that I care about know the truth," he replied, placing his hand affectionately upon his father's shoulder.

"What brings you to me this afternoon? Surely you did not arrive to share a glass of wine?" Calipee uttered as he poured two glasses of wine from the crystal vase on the table.

"No, father. I only wish. But more serious matters have presented themselves. I have been called somewhere by someone whose summons I cannot ignore, even if I so desired," Robyn said with a quite serious demeanor. "I must leave immediately."

The Baron turned to his son and said "Somewhere by someone? Can you not even tell your own father what need has beckoned?" he asked, concern in his voice.

"No, sir, I cannot. I do not wish to endanger either you or my friends in this matter. The less you know, the less you can reveal."

"You think I would ever utter a word about this if you asked me not to? If I knew it would place you in jeopardy? The fabric weaves of its own will, my son. There is often little we can do to prevent it," Calipee said, the hurt obvious in his voice.

"Father, never! I would not suggest that you would ever intend to reveal anything. But if you do not know my whereabouts, then no one would attempt to compel you to try to give me up. As soon as I am confident that you can remain safe, you will know everything. The matter I must attend to is very grave and the future is yet to be foretold. I know not what circumstances may prevail here after I am gone."

"Are we in danger, Robyn? Should we take more precautions?" he questioned, walking to the large windows overlooking the city.

"We are always in danger, father, as long as the trees are dying. Our whole world is in danger."

"Yes, it is. I feel the darkness approaching daily. What says Promanthea?" he inquired, gazing intently at his son.

"He remains silent. I glimpse only snippets of meaning from the waves of feeling he sends to me. He will not commune with me about my journey at all."

"Is that odd? Does it cause you concern? Perhaps you should not go. Maybe that is what he is trying to tell you with his secretiveness. Remember what happened when I failed to recognize the portent of my premonitions and let your mother go that evening!" the Baron said fearfully.

"No, father, I am sure not. Promanthea knows more than he wants me to know now. But, there is no question that I must leave and that I must leave very soon. Every minute I delay is a minute less that I will have to fulfill my task. My help is needed," he said earnestly. "And father?" Robyn remarked as he placed his hand on the Baron's shoulder tenderly, "Mother's death was not your fault. You had no way of knowing what would really happen that night. And besides, she was a strong-willed woman. She would have patted you on the back and told you that you worry too much. She would have gone anyway. You know that and I know that."

"Well, I suppose you are right, Robyn. But it hurts me so deeply when I think that maybe I could have prevented her from taking that journey that particular day. We had so few enemies and she had none, or so I believed. I could not have known," he said sadly. "If only life was filled with more perfect moments and fewer regrets over lost ones and ones that never had a chance to occur. But, alas, I have learned to accept what has befallen us," he said and he gazed stoically out the window. "It is difficult, nonetheless, for me to watch you hasten off into harm's way too. But, there is no preventing that which must be. Let me not keep you any longer," he said reluctantly. "I have learned how to say goodbye though it never ceases to break my heart. It is not often though that I do not know the why or wherefore of your quests."

The Baron moved to his son once more and he embraced him and kissed his cheek as if he was a young boy.

"I will contact you when I can; when it is safe. Keep your branch near you at night and I will reach you through it," Robyn said referring to the polished piece of wood that he found at the foot of his tree one day years ago, shortly after his mother's untimely death; a sure sign of his tree's compassion.

He learned that he could activate it and speak through it if he had to. It hurt him to do it as nothing else did, leaving him exhausted and vulnerable afterward. But, the hurt was only temporary, bequeathing no permanent injury upon him. Using the Lalas or a piece of it to communicate with someone who was not among the Chosen was painstaking and exacted an emotional price.

It was not often that a tree allowed a part of itself, a part of its body, to be removed and used like this. But, Promanthea recognized the extraordinary and special love that existed between this father and son and so he permitted it. This Lalas disliked it nonetheless and he made his feelings known to Robyn many a time, regardless of the fact that he offered the branch to Robyn without a request and without discussion. Robyn chose his moments of usage very carefully, making sure he did not abuse the gift. Promanthea was wise and kind but possessive, and although the Baron was Robyn's blood father, his Lalas held a different and loftier position in the hierarchy of his life, one that he protected with a passion only Robyn fully comprehended.

"Farewell, my son. May the First protect you," his father finally spoke, impassioned, moving closer to his son once again.

"I love you father, with all my heart! Protect *yourself!* Be vigilant. I will return as soon as I am able."

With those words, Robyn kissed his father's forehead, turned and emptied his wine in one gulp, then moved toward the door and opened it just a little crack in order for what he was about to say to be heard down the entire hallway. Backing up a few yards, he threw the empty goblet with great force at the oaken slab so that the sound of shattering glass echoed down the stone passageway and was noticed by everyone in this wing of the castle.

"I *will* go, father," he shouted angrily. "And I thank you not to summon me again soon! Why must you always burden me with tiresome words? I want to enjoy my life, not waste away following in your oppressive footsteps."

The Baron hung his head in dejection as his son stormed out of the room, carelessly brushing past Dustin and the serving maids with the cockiness of a strutting rooster, scattering towels and linens in the process.

"What are you staring at?" he shouted at Dustin. "Tend to my father. I am sure he needs your mothering now since he has no other woman to come to his aid."

With that final bitter admonition, Robyn flung open the iron clad doors at the end of the hall and marched into the courtyard, his cape snapping behind him. Before he mounted Kraft, he chanced a glance backward. Discreetly catching his father's eye, Robyn sent him an invisible spark of hope on the wings of a son's love as he simultaneously observed Dustin's disgusted yet disappointed expression, and with great remorse he spurred his mount toward the gates and out into the approaching darkness. He tilted his head back a bit and sighed a deep sigh of regret for the suffering he imposed upon all of his father's loyal and devoted followers. Then, he stiffened his resolve and galloped into the darkness.

Chapter Ten

Filaree swept through the castle gates with Cameron following not far behind, leapt from Nico's back and began to summon those whom she would need to help her prepare for the upcoming journey.

"Catha! Marne! Yovanda! Come, attend me!" she announced without breaking her stride. "Cameron; gather my weapons and your own as well," Filaree said, as the castle staff burst into action immediately. The urgency in her voice startled them all and they knew not to question her instructions. "Make sure they are sharpened and polished. I will see you before the sun rises, ready to travel, in the courtyard."

Cameron nodded and stood waiting for further orders.

"Well? What are you looking at me for? Begone! Scat! I have much work to do before we depart and I know you do too," she said affectionately, though she was waving her hand at him as if she was shooing away a bothersome pet.

He smiled, understanding her humor by now, but hastened away regardless, not wishing to risk turning her excitement into anger by not taking her seriously.

"Yes my Lady, at once!" he responded, honored to be depended upon so thoroughly. Cameron recognized that his Lady's reaction to this event was unlike any he had experienced from her before. He was flattered to be the one chosen to accompany her and he jumped to the task.

As she made her way hurriedly into the depths of the castle with the three other women following closely behind, Filaree continued to dispense directions, never hesitating for an instant.

"Ladies, I will be leaving for the southern reaches before dawn breaks. I must have provisions packed that will last Cameron and me for at least three weeks. Make certain that they are light in weight and economically packed. See to them after you do the things I am now asking. Yovanda! Go directly to my rooms and fetch my ebony cloak, you know which one I mean, and bring it to the library. Catha! Run and tell my mother that I will need to speak with her and Corvina in the library as well in thirty minutes."

They both burst into action at her words.

"Marne, would you fetch me some parchment and a pen and ink and meet me in the library as soon as you can?"

"Yes, my Lady," she answered, and then she too scurried off.

Glancing straightaway from side to side to make sure that her orders were being carried out by all, she stopped briefly at a large alabaster table set against the wall in the corridor leading to the great hall. After the others were out of her sight, Filaree ran her hand down the leftmost side, hurriedly searching for something. Upon finding what she sought, she sprang the latch and a panel slid down while a drawer popped open on the opposite side of the table over to which she moved with studied determination. Reaching her long and graceful fingers into the opening, she removed a brilliant dagger, the hilt of which was studded with fine gems, black sapphires and amethysts, and capped by a large ruby.

After slipping the blade into the silk sash securing her frock, she reached once more into the drawer. This time, she retracted a small ornament, black as night, carved in the shape of a tree hanging on a thin chain of spun gold. Filaree examined it quickly, nodded to herself knowingly, and maneuvered it gingerly over her head until it was quickly out of sight, inside the soft suede of her tunic. Never hesitating for an instant, she continued down the long hallway.

Upon entering the library, Filaree Par D'Avalain went directly to the wall of scrolled maps. Pushing those in the front out of the way, knocking others off the shelves in the process and completely unconcerned with the mess she was creating, she searched for what she now needed. Upon finding it, she grabbed the scroll tied with rawhide strings, dashed to the reading table in the center of the vaulted room and with both arms outstretched, swept all of the articles covering it onto the floor. Pulling the dagger from her belt, Filaree furiously slashed the rawhide bindings, spread the map out from end to end, using the dagger as a weight for one side and an inkwell to anchor the other end, and began to examine it. She had to find the fastest and best route to Baladar and the boy.

With two swift horses, her mount, Nico and Cameron's Trojan, she anticipated a week's travel time at most. But, the weather was changing rapidly now and many areas would be icy and treacherous. She would need to plot her course carefully if she wanted to keep to her plans. Some of the areas they would have to traverse were barren and forsaken, no Lalas had grown in the vicinity for tiels, and they were inhabited by wood Trolls and other scavengers even more dangerous and gruesome than the dreaded Trolls.

She realized after a cursory inspection of the terrain on the map, that there was no avoiding this pathway though, as the western route was blocked by ice floes damning the Lake of Tears and prohibiting any crossing to the south, while the eastern passes through the mountains would take too many weeks just to ascend to on horseback, let alone pass across to the other side. No. The only viable route was directly south, across the bare plains of Chilmark, through the Winding Woods, then over the Tammell hills.

Filaree traced this path with her finger down the map to the southernmost base of the hills, carefully calculating how long each leg of the journey should take. Everclear lake formed the final obstacle they would need to surmount before they would encounter the heir of Gwendolen. The lake would be the least of their worries. If they could get to that point in six days or less, then she was sure that they could reach Baladar on the desired date.

Filaree carefully rolled the parchment up, bound and tied it once again, and placed it on the side of the table. As she was straightening up the mess she made, a tall, stately woman in a gown of crimson lace, re-embroidered with dozens of white roses, high-necked with a train of white satin trailing behind her, stepped into the room. Queen Esta was a striking woman whose age no one could ever guess. She had porcelain-like skin, the color of fresh cream, with lips as shapely and red as a young girl's. Her long black hair was piled high on her head, bound with pins of silver, each intricately inlaid with ivory. She walked with dignity and grace, evoking an atmosphere of calmness and a sense of well being whenever she entered a room.

Glancing around the library, noticing the mess that her daughter had recently created, she smiled and said, "Filaree, what has become of your need for order? For one to whom everything has its proper place, you have surely strayed from your usual path."

"Mother, I am in no mood for humor right now. I have been 'called.' I must go to Baladar and the boy!" Her eyes were wide and anxious.

The Queen barely moved, but a close observer who knew her well would have noticed a slight stagger as she quickly righted herself.

"So, the time has arrived. I have hoped and prayed that it would," she said as she bent her head thoughtfully to the side. "Honestly though, my daughter, I have also dreaded this day," the Queen continued as a single tear made its way slowly down her cheek. "But, our lives have never been our own to control and our destinies are yet to be written. When must you go? How soon? What can I do to aid your preparations?"

"I must leave before dawn. I cannot wait any longer than that. I have only just mapped my path and it will take all of my skill to get to Baladar in a reasonable amount of time as it is. The trip will not be easy this time of year. There is nothing you can do to help me now, mother. Just pray for me, and for all of us."

"You will need an escort. I will call Lord Markel and have him ready a guard for you," she said as she turned to summon her chief of staff.

"No, mother! I will travel only with Cameron to assist me. The fewer people who know where I am going and why, the better. We cannot afford to be waylaid."

"Will you be safe my dear? Just the two of you?"

"I will be as safe with Cameron at my side as with an entire army. Together, the two of us will travel more quickly and more stealthily than any other pair I know of. He is the most loyal soldier in the castle. No harm will come to me if he is nearby."

"Must you go, my darling Filaree?" she said, knowing the answer fully well, but needing to ask the question nonetheless.

"You know I must. I have waited for this moment almost my entire life. You would have gone yourself, mother, had you been called ten years ago instead of me."

"Yes, I would have, I know. I would have welcomed the opportunity. But you are *my* daughter and I am *your* mother! I fear for you, and I will miss you more than you will ever know, more than you could even imagine," she said, and she moved to the side of the maiden.

The Lady Filaree and Queen Esta embraced, the Queen patting her daughter's hair like she did when she was a child.

"I will be safe, mother, I promise. Nothing will keep me from my path, and nothing will prevent me from doing my duty and training the boy. You have raised me well."

"Your father would have been proud of you, my dear. He would have told me not to worry, not to fear; that the fabric weaves of its own will. He would have embraced this moment. But he too would have been sad, and he too would have secretly wept. Did you know he cried when you were born? He so wanted a girl, unlike so many other men. But, do not ask me to play the stoic. In your presence, I will weep openly if I choose," she said, smiling for the first time.

"I love you mother. I will always love you," Filaree responded, turning her face away for just an instance in order to brush the tears from her own eyes.

"I will get news of my progress to you if I am able. But fear not, mother. Remain steadfast. I will reach Pardatha! But, now I must prepare. I have much to do before dawn."

"Yes, I know. I will do my part and put on a good face for the people. Fear not, my child. These secrets are safe with me. Now, let me fetch Corvina so that she may help with the preparations. I have been thoughtless to leave her for so long in the hallway. The good woman must be out of her mind with worry by now."

With that, Queen Esta turned and exited the room, putting on the face of power and leadership, no hint of sadness remaining on her porcelain-like countenance.

Filaree glanced out the large, leaded window at the snow-capped hills beyond. The castle turrets gleamed like diamonds from the sun reflecting off of the sheets of ice coating them. The brilliant, bright orb was low in the western sky, preparing to conceal its beauty from this part of the world until the next day. Staring intently at the sky outside, she raised her chin high, thrust a clenched right fist high into the air, took a deep breath and uttered a solemn vow.

"For you father and for you mother, I swear that I will fulfill my destiny. I will teach the boy all that I know and all that I can, and he will lead us out of the darkness into the light! I know it. I feel it deep within my soul, stronger than anything else I have ever felt before. He will save *our* world!"

Chapter Eleven

The light from the full moon was glinting off of the polished surface in front of which the tired, old woman sat motionless. Her tattered shawl hung in shreds from her arms, concealing an even more worn and soiled tunic that had, at one time, been of the finest quality. Now, the silk was threadbare and the once beautiful colors had faded, leaving it sickly and light-brownish in hue. Her black hair was a tangled mess of mats, hanging in corded ringlets over her wrinkled and dirt smeared face. The once bright eyes were watery and pale, and where there was formerly white one could only now see a tired red.

She stared with wearied eyes into the stone before her. Motioning over and over again with her hands, attempting to conjure up an image in the stone, she finally let her arms go limp, hung her head with a sigh of resignation and stood erect.

Staring up at the moon, Trialla spoke silently to herself. *How could this have happened to me? I was to be a Queen! I was to have riches beyond measure and servants and lands of my own. How could that miserable woman have escaped with the boy? She has ruined my life!*

She spat into the corner, and rubbed a tattered sleeve across her cracked lips.

Well, she got what she deserved in the end! I only wish I had been there to see it for myself. She pushed a string of hair away from her eyes with a gnarled finger. *Where is he now? I will find him! I must find him!* The old woman stood up and walked to the open window across the filthy room. She hoisted the chamber pot with her and dumped it out the opening, listening to it cascade down the sheer wall of the turret in which she was imprisoned. She counted slowly to eight before she heard it splash into the water below.

What has gone wrong?. How could he treat me this way? He promised me so much. I do not deserve this. I will find that spoiled little brat, and I will be redeemed! He will respect me and honor me. I will be beautiful again.

She remembered vividly the exact moment when King Garold died. In her captivity she relived it over and over, never tiring of the pleasure it gave her. Like the fool that he was, he stood in front of his daughter until the end thinking that would save her. Trialla watched it all. She relished those minutes, the last gasps of breath, the passing of their lives.

Garold was a noble idiot! Well, he did save Lara from the indignities she would have had to endure had he not thrust the knife into her when he did. The Queen was already gone by that time. She died first from a wound in the back, inflicted by Trialla herself. She did not get to see her husband and daughter die.

What a wonderful feeling that was, to humble that arrogant woman once and for all, she thought gleefully. *I wish she had seen my face. I wish she knew it was I who took her life from her. She should have died with that thought on her mind. Too bad, though, that none of them survive.* Had she ever expected the boy to escape, she would have kept the mother alive. She could have used her to find the child. *They were always so unsuspecting. Those fools!*

Granted, Trialla had woven strong and powerful spells with which she seduced the kingdom. And, it was not without its cost to herself! She aged years in a matter of months and she grew hoary and broken-down from her efforts. He had promised that all that would be rectified, that she would regain her youth, that she would gain eternal beauty. But, alas, here she was, imprisoned in a forsaken cell with no means of escape, living in her own filth, old and decrepit, all due to Mira, the fool who sacrificed her own life for the boy. *He is probably dead by now anyway.* But he could not be, or she would not be forced to sit here and search for him all day and all night long. *Why was he doing this to me?. Of what importance could this boy be anyway? He was only a child. His kingdom lies in ruins, and his family is dead. He was a weak, pathetic boy! I hate them all, those fools. They deserved their fate.* She cried in fits and spurts, the tears welling up in the corners of her wrinkled eyes.

I am losing my mind!. I am going crazy. I must concentrate and hold myself together. I will succeed if I do. I will find him, she promised herself as she moved toward the stone once again.

Before she even had a chance to lift her head and glance toward the sound, he was in the middle of the room. He was so beautiful, it hurt her physically to gaze upon him. The smile, the hair, the eyes, the skin---everything about him was perfect. Trialla covered her face in shame at her ugliness and backed into the corner.

He floated across the empty space, slightly above the ground, and hovered directly in front of her. His skin was almost translucent. She could see the blood flowing through his veins, his heart pumping with power. Colton dar Agonthea had many faces, of this Trialla had suspected, but to her at this moment in time, he appeared to be the essence of loveliness, the most perfect of men, what dreams are made of. His smile seduced, his touch burned her with passion, his voice shamed her with the feelings it evoked. She would do anything for him, suffer anything for him, even take her own life if he asked her to.

He made her feel embarrassed to appear to him so, unkempt and unattractive. She wanted to hide, to crawl into a hole and peer out at him, unseen. She had been unsuccessful in her efforts to locate the boy and she knew that Colton would be unhappy with her. All her exertions were for naught. She could not even conjure the faintest image of him, no matter how hard she tried.

Colton gazed upon Trialla with eyes, black as pitch, no color whatsoever permeating the emptiness therein. He lifted his arm, his perfect fingers pointing at her, and she felt her body stand erect. Like a puppet, she walked over to the window. Unable to control her limbs, she climbed the sill and stood gazing at the water far below. Her heart was pounding uncontrollably as her leg bent at the knee and she began to lean forward. As she commenced to fall, a force pulled her sharply inward and she crumbled onto the stone floor in a miserable heap at Colton's feet.

He laughed beautifully. It made her so happy to cause him joy that she would have gladly fallen if he wanted her to, if it would bring him more happiness even if only for a second in time. Her emotions were turned upside down. She could not think straight and she wanted only to please him. It hurt her so that she was unable to locate the boy; for his sake! Everything was for his sake!

"I am disappointed in you, Trialla."

Just to hear his voice made her tremble.

"You know how much I want you to find the boy, why are you doing this to me, causing me such pain and misery?"

Anguish swept through her body. She cried out, suffering for him, feeling his loss, reeling from his dissatisfaction.

"Speak to me, woman. Tell me what I must do to make you understand my need," he implored.

Trialla crawled to his feet, grasping his ankle, kissing his toes. Gathering the courage to speak, she took a deep breath and said, "I will find him, my Lord. I just need some more time. It is not easy. Mira cast him well. The trail has faded and I have been unable to pick it up again."

"Time is running out!" he thundered, his liquid features changing even as she stared at them. "I am losing patience with you, woman."

She backed into the corner, tears pouring from her eyes now, lips quivering with fear. He rose a little higher off the ground, turned so gracefully, so magnificently, that she was awestruck, and her fear faded momentarily.

"I swear, master, I will locate him. Soon, very soon, another day at most. Please do not be angry with me. I cannot bear it."

She was blubbering by then, sloppy as a child, wanting nothing other than to please him.

"Be still!" he bellowed. "Cease your prattle and get to work. I must leave on a short trip and when I return I expect that you will have succeeded in locating the boy. You have power, Trialla. Use it now, or it may depart you unexpectedly altogether," he warned.

"Yes, your Lordship. Thank you, thank you your Lordship. I will not disappoint you. I can find him. It will be soon, very soon."

He narrowed his gaze, staring so hard at Trialla that she could barely remain conscious. She was totally filled with the desire to please him; she wanted to accomplish nothing more in life. Nothing else mattered at all.

"Beware, witch, should you fail!" he said through his teeth, his features turning sharp and venomous.

Her emotions were ragged, ascending, only to topple from the heights of expectation to the depths of despair.

"Beware!" he said again as he turned to go.

Trialla could have sworn that for an instant she saw a long claw where his finger should have been. She shivered in response.

No, my eyes must be playing tricks upon me, she dismissed the thought quickly

The hours of strain and the poor light were taking their toll upon her. Colton dar Agonthea exited as he entered, silently and without a backward glance. She watched him depart, her heart breaking at the thought of his absence, pain rushing through her limbs, emptiness filling her soul.

Once he was gone, she collapsed with exhaustion. She could not control the shaking and she needed to wrap her arms tightly around herself in order not to do bodily harm. The nausea returned and her body wretched, the bile flowing, bitter and vile. Fear consumed her very being as she rocked herself in the corner of the putrid room, crying and crying, shrieking like a madwoman until she fell into a semi-coma, wasted and worn out, a wretched shell of the woman she once was.

Chapter Twelve

Reeling from sheer dizziness rather than pain, Baladar sought to right himself. From the instant he stepped through the portal, the sensations of vertigo would not go away. He was falling into emptiness, unable to distinguish up from down or left from right. In fact, he was not even sure if he was falling or rising. He felt as if he was moving, but he was not verily certain of that.

Where did Porta go?

He could not feel his steed underneath him. He looked out into forever, gazed behind him into eternity past and floated into the future yet un-lived. A second? An hour? Perhaps a tiel? How much time passed seemed almost irrelevant, as Baladar began to succumb to the sensations. He could remain here perpetually, floating, falling, rising, rushing forward into magnificent emptiness and backwards into the fullness of the past.

All his cares disappeared, his problems faded and his troubles melted away. He forgot his name, who he was, where he was. His own consciousness, his sense of self, blended into the surroundings, making him one with the environment that he had entered. The boundaries that formerly separated him from other people, other objects, the air itself, were broken. Baladar was Baladar no more.

He opened his eyes, not knowing how long he had them closed, feeling as if he had awoken from a deep and relaxing sleep, and what he saw warmed his soul. He was upon an island, or so it seemed, for he heard water gently lapping onto a shoreline from what sounded like all directions. He thought he could see sunlight reflecting off of the liquid blueness in the distance, but he could not be certain of anything.

The colors around him were so vivid that he had to shield his eyes until they adjusted to the brilliance. His equilibrium was off, and he was uncertain if what he saw was real or not. He caught glimpses of many odd and beautiful animals scurrying around, never able to focus on any one, to ascertain if they were species he recognized or not, but he suspected that many were not. The ground was lush, covered in bright green moss, soft and comfortable. The foliage was abundant and varied.

As his eyes regained their focus, he saw trees with leaves of shiny silver, creating the most gorgeous music he had ever heard as they struck one another each time the wind gusted. The air smelled as sweet as honeyberries, fresh and wholesome. Birds of all shapes and sizes flew overhead and settled in the trees, singing sweetly, creating a crescendo of song keeping time with the wind and the leaves, rising in volume as the wind blew, and subsiding as it became calm again. He was afraid at first to take a step, expecting to fall over, unsure of whether or not he could control his limbs. Then suddenly Baladar became aware of a path, clearly defined, directly underfoot. It was made of a diaphanous material, one he had never seen before, swirling with color. He knew that he was supposed to follow it and he gladly began his journey to the residence of Calista, the Lady of the Island.

This world was so different from his own. As he walked, it seemed to create itself. He could see the path winding up ahead and he followed it eagerly. Yet he could never actually see around the immediate bend until he was almost on top of it. The landscape constantly changed, always beautiful but never the same.

Finally, he saw what appeared to be a great door, anchored by nothing, standing solitary and majestic. As he approached it, it opened and suddenly he could see not only inside, the hallways, balustrades and stairways coming into view, but also a building of incredible beauty appeared around the door, looming overhead, turrets with banners flying, pinnacles of crystal, gleaming in the sun. It must have been there all along, but as with everything else on this island, nothing was as it seemed at first sight.

Of one thing he was certain, nevertheless; he was safe here, safer than anywhere else on earth, and with that certainty, he boldly crossed the threshold and entered the palace. Following the polished stone walkway, he glanced from side to side, amazed at the size of the edifice. It seemed to go on forever in all directions, but somehow he knew where he was going. Baladar reached the end of the hall and a wonderful smell wafted up once again, spice and rose and apple-melon and other odors he could not recognize.

The double gilt doors were shut, but as he touched them they gracefully swung back, revealing a huge chamber harboring a single throne of cut quartz set against the far wall, swathed in woven silks and covered with pillows embroidered in gold. Upon the throne sat Calista, in gossamer robes of violet, a single circlet of diamonds upon her delicate head. Her long, white-blonde hair framed her face and cascaded down her back. Large green eyes peered at him, radiating warmth and welcome.

Regally, she raised her left arm, beckoning Baladar to come forward. As he did so, he dropped to one knee and bowed his head.

"My Queen, you do me such honor by allowing me entry into your domain," he said reverentially.

"The honor is mine, Lord Baladar. I welcomed you once before and I welcome you again. Arise and attend me. Need opens my doors to the good and kind."

"I bring you news, my Lady. Long awaited news," he said as he walked closer to the regal woman.

Before he even had an opportunity to speak she responded.

"So, he has arrived," she rejoined without a question, but with obvious satisfaction. "It is the beginning, Baladar, the beginning. All that has come before is meaningless now. The clock starts anew."

"I have brought the ring, my Queen, as ordained. Davmiran, the heir, will be its bearer," he stated as he reached inside his tunic and withdrew the gold band on the long, thin chain.

Slipping it over his head, he reached forward and handed it to her. As she clasped it in her hand and as he released it, he felt a wave of sadness overtake him. He staggered slightly.

"Have no fear, Baladar. All who hold the ring, no matter for how short the time, regret relinquishing it. It is a natural reaction to so powerful a relic."

Calista clasped the ring in her hand, closed her graceful fingers around it, bowed her head and uttered the words, *"C'al, port maera. Bi'al Davmiran. Setha par dormia, comte ta manta."*

The ring glowed brightly, streaks of light escaping through the cracks between the Queen's fingers. She opened her hand and presented the ring once again to Baladar.

"Take this back to the boy and place it around his neck. He will awaken immediately upon its touch on his skin. Instruct him well, Baladar. Teach him all that you can. The Gem of Eternity awaits," she said to Baladar and she rose to approach him.

"I will do all that I can, my Lady. I have summoned those whom I have chosen to aid in this quest. They are in route to my side as we speak. His lessons will begin as soon as they all arrive," he told her.

"You must know, Baladar, that the Tomes of Caradon are unclear in parts. I have read the portions pertaining to the ring over and over countless times. In some places reference is made to a gold band and in others, a silver one. The pages are old and worn and hard to decipher, but I cannot tell for certain if the ring is one and the same, manifesting as gold at times and as silver at others." After saying this, she looked intently at Baladar. "Have you ever seen it change? Has its appearance varied at all?"

"No, my Lady. As long as I have had it in my possession, it has remained a band of gold," he replied.

"The elders are not in agreement on this matter. I, for one, believe that there may be two separate and distinct rings. I only wish that the ancient books were more definitive on this point. But, there is no doubt who the bearer must be. The Gwendolen heir, Davmiran as you call him, is the one who will lead the quest for the First. The prophecy would make more sense to me now if the ring were mutable and we could witness its changeable nature. But, alas, there is but one heir, so there can be only one ring for him to bear," she said deep in thought.

A moment passed before she turned and looked at Baladar again, fixing him with a deep and poignant gaze. "Make sure he learns well. His power will be great."

"I have picked his aides with great care. They are all three noble and strong. Together, we will do what we must," he said solemnly.

"Are they all three of human descent as well?" she questioned, a hint of concern coloring her voice as she leaned lightly upon the quartz throne.

"Yes, my Lady, they happen to be. I am not as familiar with comparable individuals of Elfin or Dwarven descent. And the other major races do not serve the same side as we do. Why do you ask? Have I chosen poorly?" he asked with a newly troubled tone.

"No, I have no doubt that you have chosen well and with great care, Baladar. But, there will be a role for each race to play in the quest, as is written, and I surmised that perhaps that role would begin with the boy's education. It is not foretold as such. But, all who serve the light must participate in the effort to protect, preserve and renew it. That much is ordained!" she spoke, and she closed her beautiful eyes momentarily.

When she opened them again, she caught and held Baladar's gaze with her own and spoke with quiet strength. "The trees are dying, Baladar. I feel their pain daily. It takes a tremendous toll upon me. My powers are great too, but they are being spent in other areas now. The land suffers from each tree's loss and I must compensate for that. I must strive to maintain the balance. Therefore, I cannot be of much assistance to the boy. I feel the Dark Lord's presence growing stronger and stronger. As our shields weaken, his grow in power. His arms reach out and touch all that is clean, transforming it into that which is vile and dirty. He approaches. Eventually, he will find the boy, Baladar, and he will come to him. When that moment is upon us, you must be certain that he is prepared! Realize the gravity of these times. Our future rests upon his young shoulders...and yours!"

"I will do my best, my Queen."

"Your best, Baladar, may not be enough!" she cautioned him and then she withdrew within herself momentarily.

Calista raised her regal head once more and the look upon her face this moment was distant and pensive.

"I once knew Colton, the sorcerer, very well. We had developed a close relationship, a trusting one at one point in time. He was always distant and suspicious but I was nearer to him than he was to any other. He appeared then to be good and noble, or so it seemed, in ages past when he dwelled among the life givers. But, he was plagued by dreams that relentlessly tormented him, and as time passed, they grew more frequent and unbearable for him and he had to isolate himself from the rest of us. He no longer sought my council, nor would he accept it when I approached him. He suffered mental pain that seemed to explode unexpectedly and uncontrollably, born of the negativity of his essence, manifesting itself in waves of power unleashed randomly, and all the time he refused aid of any kind," she paused momentarily, her fragile head tilted to one side, and her sparkling eyes staring at nothing, lost in a painful reverie.

"I did not fathom then just how beyond hope he was. His strength was mighty but flawed, and some of the others believed that such flaws were disgraceful. They had no compassion for his suffering and therefor precipitated his descent. I was the only one who had any sympathy for his anguish and he bitterly rejected me. His mind and mine worked in such different ways that neither of us could possibly hope to understand the other, though I tried. It pained me deeply to witness the continual deterioration of one so strong, and it frightened me as well."

Calista walked before the quartz throne, gracefully sat upon it, and her skin immediately took on the colors and appearance of the translucent rock.

"I was not fool enough to be naive about just how formidable an opponent he would become. The others were more arrogant. Colton's fall was fast and furious, as he lost control more and more often, until he was no longer welcome, until he could no longer dwell amongst us, as he not only was endangering himself, but others as well. He refused help of any kind from me and no others offered theirs."

Baladar remained standing before her, fixed in his place as if frozen to the very ground upon which he stood. It was obvious to him that her feelings for Colton were at one time mixed, and it surprised him profoundly. He had always and only thought of him as the epitome of evil and he could barely conceive of him any other way. The Lady stared at him deeply, a knowing smile upon her face, as if she had read his thoughts.

"He and I were close at one time, yes, and therefor I was the bearer of the news that he would have to leave, that he could no longer abide in our realms. This enhanced his bitterness, but he was able to cushion his plunge before his ruination somehow, finding refuge among the twisted and the outcast, feeding ravenously upon their negative energy. He never forgave us and his hate for our world is beyond measure. And his enmity for me is just as extreme, if perhaps a bit more personal," she related, a sad and ironic expression marring her beauty.

"He has spent tiels feeding off of those he has come to rule, and his power has grown and grown. Even I cannot stand against him alone, unaided by the trees who never accepted Colton from the beginning of time, sensing before we could, his fatal imperfections. And they, alas, are weakening each day now, departing one by one, relinquishing us amidst their extraordinary despair. My time too is running short. I feel the fabric wearing thin. Beware that you do not take too long to prepare the boy," she said with gravity, piercing him with the intensity of her gaze.

"I will begin as soon as possible, as soon as I return and wake him from his peaceful slumber, my Lady," Baladar answered.

"Express no sadness for the child, Baladar. His slumber is not peaceful! There can be no peace whilst the trees and the land suffer so. It is but a waste of precious time, and if he is not awakened soon then the weave will be beyond even his ability to mend it. There is no room for regret here. He did not choose his destiny, but it remains his nonetheless! His full strength will be required. He cannot be led astray by self-pity or doubt," she rebuked him in warning, her cheeks momentarily flaring crimson.

"I shall not, my Queen. I vow that I will train him well. He will be prepared properly and he will lead us forth into a new age. He will fulfill all that is prophesied for him, of that I am certain," he said with confidence.

Queen Calista stood up, majestic and wise, and walked gracefully to the tapestry hanging on the wall to the side of the throne. Raising her arm, the tapestry flew away, revealing a niche in the granite wall. With one hand, she reached in and withdrew a simple pouch of scarred leather, pulled taught with a cord of rawhide.

Handing it to Baladar, she said, "Give this to him to keep with him always. Only at the moment of gravest need may he partake of this powder of creation, made from the Lalas itself. He must choose well and carefully, Baladar. This powder will save his life, but only once. If he wastes it unnecessarily, he may doom us all."

With that, the Queen of the lake bid farewell to Baladar, kissed him on the forehead and walked back to her throne.

"Farewell, my Lady. I know that it is time for me to depart. I have lingered longer than I should have. This is but the beginning, but one last question if I may?" he asked. Calista nodded her permission. "Should the need arise, may I visit you again?" he queried, expecting the answer to be affirmative.

"I fear not, my devoted Baladar," she responded, as he paled noticeably at her reply. "I must concentrate upon the darkness now that the boy has come, and I cannot weaken. It will require all of my energies and I must not allow myself to be distracted. Perhaps some time in the future we will meet again, but I will not allow my pathways, my secret ways, to be opened to anyone until Colton dar Agonthea is vanquished or the First falls! I will do my best to aid you in ways you may never know. I will never cease my efforts on your and the boy's behalf, but I must toil in my own manner. Alas, I must do so in solitude. Remember! My shores will be sealed to all until such time as the trees are safe or a power greater than mine breaks through," she said, causing Baladar to frown with concern.

"We have talked long enough. Now go. You have much work to do. Firstspeed, my son," she said with finality and she smiled sweetly at him.

Consumed with sadness and a terrible sense of loss, Baladar realized that this answer was definitive, dictated by circumstance and fate. He turned and began his journey back home, disheartened by the thought of possibly never seeing the Lady again in this lifetime, but ultimately focusing upon his overwhelming determination to carry out his appointed task.

Chapter Thirteen

Baladar traversed the pathways back to the edge of the woods, experiencing once again the unsettling but euphoric passage to his plain of existence, when seemingly out of nowhere, Porta appeared, calm and rested. Mounting his steed, he spurred him onward expectantly. As he cleared the dense brush, he became aware that more time had passed than he had realized. To Baladar, it seemed as if only a few hours had gone by since his arrival at the island on the lake. But as he had come at night, and now the sun was nearing the horizon in the western sky, he recognized that at least perhaps nearly a full day had elapsed, if not more.

Suddenly, his skin prickled as a feeling of foreboding overtook him, and he felt an urgency to return to the castle as rapidly as possible. Expectation quickly transformed itself into concern as he rushed through the brambles, pressing Porta's sides with his heels, a reckless abandon forcing him forward. Bursting out of the woods, Baladar galloped forth to the stable gates.

Halting in a swirl of dust, he wasted no time in jumping from his seat on Porta's bare back and leaving his friend to be attended to by his stable-master. Unaccustomed to his liege Lord behaving in so rash a manner, Tanner, the master of the horses, rushed to his aid only to receive a curt nod and witness the back of his lord's robes as Baladar rushed off to the castle with hardly a word spoken, leaving him standing wide-mouthed and startled. Porta whinnied in salute to Baladar, but he was already gone.

Baladar's concern mounted as he neared the main entryway to the keep. What had been a bustling court the evening prior was now empty of everyone except some housemaids and a young page. Of course, all of the evening's guests had gone home by this time, but the aides and servants who arrived with Lord Kettin should have still been milling around. Something was amiss! He never did trust Kettin and having left him alone to his own devices in the castle was probably a mistake.

He burst into the great hall thinking of only one thing when Grogan, the head of his personal guard, rushed into the antechamber with a cortege of attendants, all fully armed and obviously agitated.

"My Lord," he said as he bowed deeply to Baladar. "I am

afraid there has been an incident in the castle during your absence. It seems sir Dalek and Lord Kettin had been drinking rather extensively after you departed last evening. They apparently began arguing rather boisterously over Kettin's interest in Dalek's niece, you know the wench named Daria with the beautiful eyes, when Lord Kettin pulled out a dagger and thrust it into Dalek's side. He died immediately, your lordship. He did not suffer," Grogan said sadly, staring at Baladar with his shoulders back and his body stiff.

Baladar felt as if someone had hit him in the stomach with the end of a jousting stick.

Dalek dead? Is the boy safe?

Not wanting to alert anyone else in the castle to the youth's presence, Baladar knew that he had to dwell here for a while and learn all of the details before he could slip away and attend the boy, no matter how difficult that might prove to be.

"Dalek? Ah, this grieves me deeply. Were you able to assess blame here, Grogan? Was Dalek at fault? Did Kettin suffer injury?" Baladar queried, wishing that it had been Lord Kettin who would soon lay upon the pyre instead of his good and loyal aid, Dalek.

"Lord Kettin feigned weakness afterwards, my Lord, and expressed outrage at his treatment under your roof, but he was unhurt. All who witnessed the incident swore that Dalek never raised a hand to the Duke's son. I interrogated those present and I have determined that Kettin provoked the attack, for what reason I could not ascertain. He harbored no ill will toward Dalek previously. He is on his way back to his father's lands as we speak. He retreated to his rooms immediately after he, pardon me your lordship, murdered Dalek, expressing no remorse whatsoever, and he alerted his attendants that he would be departing straightaway in the morning.

"He said to tell you, my Lord, and please forgive me, these are his words, not mine, that it was clear that his presence was unwelcome in your home and that he feared for his safety under your roof. He ordered me to emphasize to you that he felt his treatment here was an insult to him and to his father, and that he had to believe that you intended it to appear that way. He said to tell you that the offer of alliance he carried with him on the Duke's behalf would have to be withdrawn and reconsidered, under the circumstances. He said that other options had to be addressed and that old affiliations may have to be reevaluated, that the wind has changed direction. He said to tell you that his father would not take this incident lightly, as he, his heir apparent, was threatened and that his very life was in danger while he was supposed to be under your protection." Grogan bowed his head apologetically and waited for instructions.

"Thank you, Grogan. I appreciate your candor," Baladar responded. "I would never hold you responsible for the words of such a one as Kettin, Duke Leonardo's son. I wonder if his father was privy to who took part in these depraved actions. Kettin surely had another agenda when he arrived here, outside of the realm of a friendly visit, and I fear that Dalek suffered the ultimate fate so that Kettin could foster this ruse. I am deeply aggrieved," Baladar said with much sentiment.

Returning his attention once more to the situation at hand he then asked, "By the way, when did our uninvited guest finally depart, being that he felt so unsafe here?" While he questioned his Master at Arms, sadness and anxiety was making it difficult for him to stand inactive, but he did his best.

"He was late to rise, your lordship, and he needed time to gather his men and deal with some private matters. He demanded a hot breakfast for them all before he left, which he did not attend. I bade them farewell, nevertheless, but he was not present when I did so. He could not have rejoined the others until they were mounted and ready to go, as I never saw Lord Kettin again. The group did not embark until well after 9:00 in the morning. He was quite secretive about his leave taking prior to then, pretending that he was unsafe, and he desired that we remain well out of his reach and sight until he cleared our lands. He chided me and warned me that if I followed him he would take that as a sign of aggression and that as he was already the victim here, it would only exacerbate the ill will. He mentioned how much he disliked being spied upon, insinuating that we were watching him too closely."

Baladar looked pensive as he pronounced sadly, "I take responsibility for this situation. Whether or not what Kettin claims has any truth to it, we shall all bear the brunt of his visit. I am afraid that we will one and all learn in time what the true purpose of his sojourn here was. I should never have quit the castle until I was able to determine his true intentions." He paused for a moment, anxious to attend to other matters. "Grogan, secure the gates and post a watch. We must now be vigilant at all times until the Duke and I can meet face to face and correct this wrong, if such can be done at this point. I have some thinking to do and pressing matters to attend to. Forgive me. Temian, see to Dalek's arrangements, and make sure that he is properly handled. He was very dear to me and we shall all sorely miss him."

Baladar turned and walked away, hiding his anxiety as he slowly made his way out of the hall toward the master stairway.

Once out of sight of Grogan and his men, he bounded up the steps, taking two at a time, and headed directly for his rooms. His trepidation was mounting as he neared his private suites where the boy, Davmiran, lay sleeping. The ring hanging beneath his tunic was burning his skin, causing him to wince in pain.

Flinging the door open, he entered the chamber and gasped at what he saw. The boy was gone! His bed was empty and not a trace of him was to be found.

How could that bastard of a Duke's son have known he was even here? Baladar thought furiously. *I must find him and bring him back immediately. What chance have we without him? The world is on the brink of chaos and our one hope has been kidnaped by a fool!* he declared silently. *Does he even know what he has done? I must catch up with him and retrieve Davmiran!* he thought as he considered his options, fearing now with the loss of the boy, that the death of Dalek, his loyal and trusted aide, was merely a foreshadowing of the disappointment and sorrow that was to come.

Baladar poignantly remembered Calista's words, yet the true weight of the past day's deeds had not fully descended upon him. He was unwilling to accept that the heir would not be found. The thought was inconceivable, after having waited so long and so patiently, that he could have slipped through his fingers so quickly.

How careless have I been? To have left him unguarded no matter how serious the purpose which drew me away, borders upon negligence! Could this all have been by design? Have I fallen into a trap that may cost us all so dearly?

He started to suspect everything, even his own cogitations and inspirations, wondering if Colton had infiltrated his thoughts and his home. Calista spoke of the Dark Lord's power and of his deviousness, his ability to twist people's minds.

Has he already defeated us? Baladar began to worry. *Could it be that his victory would be so simple to achieve, that one misstep by me could possibly mean the end of the world as we know it?*

Baladar was consumed by these concerns, as he frantically planned his next move. He was not one to give up, even in the face of seemingly insurmountable odds, and he would not give up now. If the boy was to be found, he would locate him and bring him back safely to Pardatha.

The sun had set by this time, and Baladar knew that Kettin could not have traveled too far, considering how much baggage his retinue carried with it, and how opposed to discomfort Lord Kettin was. He could not travel at top speed, even after having taken the boy.

I could overtake him on Porta in a matter of hours, he thought, desperately trying to determine what to do.

Baladar was not accustomed to rashly responding to circumstances, but now he needed to make some serious decisions, and he had to make them swiftly. Moving to his desk, he withdrew the small pouch that harbored his gems. He retrieved the Lalas disk from the cabinet against the wall and set it down on the desktop. Placing the stones one by one at opposite sides of the disk, he began to hum.

As he sank into the trance of power that was required to activate the disk, concentrating upon Kettin's image, a picture began to form amidst the swirling colors within the borders of the wood. The stones flared brightly, creating an arc of light above the desk. Baladar carefully scanned the images, searching for signs of the boy.

He could see Kettin sitting upon his horse, chatting with his man-at-arms. He seemed casual and unconcerned about anything. Since there were no wagons within the entourage, Baladar could see everyone who was traveling with Kettin, and to his shock and consternation, Davmiran was nowhere to be found! He reviewed it once again, careful not to miss scrutinizing any area of Kettin's group. There was no sign of the boy!

Confusion overtook him as he searched the group once more. Nothing! Not a trace of him. He broadened the field of the image to encompass a wider radius, but to no avail. In utter dismay he let the image disappear, carefully returning the gems to the pouch and placing the disk back in the spot he had removed it from.

Perhaps I was wrong, he thought, his mind rapidly assessing the other possibilities. *Maybe Kettin did not take the boy. But if not he, then who did?*

Baladar sat down in his large chair in the corner of the room and peered out the leaded windows toward the eastern horizon.

"How could I have been such a blasted idiot!" he exclaimed out loud.

Of course the boy would not be with him any longer, even if it was he who abducted him originally. The spell that I cast upon him would have insured that all of their memories of his existence would have disappeared from their consciousness' immediately upon their departure from the confines of the city's walls. They would have left him outside the gates, unaware of his presence. Or, they would have continued to carry him with them unbeknownst to the entire party, until he fell from his horse or wandered away. He could be with them and still be safe! But, then I would have seen him," his mind raced on. *No, they must have left him behind somewhere, wandering on whatever means of transportation they had placed him on, most likely a mule or a pack horse.*

Baladar was thinking quickly now, trying to picture exactly what must have happened as they crossed the threshold of his premises. At first, he felt relieved that Kettin's evil intentions had been thwarted by his magic, but then he instantly realized that now the boy would be on his own, defenseless and vulnerable, though invisible to any humans. Humans were certainly not the only danger in the woods. His life could be in more imminent risk abandoned and on his own, than in the company of the Duke's son.

What Baladar had construed would serve to protect Davmiran, was now going to be a liability to him, perhaps a fatal one!

"I was not blessed with the young man's presence only to lose him so quickly," he muttered. "I must think, I must find him! He is in grave peril and every moment that passes enhances the risk for all of us. May the First grant me wisdom and aid my search!" he exclaimed.

If the Dark Lord indeed sent the Duke's son to carry out this evil deed, then he may be searching for him as well. Could he see through my magic? Baladar wondered, fearfully.

In despair, Baladar stared out into the darkness, questioning what to do next, shivering with concern and feeling the weight of the world upon his shoulders, while the ring continued to burn with an ever raging heat, suspended from its golden chain on the middle of his chest.

Chapter Fourteen

From his vantage point behind the tree, Elion could not understand what the soldiers were doing. They led a horse through the gates, its back draped with a long saddle blanket that looked as if it concealed something. The guards seemed to take great care in leading the animal out, but as soon as they crossed the threshold, they appeared to lose interest in it altogether, dropping the rope that they held so tightly just a moment before.

Their Lord and obvious leader turned his attention to the horizon, rather than the horse and its baggage, and laughed and slapped his man-at-arms on the back as if they were sharing some hilariously funny joke. Spurring his horse on, he led his entourage quickly across the open ground surrounding the city walls and disappeared into the nearby woods, never looking back once to see what happened to their quarry, leaving the mare behind as if it never existed. No one from the castle followed them out or bid them farewell.

They could not have been very important or cherished guests, he thought.

The unsaddled horse dropped its head to chew on some sweet grass just off the stone pathway, as the soldiers and their leaders continued on. They left the horse to wander deeper into the grass unheeded. While searching for more to munch upon further down the path, the blanket on its back slipped to the ground and to Elion's astonishment, there was a boy draped over its haunches, unmoving, bound hand and foot.

After the mare had strayed quite some distance from the city walls, Elion watched the youth fall from the horse and land, motionless, upon the soft earth now hidden from view by the tall meadow grass. The prisoner did not move at all. He lay perfectly still, even after hitting the ground with some force from his perch atop the mare.

Elion's sharp eyes took in everything, and his extraordinary hearing allowed him to eavesdrop upon the group from a great distance. No one in the entire convoy ever stopped or even seemed to notice the absence of what appeared to captivate their attention just moments before. They spoke of their return home and they made all kinds of small talk, without a mention of the horse or its inert rider. It looked to him as if the horse carrying the boy just vanished in plain sight, as if they became invisible to them all while still in their very presence. One moment they were doting upon them, and the next, they were moving on as if they were never there.

Elion watched from his hiding place until the soldiers were entirely out of sight and then he slowly walked over to the unconscious youth. As he neared the boy's side, he noticed that his beautiful navy blue eyes were open wide, but they were clearly seeing nothing. His breathing was steady, but he moved not an inch. He did not appear to be suffering from any injury and he seemed not to be in pain, but he was as lifeless as a rock in all other respects. Elion bent to listen to his breath and his Elfin instincts bristled with excitement.

This is no ordinary boy, he thought to himself immediately, his entire body tingling with energy.

He quickly pulled a small silver dagger from his high suede boot and cut the bindings on his hands and feet. Taking off his loden cape, he laid it upon the ground and carefully placed the boy on top of it. Slipping two small branches into the belt loops on either side of it, he created a makeshift portable. Using the hood as a handle, he grasped it and pulled the young man slowly through the grass into the shelter of the woods ahead, stopping only to place his dangling arms upon the conveyance so that they would not continue to catch on the brush beneath. He was so moved by the boy's presence that he barely noticed the matted trail he left behind in the soft undergrowth.

The sun was quite high in the eastern sky and there would be at least seven to eight hours of daylight left before darkness set in. Once safely hidden in the dense trees, Elion bent over the youth and examined him more closely. His skin continued to prickle as he gazed upon the stunning boy. Humans did not usually appear to him to be as beautiful as this one did. He often found their features exaggerated and misshapen, making them ugly, rather than soft and pleasant to gaze upon. Their skin was usually blemished and dirty and their eyes, the windows to their souls, were small and tired looking, in a variety of washed out colors.

This boy had skin like polished stone, smooth and unblemished, and his eyes, though lacking in recognition, were clear and extraordinarily bright. His features were so perfect and symmetrical that they were almost Elfin in appearance. His ears were not too big for a human and they were delicately shaped, although they were rounded at the top, which Elion still found strange to glance upon. His hair was silken and beautifully colored, yellow and healthy looking. All in all, this was the first human that Elion could actually say he found to be aesthetically pleasing.

But, it was not merely his appearance that struck the young Elf. In fact, that was the least significant aspect. The boy seemed to radiate power, a power he had never experienced before. It made him smile and it lifted his soul. All the weariness and fatigue he suffered during his journey, all the sadness for those he left behind and all of the anxiety he harbored regarding those he was hoping to reunite with, was washed away by his presence. The feelings were extraordinary! He was consumed with an overwhelming need to protect this adolescent human, this boy he had just stumbled upon. And the oddest thing of all was that this need felt so right and so pure. It was not born of envy, or jealousy, or hate, but of love.

It was clear to Elion immediately that the human was not simply asleep. Someone had placed a strong spell upon him, and no rudimentary conjuring would awaken him. Of this he was sure. He would need time to determine what needed to be done with him, but he would first have to get him to a safe place. Obviously, the castle was not his home and the inhabitants were not his friends. Otherwise, the departing humans would not have been permitted to lead him out, bound hand and foot, the way that they did. No one followed the group out to check on his welfare or to bid them farewell. Surely his beauty could not have been overlooked by them all. Yet, they apparently did not care about his fate.

What a strange race the human one is, he thought. He was surprised though at Baladar, the Lord of Pardatha. He had heard such good things about him from his parents and his uncle. *They must have been wrong,* he concluded, and he was glad he decided not to stop in the city on the way back home. *Destiny must have brought me here at this moment in time,* Elion thought, overwhelmed by the prescient feeling that was invoked by being in the boy's company. *The fabric weaves of its own will,* he reflected soberly. *He would have died if not for me,* he pondered. *I must find a way to awaken him and learn his purpose, his reason for being here, and why he was left to expire, defenseless and alone.*

Elion continued to think to himself and weigh the possibilities, as he pulled Davmiran gently through the woods. He made little sound himself as he walked, seeming to travel on top of the leaves and twigs, rather than through them, his steps were so light. His pointed ears twitched independently of one another, picking up all the sounds of the forest, carefully screening out those which were normal and safe and focusing in on any that might be dangerous. His sense of smell was as good as any hound he might encounter and he could easily sense danger in that way as well. But, everything was all right now. The forest was friendly and peaceful, posing no immediate threat to either him or the boy.

He stopped momentarily now and again to pull some berries from a branch or to gather some nuts from the base of a tree. Munching as he walked, he wondered how the boy would receive nourishment. He was quite skinny for a human, after all, and he could not allow him to suffer from lack of sustenance.

Elion released his hold on the cape for a moment, as he recognized a particular tree in the distance. Moving directly over to it, he used his dagger to slice a thin line in the bark of the thick trunk. Pulling a transparent receptacle made of some kind of soft, vegetation from his vest, he blew into it and it puffed up like a glass bottle bulging at the bottom. Holding it against the tree, he watched patiently as a yellowish liquid, thick and fragrant, oozed out of the slash in the bark. After the flask was about half full, he brought it to his lips, and tasted the extract.

"Ah!" he smacked his lips. *Kala sap is still one of my favorite things to drink. To be so good to the palate and so good for the body at the same time is definitely a blessing.*

Carrying the juice like substance back to the boy, he knelt beside him, gently lifted his head a bit and placed a small pillow from his backpack behind him. Opening his mouth with his free hand, he placed the flask against his lips. Squeezing it from the bottom, a small amount of the Kala spurted into his mouth. He rubbed the boy's throat until his muscles caused him to swallow involuntarily. Elion did this until a fair amount of the liquid had been downed, satisfied that he would now survive for a while without becoming dehydrated. Squeezing the remainder into his own mouth, he folded the receptacle and put it away.

By now, the sun had just about set and the wind was rustling through the leaves, indicating to him that a storm of sorts was on its way. He could smell the rain in the air. Returning the pillow to his backpack, he continued on, pulling the boy behind him. He had been journeying for many days already when he came upon this youth, and he had a ways to go yet before he would reach his destination, his home of Seramour nestled within the protective woods of Lormarion.

Elion had been away now for four years, living with the Northern Elves, mastering their lore and honing his indigenous skills at the same time. His uncle Bristar was a learned and wise leader whom his father loved dearly. Treestar had always wanted Elion to live with him and study the ways of the mountain Elves in the heights of Crispen with his elder brother. Their customs were so different from his own, and he wanted his son to have the opportunity to benefit from the knowledge of his northern kin.

He hoped that Elion would bring home with him a wisdom that he could impart to his own people, helping to lead them through the troubled times to come. His father, Treestar, was getting old even in Elfin years, and he knew that Elion was the one to take his place among his people when he could lead them no more. With the trees dying everywhere, the Elfin lands were no longer certain to be safe from danger, and Treestar wanted his son to be prepared.

As the darkness approached, even the Elves shuddered. Sheltered as they were, they had paid little attention to the world of humans. But, the death of a Lalas was felt by all living things, and so many deaths recently, alerted their leaders to the imminent threat to all the peoples of the lands. They could ignore it no more, and Treestar sent his three sons to the far corners of the globe in search of whatever knowledge they could garner from the many friends and relations he had.

Fallean and Dalaway both left when he did, and they were due to return in the same month that he was due to arrive back home, Dalaway having gone the farthest, all the way to Eleutheria, and Fallean the nearest to the island of the Sea Clans. Elion was right on schedule, if nothing hindered his travels at this point. He was anxious to return, to see his father and brothers and to share what he had learned with them all in their effort to prepare for what everyone knew was approaching from the southern reaches, and hopefully prevent it from devastating them. He left with his uncle's pledge to his father that the northern kingdoms would march to their southern brethren's aid if called upon to do so. This was heartening and it caused him much joy and comfort to be able to carry this message back to Treestar and his people.

The wind was kicking up now and although he knew he could travel at night as his vision suffered little due to the darkness and he did not tire easily, he wanted to rest and think without having to be vigilant at the same time, as he would have to be if he continued on at this time. If he could find a safe haven for the night, he could plan somewhat and still have an opportunity to observe the boy as well.

A short while later, up ahead, he thought he saw a small opening in the side of the rocky hill. As they approached it, he could clearly make out a narrow cave entrance that would accommodate them if he crouched down. He sensed no danger and he did not smell the presence, past or current, of any living thing. Pulling the boy behind him, he hunched over and entered. Inside, he found a chamber, safe and secure, within which he could stand up and move around comfortably.

Making the boy as snug as possible, he laid out his bedroll and sat upon it to ponder the events of the day. From out of his backpack, he removed a small pouch, opened the drawstring and sprinkled a fine, luminous powder onto the stone floor. Spreading it thinly with his fingers until it covered an area a foot in diameter, he struck a flint to the stone and let the sparks fall upon the powder. As they touched it, the powder flared into flame, soft and warm, spreading its heat throughout the small cavern at once. It would burn all night without replenishment, Elion knew.

He settled back against the hard wall and gazed from the flame to the face of the youth at his feet, assured that fate had brought them together, gaining confidence as the moments slipped away and believing now that even after four years of studying and learning, the boy that he had just stumbled upon would unwittingly provide the answer that they had all been searching the globe for. He sincerely felt that the future of his race, aye, of the whole planet, lay here in this dark cave, unconscious and innocent to the maelstrom building around him.

Elion closed his eyes and allowed himself to drift off into a light sleep, confident that with the dawn would come a renewal of hope, an easing of the tension caused by his acute perception of the ever encroaching darkness. He peeked through half closed eyes upon the countenance of the young human lying quietly at his feet, his eyes drawn to his presence, and he welled up with emotion once more. He watched him breathe for a few moments longer, until he finally sank into a deep and cleansing sleep, lolled by the sound of the rain that had begun to fall heavily outside of his temporary sanctuary.

Chapter Fifteen

As Cairn and Calyx emerged from the foliage to stand in front of Tomas' tree, they could hear his humming and see him huddled high up in the branches. Cairn felt as if he was violating the privacy of the moment, and he turned to beckon Calyx to leave with him, when Tomas bounded down from his perch and ran to Calyx, only to grasp on to his huge forelegs and hug him deeply to himself. Cairn approached the two of them and saw tears streaming down the cheeks of the boy.

"So, you know already?" he said somberly. "I thought I would have to be the bearer of this tragic news."

Tomas looked at him sadly, his green eyes brimming with tears. "When I first sensed danger, it was already too late. Ormachon would not let me leave. He made me stay here with him. I wanted to go to them! But, he forbid it. Did you see what happened?" Tomas spoke these words like a grown man, holding his head high, forcing back the pain and the overwhelming feeling of loss.

"No, Tomas, only the results. It was an evil enemy that attacked your aunt and uncle. There was nothing I could do. I too was too late," Cairn responded. "I gave them a proper burial, as best that I could under the circumstances. I wished to spare you the anguish of having to see them, so that you could preserve your memories of them as they were before. They were good and noble people, undeserving of their fate," Cairn said, his yellow eyes dulling with fatigue and sadness.

"I must go to the cottage. I have to say goodbye. Then we can leave," Tomas remarked with single-minded maturity.

Cairn was taken aback by the words. He assumed that he would have to coerce the boy to leave. After all, he would be leaving his tree, Ormachon, and his home all at once. Such must be difficult for a young man. But, Tomas seemed to know what he needed to do, and his confidence during this most distressing time emboldened Cairn.

"You are remarkably strong, my young friend. I am honored that you trust me enough to be willing to journey with me as your protector," he said honestly.

"Ormachon likes you. Oh, I do too, and Calyx also, but Ormachon tells me that it is you whom I must journey with now for a time. He knows! He always knows," Tomas answered, pushing his blonde hair out of his face and wiping his nose with his sleeve and sniffling, reminding Cairn that he was just a boy after all.

"Please tell Ormachon that I will not let him down. Nor you, Tomas. I have an important journey to make and it will be my favor to have you accompany me. Both Calyx and I will guard you as if you were our own flesh and blood. That I pledge to you, and to your tree!" Cairn stated boldly.

"I have to stop at the house first. I do not really have anything of my own to bring along. Ormachon says that I do not need anything from here. But there is something of my aunt's that I want to find before I go," the boy said.

"I will go with you there, Tomas, and then we can leave, if that is all right. You should not journey there alone and unaccompanied," Cairn replied.

Tomas looked a slight bit perplexed for an instant, not seeming to comprehend the potential danger that Cairn perceived. He seemed to have no fear regarding his own safety. Or perhaps, he just did not envision a situation that truly threatened him. His innocence was like a breath of fresh air and Cairn was invigorated by it even under these trying circumstances.

The boy hesitated a moment longer and then he replied, "Yes, it is. I have beforehand said my goodbyes to Ormachon. Besides, he promised me that he will be with me wherever I go, so I am not afraid."

Tomas looked around, seeming to take in everything he saw deeply and with meaning, then he looked up at the huge tree under which he stood, closed his eyes and stood still for a minute or so. Abruptly, he turned away from Ormachon and started walking toward the path to the cottage.

As Cairn and Calyx pivoted to follow, Cairn saw the entire tree rustle its leaves in farewell, shedding some as it did so which fell at his feet as he was walking away. Tomas turned and said, "Pick them up. Don't be afraid. He wants you to!"

Cairn bent down and gathered up the Lalas leaves, placed them in his pouch, bowed to Ormachon with reverence and then quickly caught up with the boy who was already some ways down the path, disappearing into the thick grass, with Calyx following closely behind.

Upon arriving at the small house, Tomas took a moment to absorb the situation, examining things closely as if he were trying to determine something or understand something that was confounding him. The look upon his face was not only sad but quizzical. He walked slowly to the fresh mound of earth that Cairn indicated was the burial site, knelt down, and bowed his head after placing his delicately sculpted fingers atop the soil. Muttering under his breath and motioning gracefully with his hands and arms, he appeared to be much older than his fourteen odd years.

He carried himself with such dignity for this young a man, under circumstances that would test a hardened and experienced adult, that it moved Cairn to the brink of tears himself. When he completed his personal tribute, manifesting a maturity far beyond what would be expected of one his age, he stood and walked to the cottage. When he completed a task, he simply moved on to the next one with renewed determination. He seemed not to linger over things, but to always move with a clear purpose. Cairn and Calyx remained a few paces behind him, respecting his solitude. He was an extraordinary youth, dealing with a situation most would find difficult to face with as much dignity as this boy did.

Stepping over some debris as he was about to enter his former home, he glanced down at the ground where his aunt and uncle had fallen for their final time. Noticing the burnt twig that had once been in Safira's hand, he smiled knowingly to himself, and then he bent to pick it up and examine it. He held it tightly in his fist and closed his beautiful, green eyes. After a moment, he released it and let it fall to the ground, appearing to be considerably pleased, having obviously retrieved some sort of information from the relic and requiring it no more.

Cairn followed him into the house, watching him as he closely examined the devastation. Very little remained in one piece after the battle. The walls were scarred and broken, the hearth was pilfered and in disarray and the floor boards were shattered by what could only have been axe blades. What he was seeking was not going to be found inside, and Tomas evidently knew that as he made only a cursory examination of the premises before he turned decisively and walked out the door. Moving briskly toward the garden in the rear of the home, he spotted a small but beautiful cloud-berry tree, its thick trunk gnarled and twisted though its blossoms were full and fragrant. After contemplating the tree for a moment, Tomas turned toward the shed behind the house and ran over to it. Fetching a short handled axe from inside, he returned to the sweet smelling tree, removed his tunic and proceeded to chop at its base, attempting to topple it, or so it seemed.

Cairn was astonished at the ferocity with which the young boy attended to this task. "Tomas? Perhaps you need not vent your anger on this innocent tree?" he offered, uncertain as to what the boy was doing.

"I seek something," he replied simply and straight forward, never pausing for a moment. "Safira directed me here with her last thoughts. I would never inflict a lasting hurt on a tree like this," he said as if such a suggestion was out of the question. "I need to find the object she has hidden," he answered, never wavering from the task at hand. "Did you see the charred branch by where she fell?" he queried while swinging the heavy axe, perspiration beading on his forehead, matting his blonde hair.

"Yes, I thought it strange when first I approached them that she clutched it so tightly still," Cairn replied remembering the moment. "Even after her life expired."

"It bore a message for me! That is why my aunt held it dear. She hoped I would find it before someone else did. Lucky for me that you were the one to discover them." He turned to face Cairn after those words, delaying his efforts for the first time. "Was it luck?" he asked, briefly catching Cairn's eyes with his own, and then immediately returning to his labors, neither waiting for nor expecting an answer. Cairn pondered the question himself, feeling even more and more assured that his encounter with the boy and his family was ordained, meant to be, and was not mere serendipity, contrary to his previous beliefs concerning such matters. Cairn had always been a strong believer in free will as the cornerstone of right and wrong and good and evil. People were responsible for their own actions, and that ultimately determined the parameters of blame and conscience. His short sojourn with this family was altering his mind-set of many years, and strangely, he was not shaken, but comforted by the boy's words and the doubts that they raised.

As Tomas toppled the stout tree, what remained was a short stump about seven inches in diameter. It appeared to be soft and viscous in its center where the boy stuck his slender hand, searching for something. The pulp gave way to his caresses, and shortly he withdrew his fingers, producing a small black velvet box. Cairn was astonished that such an object should be discovered within the trunk of a tree, being that it must have been placed there when the tree was just a seedling so that it could have grown up around it, protecting and hiding it until now.

Tomas cupped the box between his two hands and hummed a sweet melody, one that Cairn found vaguely familiar to his ears, yet could not at all recall where or when he could ever have heard it. Expending no effort to conceal what he was doing from Cairn, Tomas seemed to generate a great deal of heat from his closed palms, engulfing the box and causing it to glow as if it were white hot. The boy was concentrating so intently on this exercise, that his facial features took on the mask of a much older person, so stern and serious he had become. Cairn was transfixed by the boy's actions.

Without warning, the light flared up soundlessly and the box just disappeared! What remained was a solid silver ring suspended in the air for a moment before it fell to the earth, spinning and jingling as it hit the ground. Tomas' face relaxed and he once more looked like the child of fourteen that he was, as he bent to reclaim the ring. Examining it briefly, he slipped the tip of his finger inside the band and rubbed it over the rune like etchings therein. He drew a string of rawhide from his belt pouch, threaded it through the silver band, tied it off and placed it around his neck underneath his shirt.

"Would you help me for a minute? I am not strong enough to lift this by myself," Tomas turned and said to Cairn, pointing at the fallen tree.

"Certainly, my boy, what do you need me to do?" Cairn replied, anxious to help however he could.

As he moved next to Tomas, he could not help but notice a wound on his smooth stomach. It was strangely uniform in shape, though he was too distant to examine it closely. The boy hastily snatched his tunic from the ground and put it back on, before Cairn was able to determine whether the injury was fully healed or not. He hoped it was not a festering hurt with Safira no longer available to treat him.

"I need to raise the tree, and it is too heavy for me alone," he said as he placed his hands around the trunk, below the lowest branches.

Together, Tomas and Cairn heaved the broken tree upright, and with the youth's guidance, placed the severed tree atop the severed trunk.

"If you can, please just hold it steady for a little," Tomas conveyed as Cairn put his muscle into the task.

Tomas placed his hands around the area that he had previously hacked away at, slowly rubbing them up and down, seeming to blend the two now separate parts together as if they were made of soft clay. When he completed his kneading of the wood, he stepped back a pace, pointed the index finger of his right hand at the rejoined area and closed his eyes. Shortly, a blue-white light emanated from his finger, and as he moved the finger around the tree, the light seemed to seal the separation, mending the hurt and coercing the parts to grow back together.

Cairn watched as the tree became whole, unblemished once again, standing healthy and strong as if no one or no thing had ever done harm to it. In fact, Cairn recalled vividly the boy's words as he said earlier that he would not inflict a lasting hurt upon a tree.

Well, Cairn thought with satisfaction, *the boy is true to his word.*

"We can go now," he said, as he turned to face Cairn and Calyx, who sat relaxed and quiescent a short distance away.

Cairn cursorily inspected the area, making sure he and his company were not unwittingly leaving anything behind, and then he motioned to Calyx to join them. He placed his arm comfortably around Tomas' shoulder and guided him away. The Moulant bounded readily behind them, his fur flashing and shimmering in the sun and they all stepped into the brush, heading southward once again toward Pardatha and its expectant Lord, Baladar.

Chapter Sixteen

The boy was somewhat somber as they departed, not surprisingly so under the circumstances, but he frolicked with Calyx as time passed and he treated the big Moulant as if he was a cuddly pet. Scant words were spoken for the first few hours, until Tomas stated he was hungry. They came upon a comfortable lea, slightly sheltered by a grove of wild, tall cherry trees in full blossom, and sat down to rest and take their modest repast.

Cairn was now quite anxious to get on with his journey, having lost considerable time with the events of the past days. He took out two of the Lalas leaves, a mortar and pestle, and ground them up, adding a cup or so of sweet juice from a flask around his waist. Meanwhile, Calyx bounded off in search of his own meal.

Together, Tomas and Cairn shared the rejuvenating mixture, in what was not intended to be, but what seemed nonetheless to be, a ceremony of bonding. As they passed the liquid back and forth, they both experienced a closeness that defied reason. Cairn recognized the extraordinary power of this young man and he could not understand who he could be or where he could have come from. After all, he really knew nothing about him, as he had so little time to converse with his aunt and uncle before their tragic demise, and he barely had spoken to Tomas, although they did share some very serious and compelling moments that do often serve to connect people together. Yet, he felt so comfortable in his presence, as if he had known him forever, and these feelings of closeness were obviously reciprocated by the boy.

Again, Cairn knew in his heart that this was not an ordinary fourteen year old, his magical abilities aside. He was pleased to have him accompany him and he knew that he would serve the cause in some way when they arrived at Baladar's side, that their meeting was not chance, despite how contrary to his belief structure that seemed.

Good fortune was rearing its head amongst the ruins and tragedy of the past events, demonstrating the resiliency of life once more, reinforcing Cairn's faith even on the brink of these recent disasters. In time, he would learn more about Tomas, where he came from, who his parents were and how he came to be the bondmate of Ormachon. Now, it was vital that he concentrate upon the journey at hand.

Just south of the home of Trevor and Safira was the road that lead to the lake where the Selgays resided. After having enjoyed their brief diversion, they gathered their belongings as Calyx returned to join them, and the three adventurers set forth with a shared feeling of hope manifesting itself in their bounding gait and lack of apprehension, despite the danger that they all knew lay ahead.

As the woods thickened and the breeze, gentle at first, strengthened considerably, it reminded Cairn that they were entering the Forest of the Winds. The sun was setting, which in itself was not a concern, but they needed to traverse the forest quickly if they wished to reach the lake while darkness still reigned. The only possible way to cross the dangerous waters without being attacked was during the pitch of night.

Cairn picked up the pace, as Tomas and Calyx followed without complaint. After walking for about two miles, what remained of the heretofore blue sky was practically blocked entirely by the enormous Tangary trees whose leaves, as large as saucers, rattled in the wind. The noise became unbearable at times, as the breeze increased in velocity, and the small party maneuvered its way through the thick and tangled underbrush.

Shortly thereafter, the deafening clamor caused by the now violent gusts crashing through the treetops began to cause severe pain, pounding the two human's eardrums incessantly. Cairn removed a thick cloth from his pack, tore it lengthwise into two parts, and tied one around his head, covering his ears. Moving to Tomas, he secured the cloth around the boy as well. Calyx required no such protection, as his furry ears were pressed tightly to his head, blocking his keen sense of hearing, but relieving the pain of the, by now, extraordinarily thunderous noise.

As the wind continued to rage through the branches, large pieces of dead wood began to fall among the party, landing at times rather close to the travelers. Cairn did not fear the trees. They abided their trespassing with little affront and would not harm them, but the winds howled unceasingly, hurting their ears, making communication all but impossible, slowing their progress and obscuring the path that would lead them to the lakeside.

Calyx was called upon to guide the trio, his acute sense of smell directing them toward the water, and thus, despite the wind, he was able to lead Cairn and Tomas closer to the edge of the woods.

Fighting their forward motion, causing them to stop at times until the gusts subsided, the Forest of the Winds lived up to its name, convincing Cairn that the myths surrounding it were true, that many a man could easily enter and never return again, succumbing to the noise, fallen debris and total loss of his sense of direction once inside the densest parts. Calyx, though, would step cautiously behind a huge tree trunk, shelter his massive bulk enough to raise his broad nose into the air, and then determine the direction of the lake by the aqueous odor. Stepping into the open once again, he bounded ahead with Cairn and Tomas close at his heels.

If not for the Moulant, the remaining two would have been lost forever in the tangle of brush and brambles, eventually becoming stone deaf from the constant assault upon their eardrums. It was so hard to know if one was going forwards or in circles, or even backwards, due to the raging winds wreaking havoc on their senses. But, Calyx was an extraordinary guide and protector, and Cairn neither feared for their safety nor their ability to reach the lakeside with his loyal friend in the lead.

An earsplitting crash shattered the momentary silence, far louder than any previous disturbances. A huge tree came booming down directly in front of them, forcing the group to run swiftly backwards to avoid being crushed under its weight. After the dust settled somewhat, they deftly stepped through the fallen branches and over the prostrate trunk, as the wind immediately kicked up considerably in their faces. The air was thick with dust and debris, forcing them to protect their eyes and making breathing difficult. Cairn and Tomas huddled closely together, the elder sheltering the younger with his arms and body, while Calyx dauntlessly stood before them to deflect any large and dangerous objects that might fly into them from the accelerating explosions of wind. The Forest of the Winds clearly did not want them to leave without exacting its toll.

Forcing their way forward, capes and fur and hair standing almost horizontal to the earth, making slow and tedious progress, they finally emerged from the thickest of the forest vegetation. They still had a ways to go before they would come forth from the woods, and the sluggish pace was beginning to concern Cairn, as they needed to cross the lake before the sun rose. To be caught in broad daylight on a small raft in the middle of the lake would be suicide. They would be an easy and tasty meal for the Selgays. Well, Cairn and Tomas would be, at least. Calyx could save himself, but it would be nearly impossible for the big cat to do much of anything to save them under those circumstances. Cairn forced such thoughts from his mind, not choosing to dwell on the possible, but only upon what obstacles were here and now, real and in their direct path, as was his nature.

Driving themselves into the wind, step by step, with Cairn assisting the boy as much as possible, they finally reached what appeared to be the end of the tree line, when a disturbing silence overtook the forest within an instant, the violent gales ceasing completely. Nothing moved. Even the dust appeared to drop to the ground as if its single source of animation had been withdrawn all at once.

The small group huddled together apprehensively, their eyes darting from side to side, not knowing what to expect when suddenly, a voice louder than the previously deafening wind and seemingly emanating from all directions simultaneously, broke the short lived but ominous silence.

"Who dares to invade my lands without permission?" it thundered in an incredibly deep tone.

Not knowing where to direct his answer, Cairn turned to the deepest part of the wood and replied courageously, "I am Cairn of Thermaye." Pointing to Calyx he continued, "This is my companion Calyx, a Moulant, born of the forest, and the boy is my new found ward, Tomas of Pardeau. We meant you no disrespect in entering your realm without sanction, but I humbly regret that I was unaware that these woods were inhabited by anyone whose permission was required. I beg your sincere pardon if I was misinformed," Cairn stated respectfully.

The response came quickly and from all directions, assaulting their senses like the wind, "Well, you have been *misinformed*!" the still disembodied voice echoed. "I let no one pass through here that I do not approve of. These woods have been my home for tiels upon tiels untold, and I protect and defend them from what I and only I deem to be unacceptable!" the voice boomed in the otherwise perfect stillness of the night. "Move out into the open so I can gaze upon you. You smell human. Have you axes with you?"

"No, I promise. We have none in our company. We only meant to traverse the Forest of the Winds as it was the quickest route to the lake. We must cross the mountains and reach the southern city of Pardatha as soon as we can," Cairn replied, his voice clear and calm.

"What dire business drives you through my lands?"

Cairn was unwilling to divulge too much information, as he was not even certain to whom he spoke, but he believed that speaking no less than the truth would be unwise.

"Baladar, Lord Protector of Pardatha has summoned me in order to educate his ward. These two," he pointed to Calyx and Tomas, "are accompanying me on my journey."

"You speak honestly, Cairn of Thermaye. You seem trustworthy. I have observed you since you stepped into the forest. Nothing here goes unnoticed by me," the voice said boldly. "But the trees did not warn me of your approach. Why? Why did the Lalas not tell me you were coming?"

Still cowering a little before this unknown entity, Cairn began to search the area around them for a sign of the source. Suddenly, a swirling gust of wind appeared to their left in a small clearing about ten yards away. As the swirling increased in velocity, drawing into it leaves and twigs and anything loose in its immediate vicinity, a clear and distinct shape seemed to form in its center. The force of the suction obliged the small group to hold onto one another in order to prevent themselves from being sucked into the gyrating mass. Even the big Moulant had to anchor his paws deep into the slippery surface to avert tumbling forward.

"If you are more comfortable being able to see with human eyes who speaks to you, gaze now upon my countenance. I have many faces, most of which you would not recognize, as I am made of the wind, not the earth. But see me now, and be not afraid."

The debris coagulated quickly until a face of sorts was visible, the eyes of which were comprised of beautifully shaped leaves, twigs formed the eyebrows, while fruits, berries and multicolored leaves finished off the features. It hovered in the air before them.

"There, is that better?" the wind creature asked, seeming to warm considerably to the group.

"Thank you, yes," Cairn responded for them all, and continued, "Who are you, if I may be so presumptuous as to inquire?"

"Yes, yes, I know. Humans need names," the wind creature said, annoyed and impatient, yet somehow unthreatening. "If you wish to call me something then call me Percepton, protector of the Forest of the Winds. Since time untold I have kept these woods safe and healthy. My partnership with the Lalas has been long and fruitful.

"But, of late, evil things have entered. My borders have been violated. Those who tried have been unsuccessful, or should I say, they have not been permitted to leave once they have entered.

"Yet, my trees cry out in warning. Times are ripe with change, some good, some evil. I must determine for certain what side you three serve if I am to let you travel through my lands. Why was I not told of your approach?" he said once again rhetorically, his eyebrows arching high. "I need time. I cannot make these judgements hastily. Where is my help? Why do I not hear from the trees anymore?" Persepton cried out in anguish.

"You must wait here until I can decide what to do. I must seek advice. I must think. Don't move, any of you," he thundered as the wind picked up around the travelers and formed a circle of swirling leaves, hemming them in.

At that moment, Tomas leapt out from behind the shelter of Cairn's body and blurted out above the din of the blowing litter, while hanging on tightly to Calyx's tail, "I am not afraid of you. Why do you scare us so? We mean you no harm. If you are good and noble, then you would know that we are of noble purpose too."

The boy closed his eyes. He stood perfectly still and said, "I can sense that you are good, that you know we do not choose to disturb your lands. Please let us continue. We only wish to proceed on to the lake and have no intention of taking anything that does not belong to us," he said with such sincerity that Cairn was quite proud and astonished once again by the maturity and courage of the lad.

Tomas spoke directly into Persepton's fluttering face. "The Lalas mourn the passing of one of their own. Promanthea tells me so. I feel the pain too. Otherwise, they would have advised you of our coming," he said, sadly but with certainty.

The boy said this so sweetly and with such tenderness that Cairn raised his head, wondering to himself how much more he must know that he had not yet spoken of.

Immediately, the circle of their captivity vanished as Persepton began to speak. "Do you think so?" He sounded thoughtful. "I believe you. Yes, you speak the truth, young man, and you are wiser than your young years might indicate. I feel it now," he said, the leaves of his eyes crushed together, simulating closure. "I agree. They would have informed me themselves," Percepton said gleefully and with renewed energy. The expression of joy was short lived, though, as the reality of what Tomas described suddenly struck him. "Which tree died?" Percepton queried suddenly. "Do you know? Was it Acire or Mintar? Oh, I hope not Mintar. But it would be no better if it were Acire."

The apparition formed of the earth approached Tomas. As it reached him, Cairn was forced backwards, away from the boy. He could not move closer, repelled by the steady gusts pushing him aside as if he were a magnet meeting his opposite pole. The dust and leaves enveloped Tomas entirely, obscuring him from the sight of his companions. But, try as he might, Cairn could do nothing to prevent it. Calyx raised his snout to the air and growled, but even his sound was drowned out by the din of the moment.

Cairn could barely see Tomas' outline within the swirling mass. It appeared to him as if he was still standing, but it was impossible to be certain. The forest encircling them grew calm and the only motion he could detect was within the orbit of activity that Percepton created around Tomas. For some reason, Cairn was not fearful that harm would come to the boy. Nevertheless, the moments passed slowly, and he was helpless to hasten them. He walked as close to the sphere of motion as he could, but he was unable to see or hear anything that occurred within it.

As Cairn stood watching, impotent and ineffectual, he saw Tomas walk calmly out of the spiraling circle that was the wind creature. Percepton's crude features assembled themselves once more before them all, and then he spoke.

"I will allow you to depart, and I will give you my blessing too. Take what you need from my lands and may the First guide you and nourish you on your journey. Go now and I will await the trees' communication."

The ancient being moved slowly to the side, speaking to himself all the while.

"Yes, they would have told me if they could have. I should have known that myself. You are a very bright young man, my son, and I am getting too old, and my wits are getting dull with time. Shame, shame on me! Go. Do what you must. I have much to consider. I must prepare now. Do not waste my time any further," he exclaimed, feigning impatience. "Go! The fabric weaves of its own will, but I cannot simply stand by and watch."

After that final, penetrating remark, the apparition ceased to be, the pieces dropped to the ground, and it was once more dormant as before. Percepton was gone and a pathway had emerged in front of them that led to a clearing. They suddenly found themselves gasping at the sight of a vast expanse of azure blue water that lay immediately ahead of them.

There was a short continuance of rocky shoreline that began immediately at the forest's edge, upon which they now stood. Facing the lake, Cairn sheltering Tomas directly with his arms and body, happy to have the boy back beside him, steadfast Calyx at their side, vigilant and tense, they gazed out upon their destination. In the distance, they could clearly see the magnificent sweep of the majestic Thorndar mountains beyond which lay the city of Pardatha that harbored Baladar and the boy.

The stars were still shining brightly in the night sky, but Cairn knew that there remained perhaps no more than three hours of darkness before the normally welcome sun would rear its now dangerously illuminating head over the horizon. They still needed to construct a raft capable of transporting them across, and although Cairn was deft at such a task, it would nevertheless use up at least a precious hour of the few that they had remaining. The broken trees laying haphazardly along the shoreline were what they needed to gather, and good fortune had left them an ample supply.

"We must not tarry here!" Cairn warned.

Motioning Calyx to follow him, he grasped the end of a large, straight sapling and dragged it toward the beach. Calyx quickly understood what needed to be done and the Moulant sprang away, half pushing with his enormous paws, half rolling with his strong snout, tree after tree to the area Cairn had brought his to. Tomas, too, ran in search of more trees, smaller but stout.

When Cairn felt they had gathered a sufficient number for a raft that could hold the three of them, he began to wade in the water and pull out the strong reeds that grew upon the muddy shore. Tomas followed along and soon there was a pile about three feet high, laid out lengthwise next to the timber. Cairn meticulously began the task of weaving the reeds through the trees, securing them with a box knot that jutted up through the now forming planks. Looping a new reed through the last knot and tying it down tightly, he continued to affix one tree to the next. Tomas jumped to his aid, and clearly being a quick learner, he imitated perfectly the manner in which Cairn was constructing the conveyance.

In less than one hour, the raft had taken shape. Now, two long poles would be required to push the raft forwards and they needed to be flat at one end as well in order to serve as paddles when the water was too deep to pole them ahead. Calyx was sent to fetch the multipurpose oars, and while he was gone, Cairn took a stick of beeswax out of his knapsack, lit a dry willowtail with a spark from his flint, and melted the wax over each of the knots holding the raft together. Shortly, Calyx returned to the raft with two lengthy pieces of wood in his mouth, suitable for the task required of them. He dropped them at Cairn's feet and stood waiting for further instructions from his friend.

After the knots were securely fastened with the wax, and the strength of the vehicle was tested by both Cairn and Tomas, together, the boy and the man slid the bound wood into the lapping water. Cairn grasped Tomas' hand and helped him climb atop, following closely behind without hesitation. He then motioned to Calyx to join them, as the Moulant, although clearly uncomfortable with the prospect of leaving the solid shore, leapt aboard too.

Cairn dug the long pole into the soft mud of the shoreline and then propelled the small raft out into the dark and forbidding waters, as the two human travelers gazed expectantly ahead. The damp chill of the evening air caused the fog of their breath to billow ominously from their mouths and their skin to prickle in an anxious response.

Chapter Seventeen

Elion woke with the first rays of sunlight and hastened to gather his belongings together, not wanting to waste any time before he began his journey home. Glancing at the sleeping boy, he felt reassured once again that hope was not lost, that right here lay a key of sorts to the puzzle surrounding their recent losses. And, suddenly, he was overcome with a feeling of concern, a wariness that crept over him compelling him to be cautious and prudent in his travels to come. He could not just leave casually now and continue to travel openly and without fear. The lands he had traversed so far, though strange and foreign at times, were relatively safe. He encountered nothing more than concern on the part of the townsfolk and villagers he had occasion to befriend during his long trip.

Elion did witness the passing of a great Lalas, and the memory haunted him still, causing great anguish whenever he allowed himself to dwell upon the recollection of that day, sending him into a deep depression that he had to fight to rid himself of. That event he would tell of when he finally arrived home, and the thought of that eventuality weighed upon his soul. There would be no avoiding it though, as his father needed to know that such things were taking place among the human population as well. But, as far as witnessing the evil one's minions, he had done no such thing.

Talk of Trolls and dark lords and black sorcerers was rampant among the country folk, but as far as he was concerned, it was only talk. He had seen no evidence of Caeltin D'Are Agenathea, or Colton, as the human race pronounced it, nor his retainers anywhere within the vast lands he navigated. Although the Northern Elves heard the same stories that he heard time and time again, they too neither witnessed anything directly nor indirectly. But, the tales were increasing in frequency as time passed. Voyagers returning from the south had strange and disturbing stories to tell of creatures they observed, changes in the normal weather patterns, occasionally even decimated villages whose inhabitants were left homeless and adrift, and other happenings more terrifying than any spoken of further north.

Something was definitely wrong, and it was only a matter of time before evidence of the evil manifested itself among his own kind. Heretofore, even the Elves were disorganized, forsaking their ancient methods of communication, allowing their defenses to slacken. When the Lalas flourished, no people needed to fear, and therefore, they grew complacent in the face of prosperity and safety. But now, as they withered and died more and more frequently, Elion felt that soon none would be safe. The entire world was in jeopardy, and all the good people of the earth would forthwith suffer. He shuddered just thinking about the possibilities and how vulnerable his own kinsmen were. They had relied so heavily upon the trees, what would life be like without them?

Stop it! Stop thinking this way! We are far from there yet. And with this boy... He gazed at Davmiran *...there is hope still!*

Elion laid the lad once again on his cape and he used his Elfin sight to scout the immediate vicinity for any evidence of danger before venturing outside of his shelter. When he was comfortable that no menace lay in wait, he moved stealthily down the small hill.

Elion and the young boy traveled for two days and two nights unmolested. The woods were dense and quiet, as they encountered nothing more than a few small tree mandalins, as well as some scattered ferrins and foxes. Nothing hampered their progress. On the third day only after many hours passed, Elion allowed himself the luxury of a short rest during the daylight hours. The terrain was more open now than before, and although he and his precious companion were never fully exposed, he felt more insecure than when hidden by the trees.

Concealing himself and the boy behind a large boulder, taking advantage of the shadows cast by bright sun, he again provided sustenance to his prostrate associate. Downing a bit of invigorating fluid himself, he moved on with renewed determination.

He was making good time, and by late afternoon he began to scout for a safe haven wherein they could spend the night. As he traveled deeper into the southern lands, getting closer and closer to his home, he was also leaving the safety of the north where the preponderance of the Lalas still remained, and until he reached the northernmost outskirts of Lormarion, the Crest of the Dawn, he would be particularly imperiled.

Elion knew that he would have to cross the Plain of the Wolves under the cover of darkness, risking exposure to the nocturnal threats, rather than in broad daylight where the keen sighted animals would be upon him in an instant. His superlative skills would aid him in his navigation during the dark of night, and there would be no moon tomorrow eve to illuminate his small party. He had good fortune to thank for that. Timing would be everything, and he would have to move quickly once out in the open. He knew that would not be an easy task while dragging the boy behind him, and he hoped upon hope that the wind would be still and that the breezes would not carry his scent into the dens of the wolves.

Once across the plain, he knew that he would find safety upon the Crest. If he timed it right, the rising sun would obscure anything that moved on the ridge, and then the final approach to Lormarion would be an easy one. The Crest of the Dawn was so natural a wonder that no magic could have made it a more perfect defense for the Elves. From the heights of the city, one could see anything that approached during the morning hours, or almost anytime during the day, in fact. But should anyone be observing from the north, the breaking of dawn upon the Crest concealed anything that moved, bathing the hill in bright sunlight and veiling all activity.

This phenomenon had served the Elves well. During the Troll wars twenty-eight tiels ago, the armies that amassed in the plain to lay siege upon the city were devastated by the Elfin warriors. Under the cover of the rising sun, the greatly outnumbered forces left the city and seemingly appeared like magic before the unprepared invaders, suddenly becoming visible to them only after it was too late. Frightened and disorganized, the startled Trolls ran amok, trampling their own forces in their frenzied and scattered retreat, easy prey for the skilled archers on the Crest. The slaughter was historic and no invader had attempted a southern approach since. Elion took heart in that memory. He need only carry the boy across the plains and he would be home, and this he intended to attempt two hours before dawn, for he reckoned that it should take him no longer than that to cross if he was able to do so unhindered.

After walking a bit further, he discovered a shallow gully ringed by short but thick perridon trees which were well past their fruit bearing age. He feared not that they would attract any hungry prey of the flying type or other, being no longer desirable as sources of nourishment. Here, he and the young boy could rest in relative safety until just before daybreak. He was only a short distance from the edge of the woods, but he could not risk sleeping past the appointed hour.

He made himself a strong mixture of ground Lalas leaf and spring water, basking in the invigorating feeling that overtook his entire body and mind upon drinking it, whereupon he sat down only to rest his weary legs and gaze upon the countenance of his companion.

Hope flooded him once more as he contemplated the approaching sunrise. Soon he would be home. Soon he could begin the painstaking process of preparation. If his family did not already know of the danger that was imminent, he would so advise them. Together, they would find a way of reviving his companion, and thus they would take the first steps toward halting the approaching darkness. Elion was confident. The world would be young again and his people would live in peace and safety once more. The trees would flourish and new Lalas would be born. The Evil One would be turned back, his minions vanquished. Just looking upon the calm face of the young man under his protection invoked such feelings. Yes, Elion was confident and soon he would be home.

The valiant Elf focused his eyes upon the eastern sky. As soon as the moon faded from sight just above the horizon, he knew that he had only approximately two and one half hours of darkness left before sunrise. Swiftly securing the hood of his cloak to his belt so that he could pull the boy behind him, leaving his hands free, he began the final journey to the wood's edge.

The air was still and the sky was dark as pitch. Luck was with them. Breaking free of the final line of trees, Elion with Davmiran in tow, stepped cautiously onto the grassy edge of the plain. Swiftly crossing the perimeter, he began to pick up speed until he was jogging across the smooth grass, carefully choosing his path so as not to jar the boy following behind. He deftly sidestepped the rocks and small gullies without breaking his stride, counting on his agility and keen sight to prevent any serious harm from coming to his companion. One false step and they could both be in sincere danger. Darting from left to right, Elion proceeded at a fast clip.

Although he could not see it yet, he knew that the Crest of the Dawn was fast approaching, as he had already been on the plain for about an hour. Half the distance was already crossed and nature had been kind to them so far. The wind was barely detectable and he sensed no evidence of a single wolf. The eastern sky was beginning to brighten somewhat, and Elion was tiring now, the previous night's vigilance, lack of sleep and sheer physical exertion finally taking its toll on his body and mind.

He pushed himself forward, finding his second breath, knowing that the home stretch was soon to be underfoot. As he kept going, nimbly evading the pitfalls that would trip up any ordinary Elf, he thought he could make out the approaching ridge, marking the beginning of the Crest of the Dawn. As Elion ran with renewed determination toward his home and safety, the sun inched its way over the far skyline. The rays of light streaked out, illuminating him only slightly, as a subtle wind began to blow from behind.

With only a few hundred yards left to navigate before he reached the safety of the hill, his worst nightmare materialized before his very eyes. Darting to the left to avoid the specter before him, he saw another great, dark shadow fast approaching. Zigzagging across the remaining yardage, Elion sought desperately to outflank the gathering pack of wolves. He stopped only for an instance to hoist the boy on his back, hoping to increase his ability to maneuver without causing him harm. That moment of interruption proved to be his downfall. The circle was closed and Elion no longer had an open path to the Crest. Whichever direction he looked, he now saw the looming shape of a great wolf.

Laying the boy down and straddling his prone body protectively, Elion pulled his longbow from its sheath. Quickly notching an arrow, he pulled the bowstring taught. Hoping to be able to down the wolf directly in his path and dash for the Crest as the sun came up, he aimed and let loose his first arrow. The massive wolf collapsed in a heap, the shaft having penetrated through its large left eye. Elion hoisted the lad on his back once again and sprinted for the opening he just created by dispensing the wolf, but he was too late. Two others sprang from the shadows, obstructing his path. Not willing to relinquish hope, he drew his dagger from his belt with his right hand, all the while holding tightly on to the boy with his left, awkwardly reaching back to do so. The imbalance became too great and both he and Davmiran tumbled to the ground.

Within a moment's time, the wolves were upon them and Elion threw himself over the boy to shield him, with his dagger still in his hand. He lashed out in all directions, frenziedly striking home time and again, drawing blood he could now clearly see glistening in the light of the sun suspended in the eastern sky. His strength was ebbing quickly now and his vision was obscured by the blood and gore all around him. He could not determine how many wolves had gone down in the melee, but he knew that whatever the numbers, they were not nearly enough. They kept coming at him, becoming more daring as he weakened.

This is no way for it to end, he thought sadly. *I have come so close, so close.*

The wolves seemed to back off for a moment, perhaps to gather for a final and deadly attack, when Elion saw what he thought was an Elfin arrow rip through the neck of the raging wolf before him. Another and another, as if in a dream, the wolves went down, howling and spurting blood from massive wounds.

Elion lay over the boy by now, his dagger still clutched limply in his right hand, blood obscuring his vision and fatigue impeding his thoughts. He fought to remain cognizant, his last vision was of a charging Elf with wild white hair flying all about his wrinkled and tanned face, an undulating scream coming from his wide open mouth, piercing the now startled wolves repeatedly with his sharpened Elfin sword, his blood rage out of control.

"Father?" Elion queried as he lost consciousness. "Is it you? Is it really you?"

Possessively sheltering his eldest son from any additional onslaught, Treestar, King of the Southern Elves, observed warily as his small band of armed warriors dispatched the remaining animals. The First must have been watching out for him or he never would have happened to be atop the Crest of the Dawn this morning. Something warned him, a feeling of concern came over him last evening, compelling him to arise before the sun and post a lookout on the hill. Strangely though, the concern was apprehensive, brimming with expectation and not simply with fear. And sure enough, his instincts were correct. Just as the morning light broke over the city, Treestar witnessed a gathering of the wolves at the base of the ridge. He then saw a glinting light, as if some man made object were reflecting the rays in warning. That light turned out to be Elion's small dagger, thrusting back and forth, side to side, in his chaotic effort to protect himself and his young charge from the overwhelming enemy. Rising to the call, unaware at the time whom he would be aiding, Treestar rallied his small band and attacked.

Once he was able to discern exactly who was in danger, he was overcome with rage like nothing he had ever felt before. Perhaps it was because he missed his son so much after all this time. Perhaps it was simply because he loved Elion so dearly and the thought of losing him was too much to bear. Whatever the reason, nothing was going to stop the Elfin Lord from his goal of rescuing his issue and bringing him back safely to Lormarion, to the comfort and security of Seramour, to the warmth and shelter of his home.

When he was satisfied that the peril was over, he called upon his men to lift the unconscious Elfin youth carefully and to carry him to the Crest, cursorily examining him to make certain that he had suffered no life threatening injuries during the fray. Confident that he would survive, overjoyed at his son's return, Treestar likewise had his warriors tenderly transport the young boy who had been laying, unseeing and motionless, beneath the shelter of his son's slim body. Treestar happened to glance upon the countenance of the lad and he noticed the half-open blue eyes, the sightless gaze, and he was taken aback by the serenity it invoked in him, even amidst the overwhelming carnage of the battlefield. Hurriedly, he urged his men onward to the protection of the Crest of the Dawn, to the shelter of the now steady sun, and forth to the protected heights of Seramour.

Once the small group reached the peak of the small rise, they knew that they were completely safe from further attack should the wolves even attempt to mount a new assault. The Elfin company along with their human friend would be invisible to all below, and any party attempting to reach them from the plain would be easy prey for those watching from above. This was not the way Treestar had envisioned he would be reunited with Elion, but at least his son was safe and alive. He hoped that his bruises were not serious, but he would leave that determination up to his wife and to the other healers as soon as he could place Elion in their care. His companion seemed unharmed, though dirty and spattered with blood as well, and so strangely quiet and serene despite the mayhem that surrounded him, not appearing to be ill or uncomfortable or in pain.

Treestar wondered what disease or spell could be keeping the young man from awakening. He also pondered the origin of the youth, surprised that Elion would lead any stranger not of his own race into the safety of Lormarion. Times were changing, and the Elves were more careful than before, more wary of strangers not of their own kind, unlike the open days of the past when all wayfarers and voyagers were welcome in Lormarion. His son would never risk even the remotest chance of causing harm to his nation and family. Therefore, Treestar thought, he must have a reason for bringing the lad here, and in time he would find it out. Right now, his priority and utmost concern was to get the two of them to shelter and warmth, have their wounds dressed and their health examined and allow them some rest and nourishment.

Once over the highest point of the Crest, a pathway became clear and distinct before the small and weary party. Following it, they shortly arrived at the base of a giant Noban tree, the tallest and broadest trees of the southern reaches. Although not sentient like the

Lalas, they were noble in their own right and magnificent to gaze upon. The branches of a full-grown Noban did not begin until thirty feet of trunk rose up straight and tall from the ground. Then, the broad, heavy arms of the trees twisted and wove their growth together to form a mesh of dense and protective platforms upon which the Elves constructed their living quarters. In order to ascend to the heights of even the lowest branches, an elaborate system of pulleys and platforms was devised, and during a normal day one could see them rising and falling continuously, bringing the people and goods of Seramour up and down with ease and comfort.

The forest of Lormarion was large and spread out, but the tops of the Nobans intertwined, making it possible to travel entirely from one end of the city to the other without ever touching the ground. The bark of the Noban tree was dark brown and sleek, not textured and porous like many other forms of vegetation. It was not vulnerable to fire as most wooden things were, due to its ability to secrete a quenching sap in response to heat, as well as to its incredible density. An axe barely left a mark on the trunk of a full-grown Noban even after repeated strikes, and it was almost impossible to drive a spike into its side even with the largest of war hammers.

Thus, the Elves built their homes in the heights of the branches, protected from most everything for centuries. Lormarion flourished and the city of Seramour grew in wealth and size while the Elves prospered. They were a hard working and good people; honest, true and just. Talk of the unmatched beauty of the city circulated throughout the land, raising the tree city of Seramour to the heights of legend.

The Elves of the south kept to themselves though, and they rarely took part in the conflicts the humans were so frequently involved in. Treestar, the King of the Southern Elves, feared now that their isolation may be coming to an end. His scouts returned with warnings of unrest and illness smothering the southern regions. The evil was spreading, and he was not of a mind to hide in the treetops until it reached even the heights of Seramour.

Treestar was a brave and wise Elf, and he recognized when to be prudent and when it was prudent to be aggressive. He was anxious to hear from Elion regarding the situation in the rest of the world that he visited these past years. He needed to know if the rumors were spreading northward as well and if it was true that the Lalas were dying. He needed to think and plan, and his son would be his right hand during this process. Treestar was overjoyed at his return, although he never envisioned that this would be the manner in which they would meet once again.

When Elion first left his home many years ago, the Plain of the Wolves was not as dangerous as it now was. The Elves did not molest the dens of the wolves, and the big animals, likewise, allowed small parties to traverse their lands unhindered. No Elf ever wore a cape of wolf fur and no wolf supped on an Elfin lad or lass. Times were certainly changing and not for the better, Treestar thought regretfully. But Elion, his first born, was home once again and he was no longer without a son to confide in. The strange young man whom he brought with him radiated a compelling sense of hope, and Treestar recognized the auspicious nature of this encounter. Elion would have much to tell upon his revival and Treestar was anxious to hear it all.

Chapter Eighteen

Concordia was a wealthy land. Lying as far to the west as it did, it suffered rarely from the petty, tribal wars and human conflicts that plagued the more populated regions of the south and the east. Even further to the west lay the kingdom of the Alpen Elves of the Ice Kingdom, a strange and solitary race as different in attitude and lifestyle from humankind as from their southern and northern Elfin brethren. Their lands were frozen over all of the year long, and they built their buildings out of the ice which never melted. They learned to live and thrive amidst some of the coldest territories on the planet. They harnessed the sun, using the reflective powers of the massive sheets of frozen water, and learned how to establish a green paradise in a frozen wasteland. It was a rare occurrence to receive a visit from one of them, as they were so reluctant to open their culture to the influence of any other.

Few ventured into the far hills west of Concordia, not out of fear, but out of an understanding that they would not be welcome. It was not belligerence that made the Elves so apprehensive about contact with humans, but fear that their culture would be changed if they let the outside world in. They guarded their privacy religiously, and very few really knew much about them.

Robyn was like no others in Concordia, nay, no others in the whole of the continent, and he had made his forays into the protected lands of the west. It took him many years to develop a trust among these isolated people, but he persisted and he eventually succeeded. His visits to the kingdom of Eleutheria were ones that he deeply cherished. He learned much from them, and they grew accustomed to him and began to look forward to his sojourns into their lands as well.

He spoke of them to no one, respecting totally and completely their desire for isolation. Never would he have violated it to begin with if he did not believe that he had things of import he needed to pass on to them that would impact upon their own welfare. They were true lovers of the light and the trees in their own solitary ways. They too feared the passing of the Lalas and desired nothing more than to see it brought to an end.

There was one other reason Robyn loved his journeys to Eleutheria; he had developed a curious passion for Alemar, the daughter of the reigning King of the Elves. More beautiful than any human girl he had ever seen, she understood him like no other woman did before. To her, he was not simply a handsome, spoiled son of a noble, but a learned and caring man. He could be real with her like he could be with no others except his own father, and she cared for him for what he was, not what he appeared to be. He dreamed of her at night, and she of him.

One day, he pledged he would return and remain there for a time, when the world was a safer place and his duties were not overwhelming. Now was certainly not the time, and Robyn knew that he would have to be satisfied with his dreams for the moment.

Promanthea understood his passion and his longing, but he remained silent when Robyn asked him his opinion. With his tree, that did not mean anything discernible. Silence was not a sign of approval or condemnation from Promanthea. It was just silence.

Robyn had the luxury of a safe and peaceful homeland amidst which he could study and train. The weather was brisk, being north of the Thorndars, but the land was bountiful and beautiful. The rivers ran clear and strong, and although farming was a necessary livelihood in a civilized society, much of the population's sustenance came from the waters. Concordians were experienced fishermen and they learned to navigate the rapid waters of the Sirceloc river at an early age. The waters were abundant and the fish were plentiful.

The Sirceloc was a magnificent waterway, deep as the western ocean in parts. Winding and narrow, broad and straight, it had more faces than the many and varied people of the countryside. All the inhabitants learned to respect the water as soon as they became aware of its existence. Sirceloc could be the source of life as well as the taker.

Robyn loved the river. He swam frequently and he learned from Promanthea to venerate the water as he would the blood of life. The waters ran through the lands, feeding and nourishing the parts of the earth it passed through as did the blood of a human as it passed through its veins. When Robyn soaked in the cool waters of the Sirceloc he let his senses melt into the flow, becoming one with the liquid of life, experiencing the vast movement and soothing surge of the constantly moving and yet never depleted entity.

The water lived and breathed and spoke, and Robyn learned to hear with his tree's ears the language it spoke. It told of another side to life, a different sense of time, of motion and of birth and death. When Robyn was near the river, he was never alone. As the Lalas communicated through their network of roots spanning the earth and their intimate relationship with the soil, so too were the rivers all intertwined, feeding into and out of one another eternally.

The whole of nature was a wonder to Robyn, and his powers derived from the elements and his understanding thereof. His ability to become one with the organic was what made him an extraordinary wielder of the earth magic. The elements listened to him and they respected him as he respected them.

Upon leaving his father's side, Robyn chose to mount his horse and follow the river southeast toward Pardatha, staying close to the waters he cherished so much. Kraft learned not to fear a raging river or a waterfall, but to respect it too. Robyn taught his trusted mount to flow with the water, not to fight it, and thus, to swim like no other horse in the land. They were a formidable team, and together they would journey quickly to their destination.

Leading Kraft deftly into the shallow water, Robyn guided him toward a deep flow, eased him slowly into the clear, cold liquid and encouraged him to relax. They began to run with the current, nimbly avoiding any protuberances and picking up speed as the moments passed. Kraft tucked his sturdy legs under his belly, and Robyn lay his head on his companion's neck while resting his own legs high on the stallion's back. They traveled in this fashion for a number of hours, making tremendous headway with little exertion.

As the river widened, the water slowed and Robyn spurred Kraft back onto the solid ground. The air was chilly and a fine rain began to fall from the clouds that were suddenly accumulating more thickly in the skies above. The sun had fully set, and the new moon was bright in the clear sky, poking its face in and out of the rapidly coagulating cumulus. If they followed the river for the next two days, they would be directly north of Pardatha before the water veered in the other direction. Two more days of hard riding through the Delphan hills would leave them no further than a day's easy canter from the city gates. But for now, they would need to rest.

Robyn found a grassy knoll near a bend in the river. There he dismounted and let Kraft nibble on the sweet blades beneath his feet. Searching for a comfortable place to bed down for the night, he espied a moss-covered expanse not far to the left. Leaving his mount to join him at his leisure, Robyn wandered thoughtfully to the chosen area. He was saddened by the pain his father felt at his departure, and something reminded him of it at just that moment.

He sat down to reminisce and rest, allowing his mind to relax in the safety of the river and the trees. Robyn was invigorated by the prospects for the future. Promanthea had instilled in him the need to find a way to halt the approaching decay, and he truly felt deep within his soul, that his "calling" was the beginning of that process of discovery. He had journeyed often in the past, at times at Promanthea's request, at times of his own free will, in search of some speck of knowledge, some insight or method he had heard of somehow, somewhere, that might help him in his quest to prepare against the Evil One and his hoards, always learning, always absorbing, always growing in power. He had yet to be truly tested and that he knew only too well. The time was coming for that and he would not hasten it. Each day brought him more insight, and Promanthea's great patience steadied his soul.

Robyn lay back upon the soft moss and closed his eyes, allowing his body to refresh itself and his mind to relax and absorb the strength from the earth that so softly enveloped him, to help him prepare for what was soon to come. His deep relaxation evolved into a calm and refreshing sleep, as the night wore on. The woods were quiet and peaceful, the water ceaselessly flowed, life ended and life began, but the darkness was approaching and its shadow was spreading northward already, engulfing all in its destructive path, reversing the natural cycle of rebirth and rejuvenation and blighting the land with its evil intent.

Robyn slept on, but his dreams grew restless. The calm evaded him as the dawn approached and he tossed and turned uncharacteristically, waking Kraft whose own trepidation increased by the minute. The big stallion nuzzled his master softly, hoping to ease his apparent distress to no avail.

With a violent start, Robyn's head rose from the mossy earth. A sharp pain burst within his mind and a burning sensation quickly spread throughout his entire being. His fingers constricted into tight fists involuntarily and his toes cramped up painfully. The hurt was so severe that he feared he was dying, never had he experienced anything so acute. Before he had an opportunity to steady himself, he was overcome with a monumental sorrow, so deep that tears cascaded down his cheeks in rivulets, uncontrollably.

"Not Promanthea? It cannot be!" he shrieked aloud.

Fighting to calm himself, to maintain his sanity, Robyn thrust his fingers deep into the soft ground beneath him, attempting to draw power and sustenance from the earth, searching for a connection, a link, to his bond-mate. Initially, he recoiled from the shock, wanting to retract his fingers and break the chain that would bring him the news he craved or the news he feared. But, he endured the pain and he fought the urge to regurgitate, as he steadied his thoughts and continued to explore the sediment for a pathway of communication, though the torment never let up for a minute.

His fingers struck a root tendril that had wormed its way to him from the surrounding vegetation, and as it wrapped itself around his hand and wrist, he began to receive scattered images of a great tree, a beautiful and ancient Lalas, shuddering and decaying in its final death throes, even as he watched. The horrifying scene made him recoil in outrage at the beauty and goodness being forsaken and lost. The tree so resembled Promanthea that he reeled from the nausea this possibility generated in him, but he persisted with his observation. He had to know!

Struggling with the waves of pain that washed over him, he sent out his thoughts with as much clarity as he could muster under the circumstances. The visions in his mind were unclear and blurry, the link was not strong, but Robyn would not release it. He held on to the faint indication of sentience that he vaguely felt amidst the images he was perceiving. If Promanthea was dying, he would die too. He could not live without him! But, something told him that it was not his tree, his bond-mate. Something, an inner strength perhaps, mercifully allowed him to keep hoping and searching for the coupling that would give him the answer he craved and dreaded.

His mind-cries were shooting in all directions, reaching out in search of his friend or another with knowledge of him. No reply was forthcoming, only the spreading anxiety that the death of a Lalas elicited throughout the countryside. He felt it acutely now, and his mind was ready to burst, his vision was blurring in reaction to the pain and anguish.

Depression overcame him in violent waves, but he struggled on, maintaining all the while the bond that would ultimately bring him news. Deeper into the soil he thrust his hands, breaking his nails and cutting his skin, not wanting to lose the connection he had established, fruitlessly hoping that he would encounter a stronger link further down in the earth, when he knew instinctively that the small tendril would be sufficient if there was news to be had. Desperate for relief, Robyn gathered his thoughts with superhuman effort, and utilizing what strength he had remaining, he sent out a final plea. Alas, his efforts were met with nothing more than silence, an ominous silence suffused with loss and trepidation. In despair, he relaxed his will and was overcome with heartache.

I am here.

The words filled his head with an inexplicable softness, a mellowness that could not be compared with any other feeling he had ever experienced. The relief was enormous, just to hear his soothing voice, just to know that he was alive. Nothing could have sounded more beautiful, more sonorous or heavenly as Promanthea's voice at that moment. Robyn lay his head back, exhausted, but unwilling to relinquish the link that he had so painstakingly established.

Thank you! he sent in thought, *Thank you so much! I could not bear not knowing your fate any longer.*

Fear not for me, Robyn, though my ultimate fate is yet to be determined. But another of my kind has fallen, a great and dear friend. All the land will suffer from this. The fabric tears once again, the stitches loosen and the seams rip. I must prepare. Continue on your way and let nothing stop you. Nothing! My reach is being constricted and I will require your eyes in order to see as far as I must. Be strong, my friend. Never lose heart! I will be safe, and you must remain so too, at all costs.

With that, the coupling was shattered, the root encircling his hand shriveled away and he was left bereft of any further knowledge, yet tremendously relieved by the information he had been able to receive.

Promanthea was safe! he rejoiced while still suffering from the shock and sadness any Chosen felt at the loss of a Lalas. But, it was not his. At least it was not his tree! He was ashamed of himself for that thought, at the selfish nature of it, but he could not deny the existence of the feeling.

By now, the sun had risen above the eastern tree line and although the sky was cloudy and grey, the air was crisp and no precipitation fell upon him. He would be able to travel quickly, now more anxious than ever to reach Pardatha. Robyn, riding securely atop Kraft, made good time following the river southeast and encountering nothing out of the ordinary, nothing that caused him undue concern. The weather, although usually a bit warmer this time of year and usually brighter, was not too bad.

It took him two full days to rid himself of the terrible depression that overtook him after the encounter with the dying Lalas. It plagued him during his dreams, leaving him for the moments just before dawn, only to find him again immediately upon his awakening.

Robyn forced himself to move on, to continue his journey, fighting the desire to lie down and sleep for eternity. Although he endeavored to open his mind up to Promanthea's contact, he had no further communication with the Lalas since that fateful morning, but neither did he expect to. Robyn felt the enormous burden upon his shoulders. He knew that he would be on his own now, that the next chapter would be written without the aid of his great tree.

As he galloped through the woods, he recalled how hopeful he was just three days ago, how full of promise the world appeared to be and how empowered he felt. Now, although the promise of his soon to occur contact with the heir of Gwendolen was paramount on his mind, he was struggling with doubt, an emotion that had not plagued him in the past. The experience of witnessing the death of so great a tree, of so monumental a force, had changed him. It hardened his resolve certainly, but it also caused him to focus on just how small and insignificant he was in the scope of things, how powerless he seemed to himself now, if a tree, as great and noble as the one that passed from this earth the other day, could not even resist the coming darkness.

The powers to the south were building and their influence was spreading. He felt it in the soil, in the air, in the very trees he communed with. But, the boy had appeared as well only recently, waiting to be trained. The fabric was weaving of its own accord...a tear here, a rip there, an open seam. But then a new thread was introduced, and a new and unexpected product was created. That is how he began to perceive the process, and his hope, his faith, began to return anew. The dialectic of his thought helped to carry him from darkness to light many times in the past, and it aided him now as well.

Robyn was well aware that he could not predict what only time would tell. But, he also believed that he had a part to play in this dark chapter, and that he could effect change and guide it, if not generate it wholly on his own. He thought as he rode, swiftly and sure, and the time passed reasonably fast. His spirits lifted accordingly as he approached the plains.

He would soon have to depart from the comforting water of the Sirceloc, a source of sustenance he would dearly miss, but he accepted necessity stoically, and he was ready to move on. Ever since the "calling" had overtaken him, Robyn had no doubt that in time the future would be secure. He believed that he only needed to reach the boy's side, impart what knowledge he could to the youth along with his other teachers, and the world would begin to mend, set on the correct course, the healthy course once again. The cloth could unravel and be re-woven, and tomorrow would still come. He yet believed that. The only difference now, after the shock of the recent death of the noble tree, was that the evil was closer than before, that the moment was approaching faster than he anticipated, that he would not have the luxury of time that he expected to have to teach and practice with the young boy. The timetable he never fully envisioned to begin with would now need to be speeded up. He felt an urgency that he heretofore never felt.

All of these emotions were welling up in the young Chosen, and he worked his way meticulously through them, painstakingly climbing out of each pit of depression until he was able to put the destructive feelings behind him at last. By the time he bid farewell to the river Sirceloc, he was himself once again, though transformed forever, like the fabric of life, re-woven out of the same threads, retaining the same essence, but still subtly different. Robyn spurred Kraft onward with renewed determination toward the open hills of Delphan. Two day's hard ride over the knolls was all that remained between himself and a clear path to Pardatha.

Chapter Nineteen

Cameron met his revered Lady, Filaree Par D'Avalain, in the courtyard of the castle, prepared, as always to begin the journey she had outlined earlier. His admiration for her was unbridled. Nico, her silver grey mount, and his own horse, Trojan, the black stallion bequeathed to him as a foal by his father, stood ready, with their saddlebags packed, requisitions well chosen and their weapons carefully stowed and secured upon the horses.

When Filaree stepped onto the paving stones of the atrium, ready to mount her filly and be off, Cameron gasped in wonder at the majesty of the woman he felt honored to accompany. When they were not training, Filaree would let her golden brown hair fly loosely behind her as they rode. She had inherited the hair from her father, the alabaster skin from her mother, while her remaining features were a perfect mix between the two parents, managing to capture the best qualities of both, the combination of which resulted in an astounding beauty. Her appearance was tempered by understanding, green eyes and the warmest smile this side of the Thorndars that formed so naturally upon lips that were red and full.

Cameron did truly love his mistress, though not in an amorous way, at least that is what he told himself over and over again. He admired her and respected her, and his love for her was complete, though not the type to cause him to be jealous in a possessive manner. But then again, she hardly even looked twice at any gentleman who might be a suitable mate for her, so his emotions were never fully tested. She was like an older sister to him, although merely six months his senior. He was an only child, and she mothered him as well in the absence of his own who died when he was born. He would lay his life down before allowing her to be harmed.

Filaree adored Cameron too. She joked with him and teased him, but she knew the value of his friendship and loyalty, and she never took it for granted. He was a handsome man, slim and wiry but very strong, with curly brown hair and deep brown eyes. He towered over her in height, but he was agile and swift. Cameron could fight, indeed, and she knew that he would be a worthy opponent of anyone who challenged either her or him. His loyalty was unquestioned, and Filaree's only worry thereon was that it was sometimes an overzealous one, that it could cause him harm if he reacted in haste or overreacted to what he perceived to be a threat to her welfare. But she too loved him, as he loved her, fully and honestly and thoroughly platonically. Together, they were a formidable team, each understanding the manner in which the other fought, able to predict the other's movements and reactions, able to anticipate what strategies each would employ under difficult circumstances. They rarely had to talk in order to coordinate their movements while in battle. They danced the dance of war better than any other partners could. There was also little that they kept hidden from one another when it came to their quests, concerns and evaluations. In order to be the perfect team, they needed to keep one another totally aware of any doubts as well as confidences they may be harboring.

It was no surprise thus that few men courted Filaree and few women pursued Cameron. Most assumed that they were a pair, in all ways, and they did not seek to challenge that relationship. Both Filaree and Cameron were reconciled to that problem, knowing that when the right person finally came along for one or the other, he or she would understand the truth and not be frightened by their friendship. In the meantime, they believed that they had no time for romance anyway, and they did not regret their choices. Both had their flings on their own time and they satisfied whatever yearnings and needs they may have had, but they deemed their purpose to be exalted, and they vowed that they would not allow personal feelings to come before the greater good.

Although Cameron was never fully apprised of the heir's importance, of the reason for the "calling", he was told what he needed to be told and he did not feel deprived of information in this regard. He was a man of few words who only needed to be convinced of his purpose once in order to pursue it without hesitation. He believed in Filaree and her ability to discern the right path, and when it came to the "calling", he immediately knew that he would sacrifice whatever was necessary to aid his Lady in the answering of that call.

"Come, Cameron. We must mount and be off," she called to him.

"Yes, my Lady," he replied as he deftly hoisted himself atop his steed, after first checking the girth under Trojan's belly as well as Nico's.

They had a long ride ahead of them and the last thing that they needed was a loose saddle causing either mount irritation and thereby slowing them down. He checked the saddlebags, made certain the weapons were secure once again and then he was finally ready to depart. Filaree glanced briefly back at the castle, allowing her gaze to rise upward toward the tower where she knew her mother would be watching. Permitting her eyes to linger for only a moment, she turned swiftly away and urged her horse forward. Nico responded by breaking into a loping canter, her shod hooves clapping upon the cobblestones in a loud and rhythmic fashion, echoing throughout the courtyard, as Cameron spurred Trojan on, gingerly catching up to Filaree so that the two departed the gates side by side.

They headed directly southward, toward Chilmark, a short ride from the outskirts of the city. They planned to cross the barren plains before nightfall, entering the Winding Woods in time to bed down for the evening. The woods would offer protection of a sort, if they chose their campsite well. One could easily get lost in the forests south of the Chilmark.

The Winding Woods were so called because the trees that grew there rose in winding rows, spiraling to the top of the crest. They were so dense and thick with foliage that the traveler had to follow their path, not forge his own. The trees chose the direction that anyone who trespassed in their realm had to take. They were not related to the Lalas directly, perhaps more primitive, less conscious, but they communicated with one another in their own fashion, allowing some travelers to enter and exit safely, while trapping others indefinitely inside their twisted and confusing maze. No one had ever impugned the integrity of the trees in the Winding Woods. But, neither did one ascribe any ethical purpose to their behavior. They simply seemed to randomly pick among those who dared to enter, letting some through safely while inexplicably detaining others.

Filaree and Cameron were prepared to take the risk of entering the Winding Woods, confident that they would carefully wend their way through to the other side, and reach the Tammell hills by the third day. Their real concern was reserved for the hills themselves, inhabited by wood Trolls who rarely left the dreary territory, but took sport with anyone or anything that chose to enter their domain.

The Trolls were fat and ugly creatures, uneducated although mentally capable. They were generally lazy and slovenly, happy to trap the unsuspecting human or Elf and force him or her into perpetual servitude, until they chose to carve them up for a rare dinner. Few journeyed into the hills unless accompanied by a substantial force, and the Trolls otherwise kept to themselves for the most part. They lived in caves when available or carelessly constructed mud huts, and they scavenged for roots and mushrooms. Much to the surprise of most people and contrary to common belief, they rarely ate meat.

Trolls were generally grumpy, dirty, and dumb, but they could be formidable enemies when angered. Their stupidity made them easy to outsmart but hard to defeat if they should come upon a party unawares, as they fought blindly and with unrestrained furor, carelessly ignoring their own wounds in the process. If they were discovered by one of them as they crossed the hills, Cameron and Filaree would have to fight their way out, no doubt. That prospect they did not look forward to. They discussed these issues as they rode, stopping only to eat some fruit and cheese and to water the horses occasionally.

The plains were devoid of people and few animals dwelled upon them. The rain settled swiftly into the hard soil, leaving large crevices and dry gullies everywhere. Wherever it did not drain, it froze in standing pools during the winter months. Very little grew and there was not much that was desirable about Chilmark. It did provide the city and castle with a natural defensive barrier, as no one could hide therein due to the lack of vegetation, and it was also hard to build structures in the cracked and fissured ground. Even if an army did approach Altair and the city of Avalain, it would be hard put to camp in the plains of Chilmark and lay siege to it. They provided no sustenance to an army and no shelter from either the elements or bombardment from the castle above.

"Ride next to me Cameron. The path widens from here on and the soil is harder. Trojan will not lose his footing as easily," Filaree said.

"How do you know that the woods will welcome us, Lady, and not prevent our passing through?" Cameron asked, concerned about the rumors he had heard his entire life.

"I am not certain of anything, but I am not unprepared."

Filaree reached into her blouse and withdrew a carved pendant shaped like a tree, though black in color, hanging from a thin, gold chain.

"Do you see this, Cameron?"

"Yes, my Lady. It is quite beautiful," he responded, leaning over as he rode to gaze upon it.

"Beautiful and functional. My father gave this to me when I was a young girl. He was born here, as was I, and he spent many a day learning about the countryside. My father loved all that lived in nature, and he craved understanding and knowledge. The Winding Woods was a place where he ventured often as a young man. He told me many stories of his sojourns there." Filaree replaced the token and drew her reins in tightly, abruptly stopping her forward motion. Looking at Cameron quizzically she said, "You know, you resemble him. He was not a man of many words, but his heart was pure and his purpose clear." She loosened her grip on the leather straps and Nico proceeded forward once again.

"I am honored that you think so. Although I did not know him, I was told he was a good and noble man," Cameron replied, catching up to her again.

They were trotting now, careful not to lead their mounts into areas where the soil was too cracked and their ankles could get caught and twisted.

"The necklace I showed you was given to him when he was a boy, by Pembar. Do you remember being told of him?" she inquired.

"Yes, my Lady, but I did not believe he was real. I thought he was just a legend, a character in tales told to frighten children," Cameron said.

"Well, so did I until my father gave me this. I thought he was kidding when he told me that Pembar lived in the Winding Woods and that one day, when he was exploring near the base of the trees, he was approached by the odd, aged man. He shuddered in fear, initially, he told me. He spoke to me like a young boy. He said that he had never been so frightened in his life. I remember thinking it so strange that my father would be frightened by anything. That moment is so vivid in my mind, Cameron, it is as if it was yesterday," Filaree said, sounding childlike in her reminisce. "The already ancient man befriended him and taught him all that he knew of the trees. Pembar was a strange, old man, my father said, but he was good. His ways were different than other people's, but he served the right side and he recognized the virtue in my father. Pembar just preferred to live apart from people and that was hard for most folk to understand. And, as he aged, he looked more like a shabby, straggly tree than he did a man. The legends just rose around him."

"I heard all of the tales, but I never thought that he was real. When I was a child, Pembar was a character in a bedtime story who gave me nightmares. My father used to warn me about wandering away and getting lost in the woods. He used to tease me by saying Pembar would find me and make me his slave. I never knew or suspected that he was a real person."

"He was real, Cameron, and he gave my father this token, this black tree. He said that it would identify him as a friend of the woods, as a person that would never harm a tree needlessly. He told my father that if he wanted to learn about the Winding Woods and their ways, then he would need to identify himself to them, so he wore it always until he gave it to me. The trees there were not smart like the Lalas. They could not reason, he told my father, but they could distinguish good from bad and they reacted instinctively to their recognition. The necklace just assured him of that recognition."

"Your father spent a good deal of time in the woods?"

"Yes, quite a lot. He told me that he loved to enter and to follow the paths that the trees created. They changed each time he stepped foot in the forest. He was fascinated by them. He went to them often, and as he grew older himself, he would spend days at a time there, worrying my mother no end. He used to tell me that he learned to revere the mysterious in nature because of the forest, how it changed for no human reason, how the woods lived and grew as a unit as if the forest was really one tree rather than thousands. He was very fond of the Winding Woods," Filaree said. Talking about him brought her great joy.

"I had no idea, my Lady, that anyone ever went in and out of there often," he said, astonished at her father's boldness.

"Well, he did, Cameron. And he told me that the time would come when I would need to also. He knew, Cameron! I really believe that he knew even then that this time would come," she said contemplatively.

"So, the pendant identifies us? As friends?" he asked.

"Yes, I think that is correct. I feel that we will not be harmed or led astray. I think that the path that will open before us will lead us directly to the Tammell hills. The trees of the woods have protected our kingdom for centuries. Is it not strange to you that we have never been invaded from the south?" she asked him.

"Yes, but I always assumed that it was because of the dryness and the exposure of the plains," he replied.

"Partially, that is correct. But the woods could have served as shelter to an invading army. The trees could have provided material for war machines and ladders, not to mention weapons. But they never did...for anyone!" she commented.

"I hope you are correct, my Lady. I am not anxious to spend eternity wandering in circles when we have so much to attend to," he said only half seriously, yet concerned nevertheless.

"Neither am I, dear Cameron. Neither am I."

With that remark, Filaree spurred Nico on a little faster, gaining the lead and breaking into a canter as the ground was easier to navigate at this point. Cameron hurried to catch up, and they rode in silence at a swift pace for the next few hours.

As the sun began to set, they had reached the exact point that Filaree had planned to reach, having had nothing delay them up until now. The two travelers dismounted and let the horses graze in the short grass that ringed the edge of the plains. They provided them with water and some honey laced grain, and then they began to pitch the small tent that would shelter them for the night against the evening chill. Cameron gathered some wood and started a small fire. Filaree prepared some food she withdrew from her saddlebags and then sat down by the fire to eat, offering Cameron a dish as well once he completed his task.

"What ever happened to Pembar?" Cameron asked as if he were holding this question in for quite some time.

"My father never told me for certain. I do not know if he knew himself. But he did remind me over and over again that, as time went by, the old man grew more and more treelike and tended to remain in one spot more and more often. He said that Pembar no longer wished to move about, that, and he joked or I used to think that he was joking, he was "planting roots". If I were to guess, Cameron, I now believe that he was hinting at the possibility that Pembar mutated into a tree in the end, just as trees change into rock after centuries, but my father never actually said that," she said, while preparing the food.

"Could that be, my Lady? Do you think?"

"Anything is possible, and I do not discount the supposition. After all, what other end would have been more fitting for him? Perhaps we will find him when we enter the woods," she replied teasing.

"I suppose it is imaginable," he said thoughtfully. "The world certainly is a strange place, my Lady. But I hope that if it is true, and that if Pembar is a living tree in the Winding Woods, that he does not hold it against me that I feared him as a child and played along with the other children when they teased him during our games."

"I doubt he will remember you, Cameron. Have no fear, he was the brunt of many a joke and the bogeyman for many children, and besides, he was not known to favor boys like the lake sprites do. Perhaps some of those ladies will be visiting the woods too," she said laughingly, knowing how he always shuddered at the thought of being captured by the sprites, even until today. "If he is waiting in the forest for unsuspecting children, then I think he will pass you by. Cameron, you are no longer unsuspecting, and the last time I looked, you had grown up," she kidded.

"Yes, but when I hear you speak of Pembar, I feel like a child once again. It is good to finally know that he was kind and not evil. Now, I feel more grown up, my Lady," he said with a chuckle. "But, please, do not remind me of those pixies on the water. I will never outgrow my fear of them!" he responded seriously, shuddering at the thought.

"I was only kidding about the sprites, Cameron. I am sorry, that was unkind of me. But, I am glad that I was able to educate you with regard to Pembar. Now, let us hope that we are permitted to enter the woods, and more important, exit the other side without delay, as I hope. I will display my token prominently and with pride as we travel. Unless the trees have come under the influence of the other side, we shall be safe and our journey will continue unhampered," Filaree spoke with conviction, as she prepared to enter the tent and retire for the evening.

Cameron remained outside for a while after his charge went to sleep, watching the plains for any sign of danger. They were both not terribly concerned that harm would come to them here, so after he gave the Lady Filaree enough time to settle herself and possibly fall asleep, he crawled into the tent to attempt to rest himself as well. He heard her softly breathing as he lay down beside her, covering her with the stiff blanket so she would not be chilled during the night. He too fell asleep quickly, and they both slept soundly until dawn.

Chapter Twenty

Cairn dug the long pole into the soft mud, propelling the raft further into the lake, and the black waters parted as they sprang ahead. There were approximately two hours left before the sun would rise, and Cairn wanted desperately to be close to the opposite shore by then. Being only near to the land could be dangerous. The Selgays were vicious animals and they wasted no time in attacking as soon as their keen eyes spotted prey from their vantage points in the rocky crevices of the Thorndars above.

Calyx sat vigilantly at the stern of the raft, gazing expectantly at the dark sky. *No Selgay would have an easy time with him,* Cairn thought, while Tomas, seemingly unconcerned, was curiously humming to himself as if he did not have a care in the world.

"I love the water at night," Tomas remarked suddenly.

"Well, my boy, this water may be beautiful, but the hills harbor some very dangerous birds, and we must cross with haste," Cairn responded.

"They will not harm us," he said matter-of-factly, gazing into the water over the side of the raft.

"Can you be so sure of that, Tomas?" Cairn asked seriously, for the tone of the young boy's voice was so compelling.

"Yes, Cairn of Thermaye, they will not harm us. Besides, we will be across before it gets light," he said.

Cairn, not willing to take anything for granted, remained unsure and apprehensive.

"How do you know, Tomas? How can you be certain? I want to believe you, but I would like to know what makes you so confident?"

"I just feel it. The water is calm, nothing threatens from below and the birds are all asleep. They feasted well yesterday. A party of Trolls tried to cross from the east, heading toward the southern dukedom of Talamar. They were too slow. The birds are not hungry tonight."

"Wherefrom comes your surety, Tomas? I know that you are *different* than many other boys your age. But how do you get this information? Does Ormachon provide you with knowledge from this distance?" Cairn poled the waters diligently and made good headway under the stars. Tomas spoke so distinctly of things that most others could only speculate upon.

"Ormachon does tell me things now and then. My bond with him is strong and I hear him from a great distance. You see too Cairn, that we are riding upon a wooden raft, and anything wooden helps us communicate."

"I did not realize that. I thought that a Chosen and his tree needed to have more direct contact, even from a distance. I was led to believe that water interrupted the chain."

"No, only sometimes. This water is full of life, and thus it makes the chain stronger, not weaker. The distance is insignificant. Only in a wasteland would we not be able to hear one another at all."

Cairn was surprised to hear this, but it made perfect sense to him.

"I see. And he tells you we are safe here? He knows the birds will not attack?" Cairn asked still somewhat skeptical.

"No, he cannot predict tomorrow, or even what may occur an hour from now. Reading the future is not for a Lalas to do. But he can deduce based upon what he knows to be from what has already been. And, Ormachon knows much. His communication with the others is still strong, although it weakens these days."

"Tomas?" Cairn asked, stopping briefly from the task of propelling the craft.

"Yes?" Tomas gazed serenely upon Cairn's face, his bright eyes reflecting the moonlight now and again as it broke through the high clouds.

"How can I believe that you are only fourteen? You seem so much older."

"I am fourteen years and three months. But during all of those years, I was with Ormachon. I never knew my parents. As far back as I can remember, Ormachon was my father, and Trevor and Safira were my guardians. I knew no others," he said without emotion. "I grew up very quickly. While most boys are still nursing at their mother's breast, I was practicing the art of meditation. While other children played games among themselves, Ormachon taught me skills. I learned to read while very young and my bedtime stories were usually taken from the Tomes of Caradon. You see, Cairn, I am fourteen in years only, not in knowledge or experience," the boy concluded without any hint of arrogance in his voice. He was simply describing the situation as it had been.

"You and I are not so dissimilar, Tomas, although I was never chosen. I think I regretted that fact more as a child than as an adult.

When I finally realized that I would have to learn everything I needed to entirely on my own, I felt much better."

Tomas' eyes locked upon Cairn's face, fascinated, as he spoke.

"I dove into my studies headfirst, ravenous for knowledge. I loved to learn, and to reason. I must admit, though, that I envied those who were chosen, those who left my village for a life of companionship and challenge. Weren't you very young to have been picked?"

"I guess so. I never knew anything else. The first things I remember have to do with Ormachon."

"You are very extraordinary to me," Cairn said tenderly. "I never knew my brothers and I have no sons of my own. Although I have only just met you, you hold a very special place in my heart. I really cannot explain it. The moment I saw you, I felt as if I had known you before. I do not believe that it was mere chance that brought us together," Cairn said and then he stopped talking, not expecting a reply from the boy after his last comment, but he did not stop thinking.

This was a remarkable young man, wondrous even. Cairn knew that he was destined to bring him to Pardatha with him, that somehow he would play a major role in the events that were yet to occur. He hoped that Tomas would be able to help train the boy heir too, that he would not be reluctant to impart what knowledge he could to the other child. Cairn believed now that the odds of success were increased since Tomas had joined him on his journey.

"Cairn?" Tomas asked, sounding like a boy again.

"Yes?" Cairn replied.

"Ormachon told me I could trust you, but I knew that I could before he even told me. I do not understand many things about myself and the world. But I do know that being here now is right. I know that I have a purpose in this life, and I believe that you will help me to achieve it," he said with such touching sincerity that Cairn was visibly moved.

"I hope you can help me in achieving mine as well. We need each other, Tomas!" Cairn said, as the boy made his way to his side and hugged him tightly.

A single tear rolled down Tomas' cheek, unseen by Cairn, and he let it linger on his skin, overcome by feelings that were uncommon to him. He did not want to let go.

"Now, my son, help me to get this raft to the other side. I really do not want to test your predictions," Cairn responded, gently patting the boy on his back, also overtaken by a feeling of kinship, like a father for a son or an elder brother for a younger.

Cairn sensed the boy's reluctance to separate from him, and together they stood this way for a minute, creating an unusual picture upon this make-shift raft in the middle of the churning lake. Calyx growled affectionately from the end of the raft, sensing too the comfort and warmth that existed among the group. Tomas detached himself from Cairn after a while and made his way forward on the small transport, gazing ahead into the approaching dawn, calm and serene as ever, seeming to not have a care in the world.

Chapter Twenty-one

"Where is that son of mine?" the Duke of Talamar asked, exasperated. "I send him on an important mission, for once, as he so often requested of me, and he takes his good time in returning, knowing how vital what I sent him to retrieve is!

"This does not bode well. I fear that I should have trusted my instincts, and sent you instead. But Baladar would not have welcomed you as he must my son and heir," the Duke stated, staring out the broad, stained glass window of his study. His beady eyes scanned the horizon to the northwest, searching for a sign of the small party that set out for Pardatha eight days ago.

The Duke was unusually nervous recently, Fobush noticed, not surprised though considering the visitors that had only recently left the castle. Times were strange and dangerous indeed when envoys from the deep south are made welcome and given shelter in Talamar.

"Is that a rider over there at the edge of the woods?" Duke Leonardo asked, squinting his eyes and furrowing his brow in his effort to focus.

The Duke of Talamar was not a handsome man. He had always relied upon his cunning and in his ability to act and be charming in order to gain friends and alliances. The Dukedom of Talamar occupied the southern reaches, closer to the deep south than most other civilized areas, necessitating its leaders to be negotiators as well as statesmen. The borders were secure for the most part, and although the Altamar mountain range separated them from Colton dar Agonthea and his minions, the one major pass was negotiable at certain times of the year, and a small army could be led to the gates of the city, if driven hard enough. The entryway to that pass was well garrisoned, or so the Duke hoped. He often sent scouts to the fort in order to check up on the troops he stationed there. Being so far away from home, he knew that they would become careless, and he could not afford that. He rotated the soldiers frequently in order to avoid the danger of their complacency.

The Duke trembled at the thought of any army of Colton's occupying his territory. His one brief visit by the Dark Lord's envoy caused enough fear in him for a lifetime. The Duke of Talamar never boasted of his courage. He was given a simple task to accomplish and if done properly, he would be left alone; that is what he was told, and that was all there was to it! The Duke had no regrets about accepting the directive if it would assure that his domain would remain at peace and he and his family would remain unmolested.

If there was one thing that he despised more than anything else, it was fighting. The alliances he made were always designed to serve his self-interest. *After all, is that not what good leadership is all about?* The Duke was never a man others trusted with anything more serious than money, but his management and his ability to walk a thin line and balance upon it always, allowed his fiefdom to prosper, and his people were therefore satisfied.

The Dukedom of Talamar thrived upon trade, selling ore and lamp-burning oils to the north and east in exchange for clothing, silks and manufactured goods that his people were hard pressed to produce themselves. It was so hot in the south that food grew well, but his people rarely exerted the effort to provide enough to sell outside of their own territory. They created no crafts worthy of selling, and no artisans of merit ever originated in Talamar. They constructed no furniture of value, no artwork to boast about and there was no center of learning here as existed in other regions of comparable size. The oils that they were able to retrieve rather easily from the ground as well as from the polong trees, one type used for lamps and the other for cooking, were rare enough to assure Talamar of a continual source of material suitable for barter.

In days long past, when his great-grandfather ruled and the Lalas flourished in the countryside, things may have been different. The Duke in fact, hated the great trees anyway, so it did not disturb him that none existed on his lands any longer. He never trusted them, let alone those strange people who were "chosen" and lived their entire lives bound to a single tree. The "sacred" trees could not be chopped down and they produced no fruit or oil or even berries. He often wondered what purpose they really served, and he never liked those who ministered to them so graciously. No, he was not sad that they grew no more in Talamar. The last one died many years ago when he was still young, and he to this day would not go near the area where it once stood so arrogantly and proudly.

Well, the mighty Lalas is just a pile of dust now, while I am still the leader of my people!

And thus Duke Leonardo reasoned, worrying only that the dark power to the south would notice his prosperity and not pass him by if he ever extended his influence northward. How he would manage to pacify Colton dar Agonthea he was not certain, but he was determined not to let anything disturb the status quo in Talamar.

"Is that Kettin over there?" he asked his aide, jabbing his fat finger repeatedly at the window. "I could swear that I see a group of people at the edge of the woods. But my eyesight is not as good as it used to be. What do you see?" he asked Fobush impatiently, tugging upon his sleeve and pulling him toward the leaded glass.

"Yes my lord, I believe it is a party of men. Should I send a contingent out to meet them?" his aide responded as politely as he could.

"Yes, yes! I am anxious to see if he accomplished what I sent him to do. It should not have been too difficult a task, rescuing a sleeping boy from Baladar's keep. I wonder why Colton wants this boy so badly anyway," he mused aloud, frowning to himself. "Do you think they are related? Since when has the Evil One ever been interested in children? I thought he reserved his time and concern for beautiful women and gold. Perhaps the boy is the whelp of some whore of his," he said with rancor in his voice.

Fobush cringed at the way his Lordship spoke of Colton. He believed, as many did, that the Dark Lord had eyes and ears everywhere and that it was dangerous to even think bad things about him, or to even speak his name aloud. However, the Duke had always been a fool in Fobush's eyes, and he had no reason to expect he would behave any differently today. *But this son of his! May the First help them all if he succeeds the Duke.*

"Send the guard now, Fobush! Bring that dolt of a son of mine here to me as soon as you can. If he traveled any more slowly he would be walking backwards!" Duke Leonardo exclaimed.

"Yes, my Lord. At once," He turned immediately and left the room to carry out the orders.

The Duke of Talamar nervously walked to the window and gazed ahead, more concerned about his son's success than he wished Fobush to know. He desperately tried to see if the approaching party had the young boy in tow.

No one knew how thoroughly and totally distraught Colton's emissary had made him. He had been unable to sleep well since that fateful day. And how that despicable Ambassador got through the pass unnoticed with twenty hideous trolls at his side, he could not imagine. What good was it to have a garrison at the pass if they let anyone through without even warning him? What if he did not deliver the boy to Colton? What if the boy was not there? What could he really do to him? After all, he still had alliances with the north, with Pardatha, Avalain and many other kingdoms. They would come to his aid if he requested it of them.

If Kettin returned without the boy, then Baladar could not be angry with him, for he would have done nothing wrong. Kettin was not fool enough to leave his city on bad terms. Baladar was a strong ally and Pardatha was a wealthy and influential land. The Duke would have to ask for help, of course, but Baladar would not deny him. He was a noble ally and Leonardo knew that he would respect his promises.

Duke Leonardo was pacing back and forth across his study, growing more and more nervous as time passed, evaluating his options.

Why did he come to me? Couldn't he have gone east to Drakar or Entallen? He told me to contact him when I had the young man in my possession. He fought to maintain control of himself and he slowly opened the heavy lid of the metal bound coffer. Reluctantly reaching for the black leather pouch that Colton's Ambassador handed to him upon his departure, the Duke recalled the instructions that he was given; *Spread the powder from the pouch onto a stone table. Strike a flint to it. When the substance ignites, speak the words "Pemte couta delen gar. Ishma neander Agonthea', and step back.* The tall stranger told Duke Leonardo that he needed only to follow the counsel as provided and they would take care of the rest. He stuffed the pouch in his pocket and returned to his vigil at the window once again, remembering with a sudden shiver the chillingly empty blackness of the unwelcome visitor's eyes.

The Duke watched as Fobush led a small contingent of guards across the courtyard and out onto the plain. He followed them as they galloped off toward the group that was definitely emerging from the woods and heading in the direction of the castle.

It has to be Kettin, and he must have this mysterious boy with him. He could not have bungled this mission! It was so simple. A woman could have done it, he thought worriedly.

As he continued to fret, a heavyset lady with bright red lips and grey streaks in her curly black hair, burst into the room, her many layers of skirting brushing the floor loudly as she crossed to the Duke.

"What are you doing standing at the window like an old woman? Are you waiting for tomorrow while today has barely begun? You have gotten so lazy, Leon, I fear that I must soon have to do everything," she chastised, in a high-pitched voice.

"Hush, woman. You speak nonsense. Can't you see that I am busy?" he answered abruptly, trying vainly to dismiss her.

"Busy, my foot! Ever since that ugly man from wherever you said he was from appeared here, you have not been yourself. You run around and hide in the shadows, always looking over your shoulder as if you expect something awful to appear. What is wrong, dearest?" she inquired almost affectionately, but with genuine interest.

"I am concerned about our son, Dorothea, that is what is wrong. I sent him on a simple journey to visit a friend and ally and he has not returned yet. Can I not worry about our son?"

"Why should things be different now? You never worried about *your* son before," she replied, standing on her toes and gazing into the small mirror above the hearth. "What did you send him to do?" she questioned as she adjusted her lipstick with her index finger.

"Nothing too difficult. He had to go to Pardatha and bring some runaway boy back here with him. A nursemaid could have done the job, but I thought Kettin might learn something from the journey."

"Whom did this boy run away from and why did his own family not go and fetch him?" she asked confused, clearly unwilling to accept anything less than a square answer from her husband.

"It is of no concern to you, Lady. Now leave me be!" he retorted, attempting to end the conversation then and there.

"I will not allow you to speak to me with such a tone. Now, say you're sorry and tell me whose boy this is!" she demanded, making it obvious that she would settle for no further obfuscation today.

"If you insist, Dorothea, but don't blame me if you regret having asked this question," he responded, hesitating for a moment before speaking again. "Colton dar Agonthea!" he then said with a venomous hiss.

"What about that devil spawn? What does he have to do with anything?" she asked him, perplexed.

"Dearest Dorothea, what must I do to make you understand? The boy, the young man that I sent Kettin to fetch, is related somehow to Colton dar Agonthea! Is that clear enough for you?" he shouted and turned back to the window, hiding his harrowed expression from her eyes.

The woman almost fainted when the words her husband spoke finally registered in her mind. She quickly searched around the room for a seat and then sat down heavily in a large chair, her skirts flying up around her as she attempted to regain her breath.

"Are you serious, husband? What could possibly have possessed you to do such a thing? Have you totally lost your senses?" she asked, blotting her forehead nervously with the edge of her skirt.

"Quiet, old woman. You know not of what you speak. What would you have liked me to do? Refuse the Dark Lord's request? What do you think he would have done if his emissary returned to Sedahar and told him that the Duke of Talamar humbly regrets that he cannot fulfill your wish? Do you think he would have said 'Fine,' and gone about his business? That much of a fool I am not!" Duke Leonardo responded, totally flustered by now. "What choice did I have?"

"There must have been something you could have done. This is terrible! What are we going to do now? It will not end here, Leonar, you must know that. Once a beast like that finds a little cat to catch his mice, he will never let it go."

"I will turn the boy over as soon as Kettin brings him here and that will be the end of it! I have done nothing wrong. No one can fault me for this."

"No one but yourself!" she said angrily, slapping him with her words. "How did this 'envoy' get through our defenses? Were our guards sleeping? Since when do we welcome trolls in our home? I knew that no good would come of that visit. But, I had no idea that they came directly from the court of the Dark Lord! What a nightmare," she replied, fretting uncontrollably and pacing back and forth once again.

"Relax, dear woman, we will be safe here. Colton has no interest in us. If I need to perform a few small favors for him, what harm can come of it? We will survive as we always do. I am a good statesman, Dorothea. Have I not done well for us so far?" he pleaded, looking for some words of support to comfort himself by.

"Oh, I wish the Lalas still lived here. They would protect us!" she wailed.

"A curse on the trees!" he blurted angrily, losing his temper altogether and causing his wife to stop in her tracks, startled. "They never helped us, only themselves and their Chosen. Their days are past, my dear. The Lalas are dying and the world is changing.

Today, one must be friends with all sides, with all kinds, if one wishes to prosper. Maybe this is the beginning of a new alliance. Maybe there is a silver lining in this cloud after all."

"Silver, my foot! Do you hear yourself, Leonardo? What idiotic prater! Nothing good can ever come of an alliance with the devil. This must end here! You must never accept his entreaty again." She moved to his side, placing her arm comfortably around his now stooped shoulders. "Send the boy to him when Kettin returns and tell him that you wish no further contact with him. Tell him that it will threaten your treaties with your neighbors if they discover that you aided him. He will understand that. Surely he will be grateful that you were able to return the runaway to him, and then he will leave us alone," she convinced herself as she spoke. "Don't fool yourself, Leon. It is not possible to work with the likes of Colton, only for him. And he will chew you up and spit you out as soon as he would crush a bray beetle under his foot," she responded.

The Duke accepted her ideas and took comfort in her embrace, each seeking strength from the other.

"Perhaps you are right, my dear. Perhaps you are right. I will give him what he wants this time and that will be the end of it!" he said with finality while reaching to unlatch the pane and gaze out of the opening once more.

As the Duke and his wife continued to ease each others' concerns, the group of soldiers, led by Fobush, returned to the courtyard with their son and his retainers. Through the now open window of the study, the Duke distinctly heard the clatter of hooves on the cobblestones below, and he abruptly broke away from his wife and headed for the winding stairway. Dorothea followed closely in pursuit, her full skirts raising dust as they brushed over the floors, running to keep up with her husband and as anxious now as he was to reunite with their son.

When the couple emerged from the portico into the courtyard, Kettin was smiling and warmly greeting Fobush while he dismounted. Allowing his horse to be led away by a stableboy, he slapped his father's Master at Arms sharply on the back. Fobush was unaccustomed to such friendly gestures on the part of the spoiled and arrogant son of the Duke, and his discomfort showed by the surprised expression on his face.

"We had such a wonderful trip back, Fobush, the weather being as kind to us as we could have hoped. I pray all is well here. How are mother and father?" he asked as if he were returning from a relaxing vacation.

"They are well, Sir Kettin. I know that your father has been anxiously awaiting your return. Perhaps we should go to him right away."

"In time, good man. Let me get settled first. I have much to tell him. That excuse for a statesman, Baladar, was so disrespectful! If it were not for the fact that our return trip was so refreshing, I would be beside myself with annoyance," he remarked, unaware of just how much his father, the Duke, wanted to talk to him.

"I believe that your father wants to see you immediately, my Lord. He has requested that I escort you to him as soon as you are ready," he repeated more sternly, surprised at the nonchalance of the young lord in comparison to his father's uneasy demeanor.

"May I not wash and freshen up first? What could be so important that my father wishes to greet me while I am still smelling like a commoner? Tell him that I will attend him as soon as I bathe and change," he responded defiantly.

"You will do no such thing!" the Duke thundered from across the cobblestones. "You will come to my study immediately!" he commanded, struggling to master his unease.

The Duke glanced around furtively, searching for the boy his son was supposed to have brought back with him. Placing his arm across his son's back, he led him forcefully, and rather harshly, toward the door that would take them to the privacy of his rooms, literally pushing him forward against his son's reluctant will.

"Father, must you be so insistent? I have only just returned from a long journey and you do not even allow me the common courtesy of a bath first?" he asked angrily, offended by having been treated like a child.

"There will be plenty of time for that later, Kettin. Now, come!" he replied, sharply shoving his son forward. As soon as the door had slammed tightly shut behind him, he raged, "Where is the boy? What did you do with him? I did not see him in your group. Did you send him with another? Where is he?".

"I do not know what you are talking about, father. What boy?" He seemed bewildered by the question.

"*What boy?* How can you ask such a stupid question? Why did I send you to Pardatha? To retrieve a runaway boy from Baladar's court and to bring him back with you. Why else would I have sent you there?"

"You sent me to be your emissary and renew some old alliances. But I couldn't do that, since Baladar treated me miserably. I did make a statement though, and I let him know just how angry you would be by the manner in which he---"

"What kind of foolishness is this? Are you a complete idiot? You dare speak to me of manners? I can assure you Colton dar Agonthea will not be polite when he finds out you have returned empty handed!" he barked, spitting with anger as he spoke.

"You must reinforce the mountain pass at once, Leonar, at once!" The Duke's wife broke in. "Send another garrison. Send two!" She paced back and forth.

"What is the point? If the Dark Lord wants to reach me, do you think some soldiers will stop him?"

Kettin watched his parents without comprehension. He had no idea what they were talking about, but, he had a nagging feeling he had forgotten something. Something about a boy *had* been mentioned to him at one point or other. He just could not be certain what and when. It all seemed so vague, as if a fog was obscuring his recollection and preventing him from remembering clearly. All this talk about the Dark Lord and reinforcing the pass was baffling.

"I thought that I would at least be greeted warmly upon my return. What is going on here?" he interrupted, thoroughly confused.

"How can you have no idea what we are talking about?" his father asked, staring at him in bewilderment. "What manner of spell has been cast upon you that you could have forgotten everything we spoke about before you departed? Do you not recall at all the purpose of your visit to Pardatha?"

"I was to go and see Baladar and renew our alliance of mutual protection, as well as to advise him of the extent of our supply of polong oil we had to offer up for sale. Perhaps I was a bit remiss in executing your directives, but he was so rude to me and my men that I would have lost face in front of my entire retinue if I did not respond the way that I did. Baladar *left* the castle the night I arrived! He did not even do me the honor of supping with me. What was I supposed to do, father?" he inquired like a hurt, little boy.

"When you left Baladar, did you at least leave in a manner that will allow us to return if we need to? Can I mend the damage?" he asked.

A sheepish look replaced his son's pained expression, as he began to describe the tragic events that took place on the eve of his departure from Pardatha.

"I imagine you could if you had to," he stammered as he started to explain to his father. "I did have a slight skirmish with one of the guards called Dalek, which did come to blows. I did not initiate it, or at least I do not think that I did. You see, we were all drinking rather heavily. You know how good the Pardathan ale is? In any case, he was drunk and he attacked me, or so I remember, and I had no choice but to defend myself. No one else but he was killed," Kettin explained, as if this were all just a minor mishap.

The Duke sat down heavily in his chair, raised his arms over his head and covered his ears with his hands. "Tell me no more. I cannot bear to hear another word," he exclaimed, turning to Dorothea who was crying profusely by this time. "I must think. Begone!" he said to his son, flicking his wrist at him in dismissal. "Maybe I can find another job for you to do south of the Altamars next time. We are ruined! Ruined!" he wailed, as he bent his head into his lap, with his hands still covering his ears.

The Lady Dorothea led Kettin to the door of the room, brusquely tapping him on his back repeatedly with the broad of her palm, saying all the while, "Go, go, go! We will meet later after your father has had time to think. Quickly, Kettin, and close the door behind you."

After he left, she slammed the heavy door shut, locking it with a twist of her fingers, and then she turned to her husband. Her face was pale. "Our options have been greatly reduced of late," she said, pacing the floor and looking intently at the ground. "We must make some difficult decisions, my husband, and we have very little time. I will go to Baladar myself, if need be, and plead for forgiveness. But, what will you tell Colton's ambassador when he returns?"

Leonardo reached inside his pocket and withdrew the leather pouch the ambassador had given him. He held it as if it were a deadly serpent and, with disgust, he tossed it into the burning fire in the study's hearth. The Duke and the Duchess stood and watched it burst into flame.

"I was to use that when the boy was in my company. I will not need it presently. Why inform him now of my failure? If I had the boy, the emissary would not have needed to return. I could have brought him to the pass, and then merely exchanged him for a thank you." He felt better now that he was rid of the purse. He had carried it with him for days, afraid to remove it from his pocket for too long a time, yet repulsed by its proximity to his skin all the while it was there.

He hesitated a moment longer, arose from his chair and said with a renewed animation, "But now, since he will surely come here when he does not hear from me, I will tell him the truth; that the boy he sent us to fetch was simply not there! That is what I will say. He was not there! After all, Kettin has no recollection of ever seeing him, and I am sure those who traveled with him had not seen hide nor hair of him either or I would have heard about it by now. Strong wizardry was certainly at work in Pardatha, and I will tell him that as well. It was not our fault. We are not magic wielders here. He will sympathize with that. We will question Kettin's entire party first, of course."

The Duke stood up, hopeful again, plotting what he knew to be a precarious and potentially perilous path, but he always felt better when he was plotting something that would require his cunning and guile in order to be implemented.

"He cannot fault us for something we could not control. It will do him no good to know that Kettin could not recall his purpose and therefore blundered as he did. What blame could he possibly assess upon you and me? We are innocent. It was his mistaken information that sent us there in the first place. It was his scout's fault, or whoever told him the boy was there to begin with! I will just have to convince him of that and that is all there is to it!" he said, puffing out his chest with his new found confidence.

"Yes, dear, perhaps that will work," she said patronizingly, patting him tenderly on his back, "but, will he believe you?"

Her husband, the rich and mighty Duke of Talamar, turned and looked upon his beloved wife with terror in his eyes once again, knowing that their fate was sealed. The smoke from the burning powder that Duke Leonardo had tossed into the fire had thickened in the hearth while they were speaking to one another and was now beginning to billow out of the confined space into the open room. The fire was quickly getting out of control.

Something must be clogging the flue, he thought. As he moved toward the hearth, a black, snake-like tendril shot out from beneath the dense fumes and violently wrapped itself around his right ankle, bringing him awkwardly to his knees. Another slimy strand encircled his neck. He gagged on the floor.

His terrified wife ran toward the door only to be brought down by more of the fearsome tentacles, which girded her waist and dragged her toward the hearth. Her heels scraped noisily across the stone floor. The smoke continued to fill the room, blackening the walls and ceiling with its unctuous soot.

The Duke attempted to call for help, his horror mounting by the second, but as soon as he opened his mouth, the vile, black things filled it with their putrid essence. He was choking, his eyes bulging, while the devil's spawn wrapped itself around his arms and legs, issuing from the fire in great numbers now, dragging him closer to their source.

The Duchess clawed frantically at her neck. She was soon encased in a cocoon of thrashing, gyrating horror which was constricting by the second, making even the slightest movement nearly impossible. The filaments continued to whip out from the fireplace, strangling them. *Beloved*, Dorothea mouthed to Leonardo, her breath all but gone.

The Duke, struggling to reach her, saw the terror in her eyes. *She does not deserve this!* He prayed to die, not so much to end his own suffering, but so he would not have to see her suffer anymore, wishing, in his last moments, only for the guilt and shame to dissipate. He rued the day the Dark Lord's emissary first crossed into Talamar, remembering his terrifying sense of foreboding upon his departure. He knew in his heart, even then, that his fate was already sealed. *Was there nothing I could have done?* he wondered.

The study was thick with blackness, suffused with the stench of Colton, blanketed with evil nightmares. Duke Leonardo heard a banging at the door. It sounded far away. They were beyond salvation, now. The floor and walls, even the ceiling, were completely covered with writhing, undulating tentacles, slithering in all directions, black and putrid, performing a frenzied dance of death before their eyes.

Dorothea reached toward Leonardo painfully stretching her fingers forward. He struggled more violently to break free to reach her. Through the thick smoke, through the growing haze in his mind, he heard something. A seductive disembodied voice, suffused with a calm fury issued from the void, "I can tolerate failure and trickery in my enemies, in fact I encourage it. You might even say I enjoy it. But I will not tolerate deceit from those in my employ." The voice grew steadily stronger as it continued. "You freely accepted my request, yet you think you can deceive me! Know this -- no one can deceive me! No one!" The room echoed with the thunderous voice.

A sickly sweet smell pervaded the room. The Duke and his wife stared at one another with what little strength that they had left. An overwhelming feeling of adoration suddenly engulfed them both, coupled with dread like none they had ever experienced. The faceless voice elicited a wave of conflicting emotions that enhanced the pain and agony that they were feeling, but at the same time, caused them to take an odd pleasure in it, a masochistic gratification in their own suffering. They were almost prepared to thank the perpetrator of this horrendous deed, they had become so instantly enamored of him.

Struggling to maintain their sanity, vacillating between dread and a perverted bliss, they attempted to focus upon one another, knowing the end was near. Succumbing to waves of nausea, the Duke was barely able to lift a single finger in his wife's direction before the life went out of him forever.

The Duchess, exhausted and spent, her thick hair matted against her forehead and cheeks, her skirts disheveled and in disarray, emitted a final sigh from her swollen, painted lips, and then lost consciousness from which she would never awaken again. In an instant, the smoke and the tentacles disappeared. All that remained were the tortured bodies of the Duke and Duchess of Talamar. The room seemed strangely still. Chaos existed only outside the sturdy doors as the shouts from Kettin and Fobush battled with the steady thudding of the guards' weapons against the doors as they continued their attempt to break in.

Chapter Twenty-two

The Dark Lord's palace was both beautiful and horrifying, exemplifying the dichotomy of his evil. He coerced with seduction, then he obliterated his prey. Colton dar Agonthea, whose many names belied his many faces, was both heaven and hell to look upon. Few found it easy to deny his presence, to gaze the other way, to ignore him, while most were mesmerized by the confusing emotions his countenance, or even his voice stirred up within them.

Regardless of how one perceived him personally, Colton was the epitome of corruption and debauchery. He was the opposite of all that was good and clean and healthy in the world. Cairn of Thermaye would have said that without pure evil there could not be pure goodness. He would have attempted to explain the necessity of one such as the Dark Lord, regardless of the extent of his enmity for him, that without contrast all things would be bland, that in order to understand pure goodness, one must be able to recognize pure evil, to see them as distinct from one another, as opposites, that all superlatives required comparisons in order to be what they were.

Robyn dar Tamarand would intuitively feel the difference and see the Dark Lord as nothingness, as the void, neither right nor wrong, beyond the definitions. Robyn would call him the antithesis of life. He would characterize him as empty and meaningless, a different form of power than his own, a power that robbed life of its essence and of its beauty. He could not even allow a comparison with the forces that he was so intimately in touch with.

Filaree Par D'Avalain would never understand the Dark Lord at all. He would be an enigma to her. She could not conceive of evil that pure, that intense, that immutable. She saw things in terms of degrees; degrees of strength, degrees of skill, degrees of dexterity. She would weigh his shortcomings and evaluate his power in terms of her own abilities.

Regardless of how any one of them perceived Colton dar Agonthea, his presence was becoming more obvious. The eternal battle between the light and the darkness was reaching a critical point now, at this time in history, and notwithstanding the fact that such a conflict always underlay most changes throughout time, some were more permanent than others, some had more devastating effects than others and some provoked changes that were irreversible, that altered the entire course of history, throwing all of life itself into jeopardy. Such was the situation at this juncture.

As the Lalas passed away so did the lifeblood of the planet, as its veins and arteries that provided sustenance to all ends of the earth, withered and collapsed. The cycle of birth and death was being threatened with the passing of the great trees. Dissolution was becoming a possibility for the first time in thousands of tiels, and Colton dar Agonthea felt it, he knew it and he gloried in the prospect.

The heir to the Gwendolen throne, the young boy newly dubbed Davmiran, provided a spark of hope to all who studied the legends, the Tomes of Caradon, to all who recognized the role that he was destined to play in the epic that was unfolding before them. He had to rediscover the Gem of Eternity and to renew the strength of the Lalas. All that had transpired before, all the battles and victories, great and small, all the defeats, all the sacrifices and losses, the heartbreak and the sorrow, all the joy and happiness and glory that went to make up the many facets of life and history, had led up to this point. And Colton knew it! He knew that the heir was his nemesis and he knew that the threat that he posed to the dark side was the greatest threat that had presented itself in eons. The irony was evident. The closer he felt that he was coming to victory, the more threatening the boy became.

He believed that without the heir, what he perceived as the fabric of the Lalas folly would unravel completely. Yet he, for the first time in thousands of tiels, felt a pang of worry, a hint of discomfort, a slight wave of concern knowing that the boy had been successfully cast northward toward the heart of the Lalas' remaining strength, toward the circle of power that would attempt to shield him and nurture him, until he was ready to perform his task and venture out into the world in search of the loathsome first and the despised Gem of Eternity nestled therein. With it in their hands, Colton's plans would be ruined. All his work would be for naught, his calculating, his preparing, his painstaking progress.

He could see the puzzle as it was being pieced together and he knew the final picture would be quite different if the boy were to die. But, he had to find him first, and although his powers were vast, they had their limits, especially when it came to areas where the Lalas still thrived. If he was not in Pardatha, where was he? He would begin to search again, but this time his slaves would pay the price for leading him in the wrong direction. That pathetic old woman would have to suffer for her failures. The thought of that at least caused him a modicum of satisfaction.

The world was based upon two conflicting concepts, light and dark, the former incorporating a bit of everything, allowing for many shades and variations, while the latter tolerating nothing, requiring the complete absence of the other. Colton longed for the world to spin uncontrollably into the void, the emptiness of dissolution and nothingness, within which he would thrive, feeding off of the desolation, the oblivion of utter darkness. He was a being born of negativity, the opposite of the light. His energy was derived from obscurity and shadow, unlike the Lalas whose energy radiated throughout the world based upon the light.

All of life shared a bit of the Gem's spark and passed it on with each new birth, with each sprouting blade of grass, every germinated seed, everything and anything organic that perpetuated itself through rejuvenation, duplication and reproduction. The Gem concentrated the warmth of the universe and then spread it throughout the world. It was the fulcrum upon which all life balanced. The Gem received its potency from the heavens and magnified it, dispersing it through the Lalas to the very ends of the earth. As the sun warmed the planet and generated new and more beautiful life forms, the darkness and cold stripped the planet of energy, smothering it in the icy chill of dormancy, denying life the chance to flourish.

Colton was the darkness, he was the cold, he was the void, and the sooner he could capture and eliminate the boy, the sooner the trees would all die, the desolation would spread and life would come to an end. Then he, Colton dar Agonthea, could become one with the abyss and merge with the negative power from whence he came. He would find peace at last, out of time, out of space.

His castle, castle Sedahar, had as many faces as did he. It seemingly created itself anew each day, depending upon its lord's mood. Never less than spectacular but always foreboding, it was perched upon a barren hilltop, open and exposed, ostensibly easy prey for anyone wishing to organize a head on assault. Situated somewhat south east of Lormarion, the kingdom of the Elves, it towered over the basin that was once the Sea of Tides.

Tiels ago, a river emptied itself into that sea, creating giant waves on the southernmost shores, causing the waters to rise and fall like the great southern oceans. The river dried up ages past and the basin and gorge that were once lush with life, were now barren and empty. The gorge stretched all the way to Pardatha in the north, where the river had once originated. Lake Everclear, a wellspring of fresh water, was the initial source of both the now dry river as well as the Sea of Tides.

Countless tiels past, the lake shot brilliant blue water skywards from the seemingly limitless geysers that erupted from under its surface. All kinds of life flourished in the pure, warm waters of Everclear, and the brilliant blue liquid flowed in steady streams south to the Sea of Tides. The river's banks were lush with vegetation, and people came from miles around to relax upon its bountiful shores and gaze upon the mesmerizing water. But, one day, the water ceased to explode to the surface, the great geysers grew inexplicably still and the river slowly dried up and died, leaving the strange and saturnine lake as the solitary reminder of what once was.

A frontal assault upon Sedahar, despite the wide and open path to its gates, would nevertheless be a big mistake. The appearance of an exposed approach was a seductive invitation to death; an illusive beckoning by the forces of dissolution. The Dark Lord's city was built upon chimera and falsity. It was not what it appeared to be and no army had ever had the audacity to attack it.

Colton populated his domain with all types of living things, though their demeanor and appearance changed the longer they were enslaved, coming to look more and more like one another, regardless of their differences when they arrived at Sedahar initially. They grew into creatures of darkness; their eyes began to bulge, fingers elongated, hair fell out, while their skin turned a dark, slimy greenish-brown. Some of the enslaved appeared that way to begin with, coming from the south and being born into slavery. Those ones knew no other reality and thus performed their tasks without question, without any thought of doing anything else. The others, the ones who had led different lives previously, who had known freedom and light, found it harder to adjust.

His slaves fought the chains that Colton shackled them with at times, until they too succumbed to the idea that they would never, never be free again. Colton would not tolerate the taking of one's own life. Not because he reviled the idea, but because it was a waste of a body. He was the only one to make the choice between life and death, and when he did choose death for a subject, the remains were not allowed to decompose and become part of the cycle of birth once again. The dead were annihilated, thrown into the massive furnaces that fed the castle. But their souls were trapped for all eternity.

Underneath Sedahar was a mammoth maze of tunnels, carved out of the bedrock by the Valkor, the giant, coal eating, lizard-like animals that Colton bred since time began. They had three rapier-like claws tipping off their front legs, sharp and elongated, both capable of burrowing through the soft coal that the rock was inundated with as well as capable of gutting their enemies with one furious swipe. The organic matter in the coal is what they thrived upon. The gastric acid in their stomachs was both capable of digesting it and igniting it, thus allowing the Valkor to spew flame at will. As they burrowed deeper and deeper into the land, forming an underground world of tunnels and caverns, the population of slaves followed behind, polishing and carving and finishing Colton's domain.

The Valkor were four legged beasts with long tails, tipped with spikes. Their skin was smooth and shiny, streaked with black and green, and it sweated incessantly, dripping an incandescent greenish liquid that acted like a cooling system for the body and making the Valkor glisten even in the dark of the caves. Colton had them trained well, and when ridden by his most trusted few, they were formidable warriors. They were vulnerable only in a few places. Their fat underbellies were hardened and tough through years of scraping upon the rough floors of the caverns and the slimy skin was like a sea sponge, porous and buoyant, though almost impenetrable. All but the strongest tipped shafts bounced off of it, as it seemingly absorbed inches of the shaft before it ejected it with a force that sent it flying in the opposite direction.

The Valkor's eyes were shielded by two eyelids, one opaque and one solid. The only time they were both tightly shut was when the animal slept. The opaque lid protected the beast's large eyes from the powder created as the coal was scraped and mined. The Valkor's jaws were wide and flat, lined with two rows of teeth, the first long and sharp, able to rip through the rock bed, while the second row consisted of flat, broad molars that crushed the coal or its unfortunate prey into a pulpy liquid. Behind the elongated head of the animal was a flap of skin concealing an additional air hole, somewhat like a sea mammal's, that allowed the steam created by the combustion of the digesting coal to escape.

The surest way to cripple a Valkor was through this hole. A strong spike, shoved into the funnel-like orifice, would quickly put the beast to sleep permanently. But it was no simple task to accomplish, and therefore, the Valkor were among the fiercest animals on the planet. Colton had been breeding them for tiels, and he treated them with more care and concern than his more intelligent slaves whose welfare he casually disregarded.

To be given the honor of riding a Valkor into battle was one of the highest compliments Colton dar Agonthea would ever pay to a vassal. But, it was not granted without a steep price. Colton would not tolerate the loss of a Valkor in combat, and if one should die under its rider, the rider was doomed. Yet, anything but a natural death was rare for one of these forbidding beasts, thus assuring its rider of a lofty spot in the hierarchy of Sedahar.

Colton was in a foul mood this evening, and thus all those within striking range shuddered and cowered and did their best to remain out of his sight. So far, he had been unsuccessful in locating the boy. That stupid son of the Duke of Talamar returned empty handed to his father's castle, forcing him to eliminate the old man and his pathetic wife, teaching the son an invaluable lesson.

This foolish, inexperienced Duke will now understand just how serious I am. He will never chance failing me in the future when I will certainly call upon him to serve.

For that reason alone, Kettin's malfeasance was worthwhile. Colton knew he would have to watch out for Fobush, though. He harbored no love for the young Duke, and his loyalty would be questionable in the days ahead. Colton intended to advance upon Talamar shortly, realizing that he needed to secure the mountain pass very soon. He could certainly outwit the previous Duke's defenses relatively easily, as he had so recently proven, but a smarter foe, one less arrogant and more intelligent might pose a problem.

The terrain was difficult to traverse for any aggressor, and the natural obstacles added a tremendous advantage to the defending army. He would subdue them easily now while they were in disarray, and he could use the fragrant oil of Talamar for his own purposes. The people would also be an asset to his cause. They would not resist, he knew, and he could easily use them and sacrifice them with no regrets. The Talamarans were loyal to their own pockets and stomachs, nothing more. He would need only threaten them and they would obey, and he could use them to draw his enemy away from the true center of his concern.

Colton sat in the tower room of his palace, high above the coal, black hills of Sedahar. The air around him sizzled with manic power as he contemplated his next move. He cast his sight outwards, as far as his realm extended, searching for a sign of the heir, frustrating himself over and over again, knowing that he would not find him here in the dead lands where no Lalas dared to grow, but he searched nonetheless. He relentlessly scoured the land for a hint of his presence, until he shrieked with frustration. The foul sound echoed throughout the palace, and his slaves hid their heads and crawled under tables and behind cabinets, hiding wherever they could, terrified and forsaken.

Trialla, too, cowered in the corner of her cell, covering her ears and trembling all over. *He will not be merciful tonight,* she thought with both revulsion and excitement, *unless the answers I seek come to me forthwith.* She hoped she would have news for him this evening, as the plan she put into effect some weeks ago was now reaching fruition.

She adjusted the soiled shawl that shrouded her filthy hair, making sure that it concealed the empty socket that once held her left eye. The cute, innocent cat with the long, straggly fur that she secreted out of the castle in Gwendolen during the final moments was going to be a very important little animal. Her eye shone brightly beneath its fur, not obvious at a casual glance, hidden from view just above its own two, natural eyes. Trialla was proud of her effort here, of her sacrifice for Colton, and she knew that he would be so grateful if she succeeded. He promised to make her beautiful once again and she knew that it was in his power to restore her eye. He could do anything! She would be whole again as soon as she found the wretched boy.

The wily cat had managed to evade all the natural obstacles that it encountered on its way to Pardatha. She saw clearly now, through her own single eye gleaming hideously in its forehead, as the small animal approached the courtyard of Baladar's castle, albeit from a lower perspective than she was accustomed to. This little beast, once the playmate of the heir himself, was the perfect foil for Trialla's plans. No one would suspect the adorable thing, and its agility and cleverness would allow it to gain access to wherever it chose to go. Having known the boy intimately, the cat would surely be able to recognize his odor, and all she really wanted was evidence of his casting, a small token that confirmed that Mira, that horrible spoiler, that doting nursemaid, that accursed busybody, had in fact chosen Pardatha as his place of refuge.

It had been in Baladar's castle for some time now, searching out its former master. Now, she watched expectantly as the cat wound its way up the tower stairway, deftly avoiding most living things, quiet and light footed, lithe and crafty. She had taught it well. She laughed to herself at how easily the boy's pet responded to her training, and how readily its body accepted her eye and adapted to its presence. She had not even come close to killing it, as she feared she might when she first began to experiment with the process, the results of which were better than she had ever dreamed possible.

Trialla found it simpler than she expected it to be to "educate" the little thing afterwards. The only shortcoming subsequent to the completion of the process was that she had to endure vision without sound and without smell, an incomplete picture of reality. But, it was certainly worth it considering there was no risk of her being discovered. Trialla luxuriated in the safety of her voyeurism, anxiously anticipating the next scene, almost bursting with excitement while quivering with exhilaration at the thought of how sweet Colton's reaction to her ultimate success would be.

The darling pet, unaware of its grotesque mutation, wandered purposefully up the stairs, each corner opening up a new and exciting vista to the old witch woman huddled in her squalid quarters. As it moved purposefully from left to right searching out every niche and looking behind each piece of furniture, she tingled with anticipation. Suddenly, the cat raised its head and sniffed the air with a sense of recognition. It looked everywhere as its tail snapped quickly back and forth while it searched for the scent that reached its small nostrils. Trialla watched through the one eye, as the cat methodically inched its way forward.

She just wanted a sign, a token that would prove that the boy was there somewhere. She could not afford to be wrong, and the old woman knew that she needed proof to bring to her master, some evidence she could present him with that was indisputable. If she could only find something that would demonstrate that she had guessed correctly, that her intuition alone was worthy of his attention, perhaps he would look kindly upon her and bestow his approval upon her. She salivated at the thought of his approbation and her old body throbbed with the contemplation thereof.

"Where else would that woman have cast him if not for Pardatha?" After a pause, she continued, "The woman was a fool! She believed in fairy tales and she never tired of repeating those childish stories of the northern provinces to the heir. She fed him with nonsense about the safety that the north afforded its people, with all of those damned trees!

"They will not help her now, those relics of the past, those withered pieces of firewood! No, not now. Nothing can help either of them now. Once I find him I will be beautiful again, and I will have power, more power than they could ever have dreamed of! That spoiled boy will bow to me, as I did to his family for so many years!"

Trialla had traveled further and further down the path of insanity these past months, not seeing the darkness for what it was, not recognizing the limits of her role. She actually believed that her efforts would earn her privilege and authority, that Colton dar Agonthea was governed by the same rules that governed the rest of the world, that he would be fair and acknowledge her loyalty and labor, and finally thank her for her sacrifice.

"I must find that little brat! Go, kitty, kitty, kitty. He has to be there somewhere. Sniff, sniff, kitty. You will find him. Yes, kitty, kitty, kitty, that's right, keep going, don't stop now," she coaxed, as the little kitten wandered the quiet halls of castle Pardatha.

Out of the corner of her lone eye perched grotesquely on the top of the cat's forehead, she spotted a bundle lying under a table a short distance ahead. From the cat's viewpoint on the ground it seemed gigantic, and to Trialla it also seemed vaguely familiar. The cat crept carefully toward it, hugging the wall as it pressed forward. Trialla's excitement was growing uncontrollably with each step of the cat's paws. By this time, she was standing with her remaining one eye closed, hopping up and down expectantly, gleefully spinning as she bounced around.

"This must be it! Go closer, kitty, kitty, kitty. I recognize that cloth. Closer! That's right, kitty, kitty," she urged from her cell. "Step right on it. Good, good. Now, kitty, use your paws, move it around just a tiny bit. Yes, just like that, you dear, dear little cat."

The cat recognized the familiar odor of Mira's cape and brushed against it as if it was the woman's leg, unfolding it some as it did so. The Gwendolen crest was suddenly visible right in the middle of the back of the partially spread out cape that Dalek, Baladar's second, had carelessly kicked under the sideboard when he first brought the heir to his Lord's chamber. As the cat kneaded it with its front paws and began to roll atop it trying to get as close to the smell of home as it could, the familiar garment unfolded even more.

As soon as the emblem came into view, Trialla stopped dancing around and she stood motionless in the middle of her room, staring at the hated crest through her own displaced eye, mesmerized by the symbol of the family she despised so much.

"I have done it!" she screeched. "I found him! Mira's cape! The boy is there, as I said, as I predicted! I was right all along! I was right!" she rejoiced finally, cavorting around in her cell like the madwoman that she was.

Trialla had no way of informing Colton of what had just transpired, but she was so excited, so ecstatic at her discovery, that she moved to the door of her chamber and beckoned as loudly as she comfortably could down the narrow stairway.

"My Lord? Where are you, master? I have something to tell you! Please, won't somebody fetch him to me? Please, somebody, help! It will be worth your while if you aid me now. I will not forget you."

She began to raise her voice, frustrated at the total lack of response.

"What is wrong with everyone? Can't you hear me? Colton needs me! He will be very angry with you if you do not tell him that I have important information for him," she continued to rave.

The servants in the hallways heard what sounded much like the many other prisoners who had been incarcerated in this chamber over time. They were unmoved by the old witch's pleading and hardly noticed her entreaties. Trialla grew more and more agitated with the passing moments, shaking the small bars on the one opening in the door, kicking the heavy metal with her foot and doing more damage to herself than to the chamber.

"You idiots! Don't you hear what I am saying? I need to speak to the master! I have news for him that he wants and needs. If you do not help me, then when he finds out, he will kill you! Someone? Is anybody listening to me?" she hollered, losing all of her remaining patience in the face of overwhelming frustration.

Trialla turned away from the door in dismay and was startled to find Colton standing by the small window at the other end of the room.

"You need yell no longer, witch. I am here." His voice was so loving, yet so venomous at the same time it made her cringe even as she beamed up at him. "What is it that you have to tell me that compelled you to agitate the entire population of this tower?"

"My Lord, my master, I have done what you asked. I have found the boy!" she blurted out, bowing down before his feet, humbled and frightened yet utterly excited.

Colton focused his dark and empty eyes upon the woman, boring a hole in her bent head with the intensity of his gaze and compelling her to look up into his face. His gaze lifted her off of the ground, like a puppet on a string, and she dangled limply, her toes scraping the floor. Colton ravaged her mind, his thoughts tearing through her inanimate body. After a time, he spoke, his voice emotionless. "You have done well, woman." He let her fall softly to the floor. "Your methods make me proud." He pressed his hand to her matted hair.

The wretched lady responded to his caress like a well trained pet, crouching at his ankles, absorbing his touch.

"So, he is there after all! Your suspicions were accurate, Trialla." As he spoke her name, she preened like a mating bird, responding to every nuance in his voice.

"I try to please, master," she finally uttered, looking up at him sheepishly out of her one eye.

"That is your job, woman," he retorted.

"Will you help me now, my Lord? Will you make me beautiful again?" she finally asked, suppressing her fear and keeping her head bent to the ground.

"Are you not beautiful now?" he responded, feigning shock. "Would you allow me to gaze upon ugliness? You insult me."

"I meant no disrespect, master," she whimpered, nearly swooning with guilt. She cowered, burying her head in her filthy rags and trying to hide from his sight. "I just thought ... you might grant my wish. After I found the boy for you," she muttered, peeking out from under her tattered gown.

Colton spun around in a fury, sucking all the loose objects in the small room toward him in a whirlwind of debris. Reaching backwards with his hand, he motioned for Trialla to attend him near the window and involuntarily, her body rose and awkwardly strutted to his side.

"Do you see the hills yonder, woman?" he asked, pressing her face to the window with his power. "Beyond them lies the city of Pardatha and the boy. When the heir is safely in my hands, then *and only then* will I consider your desires." His voice was soft as velvet, but underneath, there was a sharpness that she could not mistake for anything other than the threat it was.

Colton released her and Trialla collapsed onto the floor. Colton rose an inch or so off the dirt laden surface and floated toward the now open door, never looking back, never uttering another word.

Upon his departure, the door slammed shut, violently rattling the hinges, while Trialla from her vantage point in the middle of the cold, stone floor, heard the locking pin slide into place, sealing her in once again.

She rose and banged her tired head against the cold iron of the bars until she had no strength left to continue and her head throbbed with pain, then she fingered the empty socket that once housed her eye, weeping all the while but still craving the sound of his voice, the touch of his hand, the abusive yet seductive presence of Colton, the Evil One, the harbinger of dissolution.

Chapter Twenty-three

*T*he sun rose strong and bright, cascading in a wave over the eastern hills, gradually illuminating the vastness of the forest before them. Cameron hastened to the horses while Filaree began to prepare a small, morning meal, both of them unable to take their eyes off of the woods ahead. Their sleep was restful, and they both were in good spirits as they finished their chores and sat down for a minute or two to eat and drink the refreshing cider Filaree poured from a soft flask. She fondled the black tree pendant beneath her blouse, as she contemplated the imminent ride.

"Let us be off, Cameron. The sun is up and we should not waste any more time here," Filaree said.

"Yes, my Lady," he responded as he rose and walked to Nico, placing the small, soft saddle on the mare's back and tightening the girth.

His own stallion Trojan, whinnied expectantly and he gently placed the saddle over his broad back as well.

Once mounted, Filaree removed the necklace from under her shirt and displayed it prominently, without saying a word about it. She urged Nico onward toward the opening in the trees that had only just revealed itself to her. She knew that it was not there but a moment ago. Cameron followed closely behind, though he was not as comfortable as she was and he was unwilling to stray too far from her side.

As soon as they were fully within the tree line, a musty odor reached their nostrils. It was not unpleasant in any way, but it pervaded every intake of air, making them both feel as if they were ingesting the very trees themselves. The path wound deeply into the forest, giving them no choice but the one before them. Filaree glanced backwards at Cameron to make sure that he was close behind, and to her surprise, the path they had just traversed was gone; the trees had filled in the space as if it never existed. Although it shocked her at first glance, it did not cause her concern, but rather it afforded her with a sense of security and comfort that calmed her considerably. She knew as soon as she stepped foot into the Winding Woods that there was no turning back, and now she was certain of that.

They walked on for quite some time, still able to see the sun rising in the sky through the dense treetops. The wind rushed through the leaves of the many and varied trees, creating a harmonious clatter of divergent sounds. Animals seemed to rush about, and Cameron was certain at one point that he saw a small rodent under the brush, but upon closer examination, he began to doubt his initial belief. The leaves just moved *as if* they were concealing other living things; they shifted in waves, making it seem like the foliage itself was alive both above their heads and beneath their feet. Cameron too, soon noticed that as quickly as he crossed the path ahead, the trees moved in behind him, concealing the trail and making it appear as if the walkway was never really there at all. Neither Filaree nor Cameron could actually see the movement of the trees, as the light breaking intermittently through the branches played tricks upon their vision. But sure enough, whenever either of them looked backwards, the path behind them was gone and a new and formidable wall of heavy foliage abutted them to the rear.

As they moved forward, the trees grew denser around them, the path grew narrower and the odor grew deeper and more intense. The air was greenish in appearance, as the sun filtered its way down to them through the deep vegetation. They began to feel themselves as if they were becoming a part of the forest, as if they were absorbing it into their bodies through all of their orifices, as if they would soon become green too and start sprouting leaves from their skin and pores. The black tree pendant resting upon Filaree's chest glowed with a power of its own, creating a strange aura around the two travelers and piercing the greenish glow with a warm, white radiance.

They wandered on, following the path before them, winding deeper and deeper into the depths of the woods. Cameron began to feel as if the forest was pushing him forward and closing in behind him faster than he was able to travel.

"My Lady, I get the feeling that we should be moving more swiftly, that the trees will eat us up if we do not hasten our pace."

"I know what you mean. I too feel as if they are urging us forward more quickly than we have chosen to go. Let's heed their request," she responded, and she pressed her knees into Nico's sides causing her to bolt ahead. Cameron and Trojan followed closely behind, but within a moment's time the forest was at their backs once again. They spurred their mounts on even faster, but to no avail. Filaree kept glancing back over her shoulder, hoping to find that they had gained some space between themselves and the encroaching woods, but the opposite was in fact the case.

She happened to look back upon Cameron's face, to ascertain whether or not his fear of this type of encounter was getting the better of him, and she noticed that he was swaying slightly in his saddle and that his eyes were almost half closed.

"Cameron! What's wrong? You can't fall asleep now!" Filaree pulled back on Nico's mane, signaling her to slow down, and then she reached back to shake Cameron by the shoulders. He appeared to be in a daze and was barely hearing her as she spoke to him.

"Wake up, friend. Stay alert. You mustn't doze! You will lose your seat entirely," she said, but her words had no effect and in fact, she suddenly found herself barely able to keep her own eyes open. The pungent, mossy odor was overwhelming her senses and her vision was becoming obscured.

There was a deep, greenish haze all around her now, and she tasted the leaves and the pine needles as she inhaled, feeling their essence entering through all of the openings and pores of her body and spreading quickly through her veins. Filaree shook her head once, then again, and then she raised her chin up to gaze at the shrouded sky. As she did so she saw Cameron slip limply from his saddle and land heavily upon the ground. By this time, Nico was barely advancing and Trojan too was standing with his usually strong head hanging dolefully down, almost to the ground itself, walking blindly forward.

Filaree tried as hard as she could to remain awake, fighting the impulse to let go and fall onto the soft, beckoning moss below. Abruptly, she pulled back upon her horse's mane once more, signaling Nico to halt so that she could assist Cameron. Her mare barely needed the suggestion, as she too was hardly awake any longer. Filaree knew what she needed to do, but her body refused to respond to her direction anymore, as the forest continued to close in about them. The branches were gently brushing up against her face and arms now, and they were becoming more and more dense, obscuring what little light remained. Cameron's horse, unsuspecting, reared up instead of crashing into Filaree, and then whinnied in confusion.

Filaree dismounted, or rather, slid to the ground, and with her hands upon her hips in a defiant stance, faced the wall of trees and said, "I come in peace! I wish only to cross through your realm, not make my home in it."

The trees appeared to converse with one another in a jangle of rustling vegetation and swaying movements. Through her tinged sight, she watched as the entire forest seemed to come alive with activity.

Looking from side to side now and not really knowing whom to address, she continued, "My father was a friend of the Winding Woods and he gave me this token." Weakly, she held the black tree aloft and its glow brightened the space immediately around her and enveloped her in its otherworldly radiance. "He told me that it would protect me here, that I had nothing to fear if I traveled within your realm. Did he speak the truth?"

The tangle of dense vegetation reacted to her remarks by swaying and clattering more animatedly than before.

Cameron lay sprawled upon the soft ground nearby. Graceful blades of grass were sprouting up between his fingers and around his neck and face, caressing his hands and body. Filaree looked down at her feet and saw in astonishment that tendrils, small shoots from the surrounding trees, were encircling her ankles as well and tenderly wrapping themselves around her calves while all along, what she saw through her eyes was becoming a deeper green in color.

She struggled to find the strength to stand erect, to not succumb to the desire to lie down and sleep, while never letting the black tree fall from her uplifted hand. The leaves began to rustle in the big tree to their left, yet no wind passed through the area. Then to the right she heard a similar noise, but the air was still calm. The creaking of the branches became more frequent as well, and the leaves lifted in response as if the trees were carrying on a conversation in a language all their own.

This went on for some time, and Filaree stood patiently and respectfully, having not the strength to interrupt the cacophony and challenge their hosts with human words, awake enough to merely listen. But she could not help but notice that moment by moment Cameron was becoming more and more a part of the earth and grass upon which he lay. Her concern for him mounted steadily, but she was unable to do anything to assist him at this time, contending with the problem of keeping herself awake and alert, knowing in her heart that if she gave in and closed her eyes, she might never be able to open them again.

Suddenly, as if a strong wind blew through the forest from all directions, the leaves began to whisper in their strange language all at once and the branches began to creak more and more clamorously in unison now. The sound began to spread throughout the entire woods, until the noise reached a crescendo so incredibly loud that it almost forced her to cover her ears in order to endure it. And then it all stopped as suddenly and completely as it began. The silence was so complete that it was deafening, and Filaree, with Cameron resting close at her side, raised her head nobly, her chin high above her chest, and held the black tree aloft before her, pivoting from side to side and exhibiting it for all to see.

She stood that way in utter silence for some time, swaying slightly from drowsiness, and she waited. It was so difficult for her to actually witness the trees uprooting themselves and moving that she was uncertain exactly how they appeared in places they were not just moments before. Her reflexes were sluggish and her senses were dulled, while she continued to peer out through heavy eyelids as if she was drugged.

Abruptly, a score of tall, full willows leaned away from one another and they created an opening between them in which appeared a majestic, ancient looking tree, bent and crooked in parts, yet noble in appearance. Its vegetation was still lush, yet it was sparser than some of the others. It seemed to raise its branches in recognition of the travelers and to bow in its own fashion. Filaree curtsied politely, or she thought she did, and then she straightened up once more.

The air was rank with the smell of the forest, and the filtered light was green in hue. Her feet were three inches deep in the luxuriant, moss covered ground, and she could not help but notice the fern-like shoots that had crept further up her legs. She felt as if they were drawing her downward and pulling her into the soft earth beneath her feet.

A long, graceful filament broke free from the ancient tree and made its way toward Filaree's face. Seeming to float in air, it hesitated a few inches from her eyes as if it was taking in her fragrance, attempting to assess her nature, then it briefly grazed her cheek with its soft end, painted a line of touch across her forehead and down the other cheek, and then it reached out toward the black tree held tightly in her raised hand. The stem examined the token with its contact, tracing the delicate outlines of the carving, and then it abruptly withdrew.

Not knowing why or how recognition came to her, but now absolutely certain of her identification, she uttered the name, "Pembar!"

Filaree stood transfixed and breathed in the deep, woody scent, though she was woozy and light headed. With each breath she believed that she was ingesting the very essence of the trees. All around her she could see movement and feel the currents of air billowing from tree to tree. Through glazed eyes and vision, badly blurred by the overwhelming green presence, she was almost certain that she glimpsed a human face peering from the midst of the old, gnarled tree. A broad smile came unbidden to her lips and her body coursed with a newly found energy.

She gazed downward and saw that Cameron's face was covered in a soft, moss-like down as if he was growing a green colored beard, and his arms and legs were totally covered with grass and ferns. His hair was braided with green fibers by now, and his skin was taking on a rugged, brownish tinge. He did not move at all and his breath passed over his body like the wind blowing through a tree. Yet, Filaree spoke not a word, realizing intuitively that this moment was one of testing and decision, an examination of sorts which they both desperately needed to pass. All of the trees surrounding them swayed silently back and forth in a hypnotic rhythm, mesmerizing her with their motion. Filaree watched as best as she still could as the big, old tree seemed to bow once more and then retreat behind a wall of younger, greener foliage, until it was out of her sight completely. She peered after it through the haze and obscurity, regretting suddenly and deeply its departure.

All at once, the wall of trees abutting them receded, creating a small, circular clearing around them. They slowly slipped back as if they had never been there to begin with. Filaree smiled to herself and mouthed a silent thank you to her father and to Pembar. As her vision cleared, she looked over her shoulder and saw a blue patch of sky for the first time in a while. She turned to face it and lowered her tired arm, allowing the necklace to fall gently upon her chest. The formidable wall of green was finally broken, and the sights, sounds and smells of the outside world once again overtook her, clearing her vision and sharpening her perception.

Cameron began to stir and to slowly extend his limbs, breaking the tender, green shackles that held him, while the horses lifted their heads, shook out their manes and restlessly stamped their hooves on the soft ground. When her senses regained their proper focus, she gazed out through the narrow opening at the forest's edge and let her eyes converge upon the Tammell hills that now loomed barren and desolate in the distance.

Chapter Twenty-four

Elion was exhausted. He had not only pulled the unconscious youth behind him the entire way back from Pardatha, but he had also just suffered from the emotional and physical fatigue of a battle hard fought.

It is good to be home, he thought to himself.

His father, Treestar, would not leave his side until he was safely within the boundaries of Lormarion itself, and then he was only willing to let his son out of his sight long enough to give the necessary orders to the watch towers to let the lifts down and bring the party up. Elion relaxed in the knowledge that soon he would be in the heights once again and that he would be able to rest and regain his strength once more.

He raised his head just enough to see that the youth he had carried all this way was still close by his side and being well attended to. The young Elf never doubted the care that would be bestowed upon them both, but he felt a proprietary concern for the vulnerable young man similar to what he felt for his brothers when he was near to them. Yet this time his protective feelings were strangely more intense.

One of the large platforms shortly descended from the fortified heights above, and in moments fifteen or so well armed guards quickly surrounded them and carefully assisted the wounded onto the lift. Treestar barked orders at them in an unusually agitated manner, anxious to reach the true safety of Seramour himself. Elion noticed with concern the state of readiness that the guards appeared to be in. He could not remember when armed guards had last stood as sentries upon the platforms. But, alas as he well knew, times were changing and safety was foremost on everyone's mind these days. He took some small comfort in the preparedness that he began to notice everywhere, wishing that it were not necessary but knowing in his heart and feeling it in his soul that it was.

The glowing powders lit the forest underneath the city, casting dancing shadows everywhere as the guards scurried about. When the platform carrying his companion and himself finally cleared the tops of the lowest branches, he gazed with an inexplicable joy upon the vistas before him.

The spectacle of Seramour was unmatched on earth as far as he knew, and he could not imagine a more beautiful scenario than that which he witnessed now. He raised his head a bit from the conveyance that he lay sprawled upon in order to enable himself to take in a broader view of his city, it pleased him so. As far as his eyes could see, buildings sprouted up, each one constructed of carved and polished wood, capped by a woven roof of dyed reeds or beautifully painted tiles of baked and glazed mud. The colors were light and full of life, and they were both aesthetically pleasing as well as practical. The southern sun high above the treetops could get very strong, and the pastel tiles kept the buildings cool and comfortable. The carving was extremely elaborate on some buildings, having been done by master artists over the many countless tiels that Seramour had existed, and some of the buildings rose up hundreds of feet into the sky, seeming in places to poke through the clouds themselves.

Seramour had grown greatly in size and population over the last one hundred and thirty tiels, particularly so in the last two as the country Elves sought out the shelter and safety of the heights of the city. The Noban trees were steadfast and sturdy, and Seramour grew and grew in breadth as well as height, able to absorb all who wished to take refuge therein. The avenues were paved with bricks of baked mud as well, spaced perfectly by artisans and builders who knew how to construct things with hardly any gaps in between, sealing the city entirely from the world below.

The foundation of Seramour was as solid as earthen bedrock, constructed upon the broad boughs of the Nobans whose branches were easily trained to grow in the directions that the Elves guided them. An entire city flourished in the skies above the forest and lands of Lormarion, one such as few peoples but the Elves could ever have designed and constructed.

The entry area, the location that housed the majority of the platforms providing ingress and egress to the city, was flat and wide, edged by a thick wall of foliage to the north and paved with enameled, red brick set in a pattern of scalloped arches radiating from the platforms outward. The larger lifts were designated for commerce, while the smaller ones served the families of Lormarion. The bottoms of the platforms were covered with a hard rubber-like substance, resistant to fire and weaponry, and when they were pulled up fully and locked into place, they sealed off the only openings through which an enemy could enter the city from below. Once shut and sealed, they also obscured the sun totally from reaching the ground beneath, requiring that artificial illumination be utilized below during most hours of the day. The city of Seramour itself spread out southward from this point. A broad avenue led from the courtyard surrounding the lifts that was lined on both sides with store houses, trading floors and shops. Many of the city's finest inns were located in this quarter of the city, each uniquely designed and decorated in order to lure the many and varied travelers and traders who came to visit and do business with the inhabitants of Seramour.

The manufacturing districts of the city spread out eastward off of the boulevard, and the streets therein were among the oldest and narrowest of any, winding in and out of the gnarly branches, paved with oddly shaped dark yellow stones. The Elves of Seramour were artisans of the finest caliber, producing furniture, fabrics, clothing, carpets and wine unparalleled in quality. The vineyards of the city benefitted from their proximity to the sun, and the grapes ripened and matured faster than those on the surface, providing the winemakers with multiple harvests each season.

To the west of the main boulevard nearest to the staging platforms lay the barracks and training grounds of the army, along with the stables and armories. Beyond the corrals and jousting sectors, one could see lush fields of green, rolling and curving according to the heights of the trees atop which they were built, all laden with the varied produce upon which the Elves thrived.

The mature Noban trees were mostly uniform in size, allowing the Elves to build upon their branches without fear of them growing in an unusual manner and thus disrupting the edifices constructed on top of them. They ceased to grow vertically almost as soon as their first branches sprouted from them horizontally, thus informing the Elves that building could safely begin upon them.

The homes of the gentry, the artisans of the highest level, the noble families and the palace spread out south and west of the main avenue, and being that there were limits upon how much lateral space anyone could occupy, most people utilized the sky in which to expand, building graceful structures of multiple levels rising high into the sparkling sunlight. The spires of the largest homes glittered magnificently as the sun reflected off of the multi colored tile roofs.

Occupying a space in the center of the residential area was the palace of the royal family. It was a sight to behold, with the main structure constructed of highly polished white wood, sealed by huge bronze colored doors and topped by pastel roof tiles. Its towers rose up dramatically from its central axis, creating a breathtaking display of delicately carved, gold colored, mallow wood that was both rare and beautiful. The two highest of the spires were capped by row upon row of dragon-like scales made of burnished silver which reflected the sun's rays so brightly that they mimicked the very sun itself.

Many believed, particularly among the Elfin race, that the palace at Seramour was one of the most splendid structures in all the world, and every time that Elion saw it he understood what they meant. Nothing in his uncle Bristar's lands compared to the majesty and elegance that was Seramour, though Crispen was certainly majestic and splendid in its own right. And Pardatha, a city both sturdy and secure, was no match aesthetically for this city either. It was rumored that only in the kingdom of Eleutheria would one find a city as magnificent as Seramour, and so few living beings outside of the Northern Elves themselves had been allowed to venture therein, that first hand accounts of the ice city were few and far between.

It feels so good to be home, he thought again as his father assisted him down the main hallway toward the stairs that would lead him to his own apartments and some longed for and much needed rest and refreshment.

Waiting expectantly at the end of the Hall of Dragons stood his mother, Elsinestra, Queen of the Southern Elves, majestic and fair, with floor length flaxen hair as fine as spun gold and a face that appeared as if it was sculpted from the whitest of marble. Her features were so delicate that they made the toughest of warriors stop in their tracks just to gaze upon them. She was a healer of the order of Andaxis, the most respected and talented order in the hierarchy of healers. Her talents were celebrated throughout the Elfin kingdoms and families came from miles around for the chance to have Elsinestra treat them when local healers were unable to rectify a situation, or under other unusual circumstances that required her deft and delicate touch. Her gentle demeanor coupled with her incredible intuition endeared her to all who knew her, and word of her mastery and special talents preceded her wherever she went.

At this solemn moment, she stood anxiously awaiting her son's return as the soldiers had sent word to her as soon as they were made aware of it themselves. She was prepared for the worst. Regardless of her inner feelings, she remained stoic and regal as her position required.

Elsinestra saw both her husband and eldest son emerge from the gallery and enter the broad hallway. She stood motionless, her face not revealing the deep concern she felt. The Queen wanted to rush to them and clasp her son tightly to her breast, she was so happy to have him back home. She was also eager to apply her talents to the task of his repair. She arched her neck slightly, the only outward sign she gave that indicated her apprehension, and she used her Elfin sight to quickly assess the physical state her son was in.

The wolves rarely attacked an Elf in front of the hills so near to dawn, and this fact alone troubled her deeply. But she sensed no serious damage. Suddenly, she noticed the presence of another, not Elfin in character, whose injuries were also not severe, yet whose mind was silent as if asleep.

Peculiar, she thought, as she attempted to decipher the strange quality she discerned in the unconscious youth.

Once they reached her side, she bent to caress her son and examine his injuries with her touch at the same time. He would mend easily, she perceived, the cuts being only superficial. His major ailment was fatigue, and a good night's sleep after a soothing bath in hot napa oil would work wonders on him.

"It is a joy to have you home, Elion," she said tenderly. "I would have preferred, though, that you returned in a less dramatic fashion."

"I had not planned it quite this way, mother. I am sorry if I caused you concern. It was never my wish."

"You were very brave, I have been told, my son. You make me very proud. Any way you choose to come back to me, I would not complain about as long as you are not carried in on a funeral pyre. Now, enough talk! I will examine you more closely after you wash and change. But first, let me see to your companion whose injuries appear to be more extensive than your own."

Elsinestra moved to the silent youth's side and bent down in order to place her hands on either side of his forehead. His eyes were partially open and she could not help but notice the beauty of their hue. She closed her own eyes and pressed her hands tightly against his head.

"This is no ordinary human!" she exclaimed. "He is full of power, untainted and pure! I have yet to study one such as he!"

"Elion? Where did you meet him, and why is he not conscious? His injuries are superficial and did not contribute to the state he is in." Perplexed, she gazed at Elion with deepening concern.

"It is a long story, mother, and although I know how important it is for me to impart to you both all of my knowledge in this regard, I am quite tired. Please, can you wait until then? Would you see my companion is treated with the utmost of care? I have grown rather fond of him these last few days. He is very special, mother."

They honored their son's request without another thought, and they quickly instructed their aides to assist them. Then Elsinestra took Treestar's hand in her own, looked deeply into his eyes and whispered in his ear, "Our son has brought an extraordinary youth into our kingdom and our home. I felt it immediately upon examining him. Never have I perceived such power in one so young! Could he be the one?" she asked in a hushed voice. "It is too soon for me to tell. His insensate state is not a natural one, though. Some spell captivates him."

"I gazed upon him only once, and I too recognized his uniqueness although without your depth of understanding. I wanted only to protect him from harm," Treestar said. "Are you disturbed by him in any way?"

"No, it is not a negative feeling that I am experiencing. On the contrary. But it is very potent, more intense by far than anything I have yet encountered." Elsinestra turned in order to conceal her comments from the others present. "We must let our son rest first and then learn all that we can about this boy. My instincts tell me much, but I do not wish to be hasty with them," she said to her husband under her breath. "See to their safety and comfort, Aliantar" she spoke gently to her attendant. "The human cannot protect himself." She then turned to her husband. "Treestar, rest now. We will talk soon."

"I will meet you as soon as I am able, my dear," he replied gratefully and then left the hallway for his chambers.

Aliantar escorted Elion and the boy, the latter was carried gently by two other Elfin pages, up the stairway and to the healing quarters. Elsinestra stood alone for a moment once again, trying to quell the emotion that was rising in her breast. If her suspicions were correct, and she was almost certain that they were, her son had just brought to Lormarion the most important visitor it had yet to receive in all its history. She needed to be absolutely sure though, and in order for that to occur, she would have to spend a bit more time with the blonde haired boy. It was difficult for her to still her heart before all of those present, and she was glad that she was now left alone.

Rarely had one disturbed her composure as totally as this errant young man did, and he was not even conscious! She too then left the room and made her way toward the library as quickly as she could, hoping to find some answers in the books therein while she waited for her husband to rejoin her.

Elsinestra gazed out of the polished windows, not looking at anything at all. During the past few hours her mind had been working at a furious pace, questioning, reasoning and attempting to comprehend what was happening. She was discomforted by the events of the day, but she was not disheartened. The fact that Elion, her beloved son, had returned and was safe within the castle brought her great joy. But, the presence of his strange companion seemed more compelling to her somehow and more portentous even than her own son's dramatic reappearance.

She could not help but remember a poem that her mother used to recite to her at night when she had trouble sleeping as a child. It comforted her enormously and when she was young, she repeated it to herself whenever she was troubled. Strangely, the words rose before her mind's eye now with new meaning.

> *This night may be long,*
> *But with the dawn, hope will come anew...*
> *The Prince of light will come one night,*
> *And our lives will be renewed.*
> *His shining eyes will guide us toward the wisdom evermore,*
> *And on that day, he will lead the way*
> *Outward from Seramour.*
> *So go to sleep, my darling child,*
> *Take comfort in your dreams...*
> *When the time is right, he will lead the fight.*
> *Fear the darkness nevermore!*

"Fear the darkness nevermore!" she recited aloud, with heartening emotions stirring her very soul.

After Treestar had an opportunity to clean and dress the minor wounds he received during the earlier fray, he changed his soiled clothing and hurried toward the library, anxious to meet with Elsinestra and continue the conversation where they had left off previously. He too felt the overpowering presence of the young human, still now when he was not even in the same room.

He walked up the winding wooden stairway and opened the

carved door at its end. The library was a stunning room, paneled with dark, rich woods and lined with both ancient books as well as new ones, providing them with a wealth of material to study, a virtual fount of knowledge, and with a vibrant source of entertainment for Elsinestra who was an avid reader.

"What was that you said, Elsinestra?" he asked as he entered the room, hearing only the last words.

She turned to her husband with a start, then smiled. "I was just recalling a children's bedtime story my mother used to relate to me when I was troubled and could not sleep easily. It has taken on a more significant meaning for me just now," the Queen said emotionally. "I said, 'fear the darkness nevermore,'" she repeated.

She picked up the book that lay on the wide reading table, the same one that she had retrieved from the shelves a while ago. Large Elfin runes dominated the cover. The book was old and its pages were worn and parched. He watched as she carefully flipped through the ponderous volume, clearly looking for something in particular.

He loved his wife dearly and he never ceased to enjoy just watching her. She moved with the grace of a goddess, never hastily or clumsily. Her ability to discern the root of a problem, physical or mental, was what allowed her to apply her healing trade so fluidly. She was a remarkable woman and he was proud to be married to her.

Elsinestra raised her head from her task just long enough to merely peer at Treestar as he sat down beside her, before she returned her eyes to the tome.

"All of the signs point to Pardatha, not here. I would never have expected that the boy would have ended up with us. He is human!" she said, as if that were odd, without ever looking up from the book. She turned another page slowly and began reading to herself. "Here, it speaks of the heir," she said, pointing to a worn page. "Could the boy be of the Gwendolen line? He certainly has the features. What twist of fate brought him to Seramour, so far north? Where did Elion find him?"

"Dearest, we must be patient. Our son will attend us shortly and then you will have your inquiries answered. What does the book say of the heir? Was that not just a legend, a mere fairy tale?" he inquired of her.

"The book I am looking at now is not a book for children, husband. You see what is happening all around us. We know the great trees are dying. We see the changes every day outside of the safety and shelter of Seramour. This book speaks of times like these, times of great change and sorrow, and it also speaks of hope. I was filled with hope when I touched that boy. The feeling coursed through my body. I was thoroughly energized.... inspired! I even thought for a moment that I could smell the fragrance of Lalas. Tell me that you did not feel the same?" she asked.

Treestar placed his large hand on his chin and pulled upon his beard. "I admit that I was unsettled when I first encountered him, but that does not prove that he is the boy the Tomes speak of. He may just be blessed with unusual power. Or, our hopes may be inspiring our imaginations," he said, feigning skepticism.

"You have always been a doubter, Treestar," she teased affectionately, and continued her thought. "But my intuition is rarely wrong. I know he is very special. I know that he is here for a reason. For better or worse, we too are destined to participate in the great drama unfolding around us, Treestar. I have been unwilling up until now to accept that. His appearance has already changed things," she continued, looking encouraged, but troubled nevertheless. "Surely my imagination did not cause me to radiate with power when I first encountered him."

"If so, my dearest, if you are sure of what you say, then we must learn how to help him, how to awaken him from this strange slumber. We must learn why he is here," he responded.

"I fear it is not sleep that he must awaken from, but powerful magic. We must first ascertain more about him if we wish to help and not cause him harm."

Someone tapped discretely upon the library door and then entered without waiting for an invitation. Treestar smiled warmly as his son walked to their side.

"Mother, father, we must talk!" he said immediately, and then he sat in a large chair next to Elsinestra, looking refreshed but still bruised and weary.

"Ah, we certainly must. We have so much to talk about. Are you rested, son?" she asked, placing her hand atop his and gazing intently into his eyes. "You have been away for so long. I only wish we had the leisure to relax and to hear all about your time in Crispen with your uncle, Bristar. But we have pressing matters to attend to. You will forgive me, Elion, if I ask you to save the tales of your travels for another moment," she said with a hint of regret. "There is only one aspect of your journey that we must hear about now," she continued.

"He has already affected you too, I see. And I can assure you, mother, that small talk is not what I intended to conduct with the two of you at this time," Elion said with affection. "The moment I laid my eyes upon him, I knew that things would never be the same for me again," he said, hardly having to guess at the purpose of this meeting. "Where shall I begin?" he asked as he sat down next to his parents.

Elion related the entire story to Elsinestra and Treestar, who both listened intently to each word without interruption. When he finished at the point where his father rescued him from the attacking wolves, he looked at them both with wide open eyes, hoping that they would have more answers for him than questions. Instead, he was met with silence for quite some time, while they contemplated the situation.

His mother was the first to speak. "Why would anyone let a young, helpless boy wander off unaccompanied into the woods? I cannot understand that at all," she said perplexed, her brow furrowed with thought.

"Perhaps they were unaware until later that he was gone," Treestar replied.

"They seemed not to even know that he was there at all," Elion said, his chin resting upon his slender hands.

"Yet you say they escorted him out of the gates, or so it seemed?" his mother asked.

"Yes, it looked to me as if they were aware of his presence as they neared the Noban gate, but as soon as they cleared the final portcullis, he may as well have been invisible," Elion commented, clearly remembering what he saw. "He was bound, hand and foot when I found him. They were not friends of his!"

"If he was their prisoner, where were they taking him to and why? Do you have any idea who his captors were?" she inquired.

"They wore no distinguishing clothing that I could see. They carried no banners and no crests were emblazoned upon their clothing. I did not recognize any of them. The leader though was a young, dark-haired man and he seemed very casual, unconcerned verily. He was human and of noble birth or at least it appeared that way to me by virtue of his bearing and the retinue that accompanied him. He was also very flippant, almost arrogant in his demeanor. They obviously were not worried that the boy would escape. After all, he was not even conscious."

"No one followed them out? No one cared that they were leaving?" Treestar asked.

"I do not think anyone was even watching them. There were no people on the ramparts bidding them farewell. The Ghost Tower of Pardatha was vacant of soldiers. No one escorted them out. They just rode through the gates and went on their merry way. It was all very strange. I remember thinking at the time that this 'prisoner' could not have been a very important one," the young Elf related.

"Pardatha has never been a garrisoned city. People always passed freely in and out, but one would think that someone would have been there to bid such a group farewell," Elsinestra reasoned.

A brief silence followed her last remark and then Treestar said, "Baladar must not have known that they were leaving! Maybe they spirited the boy out and no one in the city knew!"

"He was concealed by a saddle blanket when they first emerged from the keep," Elion said, squinting his eyes and remembering the events clearly. "I did not know they had a prisoner in their midst until later when the horse stretched its neck down to eat some grass and the blanket slipped off. He wasn't moving when they emerged from the city, so maybe no one knew they were leaving with human baggage," Elion continued upon the path of his father's thought. "That would explain why no one followed them out, either to bid them farewell or to regain the boy's freedom. These soldiers must have kidnapped him and his absence had not yet been discovered when I arrived!" he said.

"They would have found out soon enough," his mother remarked. "But, considering the state he was in when they carried him out, he could have been brought into the city under cover too. Maybe only a few knew he was even there. He is clearly not a Pardathan. His features are southern, probably from Gwendolen as I suspect, or some place else south of here, certainly south of the Thorndars. Possibly he was brought there by someone in order to be healed. Baladar, the sovereign of Pardatha, is known to be adept at the magical arts. Pardatha would have been a good choice."

"Or for protection! Pardatha is also a strong city in a strong kingdom. Baladar is a powerful leader. Anyone could tell the boy is special. If I were weak, I would not trust myself with his welfare. I would seek out someone who could help him," Elion commented.

"If what we surmise is so, then they will surely be searching for him by now," Treestar said. "They must be overcome with grief and concern! The discovery of his absence will only lead to anger. We must let Baladar know that we have him and how he came to be here. He must not think that we were the ones to steal him from under his nose!"

"Yes," Elsinestra said anxiously. "We must send word immediately. This boy is no ordinary human child. If I am correct, he will be sorely missed and it would be a great misfortune if we were to be blamed for the actions of another, particularly after the long history of cooperation that has existed between our two kingdoms. Acrimony now between the Pardathans and Lormarion would serve no one but the Dark Lord himself!" she asserted.

"You are absolutely correct, Elsinestra. I will see to it. Jerial will go. He is one of the best riders we have. Please, wife, compose a letter for him explaining how the boy ended up in our city. I will notify the stables to prepare a horse for him and provisions for the trip, and I will place it in the saddlebag myself. Elion, advise Jerial and organize an escort for him until he is past the plains. He must travel alone from then on. The message must reach Baladar as soon as possible and Jerial will ride as fast as the wind if left on his own."

"I will go at once." Upon reaching the door, he glanced back at his parents with a desperate look upon his face. "Please, mother, tell Baladar I meant the boy no harm. Make sure he knows that. If what we suspect is true, Baladar must be beside himself with concern by now. I pray he does not hold it against us."

What have I done? he thought to himself as he ran down the stairway. *I should be the one to carry the message to Baladar. It was I who brought the boy here to begin with. I must accept the blame by myself. If I do not appeal on my own behalf, they are likely not to believe our intentions. They will think it a ruse, a subterfuge. It is my responsibility, not Jerial's. I was the one who blundered here. I must make it right.*

By the time the young Prince reached the barracks, he knew what he had to do. His parents would be angry with him at first, he considered, but they would come to understand why he had to go himself. He brought this boy into Lormarion, into Seramour itself, the heart of the Elfin kingdom, and he was responsible for whatever happened now. He could not allow another to apologize for his actions.

Elion instructed the guards as to what had to be done, neglecting to tell them that his father requested that Jerial be the messenger. He simply told them that they were to accompany him until they reached the forest. He told them to gather the group and to wait for him by the platforms.

"Have everyone ready in thirty minutes. I will meet you there as soon as I can find Jerial. I must ask him something before we depart. Captain, do you know where he may be?" he asked.

"You will probably find him behind the Waverly Inn tossing horseshoes," the guard replied.

"Thank you. If my father should inquire as to my whereabouts, please tell him I went in search of Jerial," Elion said, not wishing to lie any more than he had to as he rushed out of the quarters. Yelling back over his shoulder he said, "Hurry now, thirty minutes, no more! We have no time to waste," and then he was gone.

Elion knew now that he would conveniently be "unable" to find Jerial, and that rather than waste any more precious time searching for him, he would be forced to take his place and carry the message to Baladar in his stead. By the time his parents found out, he would be well on his way back to Pardatha.

Chapter Twenty-five

Baladar left the comfort of his study, distraught and overwhelmed with concern. He was blessed with the responsibility of caring for the heir, and in so short a time he had already failed to live up to that responsibility. "I should never have left him here alone with that rogue in the castle. What was I thinking?"

He was distraught and frustrated. The boy had been there for merely six days, his teachers must be only just nearing Pardatha and Baladar was beside himself with worry. *Perhaps I should visit Calista again. She may know where he has gone.*

Just as quickly as it came to him, he disposed of that idea, remembering her last words to him and accepting that the task of locating Davmiran rested upon his shoulders. As he neared the main hallway, he espied an unfamiliar cat rolling head first all over a worn, green shawl on the floor. He loved animals, and at first, habit urged him to pet the feline, but he reminded himself of the pressing matters which required all of his attentions, and so he turned and headed down the stairway toward the doors, making a mental note to tell the housemaids to be more thorough in the future and not leave old garments lying around littering the floors.

I must go outside, sit outside for a while. There has to be some evidence remaining that will aid my search. He could not have just vanished into thin air.

Baladar emerged from the castle only to find himself staring at the paved courtyard, not really knowing where to begin. He walked to the Noban gate and surveyed the landscape beyond it. There were so many hoof marks, footprints and wagon wheel impressions in the soft ground alongside the roadway that he could not distinguish one from another. He did not even know if the boy was carried or dragged out of his house.

No one actually saw him depart, and Baladar had already discretely questioned anyone who he thought might have been in a position to witness a leave taking at that moment in time. But, as his guard related to him, the castle garrison was reluctant to observe the arrogant young lord's departure after the events of the previous evening. They would not take it upon themselves to insult a foreign Lord and countermand the direct orders Kettin gave them the previous evening. None save a few even knew of the boy's existence, which made Baladar's inquiries more difficult.

The nurses saw nothing, as they retired early the previous evening, having no idea that anything untoward had even occurred concerning the visiting Duke's son. Dalek alas, was dead and whatever knowledge he may have gained, died with him. No one else knew the young man was in the castle! In his attempt to protect the boy, Baladar had possibly sealed his doom and with it the future of the entire world.

He left the path beyond the gate and wandered into the tall grass, looking for a sign, looking for anything that might shed some light upon the disappearance of the boy. To the east, he had noticed fresh tracks which could only have been the marks left by Kettin and his band of "thieves" as they stole away, leaving only death and disaster behind them.

Baladar regretted the very moment he saw that young nobleman's face, the arrogant son of the Duke of Talamar. He knew it meant trouble, finding him in his home, interrupting his important work, just when he was beginning to believe that the encroaching darkness could be stopped, that there was hope for the world, his world and the one that his beloved wife cherished so much. He had failed them all!

What hurt him the deepest was that he failed Briland. He believed that if he could help forestall or prevent the death of a single Lalas, then his wife's life work would be redeemed. She was taken so soon, before they had a chance to grow old together, before they had the time to relax in each other's love. Their lives were always filled with commitments and responsibilities. Rarely could they just spend time in each other's arms, enjoying only the companionship and love they so deeply felt for one another.

Baladar began this descent into depression again, this free fall from the edge once more, after having spent so many agonizing days and nights learning to overcome it. He felt it overtaking him, the hollow feeling, the all-encompassing sadness, and he could do nothing to prevent it. The appearance of the boy, of the heir of legend, provided him with a purpose once again. The future beckoned to him, it seemed to call him directly by his name, and he welcomed the challenge of teaching the boy and of taking part in the future struggle that would inevitably take place, that was already taking place all over the land. But, as he searched the tall grasses for a clue as to the whereabouts of Davmiran, he felt his heart breaking once again.

Briland. Briland. What have I done? I have lost the two people most dear and most important to me. What must I do now to redeem myself? I fear I cannot go on like this. If only I can find a sign, some reason to believe that the boy is alive still, then I can still hope, but how could a defenseless boy, invisible to all human kind by my own doing, and unconscious, unaware of the very world around him, how could this helpless child survive? I have not only let him be stolen right from under me, I may have killed him just as if I thrust a blade through his heart myself!

There were no words to express the pain that he felt at that moment, but the world was becoming accustomed to such anguish and despondency, and each man or woman who succumbed fed the fires of the black hope that raged within the heart of Colton dar Agonthea, a cold, barren, evil hope for the dissolution of the world, for the end of the trees and verily the end of life itself.

During his reverie, he had wandered westward beyond the road. Baladar was so overcome with despair that he almost walked by without noticing the flattened turf at his feet. He glanced downward and he saw what appeared to be a path of broken blades of grass leading to the edge of the woods. Something had been dragged from here to there and he bent cautiously to examine the marks that were left. His heart skipped a beat as he immediately sensed that this could be the evidence he was searching for. But, how could he be sure?

As he looked more closely, he saw the small footprints of a child perhaps, or an Elf in the soft soil beneath the grass. Someone had surely been there recently and whomever it was pulled something through the tall grass. Baladar was down on his hands and knees searching the area for a sure sign of Davmiran, a piece of cloth, a lost shoe, a button or a clasp; something that would certify that he was there.

He followed the path toward the forest and he became more and more convinced that whoever was there had discovered the prostrate boy and spirited him away into the woods by dragging him across the field. The footprints were made by a soft soled shoe, not the boot of a soldier. And although they were small in size, they were deep and solidly planted. A child could not have carried the boy that long a distance. It must have been an Elf or a Dwarf. Neither race frequented these areas and Baladar wondered immediately what could have brought one to these woods just in time to find Davmiran lying in the tall reeds.

Baladar walked close to the fringe of trees edging the field.

Crouching in order to see if any other prints joined the ones he had already observed, he saw something that instantaneously swelled his heart with joy immeasurable; the woven bracelet that Davmiran was wearing when Baladar first examined him was lying on the ground in plain sight! He picked it up tenderly and placed it safely in his pocket.

So! The tale has not ended here. He lifted his head and laughed aloud.

Strange coincidences seemed to follow the charmed youth around, Baladar ruminated, and he seriously contemplated the possibility that it was mere chance that brought a distant visitor to these parts at such an opportune moment. He quickly relinquished that idea in favor of one that seemed to govern most circumstances surrounding the heir, both in legend and in life; fate led the stranger here at precisely the correct hour, on exactly the correct day, in order to rescue the boy from certain death.

The fabric wove of its own will. And Baladar realized almost simultaneously, that only a person of another race, an Elf or a Dwarf or, the First forbid, a Troll, would have been able to see him, now that he was certain it was the boy's impression he was tracking in the grass. The spell that he cast only made Davmiran invisible to humans! That would explain why he was abandoned so close to the gates of the city and why he was so soon forgotten by those whose purpose was to apprehend him in the first place. The two questions that Baladar chose not to grapple with during the midst of these other issues were how did Kettin know that the boy was in Pardatha, and on whose behalf did he attempt to kidnap him. The contemplation of those would have to wait for another time and another day.

As he examined the tracks more closely, he became convinced that the footprints definitely did not belong to a Troll. They were too small and light, and besides, Trolls never wore shoes upon their calloused feet. If it had been a Troll's footprint, he would have seen the clumsy scuff marks of a six toed beast, not the cautious signature of a clearly intelligent observer. A Dwarf's boots would have been heavier and broader, metal soled like a shod horse.

The marks would have been closer together and deeper still, as the dwarves had strong and short legs, and never wore soft shoes. Baladar knew he had to be careful not to impose his hopes upon the circumstances. Yet, his reasoning seemed accurate, and although he wished with all his heart that it was an Elf who found Davmiran, he also believed that, after examining the evidence, it was the most reasonable conclusion to draw.

"Perhaps the spark of hope remains lit still," he said aloud.

If the boy had to disappear at all, Baladar reasoned, he preferred that he ended up in the able hands of an Elf. The Elves were a good and noble race, and although they kept their distance from the world of men, they served the light without compromise. Their love of the trees was second to none and they would never do anything to harm one of the Chosen, or one such as Davmiran!

Baladar was growing more confident with each passing moment, and the depression that threatened to cripple him just a short while ago was once more placed in abeyance and forced below the surface. He reasoned that if an Elf discovered this unusual boy, he would have attempted to aid him, and when he could not awaken him himself, he would have gone in search of help. An Elf would not have approached the gates of Pardatha on his own under these circumstances. How could he have known that the boy was not ejected intentionally from the castle, but kidnaped by a rogue? It would have been foolish of him to return the unconscious youth to a city where it appeared he was clearly unwanted.

To the north was Crispen and to the south lay Lormarion. Those were the two nearby kingdoms wherein the Elves thrived in numbers, where the Elfin civilizations matured and grew in wealth and stature. The people of the northern Elfin nations rarely traveled out of their own realms. It was highly unlikely that one of their kind would have been so far south for any reason whatsoever. They had little in common with their mountain and southern kin, and they rarely interacted these days as far as he knew.

Baladar rejoiced in his conclusions, as he found either choice to be far better than he could have dreamed about just a short while earlier. He was already formulating a plan of action that he would initiate upon his return to the castle. He would contact Treestar, the King of the Southern Elves, a man he had met once many tiels ago. Although of different races, he and Treestar had much in common, he remembered. The two kingdoms had always respected one another's differences and had remained friends and allies for centuries, although contact between them was infrequent.

He would also send inquiries to Bristar, the leader of the northern clans, a more reclusive and secretive Elf, less trusting than his southern brother if the tales he had heard were accurate. A message would go out to Eleutheria as well, that distant mountain kingdom buried in snow all the year long, in the remote event that perhaps they had some knowledge that would assist him now.

He could not risk ignoring a single possibility, no matter how unlikely. But, he now had no doubt that he would locate the boy yet, and then he could arrange for his return to Pardatha. His schooling would have to begin a bit later than he had planned, but it would begin! He realized that he was taking a lot for granted here, that he was assuming much and that he really knew very little. But he was not plagued by concern any longer. His fear and discouragement gave way to promise, and in his heart of hearts he knew that Davmiran was safe.

From the depths of despair to the dizzying heights of hope unencumbered! I am like a child at the window of a sweet shop, not knowing whether the treats will be available to me or locked away forever behind an impenetrable door. I would have thought that I would have learned some lessons by now! Briland, forgive me. Oh, to be human, all too human.

Purposefully he made his way back to the castle, calculating his next moves while he walked down the very path created by the boy's untimely departure.

Chapter Twenty-six

Robyn rode Kraft with a new determination, crouching low on his back and anxious to cross the hills of Delphan as quickly as possible. Horse and rider were as one, streaking over the knolls, deftly evading the low growing brush and rocky protuberances. Robyn wanted to reach the flat clearing south of the hills by the second day. He planned to camp just beyond the southernmost rise and head for Pardatha early in the morning of the third. He had overcome the horrible feelings that had invaded his body and soul, and he was now ready and eager to reach his destination. If there was anything that he could do to prevent the death of another of the great trees, he would do it.

As he rode, he thought back on the years he spent perfecting his art, learning all that he could in anticipation of the days ahead. He always knew that he would play a part in the events that would mold the future, and his father made certain that nothing interfered with his development. He, too, recognized his son's special role and always attempted to provide him with an environment wherein he could develop unhindered. They both paid the price of those choices, though now Robyn knew that all the sacrifice was necessary and had only served to make him stronger.

He could not allow the trees to perish, not just his own Promanthea, but all the rest as well! The planet would shrivel up and die without the Lalas. If the boy he was called upon to train was the boy of legend, then it would be possible to alter the recent course of history if he prepared him properly, if he guided him well, if he protected him along the way. Baladar beckoned and Robyn would fulfill his obligation gladly. He rode and rode, head down, legs tight to Kraft's side, horse and rider bolting through the hills at a death defying pace.

By nightfall, he had covered more ground than even he had expected and although he was tired, he felt better as he neared his destination. Robyn dismounted and sat down behind a rather large hillock that afforded him shelter from the night winds that swept across the hills. Kraft remained close by, nibbling on the scattered clumps of grass that sprouted haphazardly all around.

Animals took care of their needs simply and instinctively, and Kraft was no different in that respect. He would eat until he was full and rest until he was refreshed. Robyn, on the other hand, was a bit more complicated. He was a well disciplined wielder of the earth magic, but he was also highly emotional and moved by passions and feelings. His sensitivity is what made him the unique individual that he was. It enhanced his power and allowed him to intuit much about his enemies and his allies, and it put him in touch with the pain and suffering as well as the pleasure and joy of the earth. He could feel death approaching and that always troubled him, and he was moved as well by the hatching of a bird, or even by the emergence of a new blade of grass.

His awareness came with a price and Promanthea had taught him how to deal with the flood of emotions that engulfed him daily. The Lalas taught his Chosen how to assimilate the movements and changes in the earth, and how to convert the raw energy created into a tool of power. He also instructed him in the methods of calming the storms, easing the transitions resulting from growth and movement as well as from death and disintegration.

Robyn became a master at manipulating the forces of nature in a positive way. He was incapable of abusing his understanding by aiding the side of darkness. Although he understood that death was a necessary part of life, he believed that it should come naturally and that no one had the right to take it from someone or something, unless it was in self defense. He was more than capable of inflicting harm on another if that person threatened the balance that he intuitively felt in all living things, and the one power that threatened it the most was Colton dar Agonthea, the Great Destroyer.

Robyn did not need to think about Colton to know that he had to be stopped. He felt it in his heart. He felt the wrongness of him, the evil that emanated from all of his actions and the negativity in all that he did and stood for, and Robyn was ready to begin the process of stopping him, a process that he knew he could not complete alone. The "calling" renewed his hope.

He yearned for the day to come, the moment when he could put all of his years of learning and training into play, into the quest for the First, for the Gem of Eternity, for the key to the death of the trees and the means of halting the disintegration that had accelerated in the past few tiels and that was now spiraling almost out of control. And that day, that longed for day, was fast approaching.

As soon as he closed his eyes, he was asleep.

The morning brought with it a strong northeast wind and a cloud strewn sky. The air was heavier, and Robyn sensed something foreign, almost alien in the breeze. It troubled him and urged him onward. Yet, he kept feeling as if he was traveling away from danger, not into it. He mounted Kraft once again and together they made their way south, hoping to ride without interruption until night approached once more and the Delphan hills were fully behind them. But, this nagging sense would not leave him and he could not ignore it. As he rode, Robyn attempted to analyze the emotions and to understand the signs. It felt to him as if Promanthea was beckoning to him, and yet he would have surely known for certain if that had been the case.

He was not going to allow anything to delay his journey now. By tomorrow evening he would be at the gates of Pardatha, or so he hoped. As the afternoon approached, the feeling was growing stronger and stronger and he was barely able to think about anything else. He decided to stop for a short while, sit peacefully and try to figure out what was happening. Once on the ground, he pressed his hands to the earth, attempting to learn from the soil what he was unable to decipher from the air. And then it came to him quickly. His father was trying to get a message to him and he was using the branch that Promanthea had given him. Now he understood why he kept feeling that his tree was beckoning in some way.

Robyn closed his eyes and hummed a deep, melodious hum that normally would bring him into harmony with his own tree, but instead he focused upon the polished token that he had given to his father. He knew the message must be urgent or the Baron would not have tried to reach him. He had informed his father about how incredibly tiring the process was for him and how much energy it required. Yet he beckoned nevertheless and so Robyn hurried to answer the call. Soon, he could almost see the face of the man who was contacting him. The image was blurry, but in his mind's eye it steadily grew clearer.

The voice came to him from within and was not audible to anyone or thing but Robyn.

Robyn? Robyn? Can you hear me, son?

Yes, I am here. I can hear you.

The mountain Trolls are on the march south. My scouts reported to me a short while ago. A massive army has descended from their city of Toth, in the hills, armed to the teeth. They carry the banners of Colton amidst their own. They are not marching to Concordia, but toward the Thorndars. I can only suspect that they are heading to Pardatha, or thereabouts. I have sent scouts to track them and report back to me on their progress.

Robyn took a moment to ponder this new and disturbing information.

The Baron, too, paused for a moment and then he asked, *Are you safe, my son?*

Yes, father, I am well. I have made good time, and I will arrive at my destination tomorrow sometime. Have no fear for me. All is well. Robyn was weakening swiftly from the contact, but he needed desperately to ask one question. *Did you know that another tree had died?*

Yes, Robyn, we all felt it. I thank the First it was not yours. I was unsure until this moment. The skies have not yet cleared of the storm clouds that followed upon its demise. Neither has the Sirceloc ceased to churn. But, we carry on. We keep our heads up, and pray for the day when the trees will sprout anew. Our hopes and prayers are with you, too, my son.

I must break this off, father. I must preserve my strength. Do not give in to the darkness. Allow it not to reach your heart. Be forever strong. I love you! he said and then he collapsed to the earth.

Robyn awoke sometime later to the feeling of Kraft's cold nose nuzzling him. He was tired and his head was aching, but he knew that he would recover soon enough. His loyal horse was persistent and would not allow him to fall back asleep. That he recognized, and he was instantly angry with himself for succumbing to his drowsiness to begin with.

The information that his father imparted to him was disturbing. If the Trolls were marching, then others must be mobilizing too. Colton was on the move and the timing of these events could not be coincidental. He had to reach Pardatha and warn them. He had to reach the heir!

Robyn forced himself to rise and climb atop Kraft once more. There was now a new danger driving him forward. The luxury of time, though scant even in the beginning, was now gone completely. He would not be able to rest again until he was within the gates of Pardatha at Baladar's side.

Chapter Twenty-seven

There was great turmoil on the ground below her window. She could hear the commotion all around her, from within the fortress and from without. Massive clouds of billowing black smoke rose from the deep tunnel domes into the air, darkening it and making the early morning seem like dusk. The underground air vents were spewing out all manner of pollution, for underneath them the engines of war were working at a mind blurring speed. The very stones of Sedahar vibrated incessantly, pulsing with power as if alive.

Peering out of the small window, Trialla was able to see row upon row of the Dark Lord's minions gathering in the fields beneath her tower room. Something serious was happening and she wanted to know what. She stuck her crooked nose through the slats covering the single opening in the side of the wall, and then she peered down to the left as far as she was able to see. Everywhere her vision could reach she saw the troops assembling. There were thousands of Orcs; great, hairless animals with black, beady eyes and dark scaly skin, all fronted by fat bellies that made them appear as if they were leaning forward as they walked. Marching to the beat of a heavy drum, shaking the ground with each step, they gathered behind a group of at least twenty, one-eyed giants the height of each being four times that of the Orcs. The monstrous creatures carried clubs tipped with metal spikes, and giant war hammers hung from belts that looked like raw animal entrails. Craning her neck to look to the right, she was astonished at how far the hordes of fighters stretched. The grounds surrounding Sedahar were teeming with activity in every direction. The ground looked like a seething mass of black insects, swarming purposefully toward their queen.

Trialla screeched with glee and she jumped up and down with excitement at the assembly below. "Let me out of here! Let me go with you! I can help too. Please, someone, release me!"

Although she screamed as loud as she could, her words were drowned out by the din created by the activity below. A heavy pounding on the earth that actually sent vibrations up even to her prison cell, caused her to look toward the far side of the plain. A massive group of Trolls, ugly and huge, beat upon the ground with their clubs, chanting something in a cryptic, guttural language she could not understand. There must have been five hundred of them, each carrying a large stick as big as the trunk of a small tree with a spiked ball attached to the end of a chain hanging from it. Some had knives in their belts, while others had axes and hammers.

Ogres, covered with studded black hides and even larger than the Orcs, converged behind them, occasionally thrashing their hated cousins with their clubs, making sure the smaller and weaker Orcs kept their distance. They snorted and belched, laughing uncontrollably at times, with their hideous faces contorted in grotesque smiles, unable to control their excitement. Every once in a while one would strike another unsuspecting companion a serious blow and then lean back upon his fat heels and cackle in glee.

The troops were working themselves into a blood frenzy and they had not even departed for the north. If not for the presence of their master, they would have turned upon one another soon enough, and an unstoppable slaughter would have ensued. But, amidst all of the groups rose Colton's banner, a fiery red sun on a stark, black background, unifying all the disparate combatants and binding them with fear and hideous promises.

There were other creatures Trialla could not identify: Green, slimy human-like things with bulging eyes and packs strapped to their backs which caused them to bend over under the weight. For every fifty of these, there was one guard atop a horselike animal, though the beast was stouter than a common horse and hairless. The riders smacked their whips and kept their captives in line, riding up and down their ranks, not hesitating to mete out punishment for sluggishness or reluctance.

Great pig-like beasts pulled wagons full of supplies, each ridden by a grotesque aberration of nature, a being with three arms, one protruding from the middle of its chest allowing it to hold the reins and still have two arms free. Battalions of tall, thin archers, more human than the rest, lined up behind an even taller leader, thin as a rail, skeletal even, who carried a long bow across his back, and a satchel filled with arrows tipped in black.

Trialla's one remaining hawk-like eye gleefully took in everyone and everything. Horns were sounding and drums were beating in a tumultuous cacophony of sounds, and in the midst of the seeming turmoil sat Colton dar Agonthea, Lord of Darkness, Emperor of Evil, Death Bringer and Vanguard of Dissolution, atop his prancing, silver steed Necro, majestically gazing from left to right and turning his horse in a tight circle, observing with satisfaction all the aspects of the assemblage. The seeming chaos was evolving into an organized machine, clearly capable of wreaking havoc upon whatever stood in its path, and it was not even nearly complete! Additional groups were forming all around the main entourage, raising banners and chanting in various tongues.

As Colton's cold, black eyes looked upon specific groups of fighters, they would immediately fall to the ground and bow down prostrate, foreheads to earth, in total silence until he lifted his red gloved hand. They would then let out a resounding cheer, weapons banging into the hard earth or clashing against one another, in an effort to make the loudest noise and salute their master with their frenzied support. Colton let his regal and domineering gaze move from company to company, thus honoring each and every unit and receiving their homage in return.

The reverence which the masses of warriors heaped upon their leader was total, and each and every participant, whether man or beast, was prepared and eager to begin its march toward total annihilation if that was what was in store. Their mindless energy was being focused upon one objective, and Colton was directing it with the precision of the master that he was.

Colton had spent centuries preparing for this moment and now it was finally upon him. He was seething with satisfaction, knowing now where he would strike first by virtue of the witch's discovery. Once the heir was captured, it was only a matter of time before the entire world would fall to his advances. The end was in sight and he could barely contain himself. He could almost taste the final victory, almost visualize the collapse, the slide into oblivion, the great dissolution. The Lalas were weak already, almost incapable of preventing his onslaught once the boy was under his control. He had come so close one time before, only to watch him slip through his hands at the very last moment. But not this time. Nothing could stop him now!

Sedahar itself had taken on an ominous hue, changing dramatically with its master's mood. The spires topping the towers appeared more pointed and deadlier, the doorways like hungry, gaping mouths and the foundation stone dripped with a reddish perspiration oozing from its seams under the hot sun.

Trialla had worked herself into a furor, frustrated by her imprisonment and unable to accept being left behind, and she was willing to risk anything at this point to be heard.

"Let me out!" she screeched. "I belong with you! I found the boy! Let me out of here! Please, you cannot leave me behind," she wailed, but no one could hear.

With what power she could still muster, she conjured a small ball of fire in the corner of her cell, nearest to the opening in the wall. Using her fist, she smashed the stool that was her single piece of furniture and then she tossed the broken bits of wood into the flame.

Someone below will see the smoke, and let me out, she hoped with delirious desperation, her twisted mind carelessly miscalculating the risks and thoroughly misjudging her captor. *He has forgotten that I am up here with all that is happening. This will remind him and he will send someone to release me. I will ride to Pardatha by his side! I will be his Queen!*

If no one noticed the smoke and flames, she might very well burn in her own fire and die by her own hand. But she could not conceive of the possibility that Colton would let that happen, after all that she had done for him. She was the one who found the heir! Trialla, no one else. At that moment, the chance she took was worth it, for life had no further meaning for her if Colton left her behind. She would rather be dead than discarded and forgotten again.

The fire was building quickly as the dry straw burst into flame, and the wood promptly followed suit. She added to the fire her worn blanket and whatever other scraps she could hastily gather that would burn brightly and with as much smoke as possible.

Shortly, the smoke was surging out of the window with considerable velocity, and the flames were licking the sides of the room, leaping from the one opening in bursts of red light.

He will soon see that I am in danger up here and then he will send someone to rescue me. She pressed against the doorway and covered her nose and mouth with her filthy shawl. She was coughing violently now as the room was filling with acrid fumes.

"Any moment now. He will see me," she spoke aloud as she clasped the bars of the window and burned her hands from the heat. She did not even feel the pain; she was too caught up in her longing and delusions.

Some of them are looking this way. He will be next, she thought expectantly, not realizing that her fingers were scorched and the hem of her gown was smoldering.

The fire could now be clearly observed from below, as the tall turret stood out starkly against the cloudy sky. She watched in anxious anticipation and waited for her Lord to notice her peril. A crooked smile crossed her lips as Colton gazed from his vantage point atop Necro at the high tower window above.

Finally! He will see me now! Her eye was locked upon Colton in rabid expectation of his redeeming glance when he simply bent his head back and laughed a diabolic laugh. He briefly caught her eye with his own and held her gaze for just an instant, and her very being was sundered. She had been betrayed. To Trialla's outrage and dismay, he spurred his horse slightly and Necro leapt forward, the troops making way for him as quickly as possible.

Colton rode away from the castle, not bothering to even look back, howling with delight as he went to examine the contingent of ebon magicians gathering at the rear of the massed army. His enhanced sense of hearing discerned the pathetic screams of the old woman as she burned to death in her cramped cell, and he enjoyed the harrowing sounds immensely. He particularly relished the moment she realized that he was not interested in her fate, and then the final, deranged howl of recognition the old witch released from the depths of her disfigured soul.

They are all fools, these humans. Even those with power, no matter how strong or meager. I have no more need for you, witch!

Soon, all that was left of Trialla the Sorceress, was a smoldering pile of ashes on a soiled floor in a dismal cell high in the tower of castle Sedahar.

This is shaping up to be a wonderful day, he thought, as he rode to greet the necromancers who had assembled to pay tribute to their father and master.

Colton's prized possessions, his scarlet sorcerers, all bowed low, prostrating themselves before him, with their crimson capes covering them from head to toe and not daring to look at Colton until he gave them permission. This group of thirteen was his special weapon, trained and nurtured almost from birth by Colton himself. Next to each one stood a Valkor, enormous next to the humans, with its eyes shielded and its body harnessed.

The sorcerers would travel behind the troops atop the beasts, not wasting their power until the back of the enemy was broken and it was time for the final advance. His red mages would enter the castle keep just before he would, preparing all who were left alive inside for Colton's arrival. It would be a beautiful experience, and he could barely contain his excitement. With these images fresh in his mind he turned away from this group, sat regally atop his horse and addressed the entire mass of warriors surrounding him.

"In one hour, we will ride to Pardatha!" he shouted, his black blade unsheathed now and raised high in the air.

The thousands gathered around him responded by stomping their feet, banging their shields, whistling, yelling, making as much noise as they could muster and causing the very hills around them to echo with the terrifying sound.

When they settled down, he said, "Our victory there will mark the beginning of the war that will bring us salvation!"

Again, the troops burst into cheers.

"Once we have begun our advance, let no creature stand in our way! Tomorrow belongs to us!" Colton proclaimed with supreme confidence, though what he really meant was that soon tomorrow would come no more.

He slid his sword back into the jeweled scabbard on his belt, pulled hard on Necro's reins causing the silver stallion to rear up and kick his front hooves in the air, and then he cantered off to the front of the savage multitude, more ready than ever before to lead his army northward.

Chapter Twenty-eight

Cairn propelled the raft through the placid water, still amazed at how calm the night was. The breeze barely ruffled his clothing and the water they were sailing upon was as still as if it was a small pond. The full moon lit up the sky, glaring off of the water and illuminating the dark, flowing liquid to the point of transparency. Voluminous, gloomy clouds hung overhead, barely moving but still obscuring the light at times, casting shadows of blackness over the entire landscape, only to have the reflected light burst through once again, shocking them with its intensity. Cairn was cautious all the while, trusting Tomas' intuition yet maintaining a vigilant watch nevertheless.

They had more than enough time to cross the lake, which would leave them at a point just south of Pardatha, situated on the other side of the narrow crest of the Thorndar mountains, just before the sun was due to rise. It would not take them more than another day's travel to reach the outskirts of the city once the threat of the water was behind them. Lake Tamaran was usually a formidable obstacle and it had protected the southern approach to Pardatha for centuries. Cairn was not yet ready to accept that their journey across would not be fraught with danger and difficulty. He was calmer than before and he had time to contemplate what lay ahead, but he remained alert nonetheless.

Certainly, his new found friend would be an unexpected surprise to Baladar, but once they met one another he was convinced that he would see the same goodness and power in the young man that Cairn perceived. He knew without a doubt that Tomas was meant to be with him when he entered Pardatha.

"Do you see the shoreline ahead?" he asked the boy after an unusually bright streak of moonlight defined the coast before them.

"Yes, I do. Is that where we are headed?" he responded.

"If we land near that spot, we will be within a few hundred yards of the entrance to the pass. When the sun rises, we should have no difficulty finding it," he commented.

A shrill sound pierced the silence of the evening, followed immediately by another and then another. The sky was splattered with shadows now, moving in circles above them, and the bright moonlight traced their images across the raft and across the water all around them. The Selgays were awake despite the darkness and they were aware of the travelers' presence upon the lake. Calyx growled defensively to himself and crouched low in the corner of the raft. Tomas looked up with a calm and unconcerned air. Cairn's skin prickled with fear and his mind quickly reviewed their options, few as they were.

"We must hurry. The birds are upon us!" he said as he urgently rowed the small craft ahead, the water being far too deep now to pole the transport forward. "It does not forebode well for us that they travel in a group. The Selgays are solitary hunters," he worriedly reasoned. "What evil purpose could have united them now?" Cairn questioned grimly.

"They will not attack. They will only watch us until we are gone from their territory," the boy remarked, so sure of himself.

Cairn drew some comfort from Tomas' words, as they issued so confidently from his mouth.

"I hope you are correct, young man. I do not really know what we can do to defend ourselves if they should behave other than you predict," Cairn replied cautiously. "Why are they roused at all with the sun still hours from the horizon? I was led to believe that they never flew during the evening hours, and never in a group!" he said, not expecting an answer.

"They are chaperoning us across," the boy said with a strange certainty. "Did you not hear me before when I said that they feasted upon a battalion of Trolls just yesterday? Although they are ugly beasts and extremely dangerous, the Selgays do not serve the Dark Lord. They preserve the balance, they do not upset it. The Selgays will let us pass. They understand the necessity," he concluded.

"I have studied all of my life. The masters have taught me much," Cairn began. "But you have just made me realize something that no teacher was ever able to," he said seriously. "I should know better than to assume that all predators dangerous to man are evil as well. They protect their own realm as we do ours. I just never thought that they could distinguish between one trespasser and the next," he remarked, humbled by the boy's simple statements.

"They are not unlike all the rest of the beasts. Unless they are forced, compelled by threat of starvation or pain, they perceive in their own way what endangers the well being of the planet. They feel things much as we do, they just cannot reason," Tomas explained.

"Your wisdom is beyond your years, Tomas," Cairn said with

respect, his eyes never leaving the circling birds. "Ormachon has taught you well," Cairn commented respectfully.

"He has been a great friend and I am grateful to him for much," the boy said modestly. "Watch, Cairn. You will see. The birds will be our escort to the other shore," he concluded, and he continued to calmly observe the great Selgays as they soared in swooping circles overhead, seemingly directing them with his focused stare as they flew.

Cairn followed their guidance, not being able to ascertain exactly where they were heading now as the clouds were continuously thickening overhead. He hoped and prayed that Tomas was correct about the big birds and that they were not leading them to a place nearer to their own homes only to save them the trouble of carrying them in their talons this entire distance.

They swerved and dipped above them, subtly changing course, heading all the time for the dark shoreline ahead. And Cairn cautiously steered the small raft, following closely behind. As the water grew shallow, he was once more able to touch the bottom with the flat sided pole he held. Sensing that their journey was drawing to an end, he thrust more vigorously into the black depths and the raft leapt forward.

Cairn pushed the long pole into the soft mud as they approached the other shore, and he directed the raft to a clearing on the rocky beach that he would have been hard pressed to find on his own in this darkness. Their journey across was as eventless as Tomas had predicted and Cairn was grateful for that. By now, the Thorndars towered above them, their sheer slopes extending in places straight down into the depths of the water, making their approach to the beach a difficult one to navigate. Calyx stood up and sniffed the air apprehensively, searching for danger ahead.

The great birds continued to circle the group, squawking and flapping their enormous wings until the wooden vehicle literally touched the shore, but leading them in all the while like a beacon of light. Then at once, as if their job was done and they were told they could leave, they circled the raft one final time, plunging so low that they nearly touched the tops of the travelers' heads, and then flew to their protected eyries in the vertical rock face and disappeared.

Cairn saw that Tomas seemed to salute them as they passed by, raising his palm upward to the night sky. In their wake, the Selgays created a veritable maelstrom, their wings beating so hard and fast that the water churned and frothed, and they had to hold onto the floating structure in order to avoid being blown overboard.

Once ashore, Cairn jumped from the raft onto the tiny piece of soft, sandy ground, with Calyx at his heels. Tomas calmly surveyed the area around them and then he too stepped to the ground. Together, they pulled the raft onto the shore as far as they were able to, gathered their few belongings and started to walk toward the rocks ahead.

"If I am correct," Cairn began, "the opening to the pass should be directly in front of us. The sandy beachhead is a dead giveaway to the location, but in the past, the Selgays made the approach during the day almost impossible. Few ventured here except in the dark of night, and finding this one spot without light has never been easy. The full moon helped me greatly tonight, as did the bird's 'permission' and more important, their guidance."

"I see the opening!" Tomas said animatedly, as he started to run to see if in fact he was correct.

At times he was much like a boy of fourteen and at others he seemed ageless. When he reached what appeared to be the entrance to the pass, he turned and called back, "I found it! Here, come over here. It's narrow, but we will have no trouble walking through."

The sun was just poking it's head over the far horizon and casting an indirect light over everything. By the time Cairn reached the opening with Calyx close behind, Tomas had bounded between the high, rock walls, exhibiting a great deal more enthusiasm now for the final leg of the journey than he had previously.

"Wait for us!" Cairn shouted ahead, having lost sight of the boy around the first bend in the rock.

"Don't worry. I am right in front of you. I won't go far," he replied, rushing along.

The scholar and the Moulant walked briskly forward, attempting to reach Tomas before he turned another bend. Suddenly, Calyx growled angrily and the hair on his back rose in response. Directly in front of them, to his utter dismay, Cairn saw Tomas on the ground, and there was a creature somewhat larger than a Dwarf but smaller than a grown human, with a short black beard dirtying its face above its leather jerkin, standing over him menacingly, pointing a sharpened stone dagger at his throat.

"Don't come any closer!" he said to Cairn, his green eyes darting back and forth between Tomas, Cairn and Calyx. "I do not want to hurt anyone. What are you doing here? No one ever comes here!" he exclaimed, staring at Calyx, his eyes wide with fear.

"Just put the knife down. We mean you no harm. I am Cairn of Thermaye. This is my friend Calyx and the one you are holding captive is Tomas," he said pointing first to the big cat and then to the lad lying uncomfortably on the earth, as he moved very slowly forward.

Tomas seemed unafraid, but he remained still nonetheless.

"We are on our way to Pardatha. This is the only route I know through these cliffs. Please, leave the boy alone. We only wish to pass peacefully," Cairn continued, his voice calm and soothing.

The creature seemed less nervous now that Cairn explained their presence, but he still held the blade much too close to Tomas' throat for Cairn's comfort.

Calyx growled a throaty growl from behind and the creature jumped, giving Tomas just enough time to roll out from under him and stand up. Before anyone could even take a single breath more, Calyx was atop the aggressor, pinning him down with his big paws, the dagger lying harmlessly now beside him.

To their great surprise, the little man began to cry uncontrollably saying, "Don't hurt me please! I didn't mean to scare you. I thought you were here to bring me back. They have been searching for me for days now, and I didn't know who you were. Your friend is short like they are and I thought he was one of them."

Cairn listened patiently to the frightened captive, when he realized that despite the beard, this was not a man but a young boy as well, and he was certainly a Dwarf, not a human or an Elf, which accounted for the beard at so young an age.

"Why are you here, sneaking up on innocent travelers? You are only a boy yourself," Cairn asked, admonishing him.

"I am Preston, and I am a Dwarf, but my father does not think that I am short enough. No one thinks that I am short enough, and they tell me that I cannot be pure of blood. Everyone makes fun of me, so I ran away. I have been living here for three days now and you are the first people I have seen," he said all in one breath.

Cairn motioned Calyx to back off a bit and he bent and picked up the knife lying at his side.

"How old are you, Preston?" Cairn asked.

"I am sixteen," he answered proudly. "And I know they must be out looking for me. My father will be very angry by now. But, I do not want to go back! I want to see the world and to be with people who don't tease me because I am too tall," he said defiantly.

"Well, I cannot speak for your father, but if you were my son I would want you back home as soon as possible. I am sure that he is consumed with worry by now," Cairn responded. "Where are you from, boy?" he asked.

"My full name is Preston Daggerfall, and my father is Brimgar Daggerfall of the Thorndar Daggerfalls. My home lies only a few hours from here, in the caves on the north side of the Scion cliffs. We have been living there for a hundred tiels," he said proudly.

"Well, Preston, I think you should go back home before you hurt someone, or someone hurts you. We have to be on our way and I am sorry, but we cannot spend any more time here talking," Cairn replied. "I am afraid that I cannot give you your blade back just yet, but I promise you that I will leave it on the path ahead and you can pick it up after we are gone," he said, as Tomas moved to his side.

"Do you want to come with us?" Tomas asked out of the blue, not bothering to consult with Cairn first.

The yellow-eyed scholar gazed at him stunned, not knowing what to say.

Tomas peered into Cairn's eyes with a look that said, *Do not look so fearful, I know what I am doing,* and Cairn kept a tight lip.

"Would you let me?" the boy responded. "I won't be any trouble, I promise," he eagerly responded.

"Yes, we will let you. Besides, I would like to have someone around my age to travel with," Tomas said honestly. "You are only just a bit older than I am," he remarked.

Cairn looked at Preston and said, "Let me talk to my friend here, first, if you would," and he put his arm around Tomas' shoulder and turned him away from the young Dwarf, whispering in his ear. "This boy is a runaway. Tomas, you should have conferred with me before you invited him to join us. His father will be searching high and low for him," Cairn said somewhat annoyed. "We cannot afford to have our progress impeded by a distraught father searching for his missing son," Cairn commented.

"I'm sorry. I wasn't thinking about those things. All I know is that he belongs with us. Some things are meant to be, and even though I should have talked to you first, I just felt that he should come with us to Pardatha. His father can just as easily find him there as here," Tomas reasoned, perplexed by Cairn's initial inability to understand this.

"I imagine you are correct about that at least. Dwarves have always been welcome in Pardatha, but what makes you think he should go with us?" Cairn asked, still unsure.

"I am sorry for being so unclear. I do not always understand myself why things feel right or wrong to me, but I just know that we should not leave him here alone. He reminds me of myself not very long ago and you helped me. I wanted to help him," Tomas responded, once more exhibiting a maturity far beyond his years.

"That was very kind of you," Cairn replied, somewhat ashamed of himself for ever thinking of abandoning the young Dwarf. "I am prepared to have him travel with us to the city, but we must contact his family once we get there, and he needs to know that. We cannot betray him later. You must tell him now that those are the conditions and then let him choose if he still wishes to come with us," Cairn said with finality.

Tomas happily agreed with Cairn's request.

The young, green-eyed human walked over to the boy who sat waiting expectantly for a decision and said, "You are going to have to let your father know where you are once we arrive. Those are the conditions and if you agree to them, then you can join our party."

Tomas spoke like a true statesman. Preston thought for a brief moment, and then replied, "All right then. It's a deal. I agree to send word to my father after we get to Pardatha. I've never been to Pardatha," he said excitedly. "Let me get my things together. It will only take a minute," Preston declared, and he rushed off ahead without waiting for another response.

"I hope you know what you are doing, Tomas!" Cairn said fondly but quite sternly as the three of them started down the path. He had never truly doubted the boy's intuition from the onset of this encounter.

This is becoming an interesting group, Cairn chuckled to himself, thinking about how unusual this all was for him, the solitary philosopher. He could not wait to see Baladar's reaction to his arrival now, accompanied as he was by his two new wards and Calyx. *He is expecting a serious cleric, someone who would instruct the heir in the ways of contemplation and reason. I hope I do not disappoint him too greatly!* Cairn laughed, comfortable with the choices he had made upon this journey, and more eager than ever to reach the city.

Chapter Twenty-nine

The Tammell hills were stark and barren. After Filaree and Cameron dragged themselves out of the woods, they collapsed, exhausted upon the ground. Cameron quickly stood up, brushing himself off as if he was covered with insects, and he refused to sit again.

"I would rather stand right now, my Lady, if you do not mind. The thought of getting that close to the soil does not appeal to me just at this moment," he said without being questioned.

"Do what you will, Cameron, but we are safe for now. I must say, we did come close to learning more about trees and foliage than I ever really cared to know," she joked in an attempt to lighten the mood.

"I am sorry that I cannot share your mirth my Lady, but I still feel as if I have things crawling all over me. I think that until I bathe in a proper bath, inside a proper home, I will feel the same. How could I ever have fallen asleep? What spell was cast upon me, do you know?" he asked hoping for some explanation.

"Not exactly, but they surely were trying to claim you for their own. You still look a little green, to be perfectly honest," she said with a chuckle, concealing her real concern that in fact his skin was still quite green as were what used to be the whites of his eyes.

"I do not find your humor funny, Mistress D'Avalain," he replied sheepishly, embarrassed by her levity. "Perhaps if it was you who woke to find yourself tangled in serpents made of grass and twigs you would not be joking so easily. Do I really look green still?" he asked, examining the back of his hand.

"Yes, Cameron, just a bit. But I am sure that it will fade with time. Besides, it matches your eyes," she remarked.

"Very funny, my Lady. I probably will not sleep again in fear of waking up looking like a tree!"

"Well, you can stand as long as you wish, but you are going to get tired. The trees are no longer our concern. We have left the forest, and the hills are all that remain between us and our destination. If we can cross them quickly without encountering anyone or thing to slow us down, we can be in Pardatha by tomorrow morning. I would not mind sleeping beyond the Tammells tonight. Just past the foothills lays a large lake, Everclear by name, the banks of which should provide us with a soft bed for our final evening on the road," she commented.

"I am ready to go whenever you are, mistress. Believe it or not, in a strange way my sleep in the Winding Woods refreshed me. I do not feel fatigued at all. The sun invigorates me," he said in a strange tone of voice.

Filaree looked carefully at her best friend and escort and she tried hard to ascertain if in fact he was all right. She could see nothing unusual in his appearance, except for the fact that he really was a bit pale and not his normal color. She assumed that it would pass as the day wore on.

"Good, Cameron. Let us go then," she said. "I can rest atop Nico. I would rather be mounted and on the move than reposing here anyway," she commented, and then she leapt on Nico's back.

Cameron climbed on Trojan and they were off, with Filaree leading the way. She carefully maneuvered the mare around the uneven terrain, avoiding the scattered holes that could easily catch her horse's ankle. The last thing either of them wanted now was a lame horse. Picking up speed, she cantered through the low brush, and then they ascended a steep hill that rose before them. They rode in relative peace for an hour or so, making good progress across the hills. Few words were exchanged, and both riders occupied their thoughts with the previous events of the day.

Filaree's only real concern was a potential encounter with the Wood Trolls that inhabited the hills. They were very reclusive creatures, preferring to be left alone to laze around and eat, rather than fight. But, if someone or something invaded their territory, they were capable of mustering their energy and going on the attack. They needed captives to help them gather their food as they despised having to work in the hot sun, and in addition their vision was not very good. Therefore, they enjoyed the rare wanderer who lost his way in the hills, trapping him and binding him with chains like an angry dog.

It was a singular day when someone escaped the Wood Trolls once caught. They coveted their prisoners and jealously guarded them from each other. Yet they flaunted their ability to sit back and do nothing while their slaves searched the hills for food. It was not a pleasant prospect as far as Filaree was concerned. But she was not going to be fooled by their trickery and fall unsuspecting into one of their traps.

She kept her eyes open and her wits about her as she rode. Water frightened them immensely, and they never ventured close to the shores of the lake. No Trolls could swim, least of all the Wood Trolls of the Tammell hills. They were too fat, and they avoided the water like they did encounters with the Dwarves whom they hated passionately.

"Let's pick up the pace while we can, Cameron. The ground here is free of brambles and we can make some good time here without much risk," Filaree said as she coaxed Nico into a gallop.

Cameron followed closely behind her, not wishing any more than she did to be left alone in these parts.

After a few more hours of uneventful riding, they spotted a grove of Perridon trees in the distance, short and thick, and Filaree headed for them hoping to rest the horses for a minute or two in the shade. Upon reaching them, she let Nico drop her head and graze and then she pulled out a flask of juice.

Passing it to Cameron, she said, "We have only a short way left to go. I am anxious to see the shores of Lake Everclear before us."

Cameron took a long swig from the flask and passed it back to Filaree.

"I wouldn't mind resting a bit longer, my Lady. My head is feeling very heavy," Cameron replied.

His voice sounded a bit distant. Filaree looked closely at her companion and became immediately alarmed.

"You look pale, Cameron. Our last experience must be taking its toll on you now," she said as she reached over and placed her hand on his cheek. "You are burning up with fever!" she exclaimed, and she jumped off Nico immediately in order to go to his side. "Here, I will help you down," she said, as she assisted Cameron to the ground.

His legs were unsteady and they crumpled under him, bringing him to the ground in an ungraceful heap. Filaree knelt beside him that same instant and propped his head up, and she began to feed him a bit more of the nectar she still held in her hand. His eyes were glazed over and she began to question whether something more than simple fatigue was bothering him.

"Do you feel anything other than tired, Cameron? You look pale and your eyes are glassy. Your head is burning," she commented with concern.

She did not bother to tell him again that his skin was even greener than before.

"I am all right. Really, just let me rest a minute," Cameron responded, but his voice was unsteady.

In the meanwhile, Trojan and Nico were taking advantage of the sweet grasses that grew beneath the trees, and they contentedly wandered around in search of more.

As Filaree bent to give Cameron another drink, a terrible odor reached her nostrils. She did not have to think for long in order to recognize the putrid smell of a filthy Wood Troll.

"Don't move," she whispered to Cameron and then she stealthily removed her long blade from its sheath. She used her body to block the vision of the beast watching from behind her.

Once the blade was bared, she turned with tremendous speed and stood ready to fight. An enormous Troll stood not ten feet from her with his club in hand, drooling with anticipation. It hesitated just one second too long and Filaree was upon it. As quick as lightening, she used the sharp tip of her sword to stick the beast twice in the stomach, causing it to shriek in a guttural voice and jump back a pace or two.

"Leave us alone and I will not harm you further," she said in a deep and serious voice.

The Troll was enraged at the hurt inflicted upon its fat belly, and it moved forward with an unexpected speed. But Filaree was ready, and she spun off to the left, turning and slicing the beast behind its right arm and eliciting another angry and hurt growl. The large animal saw Cameron lying on the ground and he chose to go after the easier prey, while still trying to avoid another stick from the one with the sword. But, once again she was too quick for it. Tapping the brute on the back with the flat of her sword, she caused it to turn momentarily as she maneuvered herself in front of it. Then she thrust her blade upward with both of her hands until it was directly under its chin. The beast was so tall that she was practically holding her sword vertically.

"Do not move another inch, or I will drive this blade home!" she said sternly.

The Troll roared in anger, but held its ground. Filaree saw the wooden club in its right hand and she knew that just one hit from it would smash her skull to pieces.

"Drop the weapon!" she said.

The Troll hesitated and Filaree pushed the sharp tip of the sword into the soft skin of the Troll's neck.

"Drop it, I said. You won't get another warning," and this time, the big brute listened, letting go of its weapon heavily. Filaree used her boot to push it to the side.

Cameron was hardly moving all this time, and she was growing more and more concerned about his condition, wanting only to best this beast so that she could attend to him.

"We do not want any trouble here. We only wish to pass through. Leave us be and we will be on our way as soon as we remount."

The Troll was surprised by this young woman's temerity, and it could do nothing other than nod its big head slightly and carefully so as not to impale itself on the sword. Filaree retreated a pace, holding her blade in front of her now and aiming it at the soft belly of the beast.

"Back up, you!" she said, flicking the blade just a bit and causing the Troll to take a few cautious steps backward.

With her left hand, she reached and shook Cameron on the shoulder, while never taking her eyes from the intruder for an instant.

"Cameron! Wake up. You have to wake up," she repeated. He opened his eyes but he could barely speak. "You must get up. We have to gather the horses and ride out of here. Can you do it?" she asked.

"I think so. I am just very tired," he responded, and he sat up with difficulty. After shaking his head and attempting to clear it somewhat, he was able to get to his feet and feebly whistle for Trojan. The horse came to him immediately with Nico close behind. "I don't know if I can get up in the saddle," he admitted.

All the while, the big Troll was eyeing them and breathing heavily. Filaree was unsure if it wanted to run away or attack again.

"You must, Cameron," she insisted.

She reached back, grabbed Trojan's reins with her free hand and then signaled to the stallion to go down on its front knees. Cameron was able to drag himself onto the saddle, though he was positioned more astride the horse than seated, and Filaree let the reins loose.

"Move back now to that tree over there," she ordered the Troll, as she pointed to a Perridon in the near distance. "And, don't get any ideas. I'll run you through with this blade as soon as I would anyone else who comes upon us unawares," she said with meaning.

The Troll obeyed, not willing to test the nettle of this upstart maiden. Cameron was barely conscious, and she was terribly concerned that he was going to slip from the horse. She pulled her belt from around her waist and secured Cameron to the pommel of the saddle with it, looping it around and through his own belt and then pulling it taught. Finally, she leapt onto Nico's back and reached for the reins hanging in front of Trojan.

"We are going to ride out of here now and I do not expect to see you follow us," she warned it as she urged Nico forward. "I am as quick with a bow as I am with a blade," she admonished.

Nico was prancing now, and Filaree had her advancing sideways as she moved out of the circle of trees to the clearing. Once beyond the bevy of trees, she picked up the pace a little, hoping to gain as much distance between her party and the Troll as she could without unseating Cameron. The beast walked to the edge of the shelter and silently watched them trot away. Then he raised his snout to the air and bellowed and the alarm echoed throughout the hills.

"Well," Filaree began, "they will all know we are here now. Cameron? You better hold on if you can. We must make it to the lake as fast as possible," she said, and she clicked Nico to a faster pace.

She could hear the hills resounding with the sounds of other Trolls thundering in response, and she hunched down on her mare's haunches and urged her forward. Looking back over her shoulder, she could see in the distance what appeared to be a dark wall moving toward them at a very fast pace. Ahead, she thought she saw the reflection of the sun off of the water, and she wasted no time in steering directly for it.

The black mass was gaining on them, as Trojan was unable to travel too quickly with Cameron hanging over him, but Filaree did not lose hope. The water was getting closer now, and she knew that if they did not stumble and if Cameron remained secure on Trojan's back, that they would make it. With only a hundred or so yards left to traverse, Filaree let caution to the wind and broke into a gallop, with Trojan following right behind.

The Trolls sensed they were about to lose the entire group, and ten of them crashed through the brush, raging across the hills in a frightening display of abandon. They were gaining on the horses, and Nico's ears twitched nervously. Trojan kept up with them the entire way, but he seemed to be falling back a little bit now. Filaree slowed her pace a fraction and Trojan rode up to her. She grabbed hold of Cameron's tunic, and together the two horses and the two travelers approached the bank of lake Everclear at a full gallop.

Into the water they crashed, creating a huge splash as they entered, and they immediately began to swim briskly away from the shore. The Trolls came only to the embankment, and there they began to beat their clubs against the ground, and jump up and down and trumpet with rage in their guttural voices, making a commotion that could be heard for miles around. But, no matter how much they wanted to capture the humans, they would not dare to venture into the water.

Filaree thrust her head into the cool liquid of the lake and let it wash away the sweat and remaining fear.

We are safe and Pardatha is just across the water now, she thought and sighed with relief.

Holding tightly onto Trojan's reins and making certain that Cameron's head remained above the water, she led the exhausted horses toward the distant shore.

Chapter Thirty

Elion mounted the spotted pony that had always been his choice when he had an errand to run or a task to complete, and he smiled to himself at the coincidence. Fate was playing with the pieces of his life once more, for out of all the ponies in the stables, his father had chosen this one for this particular journey, his favorite. He was the one meant to bear this message, and all of the signs reinforced his belief in that regard. The fabric wove of its own will, he mused.

The scroll with the dispatch for Baladar was safely tucked away in the saddlebags as his father promised earlier, and all of the provisions that he would need were packed carefully and stowed in the satchels attached to the saddle. He bid a mental farewell to his home and his parents, regretting the scanty amount of time he was able to spend in Seramour, but knowing that what he was doing was the only thing to do. The guards were atop their ponies and already prepared to depart. He led the way onto the large platform nearest to him and the all others followed behind. The captain beckoned to the sentries and moments later the platform began to descend.

Once it had reached the ground and they all disembarked, the lift rose quickly back up. Elion shivered briefly, knowing that what he was about to do could not be undone, and hoping at the same time that his parents would understand his actions.

"Captain, follow me," he ordered. "I know the way to where I must enter the woods. I was there just a short while ago and the memory of my path is still fresh upon me," he stated ominously.

The party of fifteen armed, Elfin fighters and one troubled Elfin Prince galloped off, out of the shelter of the woods and onto the hills which were now shrouded in darkness.

Elion wanted to travel with as much speed as possible for a number of reasons. He hoped to get as far away from Seramour as he could before his father discovered his ruse and sent someone after him, or even worse, came for him himself. He also hoped to escape the wolves this time, or at least he hoped to have the upper hand in the next confrontation with them. Unlike before, this group was well prepared to protect itself.

They charged down the hill and broke into a full gallop once they reached the flat terrain at the bottom. Elion led the way, dashing across the very spot where he was so recently rescued by

Treestar. His sharp hearing picked up the cries of the wolves in the distance, but they instilled no fear in his heart this time. He thought only of reaching Baladar and Pardatha, and of imparting the news to him about the boy he stole right out from under his nose. The brigade made remarkably good time. They raised a thick cloud of dust as they flew across the plains, which obscured whatever remaining visibility the moon had previously provided.

By the time the tree line was in sight at the far edge of the plain, the angered wolves were nipping at the hocks of the ponies' legs, attempting to cripple them and tumble the animals along with their riders. Captain Perian drew his long, slim blade out of its sheath. Holding it high in the air, he leaned halfway to the ground with his pony galloping at full speed, and while hanging from one stirrup he slashed at the oncoming wolf causing it to cry out in pain. It retreated yelping, with a huge gash across its snout. Another enraged member of the pack came upon him on the opposite side, and the accomplished rider swung himself over the pommel and repeated his amazing acrobatics, sending another beast scampering away with blood pouring from its neck. The other riders, though neither as gracefully nor as deadly as their captain, fended off attack after attack while inflicting crippling wounds on the maddened brutes until the remaining ones began to give up, tired and hurting from their numerous cuts and bruises. The bodies of their dead littered the plains.

The party entered the woods unharmed though fatigued from the fight. Once under the cover of the trees, Elion pulled up and let his pony rest.

"You are quite the rider, Perian. That was indeed an exhibition out there!" Elion said with sincerity.

"Thank you, my Prince. I have always found fighting to be best accomplished while astride my pony. He knows my body language, and he would never see me unseated," he replied proudly.

"You made that perfectly clear this evening. I think that you could have kept the wolves at bay singlehandedly," he said as he slid from his saddle to the soft, mossy ground. "You will have another opportunity to hone your skills on your return, for I must depart on my own now. Thank you, Perian. I am in your debt," he said before turning to the others. "Each of you, I thank with all my heart. First speed and may the Gem of Eternity light your way home," Elion said earnestly. "Please, tell my father that I will send news as soon as I am able. And Perian, tell him for me that I am grateful for the opportunity to carry his message to Baladar under the circumstances. He will understand my meaning," he said seriously.

"Surely, Prince Elion, I will do as you wish. And First speed to you too. May the Gem of Eternity guide you on your journey as well. Farewell!" he said, saluting the Elf Lord.

The group of fifteen followed their capable leader to the wood's edge, and with a final salute they broke through the trees one behind the other, and disappeared across the Plain of the Wolves. Elion watched as they faded into the darkness and he was not surprised that the beasts made no new effort to attack them. They had enough of Elfin warriors for one day. He smiled to himself and walked his pony deeper into the shelter of the forest.

Elion wanted to get to Pardatha as soon as he possibly could, and without the burden of his previous companion, he was able to travel quickly. He decided to follow the line of trees eastward and thus avoid anyone his father may dispatch to find him and bring him back to Seramour. He knew that it would take him dangerously close to the outskirts of Sedahar, but he believed that a single Elf on a small pony could easily avoid the eyes of the Dark One. Once he reached the ridge above the Valley of the Spirits, the barren and desolate river bed, he could remain in the shelter of the trees while traveling northeast to Pardatha.

His father, if he did send a search party after him, would not look for him near the Dark Lord's domain, and he was determined not to be waylaid on his way toward making right what he felt he had done wrong. Jorda, his pony, was strong and healthy and could ride straight through the night. What took him three days to travel before would take him no more than one and one half days this time.

The young elf took a deep drink from his pouch and allowed the Lalas leaf mixture to circulate throughout his body. He then offered a diluted mixture of the same liquid to his pony, who lapped it up enthusiastically. It provided both travelers with the sustenance they required to complete the journey. Climbing atop Jorda, he directed the animal down the narrow pathway through the trees. Once the trail widened, Elion encouraged his pony to ride faster and he guided him carefully and avoided the low hanging branches. He made excellent speed, covering many miles in only a few hours.

The sky was brightening in the east, and Elion needed to dismount not only to relieve Jorda for at least a moment, but also to stretch his legs and refresh himself. The woods narrowed at this point, forming a funnel of dense trees and brush. To the west was the wide open area he sought, lower in altitude than the woods, and parched and desolate, not succoring to any traveler. The once raging river dried up hundreds of tiels ago and left this barren gully behind; a wasteland that lead directly to Sedahar.

Elion preferred the warmth and shelter of the forest to the exposure of the range, even though he knew that he could travel much faster in the open. Stealth was almost as important to him as speed, for if he was caught by any unfriendly aggressor then his efforts would all be for naught. Suddenly, his ears picked up a faint sound which he ignored at first, it was so slight. When it persisted and grew louder, Elion walked toward the source, westward. He let Jorda graze for the moment and he crept to the outer trees, making sure that he concealed his movements from whomever or whatever was out there. The sounds were increasing in volume as he neared the edge of the tree wall, and he hid behind a large bush wherefrom he could observe the range below. The sun was just over the eastern horizon, rising above the treetops, and the gorge was fully exposed.

To his utter shock and dismay, he saw what appeared to be a black swarm in the distance, coming closer to where he now was by the second. He could not believe his eyes as he continued to witness the horrifying picture unfold before him. An army, larger than any he had ever seen before, was massing and preparing to move up the valley toward Pardatha. He still could not make out the banners that fluttered in the morning breeze, but he knew in his heart that it was not a friendly force. Elion watched in awe with his sharp, Elfin eyes locked upon the advance guard. When he could finally see the flag clearly, he wretched in revulsion. Before him flew the colors of Caeltin D'Are Agenathea, a burning red sun on a black background!

Elion sat stunned, his eyes transfixed upon the moving mass, and he attempted to remain calm. He surveyed what he saw, making mental notes of the numbers and makeup of the invaders, until he could keep count no longer. He was about to sneak back to Jorda when his heart froze. Amidst the advancing army were beasts, the likes of which he could not have envisioned in his worst nightmare. They were huge and their skin shone green in the dawn light, lizard like and terrifying in appearance. Every few moments, one of these horrendous freaks of nature would raise its ugly head and belch flames into the slowly brightening sky.

Elion stood near the edge of the wooded enclosure, lost in a ghastly reverie. He had heard about the hell hounds of Sedahar and he remembered being told of the ugly, stone eating beasts that Colton cherished, but he never believed that they were real. He thought they were merely legends, designed to frighten young children like the tales about the ghosts in the valley of the dead. More frightening even than the beasts themselves were their riders, red cloaked men with long arms, gloved hands and eyes as dead as the city of Odelot. Even from this distance, from the safety of his hiding place, he felt their eyes boring holes deep into his very soul, and he felt vulnerable and exposed; naked before these beasts from the underworld.

The surrounding marchers kept their distance as best they could from this repulsive group, out of fear no doubt. He counted thirteen of them in all. The riders sat far back on the haunches of the beasts, and it soon became apparent as to why. After each belch of fire, a stream of steam shot up from behind the animals head, perhaps ten feet in the air, sizzling as it rose, and then dissipating after a few moments.

He attempted to count the numbers and study the enemy, but the advancing army was far too large for that. It seemed to be endless as it swarmed into the valley, blackening the ground with its presence. He made a mental note of what he could; Trolls, Orcs, Giants, those hell hounds and their dark, blood-red riders. Elion had seen enough and the urgency he felt before was magnified a thousand fold by his observations. He had to get to Lord Baladar now without another moment's hesitation! The city must be warned, and his journey suddenly took on a new and vital significance.

Quietly he located Jorda and hastily grabbed his reins. He snuck back into the thick of the woods leading his pony as silently as he could, and when he found the path once more, he leapt atop him and left caution to the wind, riding with an abandon like never before. His chest was pounding and his heart felt as if it had been seized by another's fist and it was being ripped from his body. The wind assailed his face and the branches attacked his limbs as he plummeted headlong through the trees, disregarding the discomfort and the pain.

"Pardatha, Pardatha," he repeated to himself like a mantra, driving him forward as he raced through the forest.

Chapter Thirty-one

Baladar returned to his chambers, elated at his discovery yet concerned that he had become once again the victim of such violent and uncontrollable mood swings. He attributed them to the changes transforming the entire planet, the tumultuous forces affecting the weave. Everyone was suffering from the clash between the light and the dark, between good and evil and right and wrong. Everyone and everything. He understood that throughout time, this same war has been waged with perhaps only a respite here and there when the opposing forces were depleted and needed to rebuild, or when a temporary victory elevated one side over the other. But now, in this time, the battle had taken on a different shade. The trees themselves were dying. The entire balance was shifting, and Baladar was terribly disturbed by the new and deadly direction in which he perceived it was now leaning.

Baladar absolutely believed that the Dark Lord could be defeated and that peace could prevail, if not eternally, then for many lifetimes. He, like Cairn, understood that one side helped to define and clarify the other, that the darkness made the light all that much brighter, that an evil action stood out more clearly in juxtaposition to a noble act. But nothing other than the demise of Colton could balance the disappearance of the Lalas from the earth. And if one occurred without the other, then the entire future would be changed forever.

If the Lalas prevailed and the Gem of Eternity continued to nourish the world, then there would be a future full of promise for all to participate in. If the Dark Lord triumphed then there would be no future for any living thing, and a new reality would succeed the existing one. He feared that the loss of both forces would leave a void unlike any other that followed a period of great change and upheaval, and he knew that he could not let that happen, but in order to have a chance to prevent it, he needed to locate Davmiran.

From his desk, he removed a tiny box that was tucked into the back of a small drawer on the side. It was not unique in appearance but made simply out of a common wood and unadorned. After opening the lid, he removed three feathers from a bunch that lay inside, bound together by a silk thread. Baladar walked over to the same table that he first laid Davmiran upon when Dalek brought him to this room.

He has precipitated so many changes already.

Baladar carefully placed one of the feathers in the middle of the table and then he put the other two aside for the moment. Removing four of his precious gems from the pouch at his waist, he placed them in a square around the single feather. Concentrating intently, he closed his eyes and drew the power out from the stones. The black one sparkled first, sending a stream of jet black light upward, about two feet above the table. Next, the ruby stone flared, sending its own tendril out and up, merging with the already steady surge emanating from the black jewel. The blue and green stones erupted simultaneously, blazing with their own colors, and they too joined their floes with the others. Once they had all blended together, a meshed dome of white light hovered over the lone feather on the table, completely encasing it in the mesmerizing glow. Baladar was pleased as he opened his eyes and spoke the words of power.

"*Felac por tendil esti acqualto. Emerate bo minca stor.*"

The feather rose gracefully into the vortex of light and seemed to expand from all of its surfaces, as if it was imploding and turning inside out on itself, while growing in size at the same time. Baladar watched closely as his messenger took shape. Soon, a dove-grey bird about the size of a pigeon stood in the middle of the circle of light, turning its head this way and that. He extended his hand into the light and reached for the bird. Gently, he placed it in a small cage on the floor under the table. He repeated this process with the other two feathers, until there were two more birds of equal size and color in the cage beside the first one.

"*Termina porte,*" Baladar uttered, and the stones' light died instantly.

After returning the gems to his pouch, he lifted the cage atop the wooden slab and examined his handiwork. The birds cooed calmly, pecked at the cage and walked in circles, examining their surroundings.

Baladar took a piece of parchment and a pen from the desk, dipped the tip into the inkwell and wrote out the brief note that these messengers would carry for him. Simply, he asked if anyone had any knowledge regarding the disappearance of a young, blonde haired boy from Pardatha. He wrote that the youth was suffering from a rare and unusual illness, rendering him unconscious, and that his only cure lay in Pardatha. Baladar made it perfectly clear that the young man was important to him and that he wished him returned. He advised the recipient that the bird would carry whatever answer was offered back to Pardatha for them.

He was reluctant to be more specific in the event that the message was intercepted. It was bad enough that Dav was missing. He did not need to broadcast to anyone just how important his disappearance really was. Neither did he need to alert anyone other than the designated recipient that he in fact did not have any idea where the heir was, should the message fall into the wrong hands. He suspected that whoever did find him, would shortly recognize his special qualities independent of Baladar's inquiry, and if they did not know what he was talking about, the inquiry was innocent enough not to cause undue alarm or curiosity.

He signed the paper and sealed it with his ring, pressing it into the wax he dripped upon it. He repeated this exercise two more times and then slipped each rolled up piece into a small, leather tube, closed the end and strapped it around each bird's left leg, before returning it to the enclosure. Once the final bird was tagged, he held it up in front of his eyes and silently imparted to it the destination he envisioned. Again, he repeated this process with the remaining two.

When he was certain that each bird knew where its special target was, he reached for the first one and released it out the large window overlooking the courtyard. The small bird immediately flew off in the direction he had implanted in its tiny brain, and he watched as long as he could until it was visible no longer.

"First speed!" he said aloud as he lost the small messenger in the clouds.

Baladar hoped with all his heart that his analysis of the events of that miserable day were accurate, and that one of the birds would return with news of Davmiran. But, he would soon know for certain when and if any of them came back with the answer he craved. He reached for the next bird and was in the process of releasing it when he was startled by a strenuous pounding on the door to the study.

"My Lord! May I enter?" Grogan asked.

"Give me a minute if you will, Grogan," he answered, and he hastily placed the bird back in its cage. After he put the cage back under the table and out of sight, he closed the window. "You may enter, Grogan," he said as he moved to the doorway to release the latch.

The Master at Arms was clearly anxious to impart what information he had to his Lord, and he barely hesitated before speaking.

"My Lord! A rider has been seen galloping toward the gates. His mount is no more than a pony, but he travels with the speed of a stallion," Grogan said.

"Is he alone? Are there others following him or is he escorting anyone?" Baladar asked, hoping for a minute that Davmiran was being returned to him, that the nightmare would be over.

"No, my Lord. I mean, yes, sir. He is alone. None follow him and he is not escorting anyone. Shall I send some guards to intercept him?" his loyal Master at Arms inquired.

"He is on a pony, you said?" Baladar questioned, disappointed at the answer but now his interest was piqued.

"Yes, a dapple, and he is quite small himself. An Elf, perhaps," Grogan responded.

"Let him approach unmolested, Grogan. A single Elf on a pony cannot do us very much harm," he concluded, not wishing to frighten him off by sending out an armed escort for him.

"As you wish, Lord Baladar," his guard answered.

"I wish to question him as soon as he is within the city gates," Baladar instructed the soldier.

He was hoping that the arrival of an Elf in such a hurried manner would shed some light upon the strange events of the past days.

It could not be mere coincidence that brings an Elf to the gates of the city so soon after the boy's disappearance. Elves riding into Pardatha are strange occurrences indeed and two in so short a span of time are truly unusual, he reasoned, hardly able to contain his eagerness to talk to this visitor.

Baladar walked to the broad, leaded windows and gazed out over the city. He watched the guards assemble and calmly march toward the city wall, the Ghost tower and the Noban gate, where all visitors entered from. He was fatigued from the prior exercise, as he was every time he wielded his magic. Both his mind and his body were weary. But he was relieved that the messengers were prepared and ready to go on their journey as soon as he could release them. Perhaps this Elfin rider had some news that would brighten this day as well, he thought.

Baladar was a good man and he watched the people of his city go about their daily business in the streets below, wondering what it would be like not to bear the burdens of leadership that he had always borne. He felt so alone. He longed for Briland's presence and he missed her warmth, her smile, her beauty and her overwhelming goodness, so much so that it hurt him.

Davmiran could have been our son. He could have been the child we never had. Now, he belongs to no one, adrift in a hostile world, and his fate is unknown.

The nagging feeling that he was at fault persisted, even though he was rejuvenated by his recent discoveries. He needed to know for certain where the heir was. Baladar required more than hope to sustain him now.

Out of the corner of his eye, he spotted a group of riders escorting a black and white pony with an unmistakably Elfin rider on its back, approaching the castle walls. As they drew near, Baladar could see that the rider was flushed and drenched in sweat, and that his pony was frothing at the mouth and dripping with perspiration as well. Yet, he noticed that this did not deter the young Elf from proceeding forward at a pace that clearly indicated how anxious he was to arrive at his destination.

What news could this visitor be bringing me? Baladar wondered anxiously. *An Elf arriving from the south?* He experienced a fleeting feeling of encouragement that lifted his spirits if only for a moment. *Could it be that my theories are correct?. Could he be bringing me news of Davmiran?*

When the group disappeared into the castle proper, Baladar moved to the large chair in the corner of the room and sat down to wait. Shortly, he heard a knocking on the heavy door.

"My Lord? May I enter?" Grogan asked.

"Enter!"

Grogan walked to where Baladar was sitting and removed his helmet. He bowed his head slightly.

"The rider is Prince Elion, the son of Treestar, King of Lormarion. He says that he has urgent news for you that he cannot impart to anyone else. He wishes to speak to you immediately."

"Bring him in, Grogan. I, too, am anxious to speak with the young Elfin Lord," Baladar responded.

"As you wish, Lord Baladar," he answered, and he turned to carry out his instructions.

As he entered the room, Baladar could see that the young Elf was still perspiring profusely and clearly out of breath. It was obvious to him that he wasted no time coming here. He could barely stand up, and his clothing was stained with the evidence of a long, hard ride through a wooded area. He bowed deeply, despite his fatigue, and he waited for Baladar to speak first. His manners were excellent and even under the circumstances, he maintained his dignity.

"Greetings, Prince Elion. Sit, rest. You have traveled long and hard, as is evident. Can I offer you some wine or cider?" he asked, after sliding a comfortably cushioned chair toward the tired Elf.

"A mug of cider would be nice right now, your lordship. Thank you," Elion said politely, while wiping the perspiration from his brow.

Baladar walked to the side of the room and filled two glasses with warm cider from a pitcher on the serving table. He handed one to Elion who was still standing, and then he returned to his own chair.

"Please, sit. You look exhausted. What brings you here in such haste?" he asked, attempting to take the edge of discomfort off of the young man.

Elion sat in the high backed chair facing Baladar. The light from the afternoon sun was streaming through the large windows, illuminating the Elfin Prince in a curiously portentous manner.

"I have two things to tell you, your lordship," he began, not knowing which tale was the more important of the two.

"Please, call me Baladar and I will call you Elion. There is no need for formality here," Baladar said, attempting to relax the young visitor as best as he could.

"Thank you, your Lord... I mean, Baladar," the Elf said humbly, staring at the carpet beneath his feet. "I was on my way to Pardatha to bring you news of a former prisoner of yours..." he began, looking sheepishly now at the anxious Lord before him. Baladar felt the blood rush to his head and he literally had to fight off a wave of dizziness in order to concentrate.

"Tell me, my friend. I must know of this!" Baladar said with an urgent tone, and thus Elion continued.

"I found him outside of your walls when I was returning to my homeland from my uncle's in the north. He was unconscious and his hands and feet were bound. I thought that he was abandoned and that he would surely have died out there, all alone and unaware. I could not wake him up so I dragged him away into the woods..."

Baladar could barely contain the excitement and relief that the young Elf's words elicited in him.

"...in order to help him," he continued, believing that he still needed to apologize for his actions.

"Is he safe now? Where did you take him?" Baladar asked

sitting back, attempting to conceal his intense interest.

"I transported him back to Lormarion, my homeland, and he rests now with my mother and father in Seramour," he replied.

Baladar stood up and walked over to Elion. The Elfin Prince assumed that he would now feel the wrath of his misdeed, and he bent his head in anticipation and shame. Upon reaching his side, the Lord of Pardatha placed his hand fondly upon Elion's shoulder and spoke to him gently.

"You cannot imagine how grateful I am to you for saving the life of this youth, he whom I call Davmiran."

Elion lifted his head, and with an amazed look upon his face, he listened to the tale that Baladar then told.

"He was kidnapped from my very home while I was on a vital mission outside the gates. My first at arms was killed in the process, and when I returned I could find neither hide nor hair of him. He is a very special boy, you know?" Baladar remarked in a questioning tone of voice.

"Yes, sir, I found that out. Just looking into his eyes made me feel different," he said remembering the youth's blank gaze poignantly. "Why would anyone have abandoned him that way?"

"In order to protect him, I placed a strong spell upon him. Although the intention of the kidnapper was certainly to bring him back home with him, my conjuring caused him to leave him alone and helpless outside the gates of the city. It is more than fortunate that you happened along at such an opportune moment."

Elion wondered about the timing himself.

"I have only just prepared messages of inquiry to send to your father and uncle, and to your western kin as well. His absence has caused me much worry. This boy means a lot to me, to us all!" Baladar remarked.

Elion again lowered his head to his chest, ashamed that he had caused this kind man so much grief, yet thoroughly relieved that what he had thought was a terrible mistake moments ago, was perhaps an incredibly fortuitous twist of fate.

"So, tell me?" Baladar asked. "You were in the woods beyond the grassy fields. And then what did you see?" he asked Elion, interested in knowing everything.

"I saw a group of soldiers accompany a young nobleman out of the gates. The boy was laying across a horse, but I did not know that at first. He was covered with a blanket. As soon as they passed through the gate, they seemed to forget all about him, and his horse wandered off alone toward where I was standing. He fell from the animal, and then I saw that it was a boy after all, and when the soldiers were out of sight, I went to assist him. He was unconscious but his eyes were partially open. They were so blue," Elion said, looking now at no one, caught in the vision of that moment. "I lifted him onto my cape and dragged him into the woods. I could not awaken him, but I was able to force some nourishment down his throat."

Baladar was becoming more and more impressed with this young, Elfin Prince as he continued to tell his story.

"Was he injured at all?" he asked.

"He did not appear to be so. Anyway, I helped him to drink a little, I made a portage with some branches and my cape and then I dragged him to Lormarion," he said nonchalantly.

"You carried him all the way to Lormarion by yourself?"

"Well, I did not carry him exactly. I pulled him," he answered.

"You encountered no one on the way? No person saw you? No one molested you?" he questioned.

"Not a single person. I kept us well hidden and I did not travel a frequented path. I know the woods well. I ran into some trouble just before I got home, though, and if it was not for my father, we would not have made it. The wolves attacked us on the plains beneath Seramour, and I fought them off until my father and some Elfin warriors came to our aid. I really do not remember much from that point on, until I found myself beneath my parents' roof," he concluded.

Baladar was struck by the modesty of the youth and he envisioned this small Elf, no more than a young man himself, fighting off the wolves in order to protect Davmiran. He developed a strong liking for this boy instantly.

"You have done a wonderful thing, Elion. Are you aware of just how important a role you have played in this untoward event? You may have saved us all with your deeds. History will remember you well for this," Baladar exclaimed, more relieved than he cared to relate.

"I was so worried that you would think that I kidnaped him, and that you would therefor hate me and my people for this. I had to come here myself and apologize for stealing him from your home," he said humbly, his eyes downcast.

"You did not steal him, you saved his life! Remember that always. You were fated to be here, outside my gates, at that very moment! There can be no other explanation for it," he responded, elated with the news. "Make no mistake about it my son, it was not coincidence but destiny."

Elion looked pleased for the first time since his arrival, and it appeared as if a grey cloud had lifted from his head.

"Oh, I almost forgot," Elion said as he pulled the message from his tunic that his father sent him to deliver. "My father wanted me to give this to you. But, I think that I have probably already related to you everything he wrote," Elion said bashfully.

"I will read it later. But, tell me? Did the boy awaken or was he still insensate when you left?" the Lord of Pardatha inquired, hoping that the "magic" of Seramour may have had its affects on Davmiran.

"He was still asleep, or whatever you want to call it. My mother is a healer and she was going to attend to him, but I left before she had the opportunity. She is a fine healer. He may be better by now," Elion said with pride, believing fully in his mother's abilities.

"It is not an illness he is suffering from, my young friend," Baladar replied seriously. "I fear that nothing will rouse him from his 'slumber' until he is returned to me. I am one of but a few who hold the key to his future awareness," he concluded.

"I am sorry for taking him away from you, but I do have other important news to tell you that may make you glad he is not still here," the young Elf said, his slanted eyes downcast once more.

"What could possibly make me feel that way apart from the very presence of Colton dar Agonthea in our midst?" Baladar said jokingly, and then he regretted immediately having uttered his name.

"That is exactly what I need to tell you!" Elion began. "On my way here, below in the gorge beneath the great forest, I saw the most massive army I have ever seen. It was preparing to march in the direction of Pardatha!"

Baladar paled considerably at the boy's words.

"An army, you say? And whose standards did it bear?"

"Caeltin D'Are Agenathea's--a red sun on a black field! I saw Trolls, Orcs, Giants and Mages atop hideous, fire breathing beasts. I lost count, but there were thousands upon thousands of them," the Elfin Prince responded quickly, the words rushing from his mouth now as he raised his eyes to meet Baladar's own.

"I did not know which news to tell you first," he said.

The older man did not move. Then he laughed quietly to

himself, causing Elion to look at him askew.

When Baladar saw the young Elf staring up at him as if he had lost his senses, he began to speak.

"First you bring me news, better than any I could have hoped for regarding Davmiran, and then I am told that we are about to be invaded by a formidable force, by Colton himself. Do you not see the irony in this?" Baladar asked rhetorically.

"I beg your pardon, sir. I did not mean to say anything wrong. I did not consciously choose the order in which I imparted my news to you," he said regretfully. "Of course you didn't. I meant not to cast aspersion upon you, my boy. I have just recently been experiencing some rather disparate emotions. The fabric weaves of its own will, it seems. But the news you bring is grave indeed." He walked to the doorway, turned to Elion and said, "You are right indeed! I am glad that Davmiran is not here. Fate once again has intervened. But, I am afraid that you are now trapped here in Pardatha instead. I cannot allow you to return from whence you came with an army on the march," he commented, thinking all the while. "You should go north again, to your uncle. If you leave now, you can be there in five or six days," Baladar suggested, contemplating the options.

Elion hesitated for an instant and then said, "I would like to stay here, if you will allow me to. I would like to help in any way that I can," the Elfin Prince said, holding his head high. "I feel a part of this now, my Lord, and I would not wish to leave. That is, if you will give me permission to stay?" he asked, his slanted eyes peeking expectantly at the older man.

Baladar cogitated upon this bold, young Elf for a moment and then responded, "I would be honored to have you here, Prince Elion! Your services would be greatly appreciated. And, we have much work to do. But, you must understand the peril you will be putting yourself in. I cannot have more on my conscience than I do already," he commented, half to himself.

"I understand, sir. I understand only too well. But, I feel that I should be here, that I am supposed to be here, and I would rather not leave the city now," he replied in a mature and forthright manner.

Baladar looked him deeply in the eyes and said, "Well then, Elion, I accept your courageous offer of assistance! Now, you must clean yourself up and get some rest and nourishment or you will be of no use to anyone, but before you go, we must revise the dispatches I had prepared to send when you interrupted me," he said smiling, as he retrieved the bird cage from underneath the table.

The Pardathan Lord opened the small door and removed one of the grey doves, as Elion watched inquisitively. He detached the note from its leg and tossed it aside.

"We must inform your father that you have arrived here safely and that you will remain here for some measure. We must also ask him to keep Davmiran under his protection for the time being. Is there anything you wish to say?" he asked Elion.

"Please tell him of Colton's advance. He would want to know," Elion replied. "Also," he continued, his head downcast. "Please say that I am sorry for deceiving him, but that I felt it was necessary. He will know what I mean," the young Elf said, knowing that his father will forgive him once he hears the full story, but still uncomfortable with the subterfuge he was compelled to commit.

"Certainly, lad. As far as him knowing of our peril, perhaps you are right, he should be aware. But I do not want to involve your kingdom in the affairs of Pardatha. He may feel an obligation to come to our aid, particularly when he hears that you are trapped in the city," he responded with some reluctance.

"The Dark Lord's movements are every Nation's concern..." the Elf said with a wisdom much greater than his years, "...and if my father feels that he should march to our assistance, then that should be his choice. I will ask him to remain in Seramour and to prepare his own defenses, though. He knows that he cannot remain apart from this conflict indefinitely. What affects the weave here, will affect it everywhere eventually. He must also know just how important Davmiran's welfare is to us all. Once we explain, I believe that he will take the necessary precautions. He also knows the strength of Pardatha. He should not fear for me whilst I am here. My father is not a rash man," Elion reasoned while trying to convince himself at the same time.

Baladar smiled at him, despite the dour circumstances, and composed the communication.

"I will tell him as much as I must and as little as I can," he said.

Baladar placed the note back in its container, attached it once more to the bird's leg and then walked to the window. Opening it wide, he released the bird into the air and then together they watched it fly away until they could see it no longer.

Baladar turned to Elion and said, "I intended to question your uncle Bristar of the north, as well about Davmiran. That is no longer necessary. Is there anything you wish me to tell him now?"

He thought for a minute before responding.

"Yes, he should know of Colton's movements also. I lived with him for the past few years and I know him well. My uncle is an honorable Elf and he would be furious with me if I had knowledge such as this and kept it from him. I would be doing him a great disservice," the young Elf said wisely.

"I suppose that all the world will find out soon enough anyway. These events are but the beginning of a series, I fear. Those whose paths have run parallel all these tiels, will find them merging in the face of a common enemy," he replied. "You are wise to suggest that he should be informed as well," Baladar concluded, and he shook his head in agreement. "It is not for me to conceal the truth from the other nations. Yet, I do not wish for anyone to interpret the dissemination of information as a plea. My words must be chosen carefully."

Together they composed a short note, taking great care to word it properly and then they dispatched it in the same manner.

"It is too late to retrieve the one that I sent just before you arrived here, but it can do no real harm. Your western brethren in Eleutheria have never been too interested in the problems of our world and I have no right to seek to draw them into events that they wish to remain apart from now. They need not know of our troubles beyond that of the 'missing boy'," Baladar said, and then he returned to the center of the room.

Elion knew little about his western cousins and he thus remained silent in that regard.

"It is time now for you to get some well deserved rest! Do not argue with me about this now, my boy," Baladar said as he opened the study door and called for Grogan and some attendants.

When they arrived, he instructed them to take Prince Elion to the chambers nearest to his own and to tend to his needs. Placing his arm fondly around the Elf's shoulders, he looked into the depths of his soul and said, "You have done me two great services today for which I will be forever grateful, for which the world will be forever grateful! You have brought me news of Davmiran, the heir of Gwendolen, and you have advised me of the approach of an invading army, thus allowing us to prepare well before we may have been able to otherwise. You cannot not know how important your deeds are to us all!"

At the mention of the words "heir of Gwendolen", Elion's eyes opened wide and his jaw dropped. It all made sense to him at that moment, the feelings, the wonder, the beauty of the boy! He left Baladar's company imbued with incredulity while at the same time, charged with apprehension. He could not help but feel as if he had stepped into the very middle of a legend. He turned to go, and as he left the room he passed Baladar's Master at Arms entering the study.

He heard Baladar say gravely, "Grogan, attend me. The Dark Lord is on the march with all his minions, it seems, and Pardatha I fear, is his destination!" as the door closed behind him.

Elion followed the page down the long hallway, thinking about his mother and father and hoping that they would be proud of him. When and if he saw them again, he would explain why he had to make this journey, why he had to be the one and not Jerial whom his father had designated to be the messenger. He wanted them to know and he prayed that they would understand. He thought of Davmiran, and despite all of his previous concerns, despite the impending onslaught, despite the thought of the Lord of Darkness himself advancing upon him, a smile crossed his lips and lingered there for just long enough to make him feel better.

Chapter Thirty-two

As soon as Elion left the room, Baladar took the first step on that long, dreaded walk down the path of no return, the road that would lead to death and captivity or victory and jubilation. He gathered his ministers together and gave the orders that would change the lives of his people forever, come good or come evil.

The plans were well laid and well rehearsed, and like clockwork, they were carried out. His officers were skillfully organized and thus the word went out quickly to all the citizens of Pardatha, as well as to the surrounding towns and villages.

The bell tower in the main square of the city rang ceaselessly for one full hour, signaling the most dour of circumstances, and its warning was echoed by all the bells erected in the surrounding countryside for just this purpose; to signal an imminent invasion by a foreign force. Immediately, the citizenry began to mobilize. The herds were gathered, the horses were corralled and the children were sent home from their schools.

All of the men, women and children living outside the walls of Pardatha gathered their essential belongings and began to assemble in the main square of the city to await instructions as to where they would be domiciled. The men and boys of age reported to the headquarters of the Master at Arms and began to receive their instructions regarding the particular role they each would play in the defense of the city. The women who were trained in battle, those who were not raising children and those who were not with child, reported as well to Grogan and his lieutenants. Weapons were dispersed, responsibilities were explained and everyone rose to the call.

During times of peace, the city's population was approximately thirty thousand civilians and half again as many soldiers. Within two days, the numbers would swell to one hundred thousand. Of the sixty five thousand some odd refugees, thirty thousand would be armed and ready to fight to the end to defend Pardatha, their families and their lifestyles.

The citizens of the smaller towns and villages dotting the countryside that lay in the path of the approaching invaders would all take refuge in Pardatha, lending their support as well as straining the city's resources. It had been tiels since Pardatha was the target of aggression. But, with the trees dying all around, the people were not surprised that their safety was now in jeopardy. The darkness was bound to reach out to them, they reasoned, and they were grateful that it had been held at bay for as long as it had been.

Pardathans were sturdy folk, hard nosed and tough; hardy workers too. They would not surrender their city easily to any threat, and that could be seen in the way that they mobilized, in the manner that they dealt with the call to arms, in the determination that they expressed as they rallied their forces.

Whosoever attacked Pardatha attacked a people united, a city committed to its own preservation, to the preservation of a lifestyle of service and sacrifice for the greater good. They believed that their leader, Baladar, was a good man, and that he would advise them well and honestly. Although fear snuck up on some, it remained for the most part under the surface, and the people were not willing to let it overtake them.

They held their heads high even in the face of separation, as fathers bade farewell to wives and children, as children said their goodbyes to their families, and as familial units were sundered by the approach of the invaders. But, like a well rehearsed play, the participants all knew their lines and where they were to go to next.

There was so much activity in the city that it was dizzying. People and wagons were rushing from one end to the other. Troops were gathering and battalions were forming from within, as well as entering, already formed, from the outskirts. The nearby towns were evacuated and the citizenry made its solemn way to the safety of Pardatha. Animals bellowed, horses whinnied, people shouted and children cried.

Constantly now the horns would blow, announcing the arrival of a small army from the north, a battalion from the west, a tribe of woodsmen from the hills to the east, a troop of soldiers from across the lake, and the people of Pardatha would take note of who came to take refuge and to lend their support. The winds of war were blowing steadily through the city, the machinery was churning, and everyone, young and old, rich and poor, strong and weak, would soon be caught up in the maelstrom.

Baladar sent his scouts out to gather as much advance information as they could and he awaited news from the scouts already in place. He had the fields cleared of useful crops and the storerooms stocked to the bursting point. The battlements were manned, the towers attended and the gates would very soon be closed. Pardatha would be sealed tight and no one would be able to enter or leave unless they were opened from within, or until they crumbled in the face of an onslaught from without. The siege of Pardatha was about to begin.

Baladar walked out onto the ramparts and surveyed with sadness the preparations that were going on all over the city. He climbed the catwalk of narrow stone stairs that led to the top of the Ghost Tower. The turret was dark and musty, and cobwebbed from lack of traffic. He brushed the invisible strands from before his eyes as he ascended to the top. Adjacent to the Noban gates in the very center of the city's walls, the Ghost tower provided him with a clear view down the valley to the south.

The tower was so named by his predecessor after the death of his nephew, a young boy he loved dearly. He perished prematurely while playing atop it, and it was believed that the innocent child's spirit walked its stones still. The boy, Cotwald, mysteriously fell two hundred feet to the ground over the crenellated side, and few chose to venture up there at all anymore since that day. Baladar had planned to tear it down and to reconstruct it, if only to ease his soldiers' minds when need required them to be atop it. But he never had the time, and need surely beckoned him now.

The darkness of the tower steps abruptly ended as he climbed the remaining few stone treads and emerged into the bright sunlight. Surveying the surrounding land from this vantage point, he was able to see far into the distance. Despite the impressive height of the tower, the mighty Thorndars dwarfed it in comparison, rising behind the city and shrouded in a thick mist.

He envisioned what would take place shortly and he shuddered in anticipation. Baladar knew that the impending confrontation was necessary and that there was no alternative to what was about to unfold beneath these mighty walls. If Pardatha fell, then it would only be a matter of time before Avalain, Talamar, Concordia and all the other cities and counties followed suit. But, if Davmiran survived then hope would survive. This he alone knew, and if Colton was attacking Pardatha in order to capture the heir of Gwendolen, then he would be disappointed if and when he broke through the defenses of the city. Thus, even in victory the Dark One would lose.

It saddened Baladar that so many innocent people would have to give their lives in order for the Lord of Darkness to find out that he was mistaken, that he misread the signs and that his efforts were for naught. Baladar grieved at the thought that his beautiful city, along with the noble citizens who honored him with their service and fidelity, would have to suffer so, would have to sacrifice so much. But, the heir must survive and there was still a fighting chance that he would.

He looked out across the flattened lands southward, visualizing the Dark Lord's approach, knowing that if he arrived en masse then Pardatha could not hold out against him forever. He allowed his gaze to linger for just a moment, and he pictured his young charge innocent and unaware in Seramour, and then he turned away and descended the steep stairway once again, heading for the temple mount, the highest natural point of land in the city, where he would establish his war council and wait out the arrival of his nemesis.

Chapter Thirty-three

The horses were floundering in the churning water. Filaree's arm felt as if it was breaking as she held Cameron's lifeless head above the waves, reaching precariously across the span between Nico and Trojan and attempting to lay it high on his stallion's neck. A thick fog was settling in all around them and she could barely see which direction they were going. What she had so desperately sought as their salvation from the Trolls just a short while ago, was now killing them. The lake was growing more active, more violent with each minute, and Nico and Trojan were straining to keep their own heads up and out of the water. She could sense the fatigue that was setting in upon them all. Nico was gasping for breath, snorting and wheezing, and Trojan was struggling to keep even with her.

"It cannot end here," she said aloud. "We have come so far and we have so much work to do. Keep going, Nico. Don't give up!" she said, and she slid from her saddle into the seething waters of the lake, holding on to her mare's reins and Trojan's as well with one tired arm and leading them forward as she desperately pulled through the water with her other arm.

By this time, the mists had grown so thick that she could barely see Cameron's face behind her, and she was weakening quickly. She scanned the wall of vapor before her with her burning eyes, searching for something to rest upon, something solid that she could grasp, but she could see nothing other than mist and the endless blue-green of the swirling water.

Finally, she could go on no longer and her exhaustion was growing too difficult to fight. She had swallowed too much water and her lungs hurt from choking and coughing, while her eyes were stinging from the constant splash of the cold liquid. Trojan was no more than a head sticking out of the blackness, and tears began to flow uncontrollably when she realized that she could no longer see Cameron at all. She would not give up though, and as she fought to stay above the surge with every ounce of energy she could muster, a large wave rushed over them, sending them all thrashing forward, but instead of drowning in the surge as she now feared, they rose to the top of it. Another wave came immediately behind the last one and they rode this one too like pieces of driftwood on the tide, ending up countless feet further ahead.

Filaree thought she could hear a woman singing, but she had taken in so much water and was so fatigued, that she was uncertain whether it was her imagination or not. Again a wave carried them forward and with it the singing was clearer now; a beautiful, high pitched voice, melodious and rich. She coughed and spit and thrashed still, reaching once more for Trojan, forcing the tired horse's head up and watching as Cameron's still body broke through the water. Another wave caught them and propelled them ahead, and the voice grew louder with each surge of water.

The fog was so thick that she could not see where they were headed and she had lost all sense of direction by this time. In front of her, silhouetted against the mist, she thought she saw the image of a lady, the profile of a long haired woman suspended in the air, and the singing she heard in her head persisted. Filaree thought she was dreaming, that she was delirious. But the waves kept coming, forcing her and Cameron to the shore and driving them forward, one after the other. Another surge was upon them, this one greater than the last, and it sent them rushing headlong into the mists, when all at once, Filaree felt something brush against her legs. She scraped herself upon it and then was hurled forward once more, swallowing more water, but certain now that what she felt underfoot was solid.

Nico scrambled ashore followed immediately by Trojan with Cameron still atop his back, and Filaree dragged herself onto the rocky beach. She looked back behind her once more and she saw the silhouette of the woman yet, her chin raised upward and her mouth open, and she could hear the singing, the sweet, steady singing, and its crescendo rising and falling with the waves. It was not her imagination! She collapsed upon the hard shore, half on top of Cameron, having not the energy any longer to even check to make sure he was still breathing. She felt his heart beating beneath her head as it rested upon his chest and then she closed her eyes.

When she awoke, she opened her burning eyes, rubbed the sand from her face and tried to focus, not having the strength yet to rise. Through the blur that was her vision, she thought she saw people standing over her, surrounding them, talking, and saying things she could not quite hear. As her eyes cleared, she was able to discern faces hovering above her, asking questions, speaking words. Filaree shook her head and struggled to see through her tired eyes. Someone was moving her off of Cameron, and at first she resisted, striking out, she thought, with her fist. A soothing voice was trying to calm her and she could now make out a word here and there.

As her vision began to clear, she could see that these people were soldiers, that they wore uniforms and had swords at their belts. She struggled to free her arms from whatever was binding them, and the voice spoke more clearly now, into her ear.

"Lady Filaree? Calm down, we are here to help you," the voice repeated. "Men! Put them on the stretchers. Carefully!" it ordered. "Are you hurt? Can you tell me if you are hurt?" the voice asked.

"I think I am all right," she responded, not knowing for certain if she was or not.

She could barely feel her legs and her head was pounding.

"Your friend has swallowed too much water. My man here is attempting to revive him," he said, and she could see a soldier pushing on Cameron's chest while he held his head up with his open mouth facing the ground. Water was gushing from it onto the sand.

"He is very green in color, my Lady. We will do our best, but he does not look well," the voice said.

She sat up a little herself and realized that she was being carried down the beach now with Cameron by her side in the soldier's arms as well.

"He is breathing well," the soldier said. "He will live," he repeated to the one who had resuscitated him.

"Where are we?" Filaree asked the one giving the orders.

"In Pardatha, my Lady. You washed up on the shore and our scouts spotted your group. Your horses are yonder, over there," he pointed somewhere ahead of them.

Filaree remembered very little until the same soldier whose words she first awoke to said, as he pointed to the buildings that were coming into sight ahead, "We will be within the city walls shortly, my Lady. You can relax. You are safe for now."

She liked not the way he said "for now", but she was too tired to question the meaning thereof. She simply smiled as best as she could and expressed her gratefulness in her weakened state. The guard spoke once more and his voice resounded in her head. "Lord Baladar has been expecting you, and he has asked me to bring you to him at his headquarters on the mount as soon as you are able," he answered.

"Thank you, thank you. But, we must rest a bit first. I am so pleased to be here at last," she exclaimed, not comprehending what the guard really said. "Tell your good Lord that Filaree Par D'Avalain and her friend and companion, Cameron D'Ademar are at his service," she said with enthusiasm, however low in volume. "And that we will be pleased to join him as soon as we are able. Is Cameron breathing steadily now?" she asked with real concern.

"Yes, my Lady, but he does not appear to be well. His breath is strong, but his skin is pallid and sickly looking," the leader of the guards answered.

"He has been through much in the past few days. He needs to rest. If there is a healer who can provide him with a cup of Lalas leaf tea, I would be eternally grateful?" Filaree asked.

"I will do my best to see that your request is carried out," the soldier said.

Filaree knew that Cameron's color had nothing to do with their travails upon the lake. He had been suffering for quite some time now and the longer he remained untreated, the more dangerous his situation became.

"Please, good man, find him a healer quickly," she said earnestly. "And tell her that we just came from the Winding Woods! The healer must know that. It is vital that she know that!" Filaree insisted.

"Yes, Lady, at once!" he responded, recognizing the urgency in her voice.

She could hear him directing a runner to the castle's infirmary in order to inform them that a healer would be required immediately.

"Go with speed!" she listened to him say.

"Thank you. Thank you very much," Filaree said again and then she let her head relax upon the stretcher for the first time since she was placed there.

The soldiers carried them through the massive gates and down the main thoroughfare to the castle itself. She could see activity all around her, soldiers marching, livestock braying and scurrying around, wooden platforms being erected, and horses and tents and weapons everywhere!

"Sir? Can you tell me what is happening here? This is not the serene city I remember," she asked her attendant, surprised at the goings on.

"You do not know, Lady Filaree?" he questioned, startled by her inquiry.

"I certainly do not! We have been traveling for quite some days and we were well out of touch," she answered.

"The city prepares for war, my Lady! The Dark Lord marches

upon us with a great force behind him, even as we speak!" he said dramatically.

Filaree laid her head back down, stunned by the news.

So soon, she thought. *The Evil One hopes to capture the boy before he is ready, before we have had an opportunity to train him. Colton wastes no time when he perceives that he is threatened,* Filaree pondered, as they carried her into the courtyard of Baladar's castle. *This boy must be very powerful to move the Dark Lord to war so shortly after his arrival here,* she concluded.

Filaree bathed and refreshed herself, changed her clothes and then immediately inquired after Cameron. She was told that he was taken to the castle's healer, Ismaya, Baladar's own, and that she was welcome to visit him anytime. She wasted not a moment in requesting an escort down the long hall to the infirmaries. The guard knocked upon the door and a small, dark skinned woman opened it.

"Ah, the Lady Filaree," she said as she spotted the tall, female warrior at the entrance. "Come in. You will be pleased with what you will see," the old lady said, smiling and nodding her head satisfied.

Filaree saw Cameron sitting up in bed with a nurse along side of him feeding him a porridge of some sort from a spoon. His skin color was back to normal and he greeted her with a smile that spread from ear to ear. Filaree rushed to his side and grabbed his hand, almost upsetting the food tray in her enthusiasm.

"You are well, Cameron!" she exclaimed. "I was so worried. I thought you might be joining Pembar for a moment there," she said seriously.

"Your instincts were accurate, Lady Filaree," Ismaya said. "His blood was saturated with that of the trees. A strong brew of Lalas tea was what he required. The trees meant no harm to him. They only wanted him for their own. They recognized a good man when they saw him!" she joked.

Filaree tenderly laid her hand upon his brow. Cameron visibly reddened from her touch, but he looked pleased nonetheless.

"When the Lalas tea had a chance to spread through his veins, the venom, or should I say the serum, retreated in its face. He will be just fine now. But, had he not been treated, his blood would have been saturated past the point of repair. Do you see what accumulated on his bandages over there?" she asked, pointing to some soiled cloth that she had removed from a superficial wound on his leg.

Filaree looked in shock at the bright green liquid that permeated the material. It appeared to her as if she had taken a fresh green reed, broken it and then allowed the juice of the plant to drip onto the cloth.

"That was what his blood looked like?" she inquired, shocked by what she saw.

"Yes, it was. But, no longer. He is as well as ever. They do say that once the trees have entered your system, you are never quite the same again," Ismaya remarked, and Cameron's head turned swiftly in her direction. There was a clear look of consternation upon his pale and handsome countenance.

"Oh, not in a bad way," she explained as she saw the dismayed looks on both Cameron's and Filaree's faces. "It is said that trees of the Winding Woods develop their own relationships, much like the Lalas and their Chosen, although not in as sophisticated a manner. They do not choose just anyone to join them," she said, with her eyebrows raised while glancing at Cameron. "But, you will probably find that out for yourself at some point in time. I only speak from what I have heard," she concluded, feigning an ignorance of the matter that neither Cameron nor Filaree fully believed.

"Thank you, Ismaya. Whatever you did, he and I are both grateful. How soon before he can rise from his bed? I would like him to accompany me when I meet with Lord Baladar later," the maiden inquired.

"He is fine! I told you that. He can go with you whenever you like. It is entirely up to him. I know you are both fatigued, but you can rest later if important matters need your immediate attention. It will not harm him," she responded.

"Well then, Cameron? Are you ready to join me?" Filaree asked.

"I am, my Lady," he answered and then he rose abruptly from the cot, tossing the covers onto the floor, only to realize that he was not fully and properly dressed. He grabbed at the blanket to cover himself in front of the women and Filaree smiled as Cameron blushed a deep, deep crimson.

"From green to red, Cameron!" she exclaimed laughing. "When you return to your true color, please attend me in the hall," Filaree said, and she turned and left the room with a grin on her face that spread from ear to ear.

Chapter Thirty-four

The days passed and the preparations for war continued. Nothing was the same now as it was before. The city of Pardatha was turned upside down and inside out. The flow of people into it was greater than anyone expected, as Baladar and his ministers soon discovered. Far more feared the Dark Lord's advances than had been anticipated, and even those further to the north and out of his direct path, chose to take refuge in the city rather than be exposed out in the open.

Always in the past, the Lalas protected everyone and the comfort and security that their presence provided dispelled the fear that would have otherwise engulfed them during trying times. But now, the void that they left could not be filled, and Pardatha became a magnet, attracting all of those whose safety was threatened by Colton. The city, with its great and indestructible Elfin gates, with its noble and powerful leader, with walls as thick as a Noban itself, became the only place of sanctuary in the minds of the people, and they flocked to its womb with abandon.

All of the city's services were being strained to their limits, but no one would be turned away. Baladar was determined to leave the gates open as long as he could, admitting anyone who approached, and approach they did. Nevertheless, time was running out and the gates to Pardatha would have to be sealed soon. He would wait until the very last moment, and he knew that fateful moment would be upon them shortly.

His scouts continued to report that the enemy was approaching slowly but steadily. They informed him, much as Elion had, about the enormity of the assemblage, as well as about the composition, though in more hideous terms than the Elfin Prince had previously. Their descriptions were more detailed and even more frightening, and all the while Baladar and his ministers of war listened pensively and continued to prepare for the onslaught.

The armies were approaching Pardatha through the gorge to the south, as Elion had surmised. Colton was not afraid of being attacked on route, his forces were so huge and formidable, and he boldly and brazenly marched his minions down the open corridor to the city, announcing his arrival simply by the path he chose. A choice such as this would have been the kiss of death to a lesser equipped invader whose sheer numbers were smaller.

Baladar could send archers to the crest above the valley and attack the enemy from the safety of the heights. He could also send the rocks tumbling down into the gorge from the foothills of the Thorndars to their east. There were many options when an army approached from this direction. But today there was only one. Baladar and his ministers knew that their only hope was to garrison themselves in the city itself and then wear away at Colton each time he attempted to batter down the walls or shatter the gates. It was a plan of last resort, one that had only a slim chance of succeeding, and then only if the Dark Lord grew frustrated and bored.

Fortunately as the fates would have it, what the Dark Lord sought was not here. Baladar took great comfort in knowing that whatever the result of the siege, even if Pardatha should fall, all was not lost, hope still existed and the battle would continue. He could play that card in the end, if need be. What would Colton want with this city? He could give himself over to the Evil One in lieu of the heir. Perhaps he could save the city, perhaps Colton would accept Baladar's sacrifice if he thought it might bring him closer to Davmiran at a later date, if he believed that he could use Baladar to seek out Dav, once he discovered that his quarry was not here.

He was prepared to try anything, but it was not yet time for those decisions. Pardatha would put up a noble fight, and he was not ready to discount the possibility that this moody and taciturn invader would grow bored with the invasion if he found out that the ultimate reason for it was no longer realistic.

Baladar sat on the high backed council chair at the head of the great slab of rock that formed the table of war, around which were assembled his war ministers. The chamber had been built countless tiels ago on the highest ground in Pardatha. It was enclosed by ten pillars of the same stone as the table, forming an open oval around the group. From here, the council could see clearly down the gorge, across the forest and over lake Everclear.

Grogan sat at Baladar's right hand. Elion was given a chair to Baladar's left and greeted warmly by all audience members as he arrived. He was refreshed and dressed in light Elfin armor, amber in color, and high, tight brown suede boots, with a dagger at his belt. The other chairs were occupied by Bishop Anwel of Reston, Baladar's generals, Jerik Woodhaven, leader of the Treefighters, Baron Selfridge, Lord Icaran, the heads of the bowmen, infantry, and swordsmen, as well as by the leaders of the largest of the neighboring armies that entered Pardatha both to help defend the city and to seek protection for their families and other citizens.

An empty chair was placed next to Elion, and as the already assembled participants were chatting and introducing themselves to one another, Filaree Par D'Avalain was escorted into the chamber. All of the noise stopped immediately, as the Lady entered with Cameron at her side. She wore a long cloak of ebony velvet, embroidered with the crest of Avalain on its back. Her leggings were black leather over which she wore a white silk tunic. Tucked into a black sash cinching her waist was a dagger with a large ruby set into the hilt. Her jet black hair was braided and wound tightly around her head, and her almond shaped, dark eyes shone brightly in anticipation of what was to come.

Baladar stood up and said respectfully, "Welcome, Filaree Par D'Avalain. It is an honor to have you here with us. Your reputation precedes you."

He bowed his head slightly. The others around the table followed suit, awed by the striking looks of this female warrior about whom they all had heard so much.

"Please, sit. There is no reason to be so formal with me. I am accustomed to the rigors of a battlefield and I do not stand on ceremony," she responded. "But, thank you for your welcome," Filaree said, bowing slightly to the entire table.

She sat down next to Elion, while Cameron took up his position behind her and to her right, directly between his Lady and the Elfin Prince.

"Lady Filaree, Prince Elion and all of our honored visitors," Baladar addressed the group. "We are here for one purpose only, I fear, and that is to determine how we can defend the city and all of its inhabitants against the advance of Colton dar Agonthea and his armies. Originally, I summoned the Lady D'Avalain along with two others who have not yet arrived, for the noble purpose of training and educating the heir of Gwendolen," Baladar said, and then he paused in order for the gathering to quiet down.

The mention of the heir caused quite a stir amongst those present and they looked in wonder from one to another, and then all their eyes rested finally on Baladar.

"Yes, I said the heir of Gwendolen," he said solemnly. "Ages ago, it was written that a child would be born of the Gwendolen line..."

Many at the table nodded, remembering the stories that had been told to them as children.

"...and that child would one day seek and find the Gem of Eternity, and restore the balance to the world that the Dark Lord threatened," he continued somberly. "I believe that the child indeed was borne, and that he was cast into my arms not too long ago."

All those around the table, with the exception of Filaree, Elion and Cameron, looked shocked and could barely contain their emotions.

When the din died down, Duke Sigis asked, "Are you certain, Baladar? Where is he now?"

Everyone present anxiously awaited Baladar's answer.

"I am certain my friend, and to our good fortune, he is no longer here at this time. Rather, he is currently under the protection of our allies in the south. He resides in the heights of Seramour," Baladar answered and he glanced subtly at Elion.

Again, those around the table chatted briefly with one another and then they all looked once again at Baladar.

"Our brave visitor, Prince Elion of Lormarion, risked his life to bring me the news of the heir's safety."

This time Baladar looked deeply into Elion's eyes as he said those words. The young Elfin Prince was grateful to him for not revealing how the boy got to Seramour in the first place, and Baladar also did not feel it was necessary to explain the circumstances that surrounded the heir's disappearance.

"Treestar, King of the Southern Elves is his guardian right now, and unless we prevail here, he will be the one to train and educate him," Baladar said with a gravity that everyone present immediately felt. "But, take heart! Had he been trapped in Pardatha with the rest of us, before he was awakened and his powers had an opportunity to manifest themselves, before all of his teachers even arrived, there would be little hope for him, nay for us all," he resumed. "It is obvious to me that Colton believes him to still be here and that is why he is advancing upon us with such force. He does not wish to risk the legends coming true. He wants to stop the heir now, before he grows stronger. When the boy was first cast to me, I was able to witness his last moments, the final minutes before his guardian sacrificed herself in order to get him here.

"The Dark Lord was present then and was held at bay by a single woman, Mira of Gwendolen, a sorceress and healer who resided in the palace of the King. She gave her life to protect him. Colton dar Agonthea was infuriated by his inability to prevent her casting the boy to me. I saw his anger, as the boy slipped from his grasp. How he learned the boy was here, I do not know. I pray that we do not have a traitor in our midst. Nevertheless, once more the Dark Lord thinks that he has trapped him, and once again he will be disappointed. We must all rejoice in knowing that whatever the outcome will be, the world will yet see another sunrise, and hope will not be destroyed by the results of the next few days."

The members of the council were all nodding now, and although many had questions, they remained silent and allowed Baladar to continue.

"I named the boy Davmiran, in honor of this noble woman, Mira, who gave her life so that he could be with us today."

Baladar was silent for a moment, remembering the boy's face, his innocence and his power. After he took his seat, Filaree stood and addressed the group next.

"I have only just now learned that the boy is not here. It grieves me that I arrived here too late, but much has happened since I first left Avalain and we could not reach Pardatha any sooner. I have not yet had an opportunity to review the assets of the invader, which I will do on my own time. But, I am not prepared to assume that Pardatha cannot hold out against Colton. This city is strong and we have many troops garrisoned here. We will live to see another day, and I will yet have an opportunity to train the young Lord in Seramour," she said.

"Here, here!" Elion responded, leaping to his feet. "I walked right into the belly of the beast, and I am ready to fight my way out! I will never surrender to the Dark Lord's evil," he continued.

"I admire your enthusiasm and your valor, both of you," Baladar remarked gravely. "I, too, am not willing to give up before the fight begins. Pardatha has survived many a threat and she has many allies of all kinds. Colton dar Agonthea will not have as easy a time as he thinks whence the siege begins."

"My Lord?" Grogan asked. "May I speak?"

"Of course. Go ahead," Baladar answered.

"The city is well provisioned and the people are ready to defend it to the end. I must order the gates closed and sealed shortly, though, as our intelligence tells us that we have no more than a day before his advance guard arrives. He has sent a contingent of riders ahead to parlay, I assume. They will be the first to reach the city," Grogan related.

"I imagine that he will ask us to surrender before the fight even begins. He underestimates the temerity of our people," Baron

Selfridge said.

"Indeed! I would sooner die by my own hand than surrender to that bastard!" Lord Icaran said angrily.

"He will surely ask us to release the heir to his custody," Baladar surmised. "He will not believe it when I tell him that the boy is not within the confines of the city."

He was thinking that if a parlay was possible, he could then offer himself to the Dark Lord and perhaps avoid the terrible bloodshed thereby.

"He will settle for nothing less than total victory! If he cannot retrieve the boy, he will want revenge! He does not think as we do. The bloodlust that drives a warrior during battle is what determines his actions most of the time. He thrives on destruction. Do not think that he will accept anything other than what he wants," Filaree said.

Baladar thought seriously about what the maiden from Avalain had just asserted. He could not make the mistake of attributing to Colton the same thought process that governed his own thinking.

"I appreciate your analysis, my Lady. I had been thinking that perhaps he would take me in lieu of the heir. But you have made a good point. He would dispose of me as quickly as he would any one else. All that must matter to him now is the boy," Baladar concluded.

"My Lord, if I may, the city needs you. We all need you and the heir needs you. What good would it do to trade with the devil? He will not be satisfied until he has what he wants anyway," Grogan commented.

"We can only hope that our defense will be strong enough to compel him to conserve his forces for another time. After all, when he learns that Davmiran is not here he will certainly know that another battle must follow this one, and he cannot win it without an army. We must inflict as much damage as we can!" Elion said.

"You are correct, my young friend. Our strengths are many. And, he will not want to leave here weakened, at least not if he does so without what he came for," Baladar responded.

"Although we may be no more than a mote in his eye, we can irritate him significantly!" Bishop Anwel said.

"Even as the gods lose their patience, so must the devil's son," Jerik Woodhaven remarked.

"We must harass him and annoy him to the point where he either tries to crush us out of frustration, or he leaves," the Bishop commented. "A deadly gamble, perhaps, but one we must contemplate."

"When his emissaries arrive, I will meet them on the field, and I will tell them that what they seek is not here. Lady Filaree ? Will you accompany me?" Baladar asked.

"It would be my honor, Lord Baladar," she answered, bowing her head.

"And you, Elion, I think you have earned the right to bring Colton this news," Baladar stated.

"With pleasure, my Lord," Elion said proudly.

"Grogan, you must remain here. If something should happen to us, you are more than capable of taking over the defense of the city. Bishop Anwel? Would you add your spiritual touch to our group?"

"Certainly, Lord Baladar. I would like to bring the wrath of the mighty one down upon them all if I could, may the First forgive me," he answered.

"It is decided then. I believe that everyone here knows what they must do now. I wish to retire to my study to prepare. As soon as Colton's messengers arrive, I will have the tower bell ring three times. We will assemble in the courtyard and then ride to the gates together. Grogan! Prepare the city for the closing of the gates. It is time," Baladar concluded, as he stood up from the table and bid everyone farewell.

Some of the people remained to talk about the developments, while Elion and Filaree walked out together with Cameron close behind. Elion could not get over how beautiful this human female was. She had such a regal air about her, yet she was strong and determined. He would want to be on her side of the battlefield when the fighting begins, he thought.

"Did you see the heir yourself?" Filaree asked him as they walked.

"Yes, I was with him for quite some time" Elion answered. "He is very handsome, for a human," Elion continued, and then immediately realized how that must have sounded. "I did not mean anything by that, my Lady. I am sorry..." he started to explain.

"Do not apologize to me, Prince Elion. I find most humans to be rather gruff and clumsy myself," she said laughing, while Cameron frowned deeply from behind.

"Did you speak with him often?" she asked.

"Baladar did not tell you?" he questioned her, surprised.

"Tell me what, Prince?" she responded.

"That he is not well? That the heir is under a spell and is

unconscious?" he replied.

"He did mention that he has not yet awoken, but I assumed he meant that he was still sleeping from his journey," she responded.

"Well, he is still sleeping from his journey. But he has been sleeping for at least a week!" Elion remarked. "My mother, Queen Elsinestra, is a healer and she was about to go to him when I left her. She will find a way to bring him back to us," he said with confidence and with no lack of pride.

"I am sure she will, Prince Elion. I have heard much about her over the years. The boy is in good hands. Is he all that we have been led to believe?" she asked.

"More, my Lady. Much more," he said solemnly.

"I am anxious to meet him myself. But there is much to do here first if I ever hope to have a chance to work with the heir," she said. "Come Cameron. Walk with me." She reached out her arm for the other man to take and he gladly grasped it. Elion bowed to them both as they parted company for the evening.

Elion returned to his rooms to prepare for the parlay and Filaree, with Cameron at her side, went to the training grounds to observe the troops and await the tolling of the bells.

Chapter Thirty-five

Grogan gathered a small contingent of his best men and marched with them to the Noban gates. The stream of refugees into the city had slowed somewhat, but he could still see a long line of people, wagons, animals and the occasional soldier stretching out into the woods. He told his guards to spread out and start advising the stragglers that the gates would be closing soon. The dozen or so soldiers rode their horses out and around disseminating the news, and those still quite a distance from the city walls began to move with a renewed speed, turning what had been a relatively calm and organized procession into a tangled mess. No one wanted to be stranded outside the city with Colton dar Agonthea on the march and now so near.

The death of the beloved trees had caused so much pain and suffering throughout the countryside these past tiels. Without the protection and calming influence of the Lalas, the population sought out Pardatha and Baladar as replacements, if only temporary, for the security they had lost. The high walls and fortified gates of the city seemed the safest and most comforting alternative.

"Let's move now. Hurry up. Lord Baladar does not wish anyone to be caught outside. Move quickly," Grogan said as he rode up and down the remaining lines gathered outside, and the people responded with a renewed urgency.

After a few more hours the numbers had diminished to a trickle, and Grogan signaled his guards to assemble on either side of the huge entrance. Two of his soldiers pulled large, bone horns from their saddlebags and held them to their lips, awaiting their leader's signal. Grogan raised his arm and then with much regret, he dropped it, at which point the two guards began to blow on the great horns.

The sound echoed throughout the city, beyond the forest and across the lake. Baladar heard the sad bellowing from his study, high up in the castle tower. Elion turned, startled at first, and then recognized the signal for what it was. Filaree listened with a pensive look upon her face and Cameron walked to her side to share the prodigious moment with his Lady.

Everyone already in the city knew the seriousness of the sound, and for just a few seconds the activity that had grown frenetic in the past few days, died completely. The remainder of the guards accompanying Grogan moved to the large mechanism that opened and closed the massive wooden gates. A few stragglers were still rushing in, and when the Master at Arms was confident that no more were left behind, he issued the orders to seal Pardatha from the inevitable assault.

The majestic doors creaked and groaned and the soldiers cranked away, though they hardly budged them at first. Everyone nearby stopped what they were doing, stood perfectly still and watched. It had been so long since this avenue had been closed, that even the city elders could not remember the last time. Once the doors began to move though, the noise ceased almost entirely, and they closed silently and smoothly as if they were gliding upon a cushion of air. But with each foot of ground that they covered, the hearts of the people beat faster and faster. Finally, they met with a resounding crash in the wake of which an eerie hush spread over the city.

Pardatha became an island in the path of a storm, and the silence of those witnessing the event was like the calm that reigns before the wind hits and the lightening strikes. But as the First was their witness, the Pardathans would resist until the end, until there was no fight left within the noble city, until the very walls crumbled and fell. And their leaders knew all the while that the real hope for the world lay not with them any longer no matter how valiant and brave they fought, but to the south, among the Elves in the protected heights of Seramour. After a while, after the echoes that marked the sealing of the city had long faded away, and after the dust had settled upon the cobblestones of Pardatha, everyone went back about their business though they were all just a bit more pensive than before.

Grogan and his men slid the locking mechanisms into place, carefully and diligently set the seals that secured them and then took up their watch beside the Noban gates.

Chapter Thirty-six

By the time the dawn drew, Robyn was already up and atop Kraft and ready for the final leg of his journey. He would be approaching Pardatha directly from the north, thereby avoiding the swamps that edged the great forest. The air was cool for this time of year and the sky was streaked with long, grey clouds. Shadows roamed around the ground like great, hulking monsters chasing each other across the fields.

The air smelled oddly pungent, and with each breath he took his nose became more and more irritated, until he finally had to wrap a scarf around his face to filter his intake. His eyes began to tear and sting, and he thought that he could see a faint smoke hanging in the air around him. Robyn rode as fast as he could, covering ground swifter than most on the back of his stallion. The smoke grew more abundant and the acrid odor increased with each passing hour.

As he neared Pardatha, he was bothered by the fact that he saw no activity on the outskirts of the city. He would have expected to see the signs of commerce, of trade, of visitors and travelers. But instead, all was quiet and still. No smoke swirled from the chimneys of the scattered farm houses he passed and no animals grazed in the corrals. He passed no one on the way toward the city, and even though he was not traveling a beaten path, he could see the thoroughfares in the distance and they were still and abandoned.

His instincts told him to skirt the woods and not to gallop headlong into the unknown, and Robyn always trusted his instincts. Kraft was expressing some discomfort now due to the heaviness of the air, and Robyn spied a small pond fed by a clear, flowing stream issuing from a rocky hill to its west. It was surrounded by a knoll of thick, leafy trees. He led his steed in that direction and allowed him to drink from the pure waters for a time while he dismounted. Robyn tried to identify the odor that was in the air everywhere, but he could not place it. It had the taste of carbon, but it was more rancid and not pure at all. The air seemed to leave an oily residue all over him and he was becoming more and more troubled by it.

Robyn sat for a moment and dug his long fingers into the soft soil surrounding the pond. He reached for contact, and when he found what he was looking for, he relaxed and let his mind open up to the floes. Not in words, but through feelings did the images manifest themselves. At first he did not know what he was sensing, but the pictures grew clearer in his mind's eye as the moments passed. He dug his hand deeper into the ground, trying to reach a clearer source. A soft root twirled itself around his wrist with a comforting squeeze, and the previously confusing impressions became vivid images. He was astonished at the sheer size of the enemy's forces. The picture he received was neither steady nor systematic. Rather, he caught glimpses of beasts and pack animals, soldiers and slaves, siege engines and wagons, one after another, until they flooded his brain.

Robyn recoiled violently from the next image, but not soon enough to avoid being struck by the stench of the Dark Lord and the vision of his hideous expression of glee with which he led his forces. He saw Colton turn with a start, perhaps sensing the intrusion, and the image in Robyn's mind rapidly changed. He now saw huge, belching beasts, spreading a thick, acrid smoke everywhere, and he saw that the fires scattered all over the massive camp were emitting greasy fumes from the carcasses of the burning animals spitted over the flames.

Briefly, he saw a group of riders mounted on black steeds with cloven hooves, with hoods hiding their darkened faces, traveling separately from all the rest. They were moving in unison, and they were carrying a black banner with a red sun on its surface. They were not with the rest of the army but quite some distance from it, heading somewhere away from the main contingent. He could see the swords glinting at their belts beneath their crimson cloaks.

The entire scene was horrific, one image was worse than the next! Robyn realized that he was marching into the middle of the tempest, and he only hoped that he was not too late, that he would be able to reach Pardatha before the enemy arrived at its gates. He withdrew his hand from the earth having seen enough, and then he washed it briefly in the cool water of the pond, splashing some of the fresh liquid into his face as well. The air hung with the rotten stench and his eyes watered still. Robyn whistled and Kraft responded immediately, nudging him under the arm, as anxious as he was to leave this place.

Once in the saddle again, he rode gingerly, hugging the tree line and looking out for danger. A flock of birds sprang out of the trees before them, as the sound of horns blowing in the distance pierced the relative silence of the afternoon. He continued to ride, getting closer and closer to his destination, while becoming more and more anxious with each mile that he covered.

Ahead, rising above the treetops in the distance, he could see the temple mount extending high up over the city, the distinctive oval edifice silhouetted in the sun. Very soon now he would be in Pardatha, and he pressed forward with determination, riding Kraft hard. Robyn could see the walls to the city outlined beyond the plains, and as he drew closer, still within the cover of the woods, he saw the same detachment of riders on their coal black mounts with the cloven hooves approaching the gates.

He dismounted, led Kraft to a sheltered area overlooking the valley across from which this abhorrent group was riding, and he observed with growing concern the developments below. Instead of the hideous raven banner with the burning sun, they carried a white flag of truce, obviously looking to parlay with the leaders of the city. But, it occurred to Robyn, that when he saw them previously they were carrying swords beneath their cloaks! Something was amiss here. Riders looking to confer did so unarmed, unless some sort of treachery was afoot.

The rules of war were clearly written, however unusual, and all nations abided by them. But Colton dar Agonthea was a pariah, a being who always distanced himself from society and one who placed himself beyond the law. Robyn believed that he would behave no differently here and now than ever before. If the leaders of Pardatha, Baladar and his ministers, underestimated the unscrupulousness of the Dark Lord, then they may just fall into his trap.

Robyn watched apprehensively from his perch above the city, and he waited for the meeting to begin. His tired eyes scanned the surrounding countryside and finally came to rest upon the city once more. He noticed with surprise that the massive gates of Pardatha were shut tight, something he had never seen here before. The battlements were heavily manned, and he could see armed soldiers peering through the crenellated towers. He sat pensively on Kraft's sturdy back, awaiting the next development in the macabre drama about to unfold below him.

Chapter Thirty-seven

The bevy of crimson Mages approached the shuttered gates of Pardatha, displaying the white flag of truce. They all had heavy cowls covering their heads and shadowing their faces, and their steeds were identical in size and color, snorting and steaming as they pranced in place, leaving deep cleavages in the soft, vine covered soil upon which they walked. The guards on the battlements locked the visors down on their helmets and leaned over the high, stone walls.

One of the riders broke from the group and trotted right up to the wall, dropping the hood from his head to reveal a hairless pate and a ghostly white face. His lips were blood red as if painted onto his skin and his eyes were like solid black orbs, lifeless and forsaken. His voice chilled the very bones of the guards.

"We come at the bequest of our Lord and Master, Colton dar Agonthea, King of Sedahar, Emperor of the Southlands, and Liege Lord of the Forgotten Realms. We ask on his behalf for a parlay with your leader, Baladar of Pardatha. We come unarmed and our Master wishes us to express that he wants to avoid a long and costly war, and he hopes that Baladar wants the same. He asks that we speak directly with your Lord and convey his special messages," he said in a voice hollow and dead, as the Pardathan guards looked on in horror. "Tell Baladar that we await him on the plain," the rider concluded, and then he turned his mount around to return to the assembled group.

The lieutenant on watch, the highest ranking of the guards who heard this diatribe, gave orders for the others to remain steadfast and observe the movements of these messengers of death, while he ran to the bell tower to advise Lord Baladar of the arrival of the Dark Lord's emissaries.

Elion heard the bell chime three times, then he immediately jumped up from his pallet and dressed as quickly as he could. He regretfully left his dagger on the table next to his bow and quiver, and he headed for the door. Filaree too heard the bell and she sprang up from her slumber as well, already prepared to depart, reluctantly leaving her weapons behind, though feeling quite naked without them. As they emerged from their chambers, they met in the broad hallway and descended the stairway together on their way to the courtyard to meet Baladar and the others.

They spoke no words on that short journey but they felt a kinship that they could not explain, a bond between the two of them that developed the instant that they met and would henceforth remain between them always. Filaree smiled at Elion and he bowed his head in return, embarrassed but grateful for the closeness. Together they crossed the cobblestone courtyard and walked to the designated meeting place to await the arrival of Bishop Anwel and Baladar.

When the bell tolled, Baladar was already standing at the wide window, staring down at the plains stretching out before the closed gates of his beloved city. He was dressed in a simple tunic of white wool, with the crest of Pardatha embroidered in gold upon its chest. A brown leather belt cinched his waist, unadorned, and a cape of a darker brown velvet was draped over his shoulders. He took his large signet ring from the strong box on the shelf and placed it on the index finger of his right hand. The gold ring still hung from the chain beneath his shirt, and he felt its heat as he walked to the door. He carried no weapons when he left the study for the courtyard to meet the others. The Bishop was waiting at the bottom of the tower steps for him when he emerged from the shelter of the doorway. Together, they walked the short distance to where Grogan and the guards readied the horses.

"Greetings, Lady Filaree, Prince Elion," the Bishop said as he saw them standing by the guards. "It seems our "friend" wasted no time in dispatching his messengers. I assume we must meet with them for the sake of propriety, if nothing more," he continued.

"I have seen the Dark Lord, your eminence, and it is not propriety he admires, I can assure you," Elion replied.

"What good can possibly come of this meeting? Do you think that he has any interest in a peaceful solution here? For that matter, do we? How can we ever be at peace with him? We are like oil and water, and the only way to deal with him is to burn him off of our surface. We cannot live side by side with Colton dar Agonthea!" Filaree remarked with vehemence.

"We must meet nevertheless, and hear what he has to say," Baladar spoke calmly. "Perhaps we will learn something about his intentions. At least we will have the satisfaction of telling his couriers that the heir is not in the city. They will not want to bring him back that news! How he reacts to that information will determine what we do next. It is beyond expectation that he will turn around and go home. However he ultimately responds, we will feel the brunt of his furor in the short term, of that I am sure."

"May the First guide us through these dark days," the Bishop said, as the guard helped him onto the back of his horse.

"Indeed! We could use the aid of the Lalas now. We have no Chosen in Pardatha any more," Baladar noted with a certain melancholy, reminding himself of just how dear his wife, the last one, was to him.

"We can fight just as well without the trees to aid us..." Filaree commented proudly, "...if we must," she concluded.

"I fear that today we must!" Elion said gravely. "If Caeltin has to leave here empty handed, it will be at this city's expense," he said as he pulled himself atop his pony. "What I am concerned about is treachery! I saw his army. I witnessed the horrors that he has created and nurtured to serve him. An enemy such as this will not behave as we would."

"We must be vigilant, but we cannot sacrifice our values because our enemy has none!" the Bishop replied.

"Enough talk now, my friends," Baladar chimed in. "We must not keep our guests waiting. Let us get on with this 'parlay', but keep your eyes open, all of you! Pray for the best, but expect the worst," he said and he spurred his stallion ahead, crossing the threshold of the castle with his friends close behind.

The people of the city were lined up on either side of the avenue that lead from the castle to the Noban gates. They were solemn and looked up at the riders with hope and expectation in their eyes. Silently they each raised their right fist, one by one, as a sign of solidarity and fealty to their Lord, and he nodded in acknowledgment, feeling a deep respect and affection for them all as he rode past. The golden ring pulsated beneath his tunic and gave him courage as he marched through the city streets.

Everyone was captivated by the gravity of the moment, and the riders continued on in silence until they reached the sealed gates. The shadow of the Ghost Tower stretched out beyond the walls, creating an ominous, darkened swath of ground upon which the enemy's entourage assembled.

The Pardathan guards who had marshaled by the tower's base, parted so as to let the riders approach the small door that they would open in order to allow the horses out, one by one. Baladar was to be first, followed by Bishop Anwel, the Lady Filaree and finally Prince Elion. A single horn sounded atop the battlements signaling the start of the meeting, and the heavy latch on the door was sprung, allowing it to open inward.

Baladar emerged into the partial sunlight beyond the walls, and without hesitating, he walked forward with the other three close behind, lining up abreast of one another once they cleared the small passage. They trotted their horses into the middle of the plain, past the cobblestone pathways and paved roads that led out from Pardatha, toward the demonic group standing some hundred yards ahead. The new arrivals remained illuminated by the sunlight in stark contrast to the shrouded assemblage they came out to meet.

Once they were within speaking distance, Baladar wasted no time before beginning the inevitable interaction.

"You have entered our lands uninvited with a substantial armed force behind you. You come to the city in the name of Colton dar Agonthea asking for parlay, but you do not state your reason for invading our country. In good faith, we assemble hear to listen to your 'requests', and we expect that you are here in good faith as well," Baladar said earnestly.

The leader of the group stepped forward on his black steed, emerging menacingly from the shadows. All of his companion's cowls were up, covering their heads and faces, and as the speaker approached he let his own hood fall back, revealing a cadaverous face, expressionless, with empty eyes and pallid skin. The sunlight upon his skin made him appear almost translucent and hardly alive. They could literally see the liquid coursing through his veins in spastic bursts.

Baladar stepped forward once more on Porta and stood head to tail with this ambassador of evil. He watched him closely and was overwhelmed for a slight moment by the deathly stench of his breath, which issued from his mouth in gasps, through blackened and rotted teeth.

"Our master requests that you surrender unto him the boy that you hold hostage. He claims guardianship of this whelp, and he desires to retrieve that which is rightfully his," the sickly sweet voice said.

Baladar was offended by the preposterous assertions, but he remained calm expecting no less, and he replied to the leering beast before him.

"First of all, I fail to understand why your esteemed leader believes that he has a claim of any kind to the child. He was sent here for protection and learning. His parents are dead. He is no relation of your master's."

"His father, King Garold of Gwendolen, proffered custody upon my Lord on his death bed. I have the contract here. There can be no denying it!" his voice boomed, as he pulled a small parchment out from his belt and flicked it open so that Baladar could see the seals and signatures. "Now, please respect the covenant of the father and produce the son for us to take back to our Master," he said with finality, as he handed the paper to Baladar.

The Lord of Pardatha was becoming angrier by the minute, knowing that good King Garold would not have given his consent to such a contract of his own free will. He could only imagine the terrible death that the poor man suffered at the hands of Colton and the suffering that he must have endured before he was compelled to place his signature upon that evil piece of parchment. If the inscription was in fact Garold's, it was coerced out of him and Baladar felt no obligation to honor it.

"I am not sure that I can abide by this document," he said. "I will need to take it back to my scribes in the city to authenticate the seals and signatures. After all, Garold is no longer here to testify to your claims, and unfortunately he did not die in his sleep, as one as noble as he deserved," he said, stalling for time in order to absorb the consequences of this unexpected disclosure, while making clear his contempt for the circumstances that surrounded Garold's demise.

The envoy grew agitated, having hoped that no further discussion would have been necessary, and he acted as if he was offended by Baladar's subtle allegations.

"You dare to doubt the truth of what my Lord tells you? I demand that you surrender the boy immediately! You have no choice. The signatures are real and the boy belongs to Colton now!"

He spit the words through his rotten teeth and then grabbed the parchment from Baladar's hand.

"He belongs to no one! And, if he was here in Pardatha, I would not surrender him to you or your Master," Baladar said with a steel hard voice, while standing up straight in his stirrups.

The Dark Lord's envoy sat up in his saddle too and looked at Baladar venomously through his dead, black eyes, surprise clearly imbuing his anger.

"You say the offspring is not here in Pardatha? You lie, Baladar!" he hissed through his ruined lips.

Filaree rose in her seat, affronted by the turn of the conversation, her ire building dangerously. Elion could see the agitation she felt and he reached over and placed a calming hand atop her own. The Bishop sat sternly in his saddle, revealing no emotions.

"I speak the truth!" Baladar said in a hushed voice, and he could feel the golden ring burning a hole in his chest beneath his shirt. "He was kidnapped from here and he has been gone from this city for some time now. Your spies have misinformed you if they told you otherwise, emissary," he responded pointedly.

The ring seemed so hot, he was afraid it would reveal itself through the very fabric that concealed it.

"This cannot be so! You deceive us and you insult the Dark Lord in so doing! He will wish to speak directly with you, Baladar," the skeletal being said as he drew a long, thin blade from underneath his voluminous cape.

The others in his group immediately encircled Baladar, pulling out concealed weapons as well, two of them facing him and the other two confronting the Bishop, Elion and Filaree.

"What manner of treachery is this?" Baladar said with outrage, as they forced him away from the rest of his friends. "You violate the rules of war! Has your master no honor at all?" he asked.

The envoy bent his ugly head back and laughed a ghastly laugh, obviously finding Baladar's reference to honor amusing.

"It is you who deceive, my good Lord, with your lies about the boy. Do not speak to me of honor. And now you must come with us," he said as he urged him forward with the tip of his blade.

Filaree had no weapon with which to strike back, but she was more than capable of besting this "animal" with her hands alone, she believed. She surveyed the surroundings quickly then jostled Elion slightly, indicating with her eyes that he should take the guard on the left and that she would disable the one on the right. She was not going to allow them to leave with Baladar as their prisoner.

As she was about make her move, the leader of this hellish enemy looked at her sharply as if he knew her thoughts. He quickly raised his right hand, colorless palm upward and long, pointed fingernails extending toward her. A ball of blue fire formed, and he grasped it with his thin fingers as she watched. As he propelled it toward her, Bishop Anwel turned his horse abruptly and leapt directly in the fiery missile's path. It burst into his chest, sending him careening to the ground. He lay still, his white robes charred and smoldering, while a circle of crimson blood began to spread slowly outward across the front of his tunic.

§

Robyn dar Tamarand watched from the top of the hill as the opposing parties assembled on the plain below. He could not hear what was being said from his vantage point behind the trees, but it was obvious to him that the white flag the red robed riders presented earlier indicated that they wanted to talk to those within the garrisoned city.

Robyn watched closely as Baladar emerged from the single door which opened in the sealed gates of Pardatha. Behind him, he saw three others follow, one on a dapple pony, an Elf from the looks of him, a religious leader in his white robes of office and a woman warrior, strikingly beautiful even from this distance. He inched Kraft forward until he was directly above them, though remaining still within the cover of the trees.

He watched them talk for a few minutes but he was unable to determine the course of the conversations. Shortly, though, his skin tingled and his concern mounted when he saw four of the intruders surround Baladar and cut him off from the rest of his friends. At the same time, they drew their blades from beneath their robes, as he feared. Before he had time to react, a ball of fire burst from the hand of the speaker and toppled the white robed rider.

At the sight of this treachery, he spoke softly in Kraft's ear and instantly the stallion charged down the hill. When he reached the soft ground of the plain, he leapt from his saddle and sunk his right hand deep into the soil, searching for something familiar, something recognizable. Almost immediately, as if the earth was waiting for an invitation, a soft root comfortingly encircled his wrist, speaking to him in wordless images, and he concentrated with all his power.

Just as Robyn reached the bottom of the crest, Filaree swung her horse hard around, knocking into the robed rider before her, trying to grab the hilt of his sword before he could regain his seat. Elion immediately slid from his pony's back and attempted to run under the belly of the other rider's mount while he was distracted, making it impossible for him to strike at the Elf with his sword, while he attempted to upset the big steed from below. He trusted in his size and quickness to avoid serious injury.

Meanwhile, Baladar was being led away at sword point by the master of the group. No one had yet to see Robyn enter the fray, as he was still some distance away from them. None doubted for a moment that these henchmen of the Dark Lord would strike to kill if and when they could. Robyn sensed the tangle of vines permeating the soil of the plains upon which they were engaged in this melee. They had been planted purposefully, he perceived, and he would now make good use of them.

The fabric weaves of its own will, he mused as his thoughts merged with the coursing energy beneath the ground.

Baladar was about to make a desperate attempt to save himself, knowing that he would be better off dead than a prisoner of Colton's, when the earth erupted ferociously under his feet. Roots and vines sprang up from the ground everywhere, violently wrapping themselves around the legs of the horses carrying the emissaries of evil, and reaching up to the riders themselves with a speed that defied belief. The cloaked rider nearest to the Prince did not bother to wait for any of his associates. He had not yet been entangled by the vegetation, and he spurred his mount violently, causing him to lurch forward. Together, they bounded across the field, racing for the safety of the enemy lines and disappearing into its darkness.

Elion felt the tubers slithering all around him now, but surprisingly none touched his body. Still, he was unable from his position on the ground to chase the perfidious messenger, and he watched helplessly as he drew near to the masses assembled across the plain. Filaree embraced the opportunity this surprising turn of events created, and she sent the half-human she was jostling with falling to the ground, whereupon he was immediately blanketed by the wriggling and straining shoots. As she watched, they pulled him through the soft earth, encircling him in a living cocoon instantly and completely, until his body was thoroughly covered with dirt and grass. She could see his mouth open and from the blackness therein, he was barely able to let a final howl escape his parched and reddened lips before it filled with earth. In less than a minute more, he had vanished completely beneath the surface.

Filaree turned to the others who also stood mystified, dodging needlessly the writhing and thrashing vines which attached themselves only to the servants of their dark enemy, leaving them to gape in wonder. Baladar was sitting astride Porta, aghast at the final throes of his former captor, as the thrashing roots and convulsing filaments dragged both him and his violent steed into the bowels of the earth.

When all were gone but the one who fled at the onset, as quickly as they sprang from the soil, the vines and roots disappeared beneath the plain once more, and Baladar, Elion and Filaree found themselves standing near one another mystified. Elion's pony was close by and they could see Nico wandering back to join them from perhaps ten yards away. All that remained of the harbingers was a red cloak lying by Elion's feet and one lone sword nearer to Baladar, which Filaree rushed to retrieve.

The motionless body of Bishop Anwel lay nearest to Elion and he immediately moved to him and bent down in an attempt to assess the damage. He realized almost immediately, having spent many long days assisting his mother with the sick and injured, that the good Bishop would not recover from this wound. His breath came in short gasps and bright red blood issued from his nose and mouth. His entire robe was saturated and stained a deep red.

Baladar, having leapt from Porta's back, approached his friend next and pressed his head to the chest of the dying man. His eyes were already closed and he could no longer speak.

"There is nothing we can do for him now, but we cannot leave him here," he said. "Elion, assist me." Together they lifted the dying man onto Porta's back, laying him carefully over the horse's withers, and then Baladar mounted behind him.

Filaree spoke next, her protective instincts at play instantly. "We must hasten back to the city. Surely Colton will retaliate as soon as he discovers what has transpired."

She immediately signaled for Nico.

"Did I really see what I thought I did?" Elion asked as he prepared to return to the city.

"If you did not, then where did our enemies disappear to?" Baladar responded, as surprised by what had just occurred as the young Prince was.

"Let us not dwell for too long upon our good fortune just yet," Filaree cautioned. "They could have been just an appetizer for what lives under this plain and we may still be their main course," she said. "Let us make for the gates as quickly as we can."

As she said that, she saw another rider approaching at great speed from the hills to the north. Raising the sword she recovered from the ground, she prepared to meet this new intruder head on.

"Baladar! Elion! Go! I will hold him off."

Elion had no intention of leaving the Lady alone, and he slapped Porta on his rump, sending the horse, its rider and the now unconscious Bishop on their way to the city gates. He rushed to Filaree's side and as the rider neared, Filaree urged Nico forward with her sword raised and ready, not willing to give this new enemy an opportunity to strike first.

"Stop!" he yelled. "I am a friend. You have no reason to fear me. I saw what was happening from the hills above and I did what I could to assist you," he remarked in a voice that could only have been speaking the truth. "I am Robyn dar Tamarand, and I have been summoned here to Pardatha by its noble Lord, Baladar. I expected to arrive under different circumstances, though," he said. "But, we really should not be wasting time talking with the enemy yonder amassing," he continued, and he pointed to the valley to the south.

Baladar turned Porta around and trotted back to the group. He stood still for a moment and faced Robyn.

"You look very much like your father, Robyn dar Tamarand. I am Baladar, and it was I who bid you come here. But now, I could not agree with you more regarding our priorities," and he directed his horse toward the city gates.

Across the valley, they could clearly see the dust rising as the enemy's forces were obviously mobilizing and making their way toward them at considerable speed.

Elion took the lead on his small but deceptively fast pony, and the others followed. From atop the crenellated battlement, the guards saw them approaching and hurried to open the small portal through which they could reenter the city. The door swung wide and they burst through, while the guards speedily sealed the opening behind them.

Once the stable hands and guards reached them in order to assist the critically injured Bishop, they gathered together to rehash the events of the past hour. Cameron rushed to his Lady's side before anyone else had the opportunity, in order to make sure she was safe and unhurt.

"My Lady? I should have been beside you. I watched the entire atrocity from the battlements. Is the Bishop dead?"

"No Cameron, but I fear that it is just a matter of time for him. His wounds are surely critical. He saved my life! I owe him a great debt."

"We all do, my Lady," he said sincerely.

Baladar then turned to Robyn and said, "Your timing could not have been better, my friend," he said gratefully.

"I did not plan to arrive just when I did. Things seem to happen as they should sometimes, though I was too late for the good Bishop. But, I am afraid I must bring you more difficult news on top of the tragic events that just occurred. While I was on route here, another great Lalas departed forever from our midst. I was just barely recovering from the throes of its demise, when my father, the Duke Calipee, contacted me to inform me that the mountain Trolls were on the march in the direction of Pardatha, in great numbers. I rode as fast as I could to warn you, but it seems that they will only add to the strength of the formidable forces already encamped upon your doorstep," Robyn said somberly.

"It is no surprise that whatever evil lurks on this planet will now answer the summons of the Lord of Darkness. We are besieged by an enemy as great as any that has ever been assembled here," Baladar said with sadness and concern permeating his voice. "First, I lost Dalek my trusted aide, to treachery. And today, the Bishop has fallen as well. His hours are numbered, I fear. The battle has not yet begun and sadness and loss already engulf us all," Baladar sighed.

"We will prevail!" Filaree interjected, the eternal optimist. "The Evil One does not have the will to suffer personal defeats. We must damage him again and again, until he is so frustrated that he wastes his strengths and we can penetrate his weaknesses," she assessed, ever the strategist.

Robyn could not help but be struck by the tenacity of this beautiful woman. He admired her steadfastness, even in the face of treachery and death. Prince Elion meanwhile was looking at Robyn, wondering how this handsome young Lord had done what he had just done out on the plains.

"With all the excitement around us, I did not introduce myself. I am Elion, Prince of Lormarion, son of Treestar, King of the Southern Elves. I humbly thank you for saving our lives," he said, and he bowed deeply to Robyn.

"Greetings, Prince. But please, you have no reason to pay fealty to me. I did what I had to do and I had plenty of help. I have learned many tricks from my friend, Promanthea, the noble Lalas whom I honor and respect and with whom I share a sacred bond," he said humbly. "I have not had the pleasure of seeing the legendary heights of Seramour, but I have been told by your cousin in the west, Alemar of Eleutheria, that it rivals in beauty the ice castles of their own realm," he responded.

Elion was surprised and thoroughly impressed, to hear that this human had knowledge of, let alone a personal relationship with any one from that part of the world. He was an extraordinary newcomer to this recently assembled group.

"Your experience in that matter may be greater than my own, Robyn dar Tamarand," Elion answered.

"Perhaps so, although I claim no great understanding of their culture. I have just been fortunate to have been an invited guest a number of times," Robyn answered.

Filaree was watching Robyn closely and attempting to assess the man who harbored so many strange secrets and powers. He was too good looking to be a fighter, with his raven hair still shining despite the grime and wear of conflict. He had no apparent battle scars, and he carried himself with a delicacy that belied his abilities it seemed.

"You appear not to be the Robyn dar Tamarand that rumor has depicted you to be," she said boldly, yet with a questioning tone.

"You mince no words, Lady Filaree . And you, my Lady, seem to be every inch the warrior rumor has depicted you to be!" he responded.

She blushed at the compliment and immediately regretted both her new coloration as well as her previous slight.

"I take no offense in your comments, Filaree Par D'Avalain. My reputation has not been a good one. But alas, we sometimes suffer the pain of untruth in order to take refuge within it. It has served me well to appear to be other than I am," Robyn answered.

"I harbor secrets too, and I fear you may be correct, sir. It would be nice if I could play the delicate maiden now and again," she laughed, regaining her composure.

"It would become you as well as does the warrior Queen, I am sure," he answered with no sarcasm in his voice.

Filaree blushed again and turned her face away from Robyn in order to avoid having him see how thoroughly his presence was affecting her.

"You will surely cause her head to swell if you keep complimenting her so, Chosen. And now that we have all gotten acquainted with one another, I think it is time to be moving on. The war council must convene again immediately if we wish to prepare for the battle which will most certainly be upon us shortly," Baladar interrupted without any hint of malice.

Together, they walked across the courtyard toward the road to the mount. The grooms brought out fresh horses for them to ride to the crest and their own were taken to the stables to be brushed and fed and bedded down for the night. Kraft whinnied farewell to

Robyn and Nico did the same to Filaree. Porta threw his head high in the air and shook his mane back and forth before he too headed for his stall, while Elion's small pony followed proudly behind his larger cousins.

Chapter Thirty-eight

Colton was enraged. Those within his immediate reach fell to the ground, prostrate, and buried their heads in their arms. He ranted and raved for quite some time, spitting out venomous rhetoric, lashing out with words at the remaining red guards. The one emissary who had survived would have been better off had he suffocated quickly under the plains of Pardatha. He now hung from his heels, spitted from one end of his body to the other by a barbed, black shaft, as an example to everyone else of what will become of them if they should fail him.

"You lie, Baladar!" he bellowed in anger. "I know you lie. The boy is in the city. That wretched witch saw him. She would not have dared to deceive me. I will bring her back from the dead and look through her own eyes if I must! And a Chosen! A Chosen in Pardatha! He will regret ever having entered that doomed city, whomever he might be! The Lalas cannot protect him here," he fumed.

"You would never give the boy up voluntarily, Baladar, and that fool of a Duke's son, Kettin Dumas, saw him in the city. I felt it. The residue of power was upon him," Colton raved. "He is in the city somewhere and I will find him! Nothing can hide him from me."

He worked himself into an absolute frenzy, sending streaks of raw power arching across the heads of his terrified disciples, singeing trees and blackening rocks. He was so enraged that he could barely contain his outbursts and he caused the very earth to tremble under his feet. His face was a contorted mass of veins that pulsated through his almost translucent skin. The seductive good looks had given way to his true form; a monstrous beast, scarred and taloned, the previous facade totally abandoned in his rage.

"Rise! Rise I say!" he shouted, sending volleys of sound rebounding all over the huge camp. "We will tear the walls of Pardatha down, rock by rock. I will find the boy. He is mine! I will find him and I will destroy him if I must. Those pathetic idiots can keep me from him no longer!"

The noise was deafening as the army of Colton dar Agonthea, death bringer, prophet of doom, harbinger of dissolution, mobilized. The dust rose so high and thick from the frenetic movement of this massive gathering that it obscured what sun was left in the sky. The heavens grew dark and bleak, and a biting wind began to blow. From the temple mount, within the solemn oval of the war council, Lord Baladar, Lady Filaree, Prince Elion, Robyn dar Tamarand, Grogan and the other councilors, generals and warriors, could see the clouds of dust rising ominously from the gorge.

They had deployed the forces of the city atop the battlements. Hundreds of tons of boulders set twenty paces apart from one another, lay waiting to be thrown over the sides. Hot oil steamed in vast cauldrons , ready to be heaved onto the heads of any who tried to scale the walls. Archers with bucklers and crossbows lined the ramparts, pointing their razor sharp shafts through the narrow slits of the crenellated walls. Massive basins of flaming liquid stood next to the countless bowmen, who each carried long, tightly strung weapons atop the fortifications, prepared to rain fiery arrows down upon the attackers. Funnels carefully and strategically tunneled into the solid stone of the surface would direct the oil onto the heads of those below.

Swordsmen, some with two handed swords of heavy steel and others wielding lighter sabers sharpened on both sides, stood side by side with strong armed fighters holding long spears of light weight wood, tipped with fine points of razor sharp stone. They faced the oncoming enemy undaunted, ready to give their lives to protect the city and their families from the evil approaching.

From their vantage point atop the temple mount, the highest natural point in Pardatha, the valiant leaders of the opposition could see the opposing army advancing, seemingly limitless in size, led by thirteen fire spouting Valkor with sorcerers astride each. The minions of the Dark Lord spread out behind them, blackening the earth with their numbers. Baladar carefully watched from his chair, as did all of the others. Elion and Robyn had both had first hand experience with regard to this army, witnessing its composition from a closer range. They provided what details they could to the council as it massed beneath the walls of the fair city. No one else spoke whilst the enemy advanced, and each member of the war tribunal absorbed in his or her own fashion, the scene that was unfolding before them.

Elion related from memory just how many Giants, Wood Trolls, Orcs and other malevolent hirelings he had counted on his journey to Pardatha. Robyn, too, recounted what he had observed from the cover of the woods. And it seemed currently that the tally was even greater than before, that the multitudes had swelled as they marched, gathering all the forsaken strays they passed along the road to the city. They could all see Colton clearly now, sitting atop his silver steed, a swathe of green space separating him from any other member of his throng, making it easy to spot him amid the black sea of marching marauders.

Elion's sharp eyes discerned the cadaver of the remaining envoy first, and he said to the group, "Colton spared no time in meting out his punishment, I see."

Baladar focused his eyes as did the others, and soon enough they all saw the gruesome scene that Elion was referring to. Propped up between two massive steeds was the pierced and spitted body of the still red cloaked member of the ambassador's party, now both headless and armless.

"He was not happy with the news, I take it," Baladar remarked.

"Did you ever think he would be?" Filaree asked without expecting an answer.

"It must have infuriated him to find out that he came all of this way to capture someone who is not even here," Elion said, truly thankful for the first time that he stumbled upon the helpless boy when he did.

"Things are as they should be, Elion," Baladar remarked seriously.

"Indeed!" Robyn commented. "The heir will live to see another day," he said solemnly.

"As will we all, sir!" Filaree said determinedly.

"As will we all!" Robyn repeated earnestly, and he looked at Filaree with respect and friendship.

"My Lord, if I may?" Grogan asked.

"By all means, speak, Master Grogan," Baladar responded.

"The city is well prepared. No matter what the Evil One throws up against us, we can withstand it..." he said, and then he hesitated for a moment before continuing. "...at least, for a while," he concluded. "It will not be an easy victory for Colton," he said with resignation in his voice.

Ever the optimist, Filaree seized the moment.

"It will not be a victory at all, Master at Arms! We have strengths here he knows nothing about!" she said, and she glanced conspicuously from Robyn to Elion. "He believes that the trees have abandoned us here and that we are isolated and alone," she continued.

"The Lady speaks the truth. But, he must know by now that we have a Chosen amongst us. He witnessed what transpired below as we all did," Baladar said, looking meaningfully at Robyn as he spoke.

The Chosen closed his eyes and slowed his breath until he was deep in a trance of thought. All those around the great table looked upon him expectantly. The sun cast shadows across the stone but the scattered rays illuminated his downcast face, bestowing upon his skin a translucent appearance. Finally, Robyn raised his chin and slowly opened his eyes which glowed more beautifully than ever now, and then he began to speak.

"The Lalas will never forsake the earth, not as long as they still live amongst us. Fate has brought me here, as it has you Filaree and you Elion. We were not led to Pardatha to die, but rather to help prepare for the future. I detect the power in the very stones of the city, in the soil upon which it stands and in the gates that seal it from danger. This power will protect us tomorrow as it has today and we will prevail! Pardatha!" Robyn exclaimed, thrusting his right hand high into the air, and the others all stood and cheered along with him, raising a shout that could be heard all around.

"Pardatha! Pardatha!" they all exclaimed in unison, and the chant spread from the guardians on the mount to the soldiers surrounding the obelisks, down to the city streets and up to the battlements.

"Pardatha! Pardatha!" everyone shouted, drowning out momentarily the din of the enemy's armies, and resounding through the air up and over the city walls until the entire population of the besieged metropolis joined in and the very heavens rang with the heartening cheer.

Colton dar Agonthea ceased his raving for an instant and listened to the reverberating dirge rising above the noise of the battlefield. For just one tiny moment, doubt rose like bitter bile in his throat and he looked around to reassure himself. As the noise died down, he rose up in his saddle and while standing high on his stirrups, he pierced the air with his deep, sonorous voice, shattering the silence.

"Death to Pardatha!" he shouted venomously as his army surged forward all around him, and it would not stop again until it reached the very walls of the city itself.

Chapter Thirty-nine

Calyx, Tomas, Preston and Cairn walked single file in that order through the pass in the Thorndar's that would eventually lead them to Pardatha. The sheer cliffs protected them and shielded them from any outside intervention. The only fear that Cairn harbored was that they could not fight easily if attacked from either the front or the back, but he relaxed in the knowledge that only one warrior at a time could engage them, and Calyx would be a match for anyone approaching from the front. He, Cairn, would defend the rear should the need arise. The pass was so narrow and deep that the sky was merely a sliver of blue high above their heads.

Cairn glanced upward as shadows obscured their way, and he noticed that the heavens had turned grey and dimmed. A chill crawled up his arm and he shrugged it off like one would an annoying insect, and then he continued on his way. Calyx growled with apprehension as he too moved cautiously forward. Tomas sang softly to himself as if he hadn't a care in the world and Preston joined him, mimicking him as they walked, their youthful voices echoing against the forbidding cliffs.

The path wound precariously, getting steeper and steeper with each step. It remained narrow and tight for quite some time, rising higher and higher until it widened a bit and finally leveled off. The air was thick with dust and Cairn covered his mouth and nose with a scarf, signaling Tomas and Preston to do the same before their lungs became clogged with the floating detritus. The two boys followed his direction, and then they continued on.

They walked in silence for some time except for the singing of the young ones, and soon they found themselves standing in a circular landing, high up in the cliffs. Two alleyways led off from the space, one spiraling downward and one angling upward. Cairn pointed to the path that descended from where they stood, and Calyx headed immediately for the narrow entryway.

"We will come out from this pass high over the southern hills of Pardatha. The walls of the city are built into the cliffs and we cannot enter from the heights. We must wind our way down to the plain and then walk to the gates. Pardatha has few means of access," Cairn related.

Tomas looked at him quizzically, as if he did not understand what Cairn was saying.

"We cannot enter that way, Cairn. The gates are closed by now," Tomas said matter-of-factly.

Cairn looked at him astounded, his sharp features creased in wonder.

"Do you know this, Tomas? Are you certain?"

"Oh, yes. I am certain. I can 'smell' the enemy. We are too late," he said calmly as if he was merely commenting on something as simple as the approach of a rain storm.

Calyx was sniffing the air copiously and it was clear that he too literally smelled an alien presence.

"Too late?" Cairn asked. "Too late for what? What are you saying Tomas? What has happened?"

Preston stood close to the others, anxiously awaiting the boy's answer.

"The gates are closed and Colton dar Agonthea, the Evil One, approaches," Tomas replied with his eyes half closed, concentrating now. "He believes that my brother is in the city," he said.

Cairn was confused and he was thinking so quickly now that he could barely form the words he needed to say.

"Your brother? Who is your brother? Why would the Dark Lord seek him out? Tomas! You must answer me!" he pleaded, grabbing the boys arm and turning him so that they were face to face.

"My brother is the heir of Gwendolen, as am I," he said composed, with little emotion. "He does not know that I exist. No one knows I exist now except Ormachon and you three," he said as if this news was unimportant.

Cairn stood transfixed. He was clearly finding it difficult to respond to the boy's remarks, and he was unable to absorb all of what was being said.

"What are you saying? Please, Tomas, explain yourself!" Cairn finally demanded, not understanding fully what was being revealed to him.

Tomas looked out over the mountains and spoke, his eyes squinting and his head tilted as if he was telling a story about someone else.

"I was born to King Garold and Queen Lewellyn, but I was sick and I was sent away. They never knew me. They thought that I died. The trees brought me up, and I was given unto the care of my aunt Safira and uncle Trevor near where Ormachon grew. They knew the danger in raising me, but they did so willingly," he said, turning his gentle eyes first to Cairn and then to Preston as he spoke.

"I was told who I was when I was very young, and I knew that I had a brother, a twin." Tomas squinted once more, and then he looked in the direction of Pardatha. He turned back to face Cairn after only a moment and then he continued on with his story.

"When you arrived, I could see what was going to happen. When you were able to find me, I realized that the Dark One would be there soon too; that Colton's scavengers could not be far behind." He pursed his lips and let his head loll for an instant, obviously remembering what befell his adopted family. "It was fated to be that way. I wish that I could have done something to help, but we knew all along that when the time came, I would be unable to prevent what was to be," he continued, lifting his head nobly. "I was trained by them all, by Ormachon and by Trevor. By Safira too. My aunt and uncle were not as they seemed, Cairn," he said knowingly and with great pride, his beautiful eyes sparkling with the words.

Cairn allowed the silence to hang upon the air before breaking it, realizing how much it spoke.

"You are the twin brother of the boy I was summoned to help, the one cast to Baladar? Is that what you are telling me?" Cairn inquired, mystified, staring at Tomas.

"Yes," he replied, needing to say no more.

Cairn paused for a moment, trying to incorporate all that had just been revealed to him, and he stood, shaking his head in wonder. He contemplated this amazing turn of events for a while longer, making a few abortive attempts to say something, but stopping himself each time before any words were uttered. Finally, Cairn broke his own unintentional silence.

"Why did you not tell me this? Why wait until now?" he asked.

"I believed this knowledge would influence how you treated me. I did not wish to affect the weave," he answered seriously.

"Did you say before that your brother is not in Pardatha?" Cairn asked, somewhat overwhelmed by this entire discussion.

"Yes, I did. He is not there. I do not know why or where he is right now, but he is safe, I can feel it."

No one doubted the boy's proclamation.

"Pardatha is under attack, or will be soon. Colton seeks my brother. He believes that if he kills or captures him, then he will be free to ravish our world, that nothing else can prevent him from spurring on the dissolution he craves. He knows nothing of me," he replied, so nonchalantly it seemed almost impossible. "He has never seen either of us," he continued.

"And yet, knowing the Evil One is here, you still follow me willingly to the gates of the city?" Cairn asked, awestruck by the boy's courage.

"Of course! It is my time!" he answered, gazing at Cairn with the innocence of a child to whom any other choice would be incomprehensible.

His green eyes were open wide and stared completely guileless. Preston stood nearby watching closely and listening intently to everything being said.

"I knew there was something special about you," he interrupted, walking right next to Tomas. "I have a good sense about things like that. My father always told me that I was too sensitive, that I read into things and thought that I understood people when I really didn't. He was wrong! I knew you were different, and I knew that I had to join you on your journey. It doesn't surprise me that you are the heir, or whatever you say you are," Preston remarked, glad to have become such good friends with Tomas on his own accord.

"I, too, have no doubt you are what you claim to be. I am actually relieved to know now," Cairn remarked, shifting his position so that he was once more in the forefront of the group. "But, this changes so much. How can I let you risk your life so easily, knowing what I know?" Cairn asked, perplexed and consumed with doubts that had not plagued him before.

He looked hard at Tomas with a quizzical eye.

"You cannot stop me, Cairn. It is my fate and you know it. We are all meant to be here. You, Preston," he pointed to the Dwarf, "and you too," he said to Cairn and Calyx. "Besides, nothing has changed. We are all no different than we were five minutes ago. Is my life more valuable now? If I had died yesterday before you ever knew what my lineage was, would the results have been any different than if I should die tomorrow?" Tomas questioned Cairn as if he were the elder of the two. "If Colton walks away from Pardatha victorious, my brother will not even have a chance. The others he needs are in the city already. They cannot perish here before they even overtake my brother," the boy replied.

"And I, as your guardian, am left to decide what is best for you and the world?" Cairn asked rhetorically, feeling the weight of these decisions upon him. "I have a new responsibility, Tomas! Knowledge begets duty. The effects upon our world would be equally bad if you should perish, regardless of what I may know or not know. But the effect upon me, now that I know who you are and why we have come together, would be devastating if I did not do all that was in my power to protect you."

The scholarly man's yellow eyes blazed with passion. Calyx stood dutifully behind him, his saucer like orbs never resting for a moment while his broad nose flared as he took in all of the scents around them, remaining ever vigilant and protective.

Tomas looked upon his human friend with understanding and compassion. For a brief moment, he appeared childlike and vulnerable to Cairn. He could not imagine any harm coming to him and the very thought of it sent chills down his spine.

Tomas kicked the dry ground with his toe, sending small, swirling clouds of dust into the air around him. He watched them rise and dissipate before he spoke again.

Turning to his friend, he said in a quiet and fateful tone, "The die is cast, Cairn. We can control some things, but others are meant to be, and however we may attempt to change them would be to no avail. No, Cairn, your knowledge of my heritage changes nothing! You know what is best, as do I. You have always known what was best for me from the very first moment we met. There is no altering what must be. You can only hope to guide the floes and influence them when possible. The fabric weaves of its own will. Haven't you always said that?" he asked solemnly.

Cairn was silent. So much was happening so fast. He knew in his heart that Tomas was correct and that he could not protect him from his fate, whatever that might be. In so doing, he could be sealing it himself for all he knew. He would have to be reasonable, and yet he would have to let his heart guide him as well. All of the logic and ethics and metaphysics he devoted his life to studying heretofore was useless to him now. He knew that he had to allow this seemingly vulnerable, young man to walk into the midst of the maelstrom, come what may. He accepted that. He would not stop him, but he would do all in his power to protect him from harm.

Tomas looked deeply into Cairn's eyes for just a moment, then he abruptly turned, stepped in front of the elder man and led the way down the narrow, winding path toward Pardatha. Cairn, Calyx and Preston followed closely behind, each consumed by the moment, yet drawn persuasively and inevitably toward the future.

Chapter Forty

Colton arranged his attack in such a manner so as to exhaust the defenses of the city quickly by forcing them to repel the vast numbers of Orcs continually, for hours at a time. He had no doubt that those who fought for him would do so until the end, for they knew that retreat was a far worse option than death. Pressing the Orc army forward was a battalion of Trolls, their hated rivals, as anxious to slaughter them as those in the city itself. Colton cared not about how many he lost in the battle. He was concerned only with victory, and these initial skirmishes were designed merely to test the city's defenses and to weaken them. Each and every one of the Orcs could perish for all he cared. Their lives were meaningless to him.

Wave upon wave of dark-skinned beasts threw themselves against the stone walls of the city, only to fall beneath the weight of the boulders cast down upon them from above. Those behind them climbed atop their dead and dying brethren and continued their assault, mindless and frenzied. The soldiers of Pardatha worked tirelessly, changing shifts only when absolutely necessary, and the people of the city provided a new and continuous supply of missiles, quarried from the hard rock of the Thorndars. A chain of supply was established from one end of Pardatha to the other, originating in the caves at the south of the city and terminating at the battlements surrounding the gates. The mountains offered a limitless stock to the fighters atop the walls, and the Orcs fell by the thousands beneath the weight of the peaks' issue. Colton drove them forward nevertheless, sending them to certain doom, and they obeyed him, never questioning, never hesitating.

The mound of the dead and dying grew higher and higher, and Grogan became concerned that the ever increasing piles would eventually provide a platform upon which the beasts could climb and ultimately scale the walls. He instructed the archers to send arrows tipped with a hemp, saturated with oil and set ablaze, into the growing heaps beneath them. The rough rags of the deceased and injured Orcs caught afire quickly, and the bowmen used their long bows to send the arrows deep into the mass below. The fires spread surely, igniting the corpses from the bottom and emanating outward and upward, consuming not only those already dead, but all of the others who had scaled the piles in order to reach the walls and hack away at the stones with their clubs and axes.

The blaze grew to an enormous size, roaring and igniting the now darkening sky, enveloping the battlefield in an oily stench that even those high above could barely tolerate. But the city's defenses were effective, and although the multitudes that Colton saw fit to waste upon the walls in this manner seemed inexhaustible, the fervor with which the fat and ugly Orcs initially attacked Pardatha had now died down somewhat. They continued to climb upon the broken backs of their brothers, and their incredible stupidity kept them from assessing the consequences soon enough to prevent them from suffering the same fate.

The piles of the dead and dying grew larger by the hour, but they kept coming. The embers glowed a sickening red, and the heat was so intense that even as they neared the walls, some burst into flame spontaneously and ran around in circles, howling in pain. It was a bizarre and gruesome scene beneath the great, stone walls of Pardatha that evening.

As the sun set over the city for the first time since the attack began, the fires illuminated the night, and they burned so bright that they rivaled the light that came before, in an eerie and disorienting fashion. Baladar walked the length of the battlements, feeling the heat wafting over him, speaking words of encouragement to the determined defenders and all the time assessing the extent of the damage they were inflicting upon the enemy. The waste of life sickened him, yet he knew that he could not allow anyone garrisoned within Pardatha to feel anything other than revulsion for the attackers. Battles such as this required a steadfastness and fortitude on the part of his warriors in the face of these overwhelming numerical handicaps.

Baladar knew that these minor victories so early on meant nothing in the scope of things, but they did serve to raise the spirits of his people, if only for a short while. He knew that this one barrage was but the first wave in an endless ocean of assaults yet to come. In his heart of hearts, Baladar grieved for his people, for the illusion of victory they perceived, for the superhuman efforts they put forth while not understanding the ultimate futility of them. The one seed of hope that germinated in his heart was born of Davmiran's ability to survive despite the fate of Pardatha. Upon this, Baladar took nourishment and found reason to go on, to continue to fight against all the overwhelming odds and to maintain his sanity in the midst of this macabre dance of death.

Colton turned his back in disgust upon the efforts of his lackeys, and he rode his horse to the shelter of the tents, never once thinking to call an end to this extravagant waste of life, but rather insisting that it continue long into the night, knowing that his supply of bodies was almost endless. Unlike Baladar, he cared nothing for the feelings of those who fought for him. They were mere sparks to him used to ignite the fire and soon to die after their simple task was accomplished. All life was expendable to him. All life had to end, and the greater the tragedy, the greater the triumph.

Tomorrow he would have his men clear the battlefield of the dead if the fires did not do it for him first, and then he would attack once again with other men and other monsters. He would repeat this process until the city of Pardatha could fight no longer, and then he would find the boy. If Baladar was telling the truth and the heir was elsewhere, he would raze the city to the ground and adorn the rubble with the heads of Baladar and his councilors. There was no escaping Colton dar Agonthea, death bringer!

This boy was yet untrained, helpless and impotent, and as long as he found him before he attained his powers, before he realized his potential, there would be no stopping the Evil One either. The darkness would prevail, smothering all life, hastening the demise, and the sweet smell of victory would be his to savor eternally.

Chapter Forty-one

"We cannot simply fend off whatever he throws against us. Eventually we will tire. His numbers are too vast for us to overcome. We must do something more!" Filaree said to the council while standing beside the massive table with both of her hands resting flat upon it.

"What else have we to do, Lady?" Thembak the woodsman, asked. "We cannot open the gates and charge his lines. What further do you propose?" he continued.

"The woodsman is right, Lady Filaree. We have little choice but to defend ourselves. Any offensive action on our part would not be productive," Grogan commented from his place next to Baladar.

"He knows we cannot stay locked in here forever. He also does not care how many of his own men he sacrifices. How can we fight against an enemy such as this?" Pertar of Axlon asked from the other end of the chamber.

"I would rather be inside Pardatha than elsewhere right now, Pertar. At least we have a chance here. But we still have no plan, no strategy," Thembak admitted.

"Our strategy is simply to survive and to pray," Mistress Marna said solemnly.

Robyn had remained in the background, intensely following the direction of the conversation. He listened to every word his companions said. Finally he spoke, though it was almost as if he was speaking to himself.

"We have other means of weakening Colton's forces," he said pensively, without standing or raising his head. "Not all battles need be fought with steel and stone," he concluded, still staring blindly ahead.

Baladar turned his head in his direction, as all eyes focused upon the dark and handsome man from Tamarand.

"What have you in mind, Robyn?" Baladar asked.

"Yes, tell us!" Thembak said animatedly.

Robyn closed his eyes and clasped his hands together, forming a steeple with his two index fingers, and then he rested his elbows upon the heavy stone of the table. He seemed to be communicating with someone or something other than those in his immediate vicinity.

"I am not sure, my Lord, but the fields you planted many years ago willingly responded to my advances before. Perhaps they will do so again," he answered, raising his eyes quizzically now. There was an idea germinating in his mind. Although I cannot destroy the forces before us, I believe that I can frighten them and disorient them somewhat. If I can turn them against themselves, capitalize upon their own internal rivalries, their own fears, we can let them do some of our work for us," he finished.

"Whatever aid you may require, please request it now. I am sure that I can speak for us all when I say that whatever it is you need, we will gladly oblige, Chosen," Baladar remarked, looking at Robyn eagerly while everyone else at the council table nodded enthusiastically in response.

There was no question that everyone present trusted the Chosen from the north implicitly.

"I have some ideas that I would like to share with the council," Robyn said, and he stood up and faced the group.

He spent a good amount of time attempting to explain to the warriors and councilors at the large table what they all instinctively knew about the forces battling for Pardatha, but may not have ever analyzed quite this way before. He spoke of good and evil, of the natural and the unnatural and about the triumph of the right way and dissolution. He instructed those present on many matters that his own Promanthea had spent so many years teaching him about. He could not hope to school them in the arts that a Chosen devoted his lifetime to learn, but he could help them to appreciate the true meaning of the threat to the balance that Colton was propagating here and now.

He needed all of the leaders to feel empowered, to realize that the abilities that he manifested were available to all of them in different degrees. The dormant power in all of nature had to be harnessed if they had any hope of defeating Colton, and these council members were the most likely ones to achieve that goal.

"I have been trained to fight all of my life, and I have never used anything other than steel and my own wits. Now you are telling me that I had other resources available to me all along?" Filaree questioned, confused, though not doubting the veracity of Robyn's words.

"Did you not utilize the direction of the wind, the blinding sun, the freezing rain during your encounters, Lady? Do you not gauge your chances and take advantage of your opportunities in each and every fight? What makes you so superb at what you do? Have you not been all along intensely aware, although intuitively perhaps, of your opponent's footing, his state of mind, of all of those small assessments that give you an upper hand during the heat of battle?"

Filaree nodded, thinking about what Robyn was saying and examining the process she used when preparing for a fight.

"We Chosen are just men and women before we are trained. Our senses may be more enhanced and our intuitions may be stronger, but we are no different than any of you until we are schooled. What makes you all sentient and what brings us all here together, fighting for what we know is right, is what will allow you to harness the forces that surround us all of the time, the forces that will allow us to defeat the enemy before us, or at least to hurt him and slow his advance!" Robyn said.

"I share Robyn's sentiments," Baladar interrupted him. "And I too, in my own manner, manipulate my environment based upon the forces he is referring to. The power is here for us all. Our enemy cannot touch it. He attempts only to sever the bonds that unite us with the power. His strength comes from the void, from an absence of light, and ours comes directly from life itself."

"If any of you have ever seen the wonders of Lormarion you would know that what they speak of is true!" Elion exclaimed. "Nature is our friend and we are all a part of the circle of life. When we work together, we produce miracles!" he said excitedly.

"My Lord, members of the council," Grogan stood and addressed the group. "It is too late to learn how to fight differently than we have been trained to do. All of these ideas are new and confusing to me, and although I never claimed to be a scholar or erudite, I fail to see how these thoughts will help us today when the Trolls are knocking upon the gates as we speak," he said.

"They will help some of us, Grogan, perhaps not all of us," Baladar said with no condescension in his tone.

"We must be willing to open our hearts and minds to all possibilities now," Elion offered.

"We must face the facts here!" Filaree interrupted. "We are outnumbered. We cannot hold out indefinitely, and that's assuming we can withstand the full force of Colton's attack to begin with. If anyone is, I am the eternal optimist, but I am also quite adept at assessing my opponent's chances. In this case, I must admit that his chances are good," she said seriously.

"What has become of the stalwart from before?" Baladar questioned her with a sad tone in his voice.

"I prefer reality to illusion, my Lord. But, I never said that I am ready to give up. I will fight to the very end!" she answered proudly, "But if my optimism serves to obfuscate our ability to appraise our situation properly, then it serves the enemy and that I will not allow!" she responded determinedly.

"We must listen to all our options no matter how unusual they may seem at first," Robyn interjected, with a quiet sternness in his voice. "With my help, I believe that together we can harness the power that exists within all living things, and use it against our assailants," he said.

A hush descended over the group, as they all heard for the first time what Robyn had in mind. Some understood better than others what the Chosen one was describing, but everyone sitting at the war council was willing to do whatever he or she could do to preserve the world they loved so dearly, regardless of whether or not it made sense to them.

Baladar was a sorcerer in his own right, and although his powers were not derived from the fabric of life, the very essence of existence, as were those of a Chosen, he was familiar with the forces greater than himself and he was encouraged by Robyn's ideas. Baladar was a medium for power, not a molder and shaper of it. He could release what already existed and then focus it to perform certain tasks, which to many was no small accomplishment. Robyn though, was a master, as were all of the Chosen, and his abilities far exceeded those of Baladar.

"What would you have us do, Robyn dar Tamarand?" Baladar asked, and the others gazed expectantly upon the Chosen one's face.

Robyn focused intently upon the serious countenances surrounding him, and then he spoke in a hushed voice, "When the time comes, when the next attack is underway, we will need to clasp one another's hands around this table and meld our minds together. I will need to find a talisman, a relic, for us all to focus upon, and within it, I will concentrate all of the energy we emit. There is a good chance that the item may not survive the trial," he explained. "You will all have to release yourselves completely into my care and not give in to the impulse to remain in control. I will need your full and total trust. If I am successful, I hope to split the army in two, separate the legs from the body, and strand a part of Colton's force beneath our walls. We cannot take the Evil One on directly at this time. I know we are not ready for that, so I hope that he follows the same pattern as before and sends his slaves alone to perform his dark deeds, while he lingers in the background. By the time he realizes what is happening, it will be too late. Although we will not kill the beast, we will certainly be able to cause it considerable pain," Robyn said hopefully.

"You say that you will divide his army? How? What weapon do we have that I am unaware of that could accomplish such a task?" Grogan questioned skeptically.

"I felt before the vitality of that which grows beneath the plains of Pardatha, as I mentioned prior. Because you cannot see it, master Grogan, does not mean that it does not exist," Robyn partially answered while not intending to belittle the Master at Arms.

"What will you do with it, Robyn?" Filaree questioned, seeming to follow his train of thought.

"I am not certain, Lady Filaree. These things are often indeterminate. I can try to initiate an action and guide the forces involved. Nevertheless, I cannot always predict the exact outcome. But, I can assure all of you..." Robyn pounded upon the stone table, "...that every living thing, whether conscious or not, feels the wrongness of Colton. And everything that is alive instinctively rebels against him. I must tap into that sense, that natural revulsion, and attempt to organize it into an active weapon."

"What you say makes much sense," Baladar commented, sitting back in his chair "But, can you do this? And what risks are involved, Robyn?"

"The risks are to me alone. It is exhausting at the least, and at the worst, if I have miscalculated and the life I speak of has already been corrupted, or if Colton suspects what I am trying to do and attempts to thwart me while the link is active, I may not be able to regain my consciousness. The rest of you have nothing to fear. You will simply open your eyes as if nothing has happened," he answered.

"What are the odds of the worst occurring, Robyn?" Filaree asked with deep concern.

"I cannot tell for certain, but I believe they are against it. Colton must know that a Chosen is in the city by now, but I do not believe that he will suspect what I have in mind. When it comes to self sacrifice, he is not experienced," he said sardonically, and all those around the table including Grogan, nodded their heads in agreement. "I am willing to take the risk," Robyn exclaimed boldly.

"Master Grogan?" Baladar called the soldier's name.

"Yes, my Lord?" he answered.

"I would like you to take over the leadership of the city's defenses whilst the rest of us work with Robyn. You are my right hand and I ask that you serve me now," he requested of his loyal general.

"As you wish, my Lord" Grogan said, and he bowed deeply to Baladar.

"Should we fail, master Grogan, and should Robyn be incorrect regarding the consequences to us here..." he continued, and he looked deeply at Robyn, "...you will have to continue the fight unassisted by the council," Baladar concluded.

"I will do what I must, my Lord," Grogan answered humbly, his brow furrowed from the seriousness of the moment.

Baladar then rose and addressed the entire table.

"All of you who are in favor of attempting what Robyn dar Tamarand proposes please rise. Those opposed, remain seated," Baladar said, and he continued to stand.

One by one, the members of the war council stood and faced Baladar. There was not a moment of hesitation on any one's part.

"So, it is decided! Robyn? I turn the leadership of this council over to you for as long as is necessary," Baladar said, and he vacated his position at the head of the table.

Robyn bowed his head slightly and then traded places with the Lord of Pardatha.

"Please, be seated. We have some time yet before we need to begin. The field yonder is still empty and Colton has not yet rallied his forces," he said, glancing at the plains beyond the walls of the city. "In the meantime, I will need a token, something capable of holding the power without being destroyed by it. It should not be something of my own," he said, looking at the council members.

Filaree produced her dagger from her tunic, the ruby glinting in the morning sun, and placed it upon the table before her.

"If this would suffice, I offer it to you Robyn," she said, pushing it toward him. Thembak dug deep into his coat and placed a bronze pendant on the table, sliding it into the center of the slab of stone.

"My father carried this close to his heart, as did his father and his father before him. When he died, it was passed on to me. My people revere it highly. It was hewn from the rock of Pelagor, the holiest shrine of my nation. It is yours, Robyn dar Tamarand if you so wish!" the woodsman said.

Elion stood and removed his belt. Turning it inside out, he

popped a small wooden disk out of the back of the buckle.

"Here is my piece of the great Noban that rises in the middle of Seramour. It is a relic of great meaning to the people of my country. Use it if you so desire, Robyn," Elion said, as he walked over to Robyn and laid it on the stone before him.

Mistress Marna was the next to rise. She dropped the heavy hood that concealed her raven hair and porcelain skin, revealing a stunning woman hidden behind the somber clothing. From a hole in her earlobe, she removed a hanging cross inlaid with tourmaline and diamonds, and deposited it before Robyn.

"If this serves your purpose, my Lord, you are free to utilize it. It is an ancient piece, and the gemstones were taken from the crown of Athalon," she said, bowing her head gracefully as she raised her hood once more and returned to her seat.

All the others sat down as well and Robyn spoke to them as a group.

"I am moved by your devotion and sacrifice, all of you," he said, looking for a moment at each member of the council. "I realize that the artifacts you offer have special meaning to each of you, and that they cannot be replaced. It is a difficult decision for me," Robyn said respectfully, as he lifted and examined each of the pieces lying before him.

At the same time, Baladar rose from his chair and walked to the edge of the circle of stones, gazing outward over the city. The ring was burning his chest and he felt compelled to reach inside his shirt and raise it before his eyes. As he did so, he suddenly knew that this was the article that Robyn needed, and he turned abruptly and strode to the table.

Pulling the chain over his head, Baladar walked up behind Robyn and reached his clasped hand forward. Opening his fingers, he let the ring drop to the polished stone, and it spun and turned, dancing on the surface, drawing everyone's attention until it came to rest before Robyn's eyes. Robyn reached for it and raised it before him. The ring was hot in his hand and it glowed intensely from within. He examined the inscription inside the delicate band, and he looked at Baladar with the ring now hanging loosely from the chain wrapped around his fingers.

"You know that it may not outlast the day, Baladar?" he asked, knowing the answer already.

"It was meant to be used, Robyn, I know it. If it does not survive intact when this is over, then it was not destined to reach

Davmiran. This ring has spoken to me in its own way ever since I placed it around my neck, and it speaks to me now. Use it if you can. We both so desire it," Baladar said somberly, and then he returned to his seat beside Robyn.

"So be it, then!" Robyn exclaimed, as he rose and returned the other offerings respectfully to their owners. "We are more fortunate than I could have ever hoped. This ring harbors a power of its own, greater than anything that I have felt that is not derived from the Lalas themselves. It will help to magnify whatever power we can generate," he said. Turning to Baladar, he continued. "I will do all that I can to protect it," Robyn said, and he sat down at the end of the table, closing his eyes and enfolding the ring tightly within his fingers.

Everyone's eyes focused upon his hand and they could all clearly see a bright, white light escaping through the slits between his long fingers, streaking out in all directions.

A faint drumming could distinctly be heard in the background, and Grogan was the first to call attention to it as he walked to the northern end of the circle of stone and gazed out across the plain.

"The enemy doth approach," he said somberly, and the others turned their heads to confirm what they all knew to be true already.

Baladar walked to Grogan and placed his hand upon the big man's shoulder.

"Go now, the people need your presence on the wall. I will send for you later. Go, and may the First guide you and protect you," he said to his Master at Arms.

Grogan bowed deeply to Baladar, saluted the others at the table, turned sharply away and marched briskly out of the circle toward his aides who were waiting to accompany him back to the front.

Chapter Forty-two

Colton chose to send in three of his Valkor at this time, intending for them to weaken the gates with their hellfire, accompanied by five Giants with clubs the size of tree trunks, their tips hardened and covered in a studded, black metal. Behind the huge Valkor and the Giants, the Trolls would descend upon the walls and chip away at the stone with their heavy axes and war hammers.

He knew that the same fate would befall the Trolls, despite their size, as that which befell the Orcs if he did not protect them. So, he assembled a thousand archers on the outskirts of the battlefield, and in front of each one he had stand one of his green skinned, half-humans each holding a shield of burnished copper. The morning sun would reflect off of the shields and blind the bowmen atop the battlements, making it difficult for them to aim. Colton wanted the opportunity to interfere with the men hurling the rocks down from above, and the unhindered archers would do just that. They could pick off the defenders one by one while the assailants below did their work.

A deep sounding horn blew repeatedly over the battlefield as the morning sun rose over the eastern woods. Three huge beasts, snorting and puffing black smoke and steam from gill like openings on the back of their necks, emerged from the darkness of the enemy's lines. They were no longer being ridden by the red robed riders as they had been when Elion first gazed upon them, but rather, they were being led toward the Noban gate by these skeletal figures, followed closely by five giants who towered over them all.

The human-like Giant's faces were disfigured and contorted, as were their bodies, as if their appendages grew unevenly and their twin features such as eyes and ears did not mirror one another, but developed independently. One bore a short left arm and a preposterously long right arm. Another had no ears and one very large eye paired with a very small one. All were practically hairless on their heads, and their clothing was made of skins and furs, haphazardly sewn together. They were so massive that the warriors upon the battlements feared that they could almost reach up and grab them without climbing at all.

Surrounding the Giants and scurrying to avoid being trampled by their enormous feet, were thousands of Trolls, much larger than the dark skinned Orcs whose ashes still littered the fields. Their fat bellies hung down before them and they jiggled in a comical manner as they jostled for position around the giants. But they were formidable foes nonetheless, despite their appearance. Smarter than their cousins and much larger, they were relentless in their pursuit of an enemy, and their thick skin protected them from the pain of arrows and rocks to some degree. The Trolls' job was to swarm the walls and keep the defenders busy while the Valkor burned through the gates. The Giants were going to protect the Valkor from above.

Colton had amassed an army of Trolls that belied counting. They remained behind the first lines, waiting for orders to advance. This time, he was not going to allow the beasts to waste themselves so flagrantly. He would guide them more strategically, and send them out only when their brethren were consumed or dead, thus conserving their numbers. But first, he needed to unsettle his enemy further, to raise the specter of doubt before their eyes and to try and undermine their confidence, as was his way. He rode swiftly and regally to the Noban gate, unaccompanied.

The Dark Lord raised his mouth to the sky and yelled between cupped hands, "People of Pardatha!" he boomed, once again in his persuasive, melodious tone, "Your Lord and liege has chosen to sacrifice all of you, men, women and children, in order to maintain possession of that which is mine, that which was stolen from me some weeks ago," he shouted, but the shouts seemed to float upon the air, rather than to assault the senses.

His words were soft and seductive, as was his appearance once more. His skin was satiny and blemish free, his clothing was rich and dignified and his long hair was shining in the morning sun. Colton dar Agonthea appeared to be everything a King should be.

"I beg of you to reconsider what you are doing here. I ask only for what is rightfully mine. Why should you suffer for the sins of your leader? Give me the heir and I will leave your lands and your city in peace," he continued.

The soldiers on the battlements stood fast and sure, never taking their eyes off of the enemy. They had been warned by Baladar and by Grogan that the Dark Lord might try to deceive them with his magic, and they were not going to be fooled, even though many felt the compelling power in his melodious words. Colton's voice carried over the walls, deep into the city itself, and the common people were just as steadfast and loyal as the warriors on the walls, despite being unsettled and disturbed. They were not going to listen to the lies of the monster who besieged them and caused them to seek shelter behind the stone walls of Pardatha in the first place.

Although Colton tried his best, the Pardathans resisted what had been, to many before them, an irresistible temptation. They held their ground, covered their ears and shielded their children from the menacing utterances. Colton remained calm, and he continued to speak despite the lack of any immediate reaction.

"What would you have me do?" he entreated. "I was appointed as guardian of a young boy by his very own father, and I am being prohibited from carrying out my responsibilities. The boy is practically my son, and your Lord, who claims to be decent and kind, keeps me from him."

Colton was walking his horse back and forth before the walls, acting the part of the wronged man pleading his case.

"What manner of depravity is this?" he asked, his voice dripping with sadness while he appealed to the people. "All of this is unnecessary," he said, facing his own troops, and spreading his hands out before him.

The only response he received from Pardatha was total silence, and his frustration was mounting by the minute. It was not the silence borne of fear, but rather of defiance. He was unaccustomed to being ignored, to not having those before him beg and clamor for his favor, and it angered him, but he attempted to maintain his forlorn demeanor and his touching image.

"Do you have no pity for me?" he asked, staring up at the battlements. "Do you not see that it is I who have been wronged?" he pleaded.

Colton remained silent for a few moments, realizing finally that these foolish people would never give in; that he would have to kill them all in order to get what he wanted and needed. He was almost glad that they did not crack and that they refused to relinquish their souls to him so easily. He would enjoy their ultimate destruction even more, he thought.

"Fools!" he shouted in a new and different voice, turning sharply toward the gates, his sable hair flying wildly behind him. "You think you can defy me? Your time is up, little ones! I will see the clocks of Pardatha stilled forever. Your final moments approach!" he thundered, his voice now deep and reverberate, echoing with rage like a cry from the pit of doom itself.

He sat high upon his horse's back, staring for the final time upon the gates of the city and beyond, and all the illusions of civility and humanity that concealed the true nature of the fiend slowly peeled away like the layers of an onion, revealing what was concealed beneath the entirety of this time. His skin became pock marked and scaled, his eyes were suffused with red, his fingers grew long and pointed and, snapping back and forth from underneath his cape across his horse's rump, the soldiers above could see a long, snakelike tail. His beautiful steed was transformed as well into a cloven hoofed beast, still resembling the animal it had obviously been at one time, but now hideously different.

Colton dar Agonthea, revealed to the world in all his diabolic and grotesque splendor, turned his animal abruptly around and cantered back to his own, to the perfidious mass of depraved creatures he commanded, and then he signaled the commencement of the attack by emitting a burst of blue fire from his upraised hand that soared high into the sky.

The Valkor moved out of the ranks quickly, anxious to begin their foray, ringed by the five Giants. Grogan readied his troops as the monsters approached, and he gazed momentarily over his shoulder across the city, at the stones that formed the temple mount, praying that Robyn, the Chosen, would be successful in his efforts and that they would all live to fight another day.

Chapter Forty-three

As the blue fire streaked through the sky above, Robyn removed his boots and stockings and placed his naked feet firmly upon the soil beneath the table. He dug his toes into the soft earth and pressed his heels and soles to the dirt. Gently, he placed his left hand on Filaree's and his right atop Baladar's. The golden ring lay before him now with the chain removed. All the others clasped their hands together and bowed their heads at Robyn's instruction.

"Just let go of your feelings. Allow me to enter your thoughts. Have no fear," he said in a calming, soothing voice. "You will feel a strange push, like a soft breath of air against your forehead. Open to it, allow me in," he continued. Those sitting at the slab of stone felt what he described, and none resisted.

Robyn could sense the differences among the people, some stronger, while others were even more powerful than he expected. All of them had their eyes tightly shut while Robyn's were wide open and focused on the talisman, the golden ring. He allowed the flow of power to seep into his mind, flood his senses with white light, and he drew upon it, sucking it into his head.

The energy surged from one to the other, gaining strength as it moved closer to Robyn, feeding upon itself. Robyn could see the white light now rushing around the oval, spinning, undulating as it moved through the members of the group, accelerating as it grew. It felt to him as if he had a large hole in either side of his head and that the light was passing through it at impossible speeds, faster and faster, causing him to feel dizzy and light headed. He forced his eyes to remain open and centered, and he opened himself fully and totally to the light, becoming a vessel for its power, while his eyes became the lens through which he would focus and direct it.

He extracted the life force out of each person, blending it and fusing it together, and then enhancing it as he looked at the ring. When he could contain it no longer within his head, he directed the power through his eyes and out onto the relic, causing it to glow with the intensity of the sun.

The ring rose from the stone, spinning and twirling, humming and resonating with power, completely encircled by the energy. It spun faster and faster, matching the surging circle of light as it passed from one to the other around the table, creating a mesmerizing convergence of motion, light and sound. Robyn moved his feet slightly while never lifting them off of the ground, and he dug his toes even deeper into the soft, pliable earth.

Images were flashing brightly through his mind, bringing before his consciousness visions of twigs and branches, seedlings and seeds, webs of tangled roots, and for a brief instant, Promanthea in all his splendor, powerful and good, erupting with power. He channeled the energy through the ring, focused, enhanced and magnified by the talisman, and then he directed it back into the soil beneath him. It spread quickly and silently, rippling beneath the earth, emanating from the temple mount, toward the walls of Pardatha and beyond. It empowered all the living things it encountered, directing and extolling them to defend and protect the earth, urging them forward, animating everything it contacted.

The people in the streets of the city felt a tremor beneath their feet as the power radiated outward, and they all looked down for a moment, wondering what was happening, not frightened, but rather stimulated themselves by the residual energy passing underfoot. Robyn maintained his intense focus, feeling no fatigue, though the intensity of the power passing through him was surely taking its toll upon his physical being. He needed to provide the force with form and direction, and although he could no longer control it, he could guide it still. As it was the very essence of life itself, it thrived on its own presently, and it would perform according to its own design. He knew that he could let go now, that he had done all that he could do, and he was confident that what he had set in motion would continue until its power was spent. He sought now to protect the relic, the ring that burned so brightly before him.

With a valiant effort and tremendous strength of mind, he cushioned the fall of the ring, creating a pillow of soft, cool air beneath it. As it fell from the power, he grasped it in his magic and shielded it with his being, until the heat dissipated harmlessly and it clattered upon the stone intact. Robyn collapsed from fatigue and then fell from his chair to the ground, unable himself to witness the scene about to unfold before the great gates of Pardatha, while the others awoke all around him.

Filaree rushed to his side, and crouched down in order to ascertain his condition, with Elion close behind her. The attention of Baladar and the others was drawn to the plains beneath the walls, and from their vantage point on the mount, the council watched in wonder at what was taking place thereupon.

Chapter Forty-four

The Valkor reached the gates in minutes, flanked by five grotesque and gigantic creatures, each swinging his own club in a wild and barbaric manner. Leading each of the three fire-breathing animals was a red robed sorcerer. The beasts were muzzled, preventing them from releasing their deadly fire unnecessarily or too soon, and attached to the end of each restraint was a woven silver leash, appearing almost to be too delicate to constrain the massive brutes. They followed their leaders nonetheless, and they hung their huge heads almost on the ground as they stepped methodically forward. Each Giant's footstep shook the very earth itself, and rattled the stones and jiggled the weapons atop the walls of the city.

Colton withdrew to the back of his lines, and he could be seen clearly now orchestrating the movements of troops and weaponry from there, having no reason to be too close to the front. His stellar vision would allow him to witness and absorb all that took place before him, regardless of his vantage point.

Grogan noted with relief that the Dark Lord responded as they had hoped, and he was encouraged thereby despite the advance of the forbidding foe. At least, he reasoned, if what Robyn was attempting succeeded, then they would not have to deal with Colton during this round of the battle. He was unclear regarding exactly what to expect from the council, what shape or form their efforts would take, and he organized his men as if they were the only line of defense for the city.

A shrill horn blew and minutes later thousands of Trolls emerged from the front lines, running in their own awkward way, an ululating shriek rising within their ranks. They moved faster than would be expected from observing their disproportionate bodies, and they held their clubs and axes high above themselves as they advanced. Once before the walls, they set about their tasks methodically and determinedly. The stones began to fall upon them from the battlements, heaved over in great numbers by the steadfast defenders, and the first wave of marauders was quickly beaten to the ground.

By that time the Valkor had reached the gates, the red robed robbers had already removed their muzzles. Each beast raised his ugly head to the sky and roared, belching fire at least twenty feet into the air as he did so. The Giants pulled from off of their backs enormous, concave, platter-like shields and held them over the Valkor, obviously designed to catch whatever might be heaved onto them from above.

Grogan motioned to the soldiers surrounding the cauldrons of hot oil, and three pins were pulled from each of the mechanisms, spilling the boiling liquid down and over the walls onto the giants below. The hot oil splattered and sizzled as it dripped onto the giant's tough skin. They were forced to quickly reposition the shields in order to catch the steaming fluid. These huge monsters were surprisingly agile, despite their bulk, and the five behemoths deftly maneuvered the large bucklers so that they could intercept the dangerous liquid and then harmlessly dispose of it by dipping the shields sideways and letting it drip onto the nearby ground. They moved from side to side, catching everything that rained down upon them and the Valkor, while the lizard-like beasts began to focus their own fire on the hard wood of the Noban gates.

Grogan gestured to the archers, and they quickly stepped in front of the cauldrons as they were being refilled with oil. He dropped his arm and they loosed their steel tipped arrows at the giants and the Valkor below. The red robed magicians stepped back from the walls, lined up side by side, and sent bursts of yellow fire at the shafts as they fell, burning them to cinders before they even had a chance to reach their targets.

Grogan signaled to his men to persist despite the frustration of their efforts, hoping to at least catch one of the many beasts off guard and thus damage it significantly. He called for wave after wave of careening stones, followed by boiling oil and succeeded by hundreds of arrows. But the tough skin of the Valkor deflected any of the missiles that penetrated the giant's shields, and the Dark Lord's sorcerers continued unhampered at the job of annihilating the barbs even before they reached any target, let alone fell to the ground.

Meanwhile, the intense heat generated by the fires erupting from the bellies of the beasts were scarring the gates. The incredibly hard wood resisted the onslaught with a wondrous resiliency, but the extreme temperatures borne of the digested coal were clearly having an impact upon them. Every so often, each Valkor sat back upon its ponderous haunches, bent its long snout forward and then spewed sizzling steam from the air hole behind its head.

Grogan knew that for that one brief instant the beasts were

vulnerable, and he tried time after time to attack precisely at the correct moment, hoping to drop a heavy stone or a gallon of boiling oil onto them when it could do the most harm. The Giants were positioned well, and the Master at Arms soon recognized the futility of his men's efforts. If he was to have any success in halting the attack of the Valkor, he would need to distract or disable the giants first, and that he and his soldiers were hard pressed to do. They persisted nonetheless in their labors, unwilling to allow the invaders to rest from their defensive efforts, but the Valkor stood before the gates blasting away with their fire, resting when they chose and turning the burnished brown of the carved Noban Gates into a singed and dreary grey.

Grogan was so absorbed in his attempt to find a means of disabling the fire breathing monsters, the most serious threat to the city, that he barely noticed the lines of Trolls advancing against the walls. He was distracted from his deliberations by the heavy beating of the drums indicating their imminent approach, and he rushed to motion the other archers lining the walls to prepare for the attack. They waited for his signal, and as the Troll army rushed headlong into the walls of the citadel, they let loose their first volley.

The initial line of Trolls collapsed, taken down by the Pardathan volley, but before the bowmen could set their arrows to loose a second wave, they were suddenly blinded by a burst of reflected sunlight that was bouncing off of the burnished copper of the mutants' shields lining the edge of the battlefield. Grogan covered his eyes, shielding them from the intensity of the illumination while attempting to focus on the surging enemy ranks, but he was unable to see anything through the glare. His men removed their pointed shafts from the taught strings and aimed their bows downward, dazed by the intense brightness, while the enemy plunged forward.

The heavily armored Trolls were upon the walls before anyone could recover from their sudden blindness, hacking and chiseling at the stone. The enemy archers safely concealed behind the bearers of the copper shields, shot their arrows high and fast, taking down many of Grogan's soldiers before they could even recover from the confusion caused by the dazzling light. The Master at Arms saw his companion next to him fall from a black shaft that was now imbedded deep in his left eye, and he shouted to his men to drop behind the protection of the escarpment, realizing all too quickly the consequences of being exposed. They obeyed without hesitation, falling to the stone floor, creeping as close to the wall as possible and seeking shelter behind the heavy stone.

Another wave of arrows flew over the wall, searching out anyone who remained standing and causing serious harm to whomever still lay exposed. Meanwhile, the Giants realized the opportunity they were granted and they began to pound upon the gates with their tree-like clubs. The fire from the Valkors' mouths increased in intensity and Grogan feared that the gates would soon give way if he did not do something to prevent this onslaught. The Trolls were throwing ladders against the walls, seeking to scale them while the guards above were incapacitated. They moved with an uncanny speed, up the thick rungs, dragging their heavy bodies closer and closer to the top.

By this time, many of the men had regained their focus and they had crawled cautiously to the bubbling cauldrons of boiling oil and to the wheelbarrows filled with stones. As quickly as they could, they released the pins and sent the hot oil cascading over the sides once again, scorching the attackers and toppling them to the ground. With eyes shielded, they used forked paddles to force the ladders backward and away from the walls, causing the Trolls that had not fallen from the burning liquid to careen to their deaths on the hard surface below. Boulders were heaved over the edge, taking down many a Troll both on the ladders and upon the ground. But the mass of attackers kept coming by the thousands, throwing up more ladders than the soldiers could possibly disperse.

The pounding upon the gates was thunderous, and the men in the courtyard were pressing hewn tree trunks hard against the inside of the opening, trying desperately to resist the bulging force. They could feel the excruciating heat, even through the thick, hard Noban, and they feared that the gates themselves would soon burst into flame if they did not give way to the Giant's relentless thrusts first. Grogan, high up on the battlements above, rallied the men up and down the walls, and they rose to his call, fighting as best as they could against the enemy without.

Chapter Forty-five

Filaree stood and beckoned to Elion to follow her. She had ascertained that Robyn would be alright with time and rest, and she was anxious to get to the walls herself. Together she and the young Elfin Prince left the council on the mount and headed for the front lines. Cameron joined her as soon as she emerged from the oval of stones, holding Nico's reins in one hand and Trojan's in the other.

Elion whistled for Jorda who waited patiently nearby. The three friends mounted quickly and took off for the entry without waiting for any of the others. They sped down the hill and through the city, and they were all three shocked at the chaos that they encountered as they neared the Noban gates. All around they saw the dead and the wounded, while the living were in a near state of panic, trying to prevent the gates from caving in upon them. The temperature of the air was so high that their skin burned as they drew closer, and the deafening noise of the relentless pounding was almost unbearable.

"Follow me!" Filaree said, as she jumped from Nico's back and headed for the catwalk that she knew would take them to the place where Grogan would most likely be by now.

Elion and Cameron rushed to keep up with her, bounding up two and three steps at a time. When they emerged from the stairway, they were appalled by what they saw unfolding before their eyes. The defense was not chaotic here as it was below, but the battlefield was swarming with enemy forces, and it was immediately clear to them all that Grogan and his men were not winning the fight. Broken bodies and dying warriors were lying all around them, with no one available or able to aid them at this time. Arrows were raining down upon them all, and they could barely see out over the stone shelter of the walls due to the painful streaks of light that forced them to keep their eyes virtually shut.

Cameron spotted the Master at Arms atop the Ghost tower first, and he beckoned to Filaree and Elion to ascend the narrow steps behind him. Grogan stood beside one of the wounded he had carried up to the top, away from the immediate threat of the beasts below, and he was pulling gently at an arrow that protruded from his arm, soothing him with calm words of encouragement. His armor was singed and dirty, the result no doubt of getting too close to the flames that reached up and over the walls at times. He had a deep cut across his cheek, probably from an arrow that missed its mark, and blood trickled down his chin. As he comforted his soldier, he barked orders to the others on the battlements below in a confident and orderly fashion.

"Master Grogan?" Cameron addressed him first as he emerged from the stone catwalk onto the tower floor. "What can we do here to help?" he shouted above the din.

Filaree and Elion joined him immediately and they too waited anxiously for his answer.

"As you can see, we have our hands full. I fear that I require more than two humans and an Elfling right now," he said sadly.

"That may be true, Lord Grogan, but three fresh bodies are better than none, and soon, we hope that the council's work will start paying off and you will have some much earned relief," Filaree remarked.

"We must hold them off just a little longer," Elion said. "Look, master Grogan!" he said to him as he pointed to the city streets. "Can you not see the ripple of power?" he asked the tired leader.

Grogan wiped his brow with his sleeve and gazed quizzically in the direction that the Elf pointed. He tilted his head in confusion, sensing more than seeing what he was talking about, and then he returned his scrutiny to the battlefield.

"Whatever you have been working on and anticipating, it had better happen fast. I fear we are losing the battle and there is little that I can do to prevent it now," he answered while staring at the carnage all around him and at the endless stream of Trolls marching to Pardatha.

"Grogan? How can we stop the Valkor? We must halt their progress for as long as we can. The gates must hold!" Filaree exclaimed.

"They are vulnerable in only one spot. The air holes behind their heads are like a soft belly on a lizard. Plunge a sword into it and you reach its small brain easily. It will die quickly," he answered.

"How can we do that?" Elion asked, not expecting an answer.

"We must jump down upon their backs when they stop to rest. There is no other way!" Filaree said, as if they all should have come to the same conclusion.

"That would mean certain death to you all!" Grogan said. "How do you propose to return to the city, even assuming you can perform such a task? That would be suicide, my Lady!" Grogan responded.

"What choice have we, Master Grogan? We will all die soon enough if the gates are breached!" she answered truthfully.

"You cannot do it, my Lady. Grogan is right. It would be impossible to survive!" Cameron said to her, concern mounting in his voice.

"The Lady is correct, Cameron. We can try. If we fail, we have lost nothing, and if we succeed, we may just buy the city the time it needs for Robyn's magic to take hold," Elion said seriously.

"Is it agreed then? What other choice do we have?" Filaree asked, clearly decided herself upon the course of action she needed to take.

Elion nodded his head and then looked at Cameron. He stared at Filaree and bowed his head too, indicating his concurrence.

"Let us prepare ourselves. We have little time," she answered, relieved that she did not have to sever this threesome now. "Master Grogan, we will each require a long, sharp sword," she beckoned to the warrior. "One that will withstand the impact."

"I will get you what you need," he said grimly, and he immediately sent an aide down to fetch the appropriate equipment.

"There are three Valkor and three of us. I will ask Grogan to mount an attack on the giants guarding them, and he must also keep those damned sorcerers busy while we drop onto the beasts' backs. Our timing must be perfect," she said, looking out carefully over the wall. "They seem to take their rest simultaneously. And that works to our benefit. We can all jump at the same time," she said, as if she were contemplating a plunge into a swimming hole. "We must land carefully. It is a long way down, gentlemen!" she admonished them.

"My Lady?" Cameron asked seriously. "What plan do we follow after we kill the Valkor?" he asked beseechingly.

"We pray, dear Cameron. We simply pray," she said as Grogan returned with the equipment.

After they completed their preparations and instructed Grogan regarding what they needed of him and his men, the three valiant fighters walked to the rampart overlooking the great Noban gate. Grogan assembled the strongest of the soldiers and archers that remained nearby, and he placed a fighter next to each cauldron of oil and each barrel of stone, instructing them to await his orders. He told them of the plan, and they looked upon the three warriors with an overpowering sense of respect, though you could see the great sadness in their eyes.

Grogan walked up to Filaree and bowed deeply.

"My Lady, may the First guide you and keep you." He turned to Elion and clasped his small hand hard between his own two and spoke solemnly. "You do your race proud, my boy!" Finally, he looked at Cameron and spoke to him quietly. "The greatest gift you could give to the one you love is your life, young man," he said knowingly.

Cameron gazed at him, surprised by his depth of understanding, having thought that he had always concealed his feelings better than that, and then he smiled a conspiratorial smile before he walked to Filaree's side.

All the players were in their places when Filaree signaled to Cameron and Elion to join her on the wall. They climbed carefully up on the stones and drew their weapons.

"Follow my lead. Cameron! You take the one on the left. Elion, you the right, and I will take the middle one. We must jump just as they drop their heads. The big one in the middle seems to lead the others. Watch him closely, both of you. I will jump just a second before you two do," she said.

They all buckled their swords in place carefully, checked their belts for the knives and other weapons they required and then prepared to jump.

"Are you ready?" Filaree asked.

"Yes!" they both replied in unison.

The largest of the Valkor backed away from the wall, preparing to take his rest. Filaree raised her sword and yelled, "For Avalain!" as she jumped over the tower wall. The other two followed immediately, Elion shouting "Seramour!" as he dropped to the beast's back, and Cameron simply mouthing Filaree's name as he too fell upon the spine of the creature.

Exactly at the same moment, Grogan unleashed his weapons, drawing the attention of the giants away from the resting Valkor. The arrows flew in great numbers distracting the Mages, and the plummeting stones kept the frenzied Trolls at bay. Filaree hit the back of the animal hard and she was stunned by the impact for just a second. The beast barely noticed her as it spewed its steam skyward. With the soft flap open to allow the air to escape, she drove the shaft of the sword deep into the back of the animal's head, angling it to reach the soft brain. The Valkor reared up in pain, trying to figure out what was on its back causing it so much agony, but it was too late. The sword thrust home and the beast collapsed more suddenly than even Filaree anticipated, pinning her partially beneath its huge bulk as it fell.

Elion too, was immediately successful in his first attempt. The Valkor crumpled to the ground, its front legs giving way first, tumbling Elion over its spiked head and onto the earth directly before the gates.

Cameron though, landed badly. The animal he was attacking hesitated slightly before it dropped its head, and he alighted too far back to assault it as quickly as he needed to. The Valkor noticed his presence and flicked its spiked tail, catching Cameron on his sword arm. The blade slid from his now broken arm and came to rest between the shoulder and neck of the creature. With his left arm, he reached forward, stretching painfully. Suddenly, sizzling hot steam exploded out of the air hole, searing his face and the left side of his body. He reached with his weakened fingers and clasped the sword swiftly. Using his injured body for leverage, he rose up and pressed the hilt of the blade to his chest, centering the point above the exposed opening. With what strength he had left, he pressed the full weight of his torso against the sword, sending it deep into the body of the beast and striking home.

The great Valkor rose on its hind legs, now in its death throes, and Cameron, weakened from his injuries, slid to the ground. The animal struck him frontally with the rapier like talons of its front leg as it fell for the final time.

With Elion's help, Filaree had managed to squirm out from underneath the dead creature she had landed upon only moments ago, and they both ran to Cameron. Filaree clasped his hand in her own and bent to comfort him. His chest was torn open by the Valkor's claw and he was bleeding profusely from many places. Filaree frantically tried to stem the flow of his life blood by pressing upon his wounds with her tunic, all the while whispering words of comfort to him. Elion grabbed Cameron's sword which lay nearby, dripping with the greenish gore of the Valkor, and he stood guard over Filaree as she administered to Cameron.

"You will not forget me, my Lady, will you?" he asked with an uneven breath, struggling to form the syllables.

"Do not speak such words, Cameron. I will help you back to the wall. You will be alright," she said quietly, her face drenched with tears and lying close to his cheek.

"I am dying, Filaree, I can feel it," he said weakly.

"Don't be silly, you will be fine. Look, the bleeding is slowing," she responded, pointing to his chest and smiling through her tears, attempting to keep him from giving up.

Some slender roots and vines, like to those that had so violently and mercilessly attacked the invaders, were breaking the surface of the soil all around him, rising to caress Cameron's cheeks and gently pressing against his pallid skin. He was not an enemy to them but a trusted friend, and their soft and tender movements belied their affection for him. He barely noticed them as he spoke to Filaree .

"Master Grogan said it, my Lady—" Cameron gasped, his wounds making speech difficult. "Before we jumped, he said that I loved you. He knew it. It is true. I love you." His eyes were bright and wide.

"Hush, dearest, hush. You are speaking foolish words. Later, you will regret them," she said, brushing away the tears.

"No, I want to say them. I have loved you for years. I will never regret it. I will love you always," he said, choking now slightly as he painstakingly spoke.

"Don't talk anymore, Cameron. You are too weak, you must conserve your strength," she pleaded, laying her head softly upon his shoulder.

"Tell me you feel something for me too. Tell me you care for me?" he mumbled with his eyes half closed, as a slim and delicate stem lightly brushed a tear from his cheek.

"I do, Cameron, my love. I do love you too!" Filaree whispered, sobbing and holding his hand tightly.

Her cheek lay against his own now and she felt a smile break across his pained lips, just before his hand went limp. The end of the stem which now lay upon his mouth immediately burst into bloom, its small, budded end opening into a tiny yellow flower, magnificent to behold.

"Come, Lady Filaree. It is too late for him. We must now defend ourselves," Elion said, tapping her on the shoulder and trying to pry her away from the body of her dead beloved, as the enemy nearby gathered its wits about it once more.

"But I cannot leave him here to die, Elion. You must help me!" she beseeched him, unaware of or unwilling to recognize the truth.

"He is already dead, Filaree," he said to her softly but honestly, though sadness was consuming him. "Come, you cannot help him now," he continued in a soothing voice while he gently pulled her apart from Cameron and handed her back her sword which he had retrieved from nearby.

She resisted for a brief moment, unable to take her eyes off of Cameron's still smiling face, seeing for the first time the beautiful blossom that caressed his mouth and watching as other soft tendrils moved to protectively cover him. She smiled sweetly through her flood of tears, and then she gave in to Elion's entreaty. Filaree took a deep breath and slowly released her beloved's hand, laying it softly upon his ruined chest. She gently kissed him on his lips, frozen now for eternity with his final smile upon them. She wiped her swollen eyes and composed herself. The warrior in her took control once more, and she leaned only for a brief moment upon Elion before righting herself and striking a more defensive pose.

"Well, what do you propose, now, Elf?" she asked, ever the warrior, observing their precarious situation, though her heart was heavy with grief.

The enemy had recovered from the shock of the surprise attack and was now coming at the two of them en masse. They stood there with both of their swords raised before them, knowing that their circumstances were perilous.

"What choice have we my Lady, but to fight until the end?" he said nobly, reconciled to his fate.

Filaree stood up tall and strong, and prepared herself for the onslaught.

No sooner had they readied themselves for the assault, when the ground beneath their feet began to rumble and shake as if a wave of water had rolled under them, causing them to almost lose their balance. They watched, eyes wide, as it cascaded across the plain. The battlefield, littered with dead Trolls and living ones, lined with archers and beasts of all kinds, erupted violently from below.

About one hundred yards out from the walls, a formidable row of spiked trees sprouted from the ground and just as instantly shot up at least forty feet into the air. Dense and impenetrable, the trees spread out from one end of the gorge to the other, fencing the Trolls and archers in and separating them from Colton and the rest of his army. The new growth burst forth with such incredible speed that it defied the very limits of belief. The broad branches and solid trunks were tipped with lance-like leaves, pointed and sharp, and covered with thorns, honed and barbed, creating a solid wall against which the enemy was pinned.

Meanwhile under foot, great mounds of new earth heaved and pitched, raising the ground in spots and creating deep chasms in others, sending the archers sprawling and the Trolls running in terror. In their haste, many fell to their deaths in the seemingly endless depths of the newly formed pits, while others impaled themselves upon the sharp spikes of the trees during their frantic efforts to escape, bows and burnished shields strewn everywhere. The branches drew them in once they were snagged upon the spiny barbs, and many disappeared into the dense shrubbery, struggling and screaming in panic and disarray until their voices were muffled by their captors' deadly embrace. The once level battlefield had quickly become a cavernous arena riddled with danger, and the razor sharp tree branches prohibited any from entering or leaving.

The giants backed away from the walls one by one after realizing that the Valkor were no longer moving, and they threw their shields to the ground, swinging their clubs in violent, wide arcs, toppling the Trolls that gathered nearby. They were trying desperately with their limited intelligence, to adapt to the unexpected turn of fortune. The ground was heaving severely, while vines were bursting from the disrupted soil, twisting and thrashing about, latching on to the Trolls, binding them tightly and dragging them to the ground.

The giants' massive legs were becoming entangled in the brambles as well, and they stomped their great feet in an effort to break free, seemingly dancing a comical yet macabre dance upon the uneven battlefield. One of them spotted Filaree and Elion standing by the prone body of a dead beast, and it began to slowly move in their direction, ripping the vines from the ground as it trudged toward them, yanking its mired feet one by one out of the encumbering soil.

The city's defenders continued to heave whatever they could over the walls, careful now not to harm their own two valiant fighters below whose position was becoming more and more imperiled with each passing moment. The other four grotesque titans shortly discovered the woman and the Elf as well, and they too fought to break free of their living shackles in an effort to reach them, driven by the desire for revenge for the death of the Valkor, the ones they were sent to protect.

They moved toward them slowly, dragging the roots and vines behind them as they made their way forward. Elion and Filaree tried to run to the small portal in the wall, hoping that someone would be able to let them in if they could reach it quickly, but their paths were blocked by a red robed wizard. His eyes were hollow and black, and he raped them with his soulless stare, saying to them wordlessly that they now belonged to him, his pale lips twisting into a vicious, depraved smile. His two evil brethren soon joined him before the gates, and together they prepared to attack the human and the Elf.

As the first one raised his sickly arms to prepare a spell, Filaree thought she must be dreaming. She was certain that she could hear a trumpet in the distance. With her sword raised before her, her ears caught the sound of a shouting voice, though the words were not yet discernible.

Elion too had noticed the noise a moment before she had, his Elfin ears sharper than Filaree's, and he sidled next to her and said quietly, "My Lady, move slowly and carefully. Do not provoke them. We must stall for time."

Filaree caught his meaning and acted upon his request. "You do not really want to kill us now, do you?" she asked of the enemy, in a sweet, helpless voice.

He hesitated for a moment, unaccustomed to being spoken to rather than at.

"How will you ever get out of here now? Look around you. You are smart, you can see for yourself. If you spare us, we can help you," she said, appealing to his instinct for self preservation.

"Help me?" the skeletal figure asked, mocking her. "No one can help me!" he hissed sardonically through blackened teeth, his voice sending a chill down Filaree's spine.

The horn sounding in the distance was clearer now, distracting the crimson sorcerers momentarily, and within an instant they could distinctly hear voices as well. Something was approaching.

"Has no one ever expressed their concern for you?" she asked the cadaverous nightmare before her with as much sincerity as she could muster, trying desperately to prevent him from conjuring.

He was not inured to being addressed in such a gentle manner, and for just a moment he listened. He looked upon her quizzically, trying to discern her meaning, though he was a bit confused by the words and the kind tone. The other two demons feared to act alone and they waited for their leader's signal. All the while, the noise around them grew louder, and Filaree could distinctly make out words being shouted in the distance.

From atop the Ghost tower, Grogan, who had been joined by Baladar, perused the horizon. They had witnessed the results of the power as it swept across the field of battle, disrupting the enemy and cutting it in two as Robyn had predicted. They watched helplessly as

Cameron met his death and as Filaree and Elion battled the Valkor. Now too, they watched as the magicians approached the two brave fighters, clearly preparing to kill them.

From the east, above the plain, Baladar noticed movement. He looked closely and he saw what looked like riders coming rapidly toward the city. From atop the height of the wall he heard a horn, and he could swear that he heard someone shout, "Avalain! For Avalain!"

Suddenly as both he and Grogan watched, an imposing legion of armored warriors swept down out of the eastern hills, and they could hear their words being shouted clearly now upon the wind, "The Lady Filaree!", "Avalain!", and "For the Queen, for the Queen!" causing their very skin to prickle in response.

These riders roared across the fields, and the ground leveled itself before them in response, the power spontaneously recognizing an approaching ally. Hundreds of them furiously charged the enemy lines with their lances pointed and their swords drawn. They ravished the remaining, unsuspecting and disoriented Trolls easily, killing them to the last and chasing them across the gorge in every direction.

There was no place for the frenzied Trolls to hide, and they fell beneath the weapons of the formidable knights of Avalain by the hundreds. A group of lancers espied the giants circling before the gates of Pardatha and they moved purposefully toward them. Their great war horses covered in silver plated armor charged into the entangled legs of the huge monsters, and they jabbed them with their long spears and slashed them repeatedly with their swords.

"For the Lady Filaree!" they shouted passionately, as they hacked away at the legs of the brutes, running in circles around them, confusing them and making it impossible for them to strike back accurately.

The giants swung their clubs in frustration, missing their mark, and they turned from left to right, yelling in pain, as the riders jabbed them first from this side and then from that. Their huge legs were covered by green vines that reestablished their holds each and every time the massive beasts broke them, pinning them down and preventing them from maneuvering.

Surrounded by the ever-moving knights, the giants fell one by one, crashing to the ground. As quickly as they lost their footing, the soldiers were upon them, their mighty horses trampling the giants as the riders struck them relentlessly with their weapons. A great cheer arose from the battlements, and it echoed throughout the entire city, its crescendo building as each of the monsters collapsed.

Filaree and Elion stared in disbelief at what was happening around them, but they were not safe from danger yet. The sorcerers' heads jerked from one end of the field to the other, watching closely what was transpiring, realizing how quickly the tide of battle had turned, and they hesitated for just a moment too long, caught up in the Lady's words and the distractions of the struggle. The leader realized his mistake too late, as Filaree and Elion dove left and right respectively, just in time to avoid the blue fire that spurted from his fingers. The other two joined in immediately, preparing to send their deadly discharge into the two unprotected warriors as well. Righting themselves with amazing dexterity, Filaree and Elion raised their swords, and the Princess of Avalain and the Prince of Lormarion readied themselves for the inevitable attack.

Before the leader had an opportunity to send forth another burst of his hellish fire, black blood started to spurt in pulsating streams from his neck and body. He had been pierced by a dozen arrows that rained down upon him from above and by a single spear imbedded deep within his chest, bearing the distinct sigil of Parsifal of Avalain. The other two red robed monsters collapsed to the ground as well, also riddled with arrows and spears, and no longer protected by the Valkor or the Giants. Their powers alone were not great enough to shield them from the multifaceted assaults. Their black blood pooled around them on the hard earth, and as they drew their final breaths, their bodies turned to dust, leaving behind only their crimson capes floating in an inky morass of blood and gore.

The riders from Avalain were sweeping the battlefield now, killing all the enemies in sight, as Filaree and Elion clasped hands and watched with jubilation mounting in their souls. Parsifal, the most honored knight of Avalain and leader of the Queen's forces, leapt from his war horse and knelt before Filaree, his Princess. Another two of his men moved over to the lifeless body of Cameron, now covered by a soft, downy blanket of green, and respectfully carried it to the still closed gates of Pardatha.

"I must gather my men and move them into the city, my Lady," Parsifal said, his eyes still on the ground before Filaree. "The danger is far from past," he commented ominously.

"Rise, dear Parsifal, your timing could not have been better. We owe you our lives," Filaree said gratefully, extending her hand to him.

As he rose, he looked upon the fair maiden, and then said with heartfelt honesty, "My life will forever be fuller knowing that I helped you in your time of need, my Princess." His brilliant, blue eyes glowed with admiration. "The knights of Avalain live for such service, Lady Filaree ," Parsifal said humbly. "But, please, we must seek the protection of Pardatha. The mountain Trolls will be upon us shortly. They cannot be more than a half a day behind us now," he commented. "We rode before them the entire way to Pardatha," he explained, and Filaree and Elion looked upon one another with renewed consternation.

"Gather the troops, Sir Parsifal. I will signal the Master at Arms to allow us to enter. Quickly now, if the gates are to open for us, we cannot endanger the city," she said hurriedly, and then she turned with Elion at her side to see to the opening of the Noban gate.

Baladar and Grogan had already prepared the way for the releasing of the seals, and as Filaree and Elion approached the heavy wooden doors, the apparently seamless center gained new definition as it loosened, a long, thin line appearing down the middle, and the heavy doors slowly gave way, revealing a scorched and dirtied courtyard beyond. The Valkor had wreaked their damage upon the noble entryway, scarring it deeply, and the bottom of one gate dug far into the paved court beyond as it sluggishly moved, slightly askew. There would be time to repair, it, Grogan thought as the triumphant Elfin Prince and the beautiful Lady from Avalain approached.

The two warriors entered to the deafening cheers of the soldiers and city dwellers surrounding them. But, it was a bittersweet victory, short lived at best and overshadowed by the death of Cameron. As they walked down the broad avenue, past the rows of applauding people, they both maintained the confident smiles and walked the walk of victory, befitting their rank, but their hearts were sick with grief for their fallen comrade, and the cautious words of Parsifal resounded in their ears. Another battle was soon to begin, even before the anguish and sorrow of this one had even had a chance to dissipate.

With heads held high, Filaree and Elion made their way to the end of the avenue where Baladar, Grogan and the others waited, unaware still of the newest threat and yet jubilant therefore over the recent victory. Robyn was conspicuously absent from the group of councilors, causing their hearts to skip a beat. They were both unwilling to accept another grievous loss at this time.

Elion wasted no words, making his inquiries as soon as he reached Baladar's side.

"What news of Robyn dar Tamarand? Is he well?" he asked, as the two exhausted fighters stared intensely at the Lord of the city, waiting anxiously for his answer.

"Fear not, he is well. He is merely fatigued after his efforts. He sleeps soundly in his chambers in the castle," Baladar answered.

"And the ring?" Elion asked Baladar quietly.

"I wear it still around my neck."

Behind them, to the overwhelming delight of the crowd, Parsifal, the noble knight of Avalain, led his heroic men through the gates and into the shelter of the city. When the last man was safely inside, Grogan attempted to close the gates to the city of Pardatha once more, but he was not surprised to discover that although one slowly swung shut, the other was mired in the earth, far too heavy to lift and force any further. The perfect symmetry the Elfin craftsmanship had created that made them swing freely upon their invisible hinges, had been disturbed slightly by the previous barrage. As the mechanism ground to a halt, the great gate remained open on one side, the angle of the planes clearly aslant. The people were so overjoyed at the unexpectedly splendid outcome of the day, that they barely noticed the problem.

Grogan immediately began to organize a crew of craftsmen to repair the damage, but the urgency was not upon him as it had been of late. Jubilant over the recent victory, he allowed himself to relax, not yet feeling threatened by the impending prospect of an imminent onslaught. After all, the damage was not serious and it would not take long to right the problem. Besides, the craftsmen would now have time to clean and polish the outside as well, eliminating the despicable signs of the Dark Lord's aborted effort to destroy his beloved city.

At the end of the wide avenue, the councilors could hear the echoes of laughter and joy as they resounded off of the Noban wood of the one closed portal into the depths of the city.

"We must talk, Baladar," Filaree said gravely. She took his arm, noticing with deep concern the exposed entrance to Pardatha.

"The day's travails are not over!" she continued, and Baladar looked upon her saddened face with a renewed uneasiness as they walked through the scorched and debris strewn streets of the mighty city.

Chapter Forty-six

Colton witnessed the energy taking shape before him. He could feel its approach, and although he endeavored to neutralize it, the intensity with which it moved caused him great concern. He sought to shield himself from the might of the incursion, encircling himself in a field of force, but the wave of power struck with such suddenness and potency that his efforts were unsuccessful.

The Chosen one! he thought to himself, as he felt the swell engulfing him, making him sway in his saddle and burning his skin.

He fought to keep his seat, to not fall to the ground before his armies. From deep within himself he generated a dark power, forcing the flood of energy out of his body and soul. The onslaught of white light encased him in a liquid-like cocoon, covering him from head to toe. He knew that his power was greater than its, but he was nevertheless temporarily immobilized. He was frozen in place, as wave upon wave of emotions flooded over him and through him, bleaching the blackness of his soul, challenging his essence with the mesmerizing spell of blissful eternity.

He staggered dangerously under the weight of the barrage, violated by what would have generated blessed ecstasy in one whose heart was pure. The light surrounding him was so bright that those encircling him cowered before it and thought that their master had surely been annihilated, concealed as he was within its boundaries. During that one split second in time, the void collided with the very spark of life itself, and Colton was brought to his knees for the first time, if only for an instant. He withdrew into the emptiness of the nothingness defensively, seeking the strength and refuge that he understood, and he focused all his power upon the intrusive flow of energy.

The explosion was so massive that the very ground shook, scattering everything around him and creating a deep crater into which he and his horse tumbled. Streaks of horrifying, yellow light shot out in all directions, sending ripples of raw force through the air and out across his troops, strewing dirt and debris everywhere. From the smoking depths, Colton the death bringer, the omnipotent leader, emerged, shaken but free of the excruciatingly painful light once more. He had been taken so completely off guard by the assault, not having had enough time to prepare a suitable defense, not having expected an onslaught of this type and strength, that all he could do was benignly watch what presently occurred, impotent as the living barrier of trees sprang up before him, severing him from his front lines almost before he could fully comprehend what was happening.

The pain he felt now was a mere annoyance compared to how furious he was with himself for being such a fool. He should have known that the despicable servant of the trees would attempt to thwart him in such a manner. Weakness was not a state he was accustomed to, and he raged with a frustration he had yet to experience in all his countless tiels.

Colton never conversed meaningfully with anyone. He had no friends and no lovers. His was a solitary life befitting the Lord of Darkness, the prophet of dissolution. When he raved, he raved alone, and when he rejoiced, then too he did it in solitude. He craved darkness and silence and death, and anyone or anything that disrupted his ability to advance toward his desired end unhindered, he despised. Those who assisted him, he saw as merely a means to his coveted end. Thus, his satisfactions were few, and his endless life was a constant struggle against the very forces that kept the planet alive.

Colton dar Agonthea really sought dissolution as an alternative to this eternal journey that others called life. He wanted it all to end, and he wanted to finally free his tortured soul. He barely remembered his early days, his thoughts were so consumed with what he perceived to be the approaching end, the demise of the One Tree, the First. Whenever the power that the Lalas represented, that they manifested and transmitted, that they shared with the living of the earth, whenever that power touched his heart, he felt the searing pain all over again, and he hated them even more. He was so far removed from the clean and pure, from the healthy, that he literally writhed in agony when he encountered anything as natural and vital as what he just felt spreading across the gorge.

Colton watched the trees spring up before him. He witnessed the effects of the Lalas' power, the power of life itself, as it bloomed and grew, feeding upon all of the forces of creation that lay dormant and heretofore inert in the depths of the earth. The writhing mass of new life spread out in both directions, obscuring the city from his view and keeping him from the bulk of his horde, draining him, weakening him. The vast army he lost on the other side was insignificant. He gave it no thought. More would follow him. The world was full of those who could be tempted by his promises or intimidated by his threats. There were countless others that found it easier to give in than to fight for concepts such as honor and integrity. He saw no virtue in such ideas, and his only regrets were that his power was being challenged and that the heir was still free.

He was momentarily stunned by the strength of the light and the vitality of the power, and he suffered like a child whose breath has been taken from it by a sharp blow to the stomach. Weakened, he turned his back upon the battlefield, unwilling to let those subordinates who still remained within view witness him in this state. He rode his horse in silence, toward the distant mountains and the solitude they could provide him, knowing that he could always reassemble the army he now no longer had the desire to lead.

Colton dar Agonthea was too proud to continue fighting when he had been opposed so effectively. He had lost face and he could not tolerate that. The trees' reach was still long, and he had not originally anticipated a Chosen to be among the defenders of Pardatha. His body was fatigued and he wished only to be gone from this cursed city for a while, to rest and to regain his strength. The mountain Trolls would be arriving soon, bringing with them another wave of death and destruction. When he originally summoned them, he had hoped they would arrive during the heat of battle, adding their strength to his own assault. Colton was pleased that they did not, as they too would have been caught on the field when the power struck.

Let them do what they can for me in my absence now, he thought coldly. *Pardatha's victory will be short lived.*

The Dark Lord would remember this day until the sands in the hourglass of time themselves ceased to fall. For him, the true battle had only just begun, but now he was tired and his energy was spent. He would find another way of stopping the boy, in another place and at another moment, he thought as he rode toward the Thorndars looming before him. This was but a minor victory for the enemy, no matter how deeply it disturbed him now. The trees were dying nevertheless, and his season was coming. Nothing that occurred here would change that. As he inconspicuously slipped away, he transformed himself once more.

The dust from the battlefield had settled, leaving what would appear to anyone watching as a thoroughly harmless, solitary old man in worn clothing, sitting hunched over upon a listless, grey pack horse, walking aimlessly up the beaten path into the hills in search of nothing more than a safe haven in the mountains.

Leaderless, his vast army was in total disarray. Stricken by panic and self interest, the various elements sought what protection they could find, either by grouping together in their haste to run away, or by leaving alone and surreptitiously. They were all suddenly bereft of a reason for being there, and the confusion and fear that such serious doubt instilled within them caused all of them, even those whose mental abilities were only slightly higher than the four legged beasts that accompanied them to battle, to seek refuge elsewhere, to hide their heads in fear and shame.

They ran, disorganized and self-possessed, in all directions, escaping from their master's disgrace, a disheveled mob of anguished failures, no longer bound together by their common terror. And the trees sprouted and bloomed behind them, the mix of sublime fragrances filling the air and overpowering the stench of battle, while their succulent foliage blanketed over the carnage of war.

Chapter Forty-seven

Cairn felt the ground tremble and he stopped walking for a moment to try to determine from whence the quake originated. Calyx stood on his hind legs, extending his body its full ten feet in height, and sniffed the air. His red eyes shimmered and his coat changed color in the wind, from silver to copper, to blue. Tomas seemed to pay the disturbance no mind, as if he did not notice the ground shaking at all, and Preston followed his lead.

The quaking stopped as quickly as it began, and then the group continued on its journey to Pardatha. The pass through the mountains was narrow and winding, the walls on either side rising steeply into the air, exposing merely a crack of sky far above. They had been traveling for quite some time now, and Cairn assured the boys that they were close to the end of their travels.

Preston and Tomas had become fast friends, cavorting as teenagers do, playing hide and seek in and out of the boulders and trees that dotted their pathway. Although it was joyous to watch, Cairn urged them forward nevertheless, impatient to get to the city, fearing that what Tomas had previously foreseen had by now come true and that they would arrive at Pardatha in the midst of a battle. He wanted to reach the gates before they were closed and thus locking them out of the one place they so needed to enter. Cairn was also very eager to introduce Tomas, the brother of the heir, to Baladar. These were portentous moments, and it was obvious to Cairn that Tomas had a decisive part to play in the events to come. Even if Tomas was correct and his brother was no longer in the city, he knew that Baladar must meet this young man.

As the group progressed, the path widened and they could see more and more of the sky. The breeze picked up a bit, bringing with it a wonderful odor that flooded their nostrils, refreshing them and causing them to stop and take notice. Cairn thought it strange at this time of year, as the aroma was clearly originating from flowers and blossoms, and very little bloomed so fragrantly during this season. It was hard to be suspicious of something as splendid as this, so the group just enjoyed their good fortune and continued on their way.

"The Pardathans were always excellent gardeners and farmers. It seems that they have discovered how to cause things to grow even after their season," Cairn remarked, though he remained pleasantly mistrustful all the while.

Tomas glanced at him with that look he had grown accustomed to, the totally innocent and nonchalant child's stare, and he said the matter-of-fact words that he spoke so naturally, as if everyone should know what he knew.

"The power is at work here," he said, and then he turned to chase Preston down the path.

Cairn was used to such statements coming from the boy by now, even though it surprised him every time. He simply clarified the obvious. Almost as soon as he verbalized these facts, Cairn knew them to be true. The boy had a remarkable second sight, so astute and yet so guileless. Cairn smiled to himself, aware of how fond he had grown of Tomas in so short a time. Baladar would certainly appreciate the young man's perspective, and his intuition as well.

He looked ahead and he saw that the path curved sharply to the right. There was a large patch of sky over the hill, indicating a clearing in the distance. The mountains were thinning and they would soon be out in the open. It would then be only a short descent to the plains that lay between the Thorndars and the walls of Pardatha, and after they crossed them they would be at their destination.

Preston ran ahead and Cairn watched as he disappeared around the small bend. Tomas walked beside him and Calyx brought up the rear. As they came to the turn in the trail, Tomas hesitated and looked at Cairn with a questioning eye, as if something was amiss. Calyx bounded in front of them quickly and they could both hear a deep, heavy growl coming from his throat. Cairn cautiously inched his way along, carefully keeping Tomas behind him with an outstretched arm. They could hear Preston talking in the near distance and Cairn thought that perhaps he was playing another one of his games. Calyx continued to growl and Tomas became very still and suddenly withdrawn. Cairn looked upon him with alarm. His eyes had a glassy look to them and he seemed unaware, as if he had closed in upon himself and his body had just shut down.

"Tomas?" he whispered. "Are you all right?"

The boy did not answer and Cairn grew more troubled. Tomas sat down upon the ground as if possessed, appearing to neither see Cairn nor to hear his words. His body seemed to shimmer with a glow like a halo surrounding it, and he looked to be in a trance within the brilliance that encased him.

Cairn stepped slowly around the corner and he saw Preston conversing with a tired looking, old man who sat around a small fire. He could see his weary horse struggling to keep its head up in the near distance. Calyx was close by, his tail switching back and forth repeatedly, and he was growling from deep within his throat.

The old man looked at Preston with tired and worn eyes, and he beckoned to him to join him at his side. As Preston moved closer, Calyx sprang between them, prohibiting him from proceeding. Cairn revealed himself at that point and walked cautiously over toward the group.

"Greetings, old man. What brings you to these parts unaccompanied?" Cairn asked cautiously. "These hills are not always so safe when one travels alone."

He raised his head slowly and looked at Cairn closely with a friendly smile across his lips.

"I am too tired to be concerned about that. Besides, what worry could I cause anyone? There was a great battle below. I took refuge here. I was on my way to Pardatha to trade my carvings," he pointed to the saddle bags hanging from the side of his horse.

Their appearance surprised Cairn because he did not remember seeing them there just a moment ago, but he could have been mistaken.

"I was unable to enter the city and I had no place else to go," he said sadly.

"A great battle, you say?" Cairn inquired cautiously. "Has it ended? Was there a victor?" he asked the strange man anxiously.

"The earth itself gobbled up the Dark Lord's army. It was horrible to watch. Fantastic magic was at work in Pardatha today," he answered solemnly, staring into the fire. "And now a great forest stands where there was once only parched earth," he continued.

"And what of the Dark Lord? What of Colton?" he asked.

"I do not know, good man. I do not know," he said, and he hung his head again, weary and forlorn. "Perhaps he was gobbled up by the earth and reclaimed by the trees. I did not linger to find out."

Cairn was elated to hear this news, but something about this man disturbed him greatly. He would be thoroughly relieved to be further down the path and past him. He was also terribly concerned about Tomas, whom he reluctantly left behind.

"Calyx, relax, my friend!" he said to the big cat, seeing that he was still on edge. "See to our things for me, would you?" he asked the Moulant, pointing behind him to where Tomas sat hidden from view.

Cairn turned his head to nod in that direction, and he noticed the old man's eyes rise suddenly. Something in them caused a chill to creep over his entire body.

For a tired old crony, his reactions are quick.

"Straightaway Calyx, we must be moving on. Preston? Come over to me. We have dallied here too long already," he said, and he motioned to the Dwarf to join him.

When Preston was at his side, Cairn turned his back to the fire, bent his mouth to the young Dwarf's ear and whispered, "Go with Calyx right away and help him to carry Tomas to the path below. I will come to you when you are past this clearing. Take care to keep him concealed. I trust not this traveler."

Preston looked at Cairn and he could tell right away that something was wrong. Without questioning him, he pivoted and went to assist the big cat.

"What is your name, old man?" Cairn asked, and he moved closer to the fire, hoping to distract him from seeing what the others were doing.

"Some call me Motek. But I care not how I am addressed. Choose what you will," he replied with his grey head bent over.

"Well then, Motek, where are you headed to now?" Cairn inquired, moving to his opposite side in his effort to keep his attention off of the path that they had just come down.

"Back home," he answered, seeming to care very little about the conversation.

"And where may that be?" Cairn continued.

By this time, Calyx had crossed the clearing with Tomas prostrate upon his back and Preston walking by his side, obscuring the unconscious boy as best as he could with his own body.

"Your horse over there looks as if he could use some grain. Have you nothing to feed him?" he questioned, and he pointed over to the tired, old animal, hoping to further draw his attention away from his friends.

The old man raised his head and stared Cairn straight in the face. His lips curled up in a diabolical smile and he responded in a voice menacing and hushed, while his bloodshot eyes glowed a deep red.

"Be off with you, scholar, while you are still able! Join your friends and leave me be. You have asked me enough questions, have you not?" he said, and he turned away from him in dismissal.

Cairn's skin grew cold as ice and his body was sluggish to obey his own commands. He struggled to walk away, feeling suddenly soiled and wrong, his entire being aching, and without looking back, he hurried down the path as quickly as his legs would carry him.

He caught up to the others at the top of the hill. Tomas was standing and conversing with Preston once again, and Calyx stood protectively in front of the two of them.

"Hurry! We must be gone from here. We are not safe. That old man is not what he appears to be and I trust him not," Cairn said as he urged them forward anxiously.

Tomas on the contrary was himself once more, behaving as if nothing unusual had just occurred.

"Tomas? What happened to you before?" he asked, and he walked up between the two boys. "I cannot tell you how much you cause me to worry. What were you doing?" he questioned, feeling only a little bit better now that he was some distance away from the stranger.

"I did not want my presence to be known," the boy responded so naturally that Cairn felt as if he should have guessed this already. "It was not the right time for him to know that I am here," he continued.

Cairn looked quizzically at Tomas, hoping for more information, but he decided not to question the young man any further. He had his own baleful suspicions already, and he did not want to waste any more time talking until they all were safely behind the gates of Pardatha.

"Make haste, you two! We have been long enough upon this road and our journey is almost at an end," he pronounced, and he hurried the boys down the hill before him, looking fretfully over his shoulder all the while as Calyx, still growling, followed close behind.

Chapter Forty-eight

Grogan must find a way to close that gate. The mountain Trolls alone cannot harm us badly if they cannot enter the city," Baladar said to Filaree after she informed him of how close the marauding army was, based upon Parsifal's recent observations.

"They ride hard and fast, Lord Baladar, and they are more directed and smarter than those of their race we have recently contended with. My people know them only too well. Their country is an efficiently organized one. They are properly trained and well armed. Toth has been independent for many hundreds of tiels. Its allegiance to Colton has always been known, but the Trolls of the mountains were always content to live separate and apart, and not to confront or challenge their neighbors. At least until now," Thembak the woodsman said. "They are fearsome fighters. They also do not give up easily," he continued.

"There is not much that the craftsmen can do in so short a time. The balance of the gate is essential to its movement. Its strength lies in its symmetry, and if that is not corrected, the seals will not set properly," Elion remarked, knowing more about Elfin workmanship than anyone else on the council.

"Is it impossible then to fix it before we are attacked once again?" Thembak asked with concern in his voice.

"I am afraid so, woodsman," Elion answered seriously.

"We must do our best then to fortify the courtyard, and to make certain that the breach in our defense does not become a fatal one," Baladar commented.

"I shall see to it with your permission, Lord. My knowledge of this enemy is more intimate than that of any other here in the city. I can help design our defense, if you will allow me too," Thembak said.

"I would be most grateful, master Thembak, thank you," Baladar responded.

The woodsman saluted respectfully, and then he rushed out to begin his preparations.

"Sir Parsifal? How much time have we?" Baladar inquired.

Stepping forward, the knight bowed to the Lord of Pardatha before speaking in his deep, throaty voice.

"They travel on foot, but they move quickly. We overtook them on our journey here. In order for us to arrive in time to warn you, we had to avoid them by traveling eastward and then south. They were moving at a good pace directly toward the city. They should be here within two hours now, I suspect," he reasoned.

"Our soldiers are weary and theirs are fresh. It will not be an easy fight with the gates askew. We have come away victorious from the last battle, thanks to Robyn dar Tamarand and our valiant friends. But, he lies asleep now and he is exhausted with his energy totally spent. He will not be rejuvenated for quite a while, and we cannot look to him for help this time. I hesitate to ask more of you and the Lady Filaree," he said to Elion respectfully. "Let us all to our tasks, and may we each find the inner fortitude with which to continue. We will meet on the battlements when the horns sound the mountain Trolls' approach," Baladar said, and they all dispersed, each attending to his or her own preparations.

Chapter Forty-nine

Colton watched from the top of the hill as the travelers walked down to the gorge. He laughed to himself, knowing what they were about to encounter.

The older one seems quite worried. With a Moulant for company, he should be safe enough if he stays in the hills. Well, good riddance to them all. They will never reach their destination now anyway, even with the big cat to protect them. The Troll army will have them all for an appetizer, those unsuspecting fools.

He remembered that he had seen at least one other besides the teacher. It was a Dwarf, he assumed by the looks of him, although he was quite tall for the race. He wanted the satisfaction of watching the advent of the Trolls' attack upon the city before he left, and as he looked out upon the plain below, he thought he saw another person accompanying them as well.

The Dark Lord, tired as he was, focused his vision upon the light haired youth and wondered why he had not noticed him before. He sent out a pulse of probing energy, hoping that they were not already too far away for him to successfully discover anything, and just before it reached the one he had not seen before, the accursed scholar stepped in front of him, shielding him from Colton's scrutiny. A rush of information flooded his mind and he realized that this was not just an ordinary group of travelers. He learned nothing about the one young man, but he learned much about the purpose of the scholar's visit to Pardatha.

So, he was summoned to train the heir! What a pity he will not get the chance to fulfill his chosen obligations. Let the Trolls have him. There is some justice after all.

He had been so preoccupied when they had encountered him in the hills before, that he barely paid attention to them. Now, he felt that perhaps he had missed an opportunity to learn more about the boy he sought so desperately to capture. He watched them walk further into the trap, revealing himself only slightly as they moved forth. His abilities were impaired by the previous day's trying events, and he could still not clearly see the face of the young blonde haired boy, but something about him was familiar, though every time he tried to scrutinize him closely, his vision was oddly obstructed.

Colton was weary and ready to return to Sedahar by this time, and he was not overly concerned with these misguided wanderers. So, he watched only as long as it took for the evidence of the mountain Trolls' presence to manifest itself to the small group, and for them to realize the fatal circumstances into which they had stumbled. Grinning to himself, he observed as the older man grabbed the hands of his little followers and, like a helpless mother trying to protect her children from an attacking pack of wolves, started to run for a shelter that he would never reach.

Ah, the irony of it all, he thought and laughed out loud. *They will not live out the hour. That will mean one less chance for the heir, and one more chance for me. And now this day is beginning to bore me.*

He turned and walked back up the mountain path, without giving these innocent and doomed pilgrims another thought.

Chapter Fifty

Tomas was the first to step upon the parched earth of the gorge, having descended from the foothills before the rest of his group. Preston ran to catch up with him, and he yelled with excitement all the way.

"Tomas! Wait for me! Can you see the city?"

He had never been to Pardatha, though his home was not far from it, but he had heard about it his entire life. The Dwarf was as enthralled as he had ever been, finally stumbling upon the adventure he so yearned for. Cairn and Calyx stepped from behind the final escarpment, having cautiously brought up the rear, happy to have allowed some distance to be created between the two boys and the old man they left behind. When Preston finally did reach Tomas' side, he discovered him standing perfectly still with his eyes focused on the edge of the great forest that bordered the city to the north east. He appeared to be mesmerized, motionless and silent. Cairn and Calyx joined them, relieved to be so close to their destination at last.

The city loomed in the distance with its walls broad and imposing. They could see the towers of the castle and the surrounding buildings beyond. Cairn could vaguely make out the circle of great stones that comprised the Temple Mount high on a hill near the majestic rise of the Thorndar's peaks. The plains before the gates were conspicuously empty and there was almost no activity outside the walls, which was not how Cairn remembered this engrossing place. He had been to Pardatha before, many years ago, but he vividly recalled being amazed by the tumult that went on within the city and beyond the gates as well.

Before he could finish his thought, he was struck by a delicious fragrance wafting across the ancient river bed, the identical odor he noticed previously as they traveled down the mountain pass. He could see that the Pardathans had cultivated a new area of dense greenery at the edge of the gorge, remembering clearly how barren it had been when he was last there. The youth of the city used to play sports on the broad flats of the ravine, and he recalled how open and spacious the expanse previously was.

Calyx had his snout in the air once again, trying to distinguish between the many and varied odors that blew his way, and something was still bothering the big Moulant. Cairn stroked his immense back, trying to settle him down. He had been on edge ever since they encountered the strange man in the hills, and Cairn imagined he was still unsettled by that. They overtook Preston who was standing next to Tomas, and Cairn was about to point to Pardatha and mention his concerns, when Tomas turned to him with a fearful look in his eyes, so uncharacteristic of the boy. Cairn was immediately struck by the young man's distress, as he had so far been incredibly calm in the face of every adversity they had encountered since the day they had met, and now he was obviously greatly agitated.

"What do you see, Tomas?" Cairn asked immediately, looking toward the woods that the boy was focusing his gaze upon.

Preston also grew uneasy, as he had been standing with Tomas up until the others arrived, and the blonde haired boy had not spoken or stopped scrutinizing the far horizon since he had caught up to him.

"He has been acting this way as long as he has been standing here. As soon as we stepped foot upon this ground, he stopped speaking," Preston reiterated, alarmed.

Cairn had become accustomed to the strange boy's behavior, but he had yet to see fear disturb his ever calm demeanor.

"We must get into the city as fast as we can! One battle had already ended, but another will begin shortly. We are not safe here!" he said, still motionless.

The fur on Calyx's back began to shimmer and shift rapidly from color to color, and the Moulant growled deeply, his eyes focused upon the trees beyond the hills to the northeast. Cairn looked as closely as he could and he thought he saw a line of dust rising on the crest beyond.

"It is too late!" Tomas said quietly, his arms hanging dejectedly by his side.

"What did you say?" Cairn asked him, not believing that he heard what he thought he did. "Too late for what?" he asked anxiously.

"The Troll army is attacking now. We do not have time to reach the gates. And one gate is still open, while the other, though closed, is charred and damaged. It must have been a terrible clash and a fierce foe who could have damaged the Noban gates," Tomas answered, staring now toward the opening to the city. His usual calm demeanor had returned, though the news he disseminated was far from comforting. "Colton left his fearsome mark before he retreated, and despite his loss, he still manipulates the game," the boy mused, seemingly to himself.

He appeared once more to be deep in thought, speaking as if no others were present.

"Let us go back into the shelter of the hills then," Cairn said with urgency in his voice, as he went to take Preston's arm.

"We cannot. Our way is blocked," Tomas replied, raising his arm without even looking and pointing toward the shadow of a horse and rider emerging from the pass at the top of the incline.

"We cannot stay here, Tomas. We must run or we will be trampled, at best," Cairn said anxiously.

"It will do us no good to run, Cairn," the boy said casually now, having surmounted whatever initial fear he may have experienced and now reconciled to their fate as he saw it.

"I will not stand here and let us be overcome. If the gate is still open, we should try to reach it," Cairn said, pressing them to hurry, unwilling to just give up and be slaughtered after coming all this way.

They could feel the ground trembling as the huge army surged forward, out from the shelter of the trees and down the slope onto the plains. The bells in the city were sounding the attack and the horns were blowing the assembly. The noise was deafening as the mountain Trolls stampeded with their axes raised high in the air and yelling in their undulating tongue. They could not yet have seen the small group of travelers, but they were directly in the path of the onslaught and there was nothing they could do to escape it.

With a speed that defied belief, Calyx rose upon his hind legs and raised his mouth to the sky. A roar escaped from his throat that echoed across the valley, bouncing off of the rocks and hills all around. It was the plea of aid that he issued, the call for help that indicated the direst of circumstances; the signal that a Moulant or its charge was in grave danger. Calyx repeated the sound once again as Cairn gathered Tomas and Preston together, preparing to make a run for the city. By the looks of the situation, he did not believe that help could arrive soon enough to aid any of them now.

Cairn hurriedly glanced at the hill behind them and as he dreaded, he saw the silhouette of a man and horse, standing and looking in their direction. Something in the old man's eyes seemed to reflect the light of the midday sun, and he thought he saw a red flare burst in their direction as he moved to urge the others on. Cairn felt a wave of nausea overtake him. He felt as if something vile and inhuman had hit him in the back, and he stumbled momentarily before regaining his balance. A terrible taste was in his mouth and he spit on the parched soil in order to rid himself of it. His entire body was tingling. He felt vulnerable and violated for just an instant, but he had no time to focus upon it, and he compelled himself forward despite the stultifying sensations.

He grabbed the hands of the two boys and ran with them as fast as he could toward the one open gate, pulling them behind him. He had not the time to see if Calyx followed too, but he had to let the Moulant do what he felt was best under the circumstances. They could all see the front lines of the Troll army maddeningly rushing toward them, and it was clear to them all that they were not going to make it. They would be cut off long before they could possibly reach the safety of the city.

Their legs were tired and their mouths were dry, but they kept running at full speed. Cairn saw a small group of the enemy detach itself from the main contingent and turn in their direction. He could see their sparkling eyes by now, as the distance between them was closing rapidly. The screams of the bloodthirsty Trolls were deafening, and he could smell their hot breath. The stench was overpowering. A few more moments and the enemy would be upon them. He ran to the right, turning away from the city and trying desperately to gain some more time, when he felt Preston's hand pull away from his own.

The young Dwarf fell to the ground having caught his foot on an exposed tree root. Tomas and Cairn stopped running and went to assist Preston whose ankle had been twisted by the protuberance. They could not leave the boy there, and they both knew that there was no longer any chance of escape, so they turned and faced their destiny. Cairn stood protectively in front of Tomas and Preston with his hands raised to either side, weaponless save for a small dagger, as the fearsome Troll charged, its black face looming through the smog.

"Run, Tomas! Run! Save yourself. I will protect Preston," he screamed, but the boy did not move.

Cairn raised his knife in defense of the two young men, when suddenly the dust rose in great gusts all around them, blinding them, burning their eyes and causing them to choke uncontrollably. He heard the sound of an axe slashing the air, and instantly he felt the blade skim his arm. Pain shot through him and he sensed something warm running down his limb. He lashed out with his knife, striking soft flesh, and he heard a guttural yelp.

In the murky light of the dust ridden air, Cairn thought he must be hallucinating as he saw Tomas rise into the heavens, glimpsing his boots dangling briefly over his head before he disappeared completely into the cloud of sand and debris that swirled all around them. Preston too lifted off of the ground before his eyes almost at the same moment, and then vanished into the obscurity of the swirling sky. The dirt was violently churning everywhere, whipping his clothing forcefully and causing his eyes to bite and sting incessantly.

He could hear the sounds of pounding feet encircling him, and from every direction now he felt the hot breath and smelled the stench of the rampaging Trolls. A weapon grazed his side and he cringed in pain, striking out widely in all directions with his small hunting knife, trying valiantly to keep the enemies at bay, but not knowing even from whence they came. He heard Calyx's fearful roar somewhere in the distance, but he could not tell how close or far away he was. Warm, black blood splattered his face and he heard the frenzied yelps of the enemy as it lashed out at him through the obscurity of the clouded air. It was hard for him to focus upon his own peril, he was so distraught and worried at the absence of his friends.

Pain pierced him just behind his neck. His shoulders were pinched by something strong and sharp, trying to pull him upward. Cairn fought against it in vain, struggling to free himself from his attacker, believing that the end was finally upon him. He was unable to strike at this new enemy effectively, as his body was being pulled headfirst into the heavens. Dangling helpless and at the mercy of his captor, Cairn desperately tried to see clearly through the obscured and turbid air, but to no avail. His eyes were irritated and filled with tears and he was exhausted from his efforts, when in one split second, the sky cleared abruptly in a rush of fresh wind.

In front of him perhaps thirty feet away, he saw both Tomas and Preston suspended from the talons of two huge Selgays, whose wings beat heavily and thereby raised a blinding cover of spiraling dust in a path directly toward the city. He could see the dense feathers of the great bird-like beasts above himself as well, and on the ground below he saw a black sea of Trolls swarming toward the gates of Pardatha with their weapons drawn.

From this vantage point, he was able to watch as the massive flying mammals swooped over the walls of Pardatha and landed in the courtyard behind the battlements, depositing their passengers safely on the paved stones of the city with the gentle grace of protective mothers. The two beasts squawked loudly and then immediately ascended precariously into the sky after relieving themselves of their quarry, and then they turned toward the approaching enemy. They hesitated for a moment, hanging in the air circumspectly, and then they dove with an astonishing speed at the front lines of the attackers, shrieking in a terrifying manner as they plummeted through the sky. They looked like mighty, grey missiles streaking determinedly toward their targets.

Cairn felt his feet hit the ground and he tumbled once before righting himself. Tomas and Preston were already surrounded by townsfolk who had rushed to their aid by the time Cairn arrived at their sides. They looked upon one another in disbelief coupled with relief, and Preston limped immediately to Cairn's side to try and assess the severity of his friend's wounds. Cairn was covered in blood from the multiple gashes on his body, but he assured the other two that the wounds looked worse than they actually were and that he was fine. He was so grateful to be safely within the walls of the city and to be alive still that however severe his injures may have been, he knew that he could deal with them later.

Tomas lifted his head to peer over the masses of people encircling him at the one gate that remained open. He moved toward it, pushing through the lines of defenders until he stood directly behind the first row of them. Cairn and Preston were only a few feet behind him and the lines of soldiers, all of whom were armed and facing the open gate, standing in a u shaped line of defense, with their shields forming a solid blockade against the impending onslaught. Tomas broke through the bulwark and stood there solitary and exposed, staring first at the broken gate and then out into the gorge below. Cairn assisted Preston as he walked, his arm under the Dwarf's own, and then he joined Tomas. Everyone else watched them, not knowing what the mysterious threesome who had arrived so precipitously among them, was about to do.

Baladar and Filaree had rushed down from the battlements when the Selgays swooped in carrying these three visitors, and they too made their way into the clearing between the row of shielded soldiers and the awry gate. Baladar greeted Cairn of Thermaye warmly, and looked with confused wonder upon the blonde haired youth before him. Filaree stood beside them all, uncomfortable with their vulnerability and eager to maneuver them behind the defenses.

The fearsome Selgays had decimated the first row of Trolls, tearing them to shreds with their razor sharp talons and pointed beaks. The biggest of the animals, the one that had transported Cairn, had a mountain Troll in his claws as he rose into the sky. Diving at the marauding enemy, he heaved it into the pack and knocked down dozens of the black beasts with the dead body of their compatriot as they ran. The Selgay flapped its great wings heavily and rose up almost vertically, prepared to attack again. The remaining two formidable flying beasts were poised for another run as well, when the line of attack broke momentarily before their charge. The Trolls retreated in panic, not knowing how to defend themselves against the terror coming at them from the skies. The Selgays shrieked in response.

The great animals circled the area before the open gate, taking turns at diving down with fantastic speed on any daring savage who infringed upon the space they now possessively patrolled. A horn sounded in the distance, and then a contingent of the enemy emerged from the crowd, led by a larger Troll clad in black and crimson hides. All around him they scurried and scampered, apparently following his orders. His guttural commands were issuing from his slobbering jaws in a booming voice.

The wriggling mass of black beasts assembled behind its leader, and then from out of the ranks, the beasts pulled a host of wooden war machines, fitted with large, spearlike projectiles. As they set them up, the rest of the Troll army thronged behind them, far enough from the city to be out of the direct path of the terrifying beasts. The leader dropped his arm and the others let loose a missile. It sprang high into the air with great speed, and it just missed the outstretched wing of the front-most Selgay before it fell over the walls into the center of the city and shattered on the stones of Pardatha's streets. Another dangerous projectile struck the largest of the animals, grazing its side and sending it shrieking into the sky. The assailants were gaining confidence by this new development and the birds, their primary task completed, hovered very high in the sky, out of range of the new weapons unleashed upon them.

Tomas stared out among the warring masses, and from the west, leaping over heads and bodies and tearing through dozens of Trolls, with his huge teeth bared and his claws extended, came Calyx, bloodied but alive. He had numerous cuts along his hind legs and one ear was sliced clean through, but his eyes glowed a bright and healthy red, and his coat, though soiled, shimmered and shined in the sun. Cairn rushed to his side and hugged him around his big neck, while he examined him from head to tail with his wearied yet worried eyes.

Once the Moulant was safely inside the city Tomas, who still remained standing in the path of the charging Trolls, turned his gaze upon the gate. His eyes locked on the carved Noban and he concentrated deeply. The ponderous gate shook slightly and then began to slowly creak shut. It moved heavily, scraping the ground as it neared its counterpart. As it progressed, it lifted slightly and began to move more freely and fluidly. Tomas did not let his intensity falter until the gate was fully closed. It met its twin with a resounding bang, and then Grogan and his attendants immediately rushed from the crowd to set the seals, finishing the job and locking it tight.

A great cheer arose within the city and Tomas, expressionless and weakened, leaned heavily upon his friends Cairn and Preston, who had meanwhile pushed their way through the ranks and returned to his side. Calyx sat next to them, licking his wounds, allowing his compatriots the luxury of space, since none but the bravest of the common folk would dare approach them with the big cat so close by.

Calyx raised his nose to the sky and roared his acknowledgment and thanks to the Selgays, sending the few, bold Pardathans who had gathered nearby to gaze upon the Moulant with wonder, running for shelter. The great Selgays shrieked in response and then soared into the clouds, back toward their homes in the Thorndars. Preston turned his face to the sky and waved, while Cairn looked up and smiled. He wanted only to preserve the image of these departing allies in his mind's eye and sustain the feeling of gratitude in his heart forever.

Chapter Fifty-one

Baladar did not have the time to properly thank the young man who had accompanied Cairn into Pardatha so fortuitously. The Trolls, maddened first by the Selgays and now by the gates closing in their very faces, attacked with a vengeance. The big machines that shot their missiles at the giant birds now took aim upon the rooftops of the city, sending blazing shafts over the high walls and deep into the heart of Pardatha. Fires burst out in many places, and the people of the city mobilized in order to prevent widespread damage.

The Troll army attacked in waves, accompanied by barrages of burning projectiles. The soldiers upon the battlements were still weary from the previous fighting, but they fought as well as they could. The bowmen continued to down the enemy from their vantage points behind the crenellated towers. But as the battle wore on, the Trolls became more aggressive. They rolled out even larger machines and used them to hurl huge stones into the city, shattering roofs and crushing bones. They remained just out of the reach of the archers' arrows and they were thus free to act with impunity.

This enemy was smart and well organized. Its leaders took their time and planned their assaults, rather than wasting their numbers futilely. The assault continued in this manner for hours, and it was taking its toll upon the city of Pardatha. The fires were burning in some places uncontrollably and many buildings were crumbling under the barrage of rock and stone. Although Grogan mounted a noble defense, Baladar could see the signs of fatigue setting in.

The Trolls continued their steady bombardment, and now they began to aim their rock hurling devices against one spot on the wall. A single blow to the thick stones of the fortifications would not do any harm, but this continuous attack, coupled with the exceedingly perfect aim that their weapons afforded them was causing great concern among the councilors. The relentlessness with which the Trolls mounted their assault was disconcerting. They could continue on in this manner for a long time, wearing down the city's defenses and morale. And more importantly, the wall was showing signs of giving way to the perpetual cannonade, no matter how slowly.

Baladar convened the council late in the afternoon and he invited Cairn to join them as well, along with his two charges, Tomas and Preston. Robyn dar Tamarand had not yet fully recovered from his previous exertions, but the remainder of the council members were present. Baladar had not had a real chance to meet his newest guests yet. In fact, he was so consumed with the defense of his city that he had not even gazed closely upon the faces of all of his visitors, but a vivid image of Tomas lingered in his mind since the moment he first saw him.

When Cairn entered the circle of stone accompanied by Tomas and Preston, Baladar was visibly shaken and he could barely contain his astonishment. No one but he and Elion remained in the city who had seen Davmiran at close range, and this boy could be his twin. Elion gasped when he arrived and was too surprised to even take his seat. Filaree looked at the two of them in shock, never having had seen either of them react so dramatically to anything, despite all that they had recently been through.

"What is it, you two?" she asked of them in wonder. "You both look as if you have seen a spirit," she commented.

The other councilors waited anxiously for an explanation for the odd behavior of their leader and the young Elfin Prince. Cairn suspected the reason for their reaction immediately, and he chose not to keep them in suspense any longer.

"Greetings, good people. For those of you who do not know me, I am Cairn of Thermaye. I was summoned here by your Lord Baladar, for the purpose of acting as a teacher to the young heir of Gwendolen. I had received information earlier that he was not presently here in the city, but I was determined to reach Pardatha nonetheless. I have brought two travelers with me, if it pleases you," he continued humbly.

"We have been journeying for many days and we have much news to share with you that we have gathered on the way. Oh, by the way, if you have not already learned for yourself, my friend Calyx is here as well," he said, pointing to the cat-like beast reclining beside the stones. "This boy is Preston, of the Thorndar Dwarves," he said, laying a gentle hand upon the boy's shoulder. "And this is Tomas," Cairn said warmly, putting his other arm around his back. "They are like family to me, and I hope that you will welcome them among you as you do me," he finished, still standing.

Baladar had not closed his mouth since the three walked into the council chamber. He stared continuously at Tomas, and he finally could not contain his wonder any longer. Finally, he stood up and spoke.

"I am sorry to have to bypass the formalities of so anticipated a visit, Cairn of Thermaye, but I must ask this question forthright and straight," he addressed Tomas directly this time. "Forgive me my son, if I appear to be aggressive, but you bear a striking, even an uncanny resemblance to the boy I call Davmiran, the heir of Gwendolen. It cannot be mere coincidence." Turning now to Cairn he asked, "What do you know of this, Cairn, my friend? Please, enlighten us."

When he was finished speaking he sat down once again.

"It is a long story, Lord Baladar, and I am afraid that now is not the time to tell you everything you must eventually learn. But, the resemblance is true. This boy is the twin to the heir."

The table erupted in gasps all around. Cairn waited for them to calm down and then he continued speaking.

"He was raised by a woodsman and his wife, Trevor and Safira, into whose care he was entrusted when he was a new born babe. Alas, they are no longer alive to bear witness. On my way to Pardatha, I *stumbled* upon his uncle, who was kind enough to invite me to his home. Tomas and I have been together ever since," he paused.

"You are surely his twin!" Elion remarked, examining him closely. "The eyes are identical, though of a different hue. And the face! Dav's hair is longer, albeit," he said smiling.

Tomas stood up slowly and allowed his brilliant green eyes to wander from person to person around the large table, until they finally rested upon Cairn.

"It is as he says," he began. "He has been more than a friend to me, and I will be eternally grateful to him. And Calyx and Preston too," he continued. "My brother does not know that I exist, although I am sure that he has felt my presence often, as I have and do his. I have been aware of him ever since I was a small child, but I was taught about my past purposefully, while he was deprived of this knowledge purposefully as well. I am anxious to meet him. There is much that we must do together. I know that he is no longer here in Pardatha. I have known that ever since he left the city. I also sense that he is not thinking, that he is in a state of unconsciousness. Is he safe? What can you tell me of him, Baladar?" he asked with deep emotion.

Baladar stood and looked seriously and meaningfully at Tomas. The words did not come easily to his mouth, as he was overcome by the events unfolding before him.

"He is safe, Tomas. Quite safe. And, forgive me for answering you first without offering you our warmest greetings and welcome to Pardatha, but I thought that you needed to hear that," he rejoined, preparing to continue. "The noble young Elf, Elion..." Baladar nodded in his direction, "...rescued him from certain death in the hands of our enemy, and carried him all of the way back to Lormarion, where he rests, protected in the heights of Seramour," Baladar stated with pride.

Tomas' expression barely changed, but he was greatly relieved and he closed his large eyes for just a minute, in order to fully absorb the information that he was just given.

"I am grateful to you, Prince, for what you did. I would like to hear more about it some time soon," he said to Elion, respectfully. "But, what of his health?" he asked with mounting concern.

"As to his state of mind, he arrived here unconscious. As you know, the King is dead! His family -- your family, Tomas -- was attacked by Colton, and the brave woman who raised him, Mira, was able to cast him to us here, at the ultimate cost to herself. I have the token with which to awaken him, and I was returning to Pardatha after having visited Calista, the Lady of the Island, in order to imbue the token with the power it required, when I discovered him missing."

Baladar's face clouded with concern, remembering the awful feeling that took root in his soul upon learning of Dav's absence.

Elion stood and interrupted for a moment.

"I was returning to Lormarion from my uncle Bristar's in Crispen when I stumbled upon a retinue of riders leaving Pardatha. They led a horse out of the gates draped with a blanket, and then they left it there to fend for itself as if they had forgotten about it completely. They departed in one direction and the horse wandered undirected into the field near where I was hiding. To my surprise, I watched as a boy fell from the saddle onto the earth. I went to aid him and I discovered that he was unconscious." He looked at Tomas, and then continued his description of the events. "I knew that I could not leave him alone and unprotected. I felt uncomfortable for some reason about bringing him back into the city, so I sort of pulled him all the way to Seramour. I left him in the care of my mother. She is a healer of great prowess, and I am sure that his physical ailments at the least have been well attended to by now."

Elion finished, seeming to wonder himself at how odd it all sounded now.

"When Colton attacked, I was relieved that Davmiran was not

here. Until then, I felt as if I had let you all down," Baladar said, remembering those hours with remorse.

"Things are as they should be," Tomas said. "When it is safe to do so, I will travel to Lormarion and meet my brother," he commented matter of factly.

Baladar had many questions, as did the others who had been summoned to train this boy's brother, but then was not an opportune time to ask them all. Baladar rose once more and spoke solemnly.

"These are dangerous days. We do not have the luxury now of learning all we would like to, as the Troll army is pounding on our walls. We have been through much these past weeks, all of us," he said, looking around the table. "And I fear that the battle has only just begun. The Dark Lord has not been defeated, as we all know. He will return, and he is determined to locate Davmiran. It is only a matter of time before he does. We must deal with our immediate problems, and then we can begin to address the future," he concluded.

"If we do not do something soon, there may not be a future for us here!" Filaree said, defiantly. "It is well and good that the heir has a brother and that we are all learning our history lessons, but have we forgotten just how dangerous our enemy is?" she asked, reminding everyone present of her recent loss. "I think that we should concentrate on our defenses now and leave the niceties for another time," she finished.

Tomas looked upon her with great sadness in his large eyes, and he moved to her side. She held her head in her hands, and he was looking down at the stone of the table. He placed one hand upon her shoulder and she gazed up at him as a single tear ran slowly down her cheek.

"I am sorry for your loss, Lady Filaree. You must have loved him very much," Tomas said comfortingly.

Filaree never really acknowledged Cameron's death. She had not allowed herself to cry since the tragic moment, and she refused to think about his absence during the battle. But, now that Tomas brought it up and said the words out loud, she could no longer pretend that it was not true. Her eyes welled up with tears and she laid her hand over the boy's, grasping it and squeezing it hard. She looked into his eyes and found warmth and comfort there, and she smiled a sweet, sad smile.

"Thank you, Tomas. Your words mean a lot to me," she said

under her breath. "I am sorry if I was too harsh before," she replied.

"We are all tired, Lady," Baladar said.

"But Filaree is correct. We must find a way to defeat our foe nevertheless," Thembak reiterated, feeling the urgency of the circumstances.

Tomas and Filaree continued to stare at one another for a short while, and then the boy returned to his seat.

Her eyes followed him until he was sitting once more, then she looked around the table and spoke once again.

"These Trolls are strong and smart. Our greatest danger is the possibility that the wall will collapse under their barrage. We must find a way to disable their catapults."

Her voice had regained the strength and composure that characterized her manner.

"She is accurate. A siege we can withstand. Without a new source of supply, they will eventually return to their homes in the mountains. But, if they breach our defenses, both sides will suffer great losses," Mistress Marna commented. "Any breach will renew their hope. It would only prolong the battle. The Lady of Avalain is correct. We must stop the cannonades at all costs," she agreed.

"If our archers cannot shoot that far, and if we do not send a force outside the gates to attack them directly, how do you propose we disable the catapults?" Pertar of Axlon asked.

As the group pondered this difficult question, Robyn dar Tamarand walked into the oval unnoticed by the others.

"What is this I am being told of another attack?" he interrupted the conversation. "Why was I left to sleep for so long if the city was in danger?" he asked loudly.

The others stopped what they were doing and looked with relief upon the face of the man who had sacrificed so much to save them not very long ago.

"Robyn?" Lord Baladar asked. "You are looking well rested. How do you feel?" he inquired.

Robyn walked to his side and he looked with great curiosity at the new faces circling the table. His eyes were shifting rapidly, first from Tomas' face, then to Preston's, then to Cairn's and back again.

"I feel quite well, Baladar. Thank you for asking. Now, please tell me who attacks us presently? I thought we had rid ourselves, at least temporarily, of the danger," he asked, his gaze resting upon Tomas.

"The mountain Trolls marched in from the north after the last of Colton's lackeys dispersed. But, you missed more than their arrival, Robyn," Elion answered for him.

"Yes indeed, you did. Our new friends were of great help in closing the Noban gates. One was damaged in the battle and we could not budge it. Their arrival was quite serendipitous," Baladar remarked.

"How long must I wait to be introduced then, so that I can offer my gratitude as well?" he asked, extending his gaze toward the three newcomers. "I am Robyn dar Tamarand, Chosen of Promanthea. It is my pleasure to meet you," he said, as he reached his open hand to Cairn, the eldest and closest of the group, and then to Tomas and Preston in turn.

"I am Cairn of Thermaye, teacher, this is Preston of the Thorndar Dwarves, and this is Tomas, Chosen of Ormachon, the heir of Gwendolen," he said portentously, introducing him in this fashion for the first time.

"Brother to the heir, you meant to say, I believe," Baladar interrupted.

"No, Lord Baladar. I said exactly what I meant to say. Tomas is the elder, if only by minutes. He is the true heir," Cairn replied boldly.

"Is this true, Tomas? How can this be? Are you certain?" he asked.

"I was raised by Trevor and Safira, and they told me of my birthright. Ormachon has reinforced that knowledge in his own way. But, as there is no Gwendolen any longer, there is no longer a crown to be worn. I would prefer just being called 'Tomas', if no one objects. I never knew my real mother and father, although I knew of them always. But, I do believe that my brother, Davmiran as you call him, would have been the one to assume the throne, not me," Tomas said humbly.

Robyn addressed the group.

"A Chosen never lies, as you all know, so we will no longer need to question the statements just made. This young man is correct, regardless, in his assessments. We need not settle issues regarding the ascension at this moment. We have other more pressing matters to deal with," Robyn said forcefully, wishing to reserve these deliberations for another, more private opportunity.

"I would not normally question a Chosen under any other circumstances, Robyn..." Baladar began, "...but this subject concerns us all here, nay, everyone, everywhere so deeply that to avoid suspicion and doubt, I feel compelled to ask for more information. Forgive me, Robyn. Forgive me Tomas. I mean no disrespect. I do not doubt your words, but what proof do we have. The only ones present at the birth are dead. We cannot afford to win a war and then find ourselves confronted by a divided countryside. I apologize for dwelling upon these issues, but I was entrusted with the job of educating and training the 'heir of Gwendolen', and I must know just what I am to do now." he remarked, though he had to admit that he was mesmerized by the boy's gaze.

If he did not believe he had an obligation to ask these difficult questions, he would not have. Sitting beside this beautiful boy, Baladar disliked the role he assumed, and it felt wrong to doubt his words. He was emotionally and physically moved by his very presence. The boy radiated power and a wholesome, healthy essence. Being in his presence made him feel alive and rejuvenated. He wanted so much to believe everything he was being told.

"The Tomes of Caradon allude to what could be interpreted to be two rings, one gold and one silver. They speak ambiguously about the heir, and they are characteristically unclear and obscure in their way. If there are two rings, then perhaps there are two heirs," Mistress Marna said.

Cairn was not disturbed by the council's reluctance to immediately accept the truth of the words he spoke. These were such important matters, that it was their responsibility to question everyone and everything. Rather than being upset, he was smiling slightly as he looked at Tomas.

"I think Mistress Marna has made a valid point," Cairn commented, and Baladar nodded his head in agreement. "The purpose of my trip here was to educate the heir. And you, Filaree, and you Robyn, were also summoned in order to educate and teach the heir. Can we not do that whether there are two heirs or one? Need we even answer all of these questions here and now?" Cairn asked.

"He may be right. Perhaps there can be two. In fact, there have been Kingdoms ruled by twins before," Pertar remarked.

Tomas was sitting and listening to all of this, and he understood the concerns of the councilors as well as Cairn did. It did not disturb him at all. Robyn seemed to be more defensive than even Tomas himself was.

"The Tomes have always been obscure. It has been left to us to interpret them. Two rings or one ring that changes color? No one had been able to determine the answer to that. Tomas? Can you enlighten us?" Robyn asked.

The young boy slipped his graceful hand inside his tunic and removed a silver ring that shone with the intensity of the sun.

"Is this what you wanted to see?" he asked innocently. "This is the ring of which you speak. And Baladar has its twin, the golden one. I am, you have said, identical to my brother in all obvious aspects of my appearance, yet my eyes are green and his are blue. These two rings..." he pulled the chain over his head and placed it on the table before him "...are identical, despite their color."

Baladar too, removed the ring he held from around his neck, and then he walked to Tomas' side and placed it next to the other one on the thick, stone slab. They were as similar as two separate objects could be, and Tomas' comments were finding interested ears.

"Robyn? Please look at them with your own eyes and tell us all if you see any differences between the two other than the color," Tomas requested.

Robyn lifted them both, placing one in each palm, and then he examined them closely. The inscriptions inside were as identical as possible. The weight, the size and the width were all the same.

"Twins, they are!" he concluded, and he put them back down on the table.

"Your point is well taken, Tomas," Baladar remarked, satisfied and greatly relieved. "I am convinced!" Baladar said decidedly. "If you, Tomas, tell me that you believe that you and your brother both share equally the birthright of the Gwendolen's, then I will accept your word for it and I will speak of this no more," he said, and the others all avidly nodded their agreement.

"Baladar, members of the council," Tomas addressed the table. "I have always known who I was and where I came from. And I knew that I was not like the other children with whom I came into contact. My aunt and uncle never concealed the truth from me, but they were never comfortable talking to me about my future. Ormachon taught me other things, but he too was vague and secretive regarding what life had in store for me. I have felt my brother's presence every day of my life, and I feel now as if I have known him forever. I would give my life for his, without hesitating. My love for him is as great as any love I know," Tomas said compellingly, moving one or two of the assembly to tears.

"You need not fear that he and I will ever disagree. We were born of the same purpose and we share in the same power. I am hopeful that his teachers can help him to fulfill his destiny," he said, looking intensely at the three travelers. "I will aid them in any way that I can. And perhaps they can aid me as well. There is much I do not know," Tomas said with such tenderness and feeling, that no one could possibly doubt his sincerity.

Filaree pounded her fist upon the table.

"Well spoken, Tomas. We need have no further discussions about this matter now. We could neither add to nor enhance your eloquence," she said respectfully. "Gentlemen and ladies, if you will, can we now get back to the urgent situation at hand? We have a war to win!" she concluded, as the group sat reassured and ready to plan its next move.

Chapter Fifty-two

The Trolls had become more aggressive during the past few hours, sending forays of armored soldiers to the wall where the missiles were relentlessly pounding away. They were protected by other Trolls in tough leather armor, who held panels of protective shielding above them. When they reached the walls, they used picks and hooks to gouge the stones loose from the foundation.

The constant pummeling by the rocks was having its effect, and the thick wall was wearing down in the one area that the Trolls focused so intensely upon. The defenders were able to scatter the enemy time after time, but as soon as they retreated, the big catapults began to fire their projectiles once again. It was a never ending cycle and Grogan was unsure what was doing the most damage at this point.

Originally, he had almost welcomed the Trolls and their picks, thinking it was the better alternative, but when he saw how easily they seemed to remove the loose stones from the barraged walls, his opinion changed. The wall was giving way and he seemed unable to prevent it. As each of the fires in the city was brought under control one by one, it was only a matter of moments before a new conflagration flared up. This unremitting bombardment was wearing everyone out, and even though they were barely fighting, the effort to extinguish the numerous fires and to deflect the constant battery of stones and shafts, so soon after an exhausting battle, was almost too much to maintain.

Baladar rode down to the gates with Filaree, Cairn and Robyn at his side. Tomas and Preston remained behind with Elion so that they could talk and so that Tomas could learn more about his brother from the young Elf who was the last to have seen him. On their way to the battlements, they were surprised by just how much damage the city had sustained while they conferred on the mount. Fires were breaking out everywhere, and the townsfolk were running from here to there, passing water in chains and dousing whatever they could. Some of the buildings were already burned to the ground, while others were beyond saving and were being left to burn out by themselves.

"Our stock of water must be running low. The wells are not limitless," Baladar noted with concern.

"Have we no means of replenishing the supply?" Filaree inquired.

"It will do so by itself in time, Lady, but we must begin to ration it now before it runs out. I will instruct the city master to organize a plan to restrict any unnecessary use," he responded, making one of numerous mental notes as he rode.

As the four of them drew closer to the gates, they heard the incessant pounding and they saw the heavy, stone projectiles arch through the air as they flew toward the city.

"The situation is far worse than I expected, Baladar," Robyn commented while scanning the area. "The gates remain intact, though," he noticed thankfully.

"Thanks to Tomas and good timing," Cairn said.

"Thanks to you too, Cairn!" Filaree interjected.

"We have only a few more hours of daylight. When night comes, it will be even harder to impede their progress. We can barely stop them now!" Baladar commented, observing the worsening situation as they neared the front.

The Lord of Pardatha was shocked by the carnage he witnessed. It occurred so quickly and it was so extensive that he feared the coming hours. He saw the dead and the dying everywhere, victims of both the fires and the deadly missiles dropping out of the skies. He was determined to find a way to stop this bloodshed and to end the fighting.

"The condition is far graver than I suspected, friends," Robyn said. "If this continues unabated, either the city will be a mass of charred ruins, or the walls will crumble upon us...or both!" he reasoned.

"Is there nothing you can do to aide us this time?" Baladar inquired desperately.

"I only wish that there was. Without my full strength, anything I attempted to do could hurt us as easily as it could help. I am not presently strong enough to control the power. My senses are not receptive now. An incursion of force such as I experienced before has left me numb somewhat still. I am afraid this will last for a while. It would be reckless and irresponsible for me to try now, though I am tempted nonetheless," Robyn replied. "It is possible that my efforts would aide the enemy more than they would help us. I cannot take that risk," he concluded reluctantly.

"I cannot simply watch as my people die and the city is reduced to ruin! There must be something we can do," Baladar lamented quite tempestuously, growing more and more worried as they rode on.

"These invaders are possessed by the same evil that drives Colton dar Agonthea. They cannot distinguish good from bad and right from wrong. The only thing that they will respond to is fear. Pain will not even deter them from their path. Their master drives them ceaselessly toward the void, and he promises them freedom when they reach it. They are blinded by his vision," Cairn commented.

"Each missile strike emboldens them. Each fire that breaks out gives them more courage. They see that we are suffering and they believe that we are helpless to prevent it. They can taste victory and it is driving them wild!" Filaree commented.

Baladar listened intently to what Robyn, Cairn and Filaree had all just said. He agreed with them in their assessments, and a plan began to take shape in his mind. He was so saddened and frustrated by how seriously damaged the city was and by how many good citizens had lost their lives already, that he could barely look upon the havoc any longer. It broke his heart and devastated his soul.

As he wandered the rubble strewn streets, he felt impotent and helpless. Women and children too were falling under the weight of the stones and succumbing to the rampant fires. This battle would spare no one. He dared not contemplate what a total breach of the walls would unleash upon the innocent citizens of Pardatha. Baladar looked from side to side as if in a dream, powerless to aid the suffering, and a little part of him died with each tragedy he was forced to pass by.

He thought of his wife, of Briland, and of how much this city meant to her, how fully and totally she loved the people of Pardatha and he could not bear witnessing the havoc and waste for another moment. The beauty she had helped to create was being systematically decimated, and Baladar began to see the assault on his adored city as an assault on the very memory of Briland herself. He had to stop it somehow!

They had all reached the gates by this time and they dismounted, ready to ascend the battlements and to survey the plains below. Filaree, Robyn and Cairn stood by the horses, talking in a small group.

"You said something a moment ago that might help us," Robyn said seriously, gaining their attention immediately. "You said that the only thing that they respond to is fear. If we can frighten them, if we can determine a way to undermine their confidence and to raise the specter of doubt in their minds, perhaps we can at least stop their advance. Fear motivates them more than most anything else," he concluded.

"Without the guidance of the Dark Lord, they will be vulnerable," Cairn agreed.

"What weapons have we in Pardatha that can have such an effect?" Filaree inquired, doubtfully.

Cairn, Robyn and Filaree were so deep in conversation that they did not notice Baladar as he slipped away. Rather than climbing the battlements to survey the battlefield, he discretely walked toward the shelter of the gate house, scurrying inside before anyone saw where he went. He was confident that the group he left behind would do whatever they could, even in his absence.

Baladar was growing more and more disturbed by the developing situations around him. He knew that there was little he could do from within the city walls, and he was not going to send any more of his soldiers to a certain death outside the gates. The mountain Trolls had planned their attack very well, and these powerful shooting machines that they must have carted all the way from the northern hills at great physical expense, were neither anticipated nor easy to defend against.

He had underestimated the strength of this enemy, thinking that once they had stopped Colton himself, if only temporarily, they would have a respite from the tragedy of war. He miscalculated, and in his exuberance over their previous victory, he convinced himself that he neglected to keep a vigilant enough watch, and therefore he blamed himself. Now, citizens of his city were dying and there was no positive end in sight.

If he could sneak out of the city unseen and covertly make his way to Everclear, then he could try to enlist the aid of Calista, the Lady of the Island. Surely she would understand his need and the need of his people, and perhaps she could help in some way. The last time that he visited her, he was filled with great hope and expectation. The young heir was beneath his roof and he had summoned those who would begin the process of educating him and training him. Now the situation was quite different, and he refused to allow himself to despair before he attempted all that he could to help his people.

Calista was his one, last hope. He declined to accept her final admonition to him not to return the last time he left her. Baladar believed in his heart that she would allow him entry onto the island, that this noble woman would not refuse his plea. His entreaty was based upon dire need, and he believed that she could not but understand that and respond. Calista appeared to him to be the only source of light capable of blotting out the darkness that now mortally threatened the very future of Pardatha.

He perceived the golden ring, hot beneath his shirt, as if it was speaking to him in a language he did not understand. So much had occurred these past few days that it was hard to absorb it all. He felt at times as if he was riding a wave on the ocean of life that was growing with each passing moment, gaining in size and strength, knowing that he was but a passenger, subject to its building and breaking. He needed now to take action in order to assist his people, and he could not allow himself to simply be tossed and turned aimlessly upon the waters.

He could sit no longer in the city and watch as it slowly crumbled, dashing the hopes and prayers of every good and decent living being as it fell to pieces. If there was any chance of halting the enemy's progress, he had to grasp for it now. It was his responsibility!

How I wish Briland were here to help guide me on this difficult path, he thought as he hastened down the dark corridor.

No one saw him as he donned a plain, grey cloak he found amongst the guard's belongings. His dagger was at his belt, and he raised the simple hood over his head, concealing his features. He could not ride out of the city from this place, as his movement would surely be noticed. But Baladar knew more about Pardatha than anyone, and he remembered how Briland would sneak out to commune with Snihso, her tree, whenever she could not use the Noban gates for one reason or another.

He had to double back on his previous path toward the stock yards, northeast of the city. There, he remembered a small tunnel that opened to the outside from within a shrine that had been out of use for tiels. His wife, Briland, had used this hidden portal to surreptitiously exit from the city if the need arose. He had accompanied his wife through this passageway once, on a beautiful, star filled evening, and he remembered fondly how they emerged from the tunnel arm in arm, the brilliant canopy above lighting their way, and walked together to the clearing where Snihso grew. He remembered watching her that evening as she climbed into the arms of the tree she loved so dearly.

She was so beautiful, he recalled vividly. She had always wanted him to understand, as best as one who was not chosen could, the relationship she had with her tree, and she pleaded with him to join her at times, even if it meant that he just sat in the background and watched or read or thought. Briland was so concerned that he not be jealous of Snihso and that the three of them live in harmony as much as that was possible. Her tree seemed to understand, and it allowed for this singular relationship, this sharing, to continue, something which was so unusual for a Lalas, knowing in its own intuitive way that the bond of love between Briland and Baladar was a very special one.

These memories flashed through his mind as he made his way to the old building that housed the ancient, out of use shrine. The people were rushing back and forth, some panic-stricken, some determined, yet all looking to help as best as they could nevertheless. He brushed past them all, his head bowed and his features concealed, until he found the isolated, abandoned building that he sought. After he discreetly entered through the decayed doorway, he moved quickly to the back of the room and pushed a dust strewn table and a broken and discarded statuette out of the way. A worn tapestry hung from one corner on the wall behind the abandoned podium and he walked toward it. A mouse scurried across the floor, leaving a long, thin trail in the dust, but Baladar barely noticed it, caught between his determination and reverie. He reached for the cloth and anxiously pushed it to the side, looking for the area in the wall upon which he had to press to release the latch. The particles clouded the air from the worn ornament and he fanned his hand in order to see.

Baladar ran his fingers down the rough wall, feeling for the slight indentation that he sought. When he found it, he depressed it slightly and the doorway revealed itself. He needed to put all of his weight against it in order for it to give way, as the hinges were rusted and old and it had not been used for so long. It creaked open and a gust of damp, musty air wafted over him.

When he was safely inside the tunnel, he reached to the left, remembering the hollow in the wall where Briland always kept an unused torch in the event she forgot to carry one with her. He smiled a sad smile as his fingers discovered what he had hoped they would, and he struck a small flint he had in his pocket against the stone wall and lit the light. The dry cloth burst into flame and then settled down to a deep, amber glow. Anxiously, he pushed the heavy door shut and walked down the pathway.

The tunnel lead directly under the thick wall of the city and eventually terminated in the woods beyond the plains. It would not take him too long to reach the end and he did not anticipate that anything would disturb his progress down here. He jogged carefully, as the years had deposited more debris upon the floor than had been there previously.

After he reached the clearing near where Snihso once grew, he would turn south and then walk directly to the lakeshore. Everclear was not easy to approach, he knew. It was certainly possible to draw near to what appeared to be the shore, only to discover that it was just an illusion. If Calista did not want intruders to find her realm then they did not, and he needed so desperately to be welcomed into her dominion this night.

Baladar hoped that he would not have to return to the city as forlorn and dispirited as when he left. This was his last chance to save the people he cared so much about; his last chance to end the horror and provide all the people he knew and loved and tried to protect, with a safe and secure future. It was his last chance to do what his wife had given her life for; to help his people remain steadfast on their journey down the one true and noble path.

If he could only stop this assault upon Pardatha, it would give him the time necessary to see that Cairn, Filaree and Robyn arrived at Seramour and revived the boy. Baladar wanted so much to accomplish this task. He believed that with the arrival of Tomas and the silver ring, the prophecy was becoming clearer. The Gem of Eternity could be found and the Lalas could be saved. He needed the Lady's help, for he saw no other way of liberating Pardatha, and if the city fell, then all of his hopes for the future would be crushed beneath the tumbling stones of his beloved home.

Baladar reached the end of the tunnel without ever having realized how far he had traveled, he was so engrossed in his thoughts. He knew that none of the enemy would be anywhere near the trap door that would let him out in the wooded area near the lake. It was too close to the place where Snihso had once lived for anyone to trespass therein. Baladar himself entered that area with great trepidation.

He pushed on the heavy slab of stone that covered the opening and it sprang back on its hinges, sending a cascade of dry leaves and broken twigs tumbling onto his head. The earth around the exit was uneven and dangerous to traverse. In the near distance, he could see the vast hole in the ground that was once his wife's tree. It was barren of all new growth and desolate beyond belief. His heart rose in his throat, as he stepped gingerly onto the lifeless earth.

What a terrible shame. Sadness and regret welled up inside of him and caused his breath to come to him in broken gasps.

He knew that he needed to move away quickly from this spot, before the devastation and despair overcame him once more. He scanned the area, remembering vividly the beauty that enveloped this place in days past. He fought the strange desire to enter the crater, the hollow, left by Snihso, knowing that it would spell his doom if he did. The gaping hole seemed to beckon him, to call him even by name. He was certain that he heard voices summoning him. Baladar strained to turn his eyes away and he compelled his feet to take the steps that would bring him out of this forsaken space.

As soon as he turned his back upon this sorrowful scene he felt a little better, as his true purpose was once more looming before his mind's eye. He reminded himself over and over again of his reason for coming here and of the people back in the city whose hopes rested upon his shoulders. He imagined his wife walking with him, hand in hand, and he raised his head and stepped determinedly away, painstakingly placing one foot in front of the other.

Soon, he saw new growth beneath his feet and he smelled the sweet smell of berries and blossoms. His spirits lifted as he made his way to the portal that would lead him to Calista.

As he walked through the forest, the path he followed wound and rambled and he lost his sense of direction entirely. He remembered the last time that he had visited the Lady of the Island and he was therefore not distressed by his perceptual confusion. In fact, knowing that he neared the realm of the Lady rejuvenated him despite how disoriented he seemed. He could have sworn he had already passed by this tree before and that he was retracing his steps without having doubled back. It seemed impossible to him, yet he accepted the paradoxical nature of the entire forest, and he kept walking.

Calista had told him the last time that he had visited her that her lands would be closed to all outsiders from then on. He hoped that she would recognize his dire need and allow him to enter this night, and he plunged onward.

Suddenly, he saw the portal before him, a doorway suspended in mid air shimmering in the light of the afternoon sun. He girded himself against the sensations that he knew would accompany his plunge through the opening, and without hesitating even slightly, he walked through it. He immediately lost all sense of space and time. He could no longer tell up from down or forward from backward, and he could not even feel the ground beneath his feet.

In his ardor to save Pardatha, Baladar did not notice that the edges of the portal were blurred and indistinct. As he tumbled through the emptiness of this aperture, he thought only of Calista and the help he longed for her to provide. Not knowing whether he was facing up or down, he finally hit solid ground and righted himself instantly, and then he saw a winding path spread out before him and a calm shoreline at his back.

He had reached the island of the Lady once more, and he was so grateful to have been admitted, that he was blinded to the changes all around him, concentrating only on his great need. He followed the walkway, not noticing that the air was as still as could be and that no birds sang and no animals moved through the underbrush. The flowers had no odor and they were drying upon their stems. The grass beneath his feet was parched and brown, but he walked on without seeing, thinking only of his purpose. The silver leaves of the beautiful trees lay in soft piles on the ground, quiet as the night, no breeze to rustle them.

He reached the gates of the Lady's palace and they lay open already, so he walked through, consumed by his objective He saw the turrets and the towers rising around him, but they were shrouded in shadows and the banners atop them hung limp and lifeless. The light was dim and a thin layer of dust covered everything, blanketing the tiles of the floor with its dullness, rising in soft swells as he walked over it, but his eyes were blind to all but his goal.

When he reached the end of the long hallway, he found the double gilt doors standing open already, and he entered the chamber where Calista had met with him before, searching for a sign of the Lady of the Island. The crystal throne at the opposite end stood just as he remembered it, less vibrant, less alive, but he did not regard it. Baladar was thinking only of the help he needed and he was so obsessed with this objective that he could focus upon nothing else.

His eyes darted from left to right, searching for a sign of Calista, and in his desperation to seek her out, he finally began to realize for the first time that things here were not the same as they were before. It was as if he was looking through a thick piece of glass, an opaque window. Everything around him was dull and colorless and no longer beautiful and magical as it had been once before. The shock of the change was almost too much to bear. He could hear nothing and he could smell nothing. All the power that he had experienced here previously was absent. And Calista was nowhere to be found. Despair struck him like a severe blow to the belly and he gasped momentarily for breath. He doubled over in pain, struggling to maintain his equilibrium.

Baladar's concern was staggering as he finally realized the extent of the changes that had overtaken this once vibrant and effusive place.

Am I too late?

"Calista?" he called out. "My Queen? Are you here? Can you hear me?" he shouted, and not even an echo answered him back.

He walked toward the quartz throne that had been so dazzling before, so comforting in its wondrous beauty, and he saw with great relief the hem of a dress extending beyond the legs of the great chair, but it was a faded violet in color rather than vivid and alive as before. Calista stepped from behind the throne and revealed herself to him. Her beautiful green eyes still sparkled brightly and her long blonde hair framed her magnificent face, but the gossamer silk of her gown hung limply around her thin body.

"I am not the source, noble Baladar. I am but a conduit," she said to him in a soft, melodious voice, staring deeply into his eyes, not needing to be verbally questioned in order to reply.

He bent down on one knee, bowed his head before her, shocked and saddened by the deterioration that he now saw clearly all around, and he listened intently.

"As the trees die, I become further and further removed from the wellhead of the power, from the First, and the Gem's potency."

Baladar raised his head and looked upon her with adoration tempered by an overwhelming sense of sorrow, and he listened intently.

"My time here is almost done," she said with regret in her voice, as a shiver ran down the spine of the man before her.

"Colton too is but a vessel and a channel for the void. He is a harbinger, but neither is he the source. He can be surmounted, Baladar!" she continued with a weakened voice.

"You have leaned upon me as it should have been, but I am but a railing, a resting spot. You cannot rely upon me to hold you up," she said.

"But, my Lady! You have guided us for so long, in ways we

never even knew. How are we to go on without you?" he dared to ask imploringly, never dreaming that her days could be numbered.

"You know what must be done. The First must be found and the Gem must be allowed to radiate freely once again. The darkness which shrouds it must be destroyed before the light dies," Calista said, more weakly now than previously.

She closed her eyes briefly and bent her head. When she reopened them, they were just a tiny bit duller and her skin was growing noticeably paler too.

"The void encroaches Baladar, and you have the means to turn it back," she said.

Baladar thought for a minute before speaking again.

"My Queen, there are two rings and there are two heirs," he said in a whisper, knowing the import of this news.

"Two, you say?" she asked, her face tilted in consternation. "I should have known. I have been kept from the source for too long," she said, and she smiled to herself. She hesitated before speaking again. Calista closed her eyes momentarily, obviously thinking deeply. "The meaning is now clear to me, dear Baladar, and it bodes well for you, indeed, for us all," she said after a brief respite.

She began to recite a poem that Baladar recognized from the Tomes.

> *"When darkness reaches out to light*
> *and clashes brightly in the night,*
> *When the trees decide to grow no more*
> *and all the Kingdoms march to war,*
> *When the sky grows dull and the winds grow still,*
> *When the noble begin to lose their will,*
> *When wrongness marches against what's right,*
> *and cities fall beneath its might,*
> *Then what was one will become two,*
> *and the quest for the Gem will begin anew."*

"Do you see, Baladar?" she said. Her eyes were sparkling brightly now. "It is beginning. I did not know the meaning before, though I have read those lines thousands of times." She walked to the crystal throne and sat down, resting her thin arms weakly upon it. "Two rings and two boys," she said contentedly to herself. "It is as it should be! The fabric weaves of its own will, Baladar. But, you must guide it well, smooth it out when you are able to, coax and caress it toward the ends we all desire. So much, nay everything, is at stake!" she said quietly, the words issuing slowly from her mouth.

"My Queen. If I am to help the boys and set them on their quest, I must first be permitted to unite them and awaken Davmiran. My city is under siege and we have not the power to stop it. Is there nothing you can do to help?" he appealed, fearing that at this point her weakness may have become too great.

"My present life on this earth is at an end, Baladar. I fear not for myself any longer," she said, still deeply immersed in her reverie while her beautiful eyes stared out at nothing. "But you must return to the city as quickly as you are able to," she said fragilely. "I will do what I can." Her skin was growing paler by the minute, fading before his saddened eyes. "Alas, what I am still capable of may not be enough. Behold what becomes of my realm," she said, and she swept her fragile arm in a semicircle about her. Her beautiful face had a startlingly sad expression upon it. "Soon it will be no more, removed from space and time as if it never existed. Go now! Time is running out," Calista said with an urgency heretofore undetected. "Remember my son, have courage always! Fear can torment you and it can drive you to the very edge of sanity, but it can never rule your heart," she concluded. Her eyes were glowing with an intense power despite the weakened condition of her body. "Remain steadfast on your course. Always follow your heart!"

Baladar stood and reached for her hand. It was almost cold to the touch, but it was still soft and invigorating to clasp nonetheless. He brought his lips to it and he kissed it with as much feeling as he had ever felt for anyone other than Briland.

"Farewell, my Queen," he said, moved almost to tears, bowing before her and savoring what he knew were the final moments.

"May the First guide you and protect you always, Baladar. Farewell my honorable man. Be brave," she admonished him fondly and closed her eyes, while her other hand lay upon his bowed head.

Baladar released her frail fingers, turned quickly and then left the throne room as fast as he could without ever looking back. He did not know what, if anything, Calista could possibly do in her weakened condition, but he trusted her and he respected her so thoroughly that he did not question her instructions. She would do what she could, of that he was certain, if it was not already too late.

He started to walk down the great hallway, and before his very eyes, it began to shimmer and fade; to lose the very solidity that kept him from tumbling into the void. He ran now, fearing that everything would collapse beneath his feet; that it would dissolve, and that he would fall into the blackened emptiness and never get back to Pardatha.

When he reached the golden doors, they hung loosely from their hinges and beneath them was a vast emptiness. He was afraid that if they separated from their frame, they would fall away into space. He hurried across the disintegrating threshold and hastily made for the path before him. The leaves were falling thickly everywhere, creating a silver snowstorm all around him. He had to jump over crevices, beneath which was nothing at all. He rushed through waves of falling trees that made no sound as they tumbled, collapsing heavily behind him as he passed them by. This world was imploding, not simply disappearing. Its magnificence and awesome beauty was being sucked into the vacuity of the void, sundered forever, as if it never had existed at all.

The colors of everything were fading gradually as he careened down the path, getting paler and paler, until he could barely distinguish between the different objects that surrounded him. He saw only shadows of what once was, and even the shadows were pale and indistinct, evanescent and barely discernible. The blanket of moss and grass upon which he stepped disappeared beneath his feet, and he hurried over merely the suggestions of solidity, while his feet miraculously remained level. The silence was almost unbearable and it was only enhanced a million times over in contradiction to the violent activity he saw everywhere. This world was ending, and Baladar knew that he had to leave it before it disappeared completely or he would melt away with it and vanish forever into nothingness.

He ran and ran until he found himself once more before the portal through which he had earlier entered the realm of the Lady of the Island. He stepped through it and was immediately sucked into the vacuum of space, his body turning and twisting and spinning uncontrollably. He instantaneously lost his sense of balance, his equilibrium disrupted entirely. But he allowed himself to fall and to rise again, to tumble and to turn and to rush headlong into the void. He let go for a while, not knowing if he would ever return to the world once more, and he lost all track of time in the process.

He lost consciousness for what seemed like a short span though he was unsure exactly of how long, and he awoke to the distinct sound of a horn blaring in the distance. As his eyes began to focus once again, he regained his balance and righted himself. He recognized the path before him, and urgency compelled him forward.

Baladar ran at full speed through the forest, past the hollow, the chasm that was once Snihso, until he discovered once again the trap door that would lead him into the tunnel. He threw it open violently, gasping for breath by this time, and he jumped into the hole. Not wasting even a moment to find the torch he left at the door, he ran through the darkness, bumping into walls of hard dirt and falling occasionally, racing down the darkened passageway, until he reached the stone doorway that marked the end of the shaft.

Baladar pushed on the indentation that would release the lever and allow the hidden door to open. Without any thought of concealing his actions, he pressed heavily upon the stone, throwing it loudly open, and then he crashed through the doorway into the room. He collapsed in an exhausted heap on the floor, panting heavily.

Chapter Fifty-three

The noise from the catapults was the first sound he was able to distinguish, and it motivated him to rise and return to the battlements. He made his way rapidly through the rubble strewn streets, and as he approached the guard post that would take him to the towers, he heard a voice call to him from above.

"My Lord? Where have you been? We have searched everywhere for you." Grogan yelled down at Baladar.

"Let me join you and I will explain," he yelled back, panting between his words while brushing the dirt and debris from his cloak as he rushed up the winding steps.

When he reached the top, he was met by Filaree, Cairn and Robyn. They looked expectantly upon him, each of them relieved to see him again, as he immediately began to recount the events of the past few hours. After he completed relating his recent experiences with Calista and they all took a moment to absorb what he said, Robyn was the first one to speak.

"I deeply regret that I have not had the opportunity to meet this astonishing woman. Alas, I now never shall," he said sadly. "We are all dangling over the threshold of a new age. The present as we know it is falling away piece by piece. What was only moments ago a part of our reality is now mere legend. She will be sorely missed."

"Is there nothing we can do to help her?" Filaree asked.

"I fear not, Lady Filaree. It is beyond our power. We must do what we can to help ourselves. 'The fabric weaves of its own will'," he repeated solemnly to the group what Calista had so poignantly said to him earlier.

"Do you think she can do anything to aid us at this point? The wall yonder is weakening by the minute. I pray it is not too late even if she still commands some power," Cairn said as he gazed at the battleground.

Baladar was looking out over the fortification as well, at the newest barrage of stones that was being cast upon it, and he was alarmed at the extent of the damage to the broad wall. In his short absence it appeared to have weakened considerably.

"I suspect that it may be, my friend. She is gravely impaired from the same force that drives our enemy with such abandon. She had little strength left to devote to our plight, I fear."

Baladar answered these queries with tremendous resignation in his voice. He walked wearily to the edge of the wall and stood near the tower, gazing out toward the western horizon with his eyelids half closed, deep in contemplation, forlorn and distraught. He still had the image of Calista in his mind and he shook his head sadly at the thought of what she had become. Next to Briland, she had been the most inspiring woman in his life, and he always believed that she would live indefinitely. Shortly now she would be gone too, lost to the earth forever, her flame snuffed out too soon by evil and corruption.

Out of the corner of his eye he glimpsed a group of soldiers flocking to the eastern end of the wall, revealing themselves dangerously to the enemy in their exuberance, and he wondered what new horror was about to envelop them. Others joined the group, and soon they were all pointing in the direction of the lake beyond the forest, the Lady's lake.

Robyn was the first to see it since his eyes were among the sharpest of the group. Under the light of the setting sun, he could clearly see great spouts of water gushing up from the center of the lake. And as everyone watched awestruck, the island that was usually shrouded in fog and mist seemed to rise up out of its obscurity. Its hidden shores broke the surface of the lake and sent massive waves of liquid emanating outward in all directions that gained strength and speed with each foot of ground they covered.

As the island ascended like a new born volcano rising out of the ocean, the trees, grass and earth all fell away into the gushing fluid, leaving a pillar of gleaming quartz exposed for all to see. Geysers were shooting hundreds of feet up into the air and bursting violently into the darkening sky. The lake was seething and bubbling furiously, rising up over its shores and emptying endless gallons of rushing water out of its limitless basin.

Soon Filaree, Cairn and Baladar could see it as well. Water was spilling out more rapidly now, cascading through the trees and down the hill into the gorge below. They could hear explosions also as thousands of gallons of water shot skyward and then landed heavily all around, shattering whatever they hit with the impact. The catapults ceased firing, and the frightened Trolls watched the hills above them, as their panic mounted with each passing moment.

The bulk of the Troll army was camped at the base of the woods with the steep, side walls of the now barren river abutting their backs, in a place that they had believed was far enough from the city to be out of reach of its archers and therefore safe from attack. But the entire force was now directly underneath the path of the rushing water. The seething liquid began to surge over the crest of the hill and to plunge onto the heads of the unsuspecting Trolls below, creating a rapidly flowing waterfall above and behind the Troll army. The deluge was so incredibly heavy and so totally unexpected that it knocked over everyone and everything in its path. The water picked up speed at an alarming rate as it traveled and it quickly enveloped the entire army and sent it hurtling headlong down the valley.

An endless torrent of water continued to gush over the hill, building in speed and intensity, flooding the ravine and turning it into a turbulent river once again. The high sides of the gorge contained the surging flood, while the rising water washed away everything it came into contact with. It carried the instruments of war and the warriors themselves down the valley, broken and drowning in the heaving current. It slapped up against the very walls of Pardatha themselves and soaked the soldiers on the battlements in its wake, though its main flow reached no higher than the middle of the battlements. The city appeared to be floating, perched upon a hillock— a solitary haven amidst a now watery grave.

The water continued to flow unhampered for what seemed like an eternity, clearing the battlefield like a wet cloth swiped across a tablet of chalk, washing it clean. All of those atop the battlements could see the water shimmer and glow as it rushed past the city, and many could swear that they saw vivid colors streaking through the muddy morass, sparkling and glimmering below them as it coursed past. It looked to some as if a long train of gossamer silk was being pulled down the valley and spreading out in the murky water beneath the walls of the city.

Baladar stared closely at the gushing stream and he too saw the ribbons of light radiating beneath him, the colors so characteristic of Calista, his revered Queen, and he said a silent prayer for her, the Lady of the Island, the guardian mother of Pardatha. He mouthed a hushed farewell to her, as the mesmerizing colors cascaded by and disappeared into the greater flow.

Just as suddenly as it began, it ended. The water ceased to rise any longer, having completely emptied its fount upon the world. The lake settled down upon itself until it was as calm as a pond on a wind free day. What remained erect was only a solitary summit of beautiful rose colored crystal protruding above the now still surface, which diffused the light from the setting sun into hundreds of rainbows that danced and sparkled magically across the walls of the city. And then a strange calm overtook the valley, and shortly the noise of the water rhythmically sloshing from bank to bank was the only sound to be heard.

All traces of the mountain Trolls were gone and washed away forever. Baladar stood atop the walls of Pardatha flanked by Cairn of Thermaye, Robyn dar Tamarand and Filaree Par D'Avalain. With their arms entwined, standing shoulder to shoulder, they surveyed the battlefield, and four pairs of hopeful eyes looked out at the water, but saw far, far beyond.

Epilogue

During the next few months, the city and its surroundings experienced great changes. The water receded somewhat, but the river continued to flow beyond the walls of Pardatha. Lake Everclear became a place of serenity and calm where people went to meditate and worship, and the great forest surrounding it grew thicker and more lush with each passing day.

Lord Baladar, Lady Filaree, Robyn, Cairn, Prince Elion, Tomas and Preston spent many hours and days communing with each other, learning what they could, solidifying their relationships and strengthening the friendships that would prove later on to be so important to the future of their world. They could be seen taking long walks throughout the city and the surrounding hills in pairs and in small groups, and they were all greeted warmly and respectfully by everyone they met.

Spring brought with it an abundance to the landscape that Pardatha had not seen for many tiels. Fresh growth sprouted everywhere, particularly on the banks of the newly formed river, and the formidable trees that now divided the plains from the hills beyond, continued to blossom ceaselessly, and they grew denser and thicker with each passing day. The barrier that they formed became a shield against the enemy from the south as well as a place of comfort and safety for the people of the city. The petals from the ever-blooming flowers fell like snow flakes upon the moist and fertile soil and created a realm of fantasy for the young lovers of the city, a place to which they flocked; a place of beauty, love and peace. Small boats could be seen upon the young river almost all the hours of the day, and the citizens of Pardatha were immersed in a new sense of tranquility that they had sorely missed and now greatly appreciated.

The pillar of quartz that stood as a monument to Calista of the Island, radiated a myriad of dazzling colors during the daylight hours, and it was a beacon upon the calm waters of the lake, reflecting the moonlight during the dark hours of the night.

Cairn, Filaree and Robyn planned their trip to Lormarion, and they decided that Prince Elion would guide them, accompanied by Tomas, Preston and Calyx, naturally. Baladar reluctantly relinquished the golden ring that Calista had endowed with the power to awaken Davmiran, into the care of the Prince of the Southern Elves, the only other member of the party who knew Davmiran personally and the one who had unwittingly saved him from suffering the ordeal of the recent battle.

The Lord of Pardatha did not feel that he could abandon his city for as long as it would be necessary to train and educate the heir, and he felt that his rightful place was with his people. Elion was honored by the responsibility, and he promised to guard the ring with his life until his return to Seramour where he would use it to bring Davmiran Dar Gwendolen back into this world that needed him so much and waited so patiently for his return. They all pledged to come back to Pardatha with the twins as soon as they could, and it would be from here that they would plan and begin their quest in search of the First and the Gem of Eternity.

Baladar made his strange and wonderful birds available to his associates so that they could communicate with their loved ones back home. Word was sent to King Treestar and Queen Elsinestra that their son was safe and that he would be returning to Seramour with his new friends. Baladar received a reply from the Elfin nation that expressed both gratitude that all turned out as it had as well as hope for the future. Davmiran was safe and healthy, but he remained oblivious to all that occurred around him despite the best efforts of Elsinestra in her capacity as his healer. They waited in the Heights anxiously for their son's return.

One afternoon, when the sun was high in the eastern sky and the people of Pardatha basked comfortably in its warmth, a group of Dwarfs appeared on the hills behind the city, led by a strong looking man with a dark, braided beard, woven with silver threads, that hung almost to the ground before him. The leader beat upon the hard stone with the hilt of his heavy axe and announced his presence to the city.

Brimgar Daggerfall was reunited with his son Preston in the presence of his new friends, and he was told of his recent exploits as well as of his future plans. The young Dwarf had gained an honest sense of confidence since his encounter with Tomas, Cairn and Calyx and he had matured into an admirable young adult in this short span of time. His father looked upon his son with a new respect and a growing pride, and he assured him that his physical stature would never again be spoken about with anything less than the highest of regard. Brimgar was welcomed into the city, and he spent a fortnight communing with Baladar and the others and spending some much needed time with his now distinguished son. When he departed the city, he left with his pledge of support for the new alliance solidly on the table, along with strong words of love and encouragement for his son and his son's companions.

Filaree sent the sad news of Cameron's death back to her mother in Avalain, and she promised to return home as soon as she was able to, though she advised her mother that it would be some time before that would be possible. Queen Esta responded with words of her undying love, and placed no filial or emotional demands upon her daughter, other than that she not allow her grief to harden her heart. She promised Filaree that the city would set aside a day of mourning in honor of Cameron, and that his sacrifice would be remembered always. She affirmed her and her country's commitment to the alliance and vowed to do whatever was required to help defend against the encroaching darkness.

Robyn dar Tamarand spent a quiet and solitary afternoon in deep meditation, linking with Promanthea and communing with him in his own unique manner. His tree still radiated strength and vitality, and his fears that Promanthea would succumb to the despair that took the lives of his brethren were temporarily assuaged. He then communicated through his relic briefly with his father in order to ascertain his state of health and to reassure him of his own.

His father notified him that inquiries had reached him from the western Elves, specifically from Alemar, daughter of the Alpen King, as to his whereabouts and his well being. Robyn declared his love for his father in no uncertain terms, and he asked him to reply to the Elves on his behalf and advise them of the developments in the south, and to tell them that he would visit as soon as time and circumstances permitted.

He also urged his father to remain ever vigilant and to not allow his countrymen to despair, despite the continuing demise of the trees. He requested of his father that he inform the people of the struggle in the south and of the efforts that were being made on everyone's behalf to eradicate the pestilence that had stricken the land, in the hope that this knowledge would help to strengthen and maintain their resolve.

Cairn and Calyx spent their leisure time walking through the forest above the lake and gazing upon the crystal as often as possible. For the first time since he departed his home, Cairn spread out his game of life and studied the pieces, learning what he could about the events to come, speculating and devising, analyzing and planning, examining the contingencies and deducing the possibilities therefrom. All those he cared deeply about were here with him in Pardatha, and Calyx aside, he felt blessed by his new found friendships, particularly Tomas'.

Tomas and Preston had a brief opportunity to be boys once again. They frolicked in the hills above the city, swam in the warm waters of the river, fished, laughed and genuinely enjoyed their respite from the stress and strain of the trying weeks that preceded this hiatus. Tomas' green eyes glittered with life, and he seemed to grow in strength and beauty with each passing day. Preston, perhaps due to the good food and the exercise, also continued to grow, although to his own chagrin, mostly in height. It seemed as if he was destined to be the tallest Dwarf ever to come out of the Thorndars

Baladar spoke with each of his charges, advising them and cautioning them, teaching them what he knew of the legends and the words of the Tomes of Caradon, and he repeated to them all that he could of what Calista had imparted to him. He entrusted the powder of creation in confidence to Cairn, telling him of Calista's words and enjoining him to guard it with his lifeblood and to use only on behalf of one of the heirs, and then only if the situation was one of life and death. He imparted to them all the knowledge that he could about Colton dar Agonthea, and the mind of this monster as he understood it.

Baladar assured them all that he would work ceaselessly during their absence to learn whatever he could from the great books and histories, and that he would communicate with them whenever possible. He was torn between his responsibilities to his people in Pardatha and his imperative to prepare the heir. But, he knew in his heart that he was not meant to be a principal player in the game that was now beginning. He had enacted his part in the casting and in the calling, and now it was time to pass the torch on to the others.

Baladar was never more confident in anyone or anything as he was in this diverse and extraordinary group of individuals. He knew that Briland too would have agreed with this analysis, and he believed that her essence was still present in this world in some form or other, and that the goodness and strength that characterized her very being would accompany the two boys, and all of the others, on their perilous and all important journeys to come.

They all lingered in Pardatha a little longer than they knew they should have, savoring the days and the fleeting last moments, while relaxing as best they could. Everyone knew when it was time to leave and they barely had to discuss it. Early one morning, just before the leaves began to turn and the fall winds began to blow, the group of adventurers assembled in the courtyard of the castle with their bags packed and their horses saddled and ready.

Baladar joined them in this pre dawn hour and bade them all an emotional farewell. He had made certain that they were well provisioned, and he took great care in seeing to their travel needs. The trip to Lormarion would not be a difficult one, and it was understood that they would communicate their progress along the way.

When everyone was mounted and ready to go, Baladar led them to the open gates atop Porta and he watched intently as they rode toward lake Everclear, up and over the ridge above the newly named River of Tears and then through the forest on the opposite side. He stood there unmoving until they disappeared from view, and then he turned Porta around and walked solemnly back through the Noban gates, overcome by emotion, knowing that a great age had ended, though certain that a new one was about to begin.

List of Characters, Items and Places

A

Acire. Lalas tree. Tenth tree to die. Theran's Bondmate.
Adrianna. One of the forsaken women. Colton's evil worker.
Alemar. Elfin Princess of Eleutheria. Daughter of Whitestar and Aliana.
Aliana. Elfin Queen of Eleutheria. Whitestar's first wife. Alemar's Mother.
Alicea. Alemar's great, great, great, great grandmother. Iscaron and Kala's daughter.
Aliya. Queen of Crispen. King Bristar's wife.
Angeline. One of the twelve Sisters of Parth.
Armadiel. Snake of Recos.

B

Baladar. Ruler of the city of Pardatha in the Thorndar Mountains. Husband to Briland.
Behani. One of the Drue.
Beolan. Elfin Prince of Crispen. Bristar and Aliya's son.
Bethany. One of the twelve Sisters of Parth.
Blodwyn. Chosen of Lalas Lilandre.
Briland. Chosen of Lalas Snihso. Lord Baladar's wife.
Brimgar Daggerfall. Thorndar dwarf. Maringar and Preston's father.
Bristar. Elfin King of Crispen. King of the Mountain Elves. Aliya husband. Father to Beolan.

C

Cairn of Thermaye. One of the three called to educate Davmiran.
Calipee dar Tamarand. Baron. Laord of Tamarand. Robyn dar Tamarand's father.
Calista. Lady of the Island. One of the Council.
Calyx. Moulant. Cairn's friend and protector.
Carlisle. Chosen of Lalas Mintar.
Caroline. Daughter of Conrad and Sophia.
Carthane. Lalas tree. Paras' Bondmate.
Caryssa. Sea Elf.
Colton Dar Agonthea. The Evil One. The Dark One. Lord of Sedahar. Premoran's brother. Called Caeltin D'Are Agenathea by the Elves.

C (continued)

Connor. Chosen of Lalas Catalan.
Conrad. Father to Caroline.
Courtney. One of the twelve Sisters of Parth.
Crea . Chosen of Lalas Wayfair.
Crispen. Kingdom of the Mountain Elves.

D

Dahlia. One of the twelve Sisters of Parth.
Dalloway. Elfin Prince of Seramour. Youngest son of Treestar and Elsinestra.
Dashiel. Chosen of Lalas Nemaroe.
Davmiran. One of the twins. Tomas' brother. Garold and Lewellyn's son.
Dorothea. Duchess of Talamar. Wife of Leonardo.
Drue. Protectors of the Hollows. Came into existence after the death of the first Lalas.

E

Edmond. Chosen of Lalas Xia.
Eleutheria. Ice City. Kingdom of the Northern Elves.
Elion. Elfin Prince of Seramour. Eldest son of Treestar and Elsinestra.
Elsinestra. Elfin Queen of Seramour. Treestar's wife. Elion, Fallean and Dalloway's mother.

Emerial. Elfin Queen of Eleutheria. Whitestar's second wife. Mother to Kalon.
Emmeline. One of the twelve Sisters of Parth.
Esta par D'Avalain. Queen of Avalain. Filaree's mother.
Etan of Balstair. Knighted by Margot, forsaken by Colton.

F

Fallean. Elfin Prince of Seramour. Second son of Treestar and Elsinestra.
Farrow. Lalas Tree. Bondmate of Harton.
Filaree par D'Avalain. Princess of Avalain. Daughter of Esta. One of the three called to educate Davmiran.

G

Gretchen. One of the twelve Sisters of Parth.
Gwendolen. High Kingdom. Kingdom that was destroyed by Colton. Birthplace of the twins.

H

Harlan Goodheart. Discoverer of the darkening.
Harton. Chosen of Lalas Farrow.
Hollows. Forbidden places.

I

Iscaron. Ancient Elfin King of Eleutheria. Kala's husband.
Ishdomar. Lalas tree. Third tree to die.

J

Jocasta. One of the twelve Sisters of Parth.

K

Kalon. Prince of Eleutheria. Half brother of Alemar. Whitestar and Emerial's son.
Kettin. Lord of Talamar. Son of Leonardo and Dorothea.

L

Lana. Princess of the Sea Elves. Daughter of Windstorm.
Leonardo. Duke of Talamar. Husband of Dorothea.
Liam. Chosen of Lalas Oleander.
Lilandre. Lalas tree. Bondmate of Blodwyn.
Lormarion. Kingdom of the Southern Elves.

M

Marathar. Lalas tree. Bondmate of Pithar.
Margot. One of the forsaken women.
Maringar Daggerfall. Thorndar dwarf. Eldest son of Brimgar Daggerfall. Preston's brother.
Markal. Lord. Master of Arms in Avalain.
Marne. Loyal friend and personal aide to Queen Esta.
Merala da. Capital city in the Sea Isles.
Mira. Nursemaid who raised and protected Davmiran.

M (continued)

Mintar. Lalas tree. Bondmate of Carlisle.

N

Nemaroe. Lalas tree. Bondmate of Dashiel.

O

Odelot. The Dead City.
Oleander. Lalas tree. Bondmate of Liam.
Ormachon. Lalas tree. Bondmate of Tomas.

P

Paras. Chosen of Lalas Carthane. Became sick and broke his bond with Carthane. Went to Praxis.
Parsifal. Leader of the Knights of Avalain.
Pembar. One who mutated into a tree. Resides in the Winding Woods outside Avalain.
Percepton. Protector of the Forest of the Winds.
Phero. Chosen of Lalas Relamon.
Pithar. Chosen of Lalas Marathar.
Premoran. Wizard. One of the Council. Brother of Colton. Keeper of the shards.
Preston Daggerfall. Thorndar dwarf. Son of Brimgar Daggerfall. Brother of Maringar.
Promanthea. Lalas tree. Bondmate of Robyn dar Tamarand.

R

Relamon. Lalas tree. Bondmate of Phero.
Rella. One of the twelve Sisters of Parth.
Robyn dar Tamarand. Chosen of Lalas Promanthea. One of the three chosen to educate Davmiran. Son of Baron Calipee.
Rose. One of the twelve Sisters of Parth.

S

Safira. Wife to Trevor. Raised Tomas.
Sedahar. Colton's home.
Seramour. Treetop city in the Kingdom of Lormarion. Home to the Southern elves.

S (continued)

Sevilla. One of the twelve Sisters of Parth.
Sidra. Sorceress who declined to be bonded with Promanthea.
Silandre. Mountain in Crispen.
Snihso. Lalas tree. Bondmate of Briland.

T

Tallon. Town of the Chamber of the Roots.
Tamara. One of the twelve Sisters of Parth.
Teetoo. Weloh (last of the race of winged humans). Friend to Premoran.
Theran. Chosen of Lalas Acire.
Tiel. The equivalent of six years.
Tobias. Chosen of Lalas Torenth.
Tomas. One of the twins. Chosen of Lalas Ormachon. Brother of Davmiran. Son of Garold and Lewellyn. Raised by Trevor and Safira.
Tomes of Caradon. Recorded history of the land as well as premonitions for the future. The Great Books.
Torenth. Lalas tree. Bondmate of Tobias.
Treestar. Elfin King of Seramour. King of the Southern Elves. Husband to Elsinestra. Father of Elion, Fallean and Dalloway.
Trevor. Husband of Safira. Raised Tomas.
Trialla. Evil sorceress in league with Colton.

V

Violet. One of the twelve Sisters of Parth.

W

Wayfair. Lalas tree. Bondmate of Crea.
Whitestar. Elfin King of Eleutheria. King of the Northern Elves. Husband to Emerial. Father of Alemar and Kalon.
Windstorm. Elfin King of the Sea Isles. Brother of Elsinestra. Father of Lana.

X

Xia. Lalas tree. Bondmate of Edmond.

Gary Wassner was born and bred in New York. He is a Phi Beta Kappa graduate of Harpur College, SUNY Binghamton. He has a Masters Degree in Philosophy with a concentration in ethics and 19th Century Continental Philosophy. He joined his family's business many years ago and is currently the President and senior partner of Hilldun Corporation, a commercial finance company in New York City.

Mr. Wassner resides in New York with his wife, Cathy. He has three sons, Brien, Cristopher and Cole; four dogs, Trevor, Zoe Rose, Diesel and Marilyn Monroe; and one cockatiel. As a family, they travel the world extensively from the North Cape of Norway to Moscow, and from Italy to the Caribbean island of St. Barthelemy.

He is currently a moderator and administrator for Science Fiction and Fantasy World (www.sffworld.com) for which he also writes book reviews. Recently, he was a conference panelist at the World Fantasy Convention in Minneapolis where he read from his *GemQuest* series.

He is currently working on the fifth and final book in the *GemQuest* series.

About Windstorm Creative and our Readers' Club

Windstorm Creative was founded in 1989 to create a publishing house with author-centric ethics and cutting-edge, risk-taking innovation. Windstorm is now a company of more than ten divisions with international distribution channels that allow us to sell our books, games, music and films both inside the traditional systems and outside these paradigms, capitalizing on more direct delivery and non-traditional markets. As a result, our books can be found in grocery superstores as well as your favorite neighborhood bookstore, and dozens of other outlets on and off the Internet.

Windstorm is an independent press with the synergy and branding of a corporate publisher and an author royalty that's easily twice their best offer. We have continued to minimize returns without decreasing sales by publishing books that are timeless, as opposed to timely, and never back-listing our books. We stand adamantly against book stripping.

Windstorm is constantly changing, improving, and growing. We are driven by the needs of our authors–hailing from ten different countries–and the vision of our critically-acclaimed staff. All of our books are created with the strictest of environmental protections in mind. Our approach to no-waste, no-hazard, in-house production, and stringent out-source scrutiny, assures that our goals are met whether books are printed at our own facility or an outside press.

Because of these precautions, our books cost more. And though we know that our readers support our efforts, we also understand that a few dollars can add up. This is why we began our Readers' Club. Visit our webcenter and take 20% off every title, every day. No strings. No fine print.

While you're at our site, feel free to preview or request the first chapter of any of our titles, completely free of charge.

Thank you for supporting an independent press.

www.windstormcreative.com
and click on Shop

GemQuest

Demand more from your legends.
GemQuest is epic fantasy
for the discerning reader.

Visit www.windstormcreative.com/windstorm/sff.htm for more.